THE HUNTED

P.R. BLACK

HEAD
ZEUS

An Aries Book

First published in the UK in 2022 by Head of Zeus Ltd,
part of Bloomsbury Publishing Plc

9 7 5 3 1 2 4 6 8

A catalogue record for this book is available
from the British Library.

ISBN (PB): 9781801105361
ISBN (E): 9781800249394

Typeset by Siliconchips Services Ltd UK

Printed and bound in Great Britain by
CPI Group (UK) Ltd, Croydon CR0 4YY

Head of Zeus Ltd
First Floor East
5–8 Hardwick Street
London EC1R 4RG

WWW.HEADOFZEUS.COM

For Nan

FRIDAY

I

At some point after wiggling the last drops of petrol out of the nozzle into her tank, it occurred to Shell that she was free, and she should be happy about that.

She gazed at the jagged black mountains towering over the forecourt of the petrol station, and thought: *It looks like they're jostling each other to be the first to squash me.*

She had forsaken her own well-beaten runabout car to take what her husband Ewan had called The Wagon, with a touch of pride, not to say possessiveness, and he had been uncharacteristically touchy about this. 'Please bring her back in one piece,' he'd said – not quite joking.

She knew he'd said this to provoke her a little, and to snap her out of it. Shell would have struggled to define 'it', but she knew it was there. Not quite remorse, not quite guilt, not quite apprehension. 'It's only three days, Shell,' Ewan had said. 'Three days with your besties. When was the last time it happened? Your hen party?'

'I suppose.' Shell sighed. 'And they were arseholes then. Think they'll still be arseholes?'

'They'll be the best arseholes a girl could ever wish for,' he'd told her. 'Have a nice time.'

'Just nice?'

'Have a *great* time. That's underlined. Thick black marker. Have a *great* time.'

The guilt, remorse, apprehension wasn't for Ewan, of course, but for their three musketeers, who seemed to haunt the empty space at the back of the four-wheel drive, their absence causing an ache. They had been bemused rather than upset, though Lewis had been a little bit weepy at the prospect of Mummy going to the island without him. Ewan had wound their youngest up a little, and had dropped a few references to the Loch Ness monster, who Scooby-Doo had been pitted against on one of the boys' favourite videos. For all Scooby and the gang's antics, red-eyed, full-throated Nessie had frightened the boy a little bit.

'Don't be silly,' Shell had told Lewis, holding him close. 'There's no Nessie. Well, even if there is… he doesn't swim in the sea.'

'Are you going in the sea?' Lewis had said, more curious than anxious, now.

'I hope not, sweetie. They've got a nice ferry to take me across.'

After she pulled away, with her boys waving from the driveway, she felt that little tug. She'd been away before; she'd even gone for a spa day with Leah – and not a few cocktails before, during and afterwards – but the truth was that Shell had gotten out of the habit of going out, going to the pub, being sociable. Fifteen… even ten years ago, no one would have been more surprised about this development than Shell. She'd lived for it, from school days onwards. It had crystallised into harder drinking at university, away from her core school mates, the ones she was on her way to meet now… Their own little club, with its own little name.

'The Owl Society,' she said aloud, smiling.

But then she'd met Ewan, and everything had changed. All her own work, really. No one to blame but her. Shell had thrown herself into rearing her sons the same way she'd gone into anything else – one hundred per cent. All in. She'd changed. Hence the guilt, the remorse, the apprehension.

And yet, filling up The Wagon at a petrol station that had no right being in such a beautiful valley, with mountains, trees, moors and sky piled up in her line of sight, and the wind stirring the hair at her scalp, with a cold sun chipping away at the cloud cover above, she'd allowed herself that treacherous sense of freedom. 'Storm's passed the other direction,' the woman behind the counter told her, nodding towards a departing mass of bruised skies above. 'Looks like you're in luck.'

'I'll take a lottery ticket as well,' Shell had said, with a wink, and the woman had roared like it was the funniest thing she'd heard all day. It was possibly the *only* thing she'd heard all day, Shell mused, aside from the tinny sound of a museum-piece FM radio set over the woman's shoulder. But the exchange had gladdened her.

Driving off through the valley, with the ferry terminal getting ever closer, Shell began to think of the girls, and what it might be like to catch up with them now that middle age was getting too close to be ignored – and too close to be hidden, either, she thought ruefully, noting the crinkles at the corners of her eyes in the rear-view mirror. Definitely not laugh lines, no matter what anyone said.

Leah, she could talk to, but then there was Toni and the doubtless social-media-ready life she led... and dear God, Debs. Always entertaining, Shell supposed – but then some people found car crashes entertaining. Mouse too, of course... Her heart leapt. Wee Mousie Mouse. She must remember not to call her that to her face. No one called her Mouse to her face any more... Or did they?

Shell sang along to the tunes, confident in the satnav's solid yellow lines and arrows, pointing her along what was surely the best A-road in the world. Shell had even become nervous about driving during her child-rearing interregnum years – and what the hell was wrong with that? She reproached herself – sticking to the shopping and nursery/school runs, letting Ewan do the holiday and day-trip driving. She'd never been like that. Perhaps it was a part of her brain that had burned out; that had known to step aside and let someone else take the stress. She'd loved driving, had learned when she was seventeen. In fact, the girls had made full use of her services when they'd first started creeping into nightclubs and pubs that they really shouldn't have. But Shell had been glad of it. Never a fan of taxis...

She suppressed an image of Debs throwing up in the back seat of her dad's Volvo from long ago, and sang along to her Britpop playlist. Cast – her favourite. Pulp of course. Even Ocean Colour Scene, which had edged a little bit too much towards the Big Brother Rock end of the spectrum, along with Oasis... Britpop had been old when she was young, but it was the sound of wanting to be older, going to shows, dreaming of being in bands herself. As a motivational tactic, it worked; top of her voice, louder than the stereo, until she cranked it up, that is. The Wagon became a throbbing, thumping love bus, heaving up and down the A-roads. It was almost the wilderness, if you didn't count the pylons...

Shell's heart had swelled in the fifty minutes or so it took to reach the ferry terminal, where the valley became less craggy, and ancient houses began to creep in along the roadside.

She was soon parked in, had her ticket scanned, and parked The Wagon inside the belly of the boat. This is the part where her anxiety had threatened to return, and she'd feared struggling to squeeze The Wagon into a tight space, but there were plenty of spare bays. With a giddy feeling in her stomach, she felt the deck shift a little under her feet as she climbed the stairs. Then she was topside, the wind at her back, the promise of open water thrilling her even in its choppiness.

Am on the way, she texted to the group. And she shared a picture: the sea, with the islands in the background, picture-postcard perfect. *Ahoy, me shipmates!*

They had responded true to form. Leah first: *Squee! See you soon xx*; then Toni, with a picture of a toytown plane with twin propeller engines: *See your boats and raise you, hon*; ('Tart,' Shell muttered, not ungraciously); Debs with a picture of a gin and tonic, no text; and from Mouse, an emoji that could have been a smiling cat.

Once the boat started and the land moved away, Shell remembered something she'd seen or read; something about casting silver into the water, for luck. She did have some change in her pocket, a relic from the last time she'd gone to the vending machine at the gym; she hurled it into the air, after checking there was no one to see her silly act of abandon. She did not see the coins strike the water, the moment of impact swallowed in the white wash of the wake.

Looking forward to it now, she thought. Then she thought of Debs' gin and tonic; remembered there was a bar on board; then, with a sigh, remembered Ewan wasn't here, so Ewan wasn't driving. Meaning she was. Oh well. Soon enough, she thought.

The crossing to the island took a little longer than Shell anticipated. She had done a bit of sailing as a student, but even so, she was surprised by how long it took to get there given how soon the island had appeared on the horizon. It was as if the land mass was effecting a slow retreat, but losing ground to a faster pursuer. She was in the car and ready to go when the ferry docked at a simple concrete protrusion reaching off a rocky shelf and into the sea. An immense mountain hid the rest of the island, but the road round about was flat, and easy to navigate. Shell was grateful to be disgorged into the light, and even more grateful to remember, at the last moment, that she should be turning right, not left, to get onto the road to Owl Tree Halt.

The dark clouds had returned, and even The Wagon, in all its fat-arsed bulk, rocked a little in a sudden high wind. The mountainside was denuded of trees on this part of the island, and the grass and mosses turned a sickly green in the spotlights of the late afternoon sun. There was something thrilling about the tiger-stripe effect of the light, followed by the dark fingers stealing across the face of the hill, then the light, again. *Nearly summertime*, she thought; *nearly time for the better days.*

The satnav told Shell she was less than three miles from Owl Tree Halt when she saw the hitch-hiker.

It was clearly a woman, which made Shell think. She hadn't

seen any hitch-hikers since she was a child, and she had also seen many movies and read many books, and so upon approaching the dark figure by the side of the road, she had thought to treat it as she would a charity worker with a clipboard on the high street. Then she saw the frantic movements of the hands, a second before she glimpsed a small hatchback car in a lay-by, with its hazards still on.

The woman's face was stricken, as Shell passed. *Help*, the woman had mouthed, as The Wagon rolled past. Then once more: *Help*.

Shell didn't hesitate. Checking there was no one about to roll into her from behind, she brought The Wagon to a stop, turned in the road in a single tight arc, went past the hitch-hiker, then turned again to stop right beside her.

A woman of about Shell's age, covered from the neck down in livid purple waterproofs, bent down to speak as she lowered the passenger-side window. Underneath a beanie hat, her thick black eyebrows bullied a somewhat blunt, though still cute face. Shell experienced a strange moment of recognition, then quickly dismissed it when the woman spoke in an American accent.

'Hey, thanks for stopping! I was beginning to worry no one was going to stop. I've had a bit of trouble with my ride, over there.'

'Has it broken down?'

'Yeah,' the woman said, vaguely, gazing up and down the road. 'Yeah, something wrong with it, honey.'

'You're welcome to use my phone, if you like,' Shell said.

'You know, I already spoke to the breakdown company and they were like, "Uh, we can't get anyone out there for hours," and I'm like, "Dude, is it even going to be worth me sticking it out here? I've got somewhere to be, you know?"' The hitch-hiker was a little bit too loud, but Shell still felt concern for her. There was a naivety to her, even though she was long out of her twenties. She was thick-set, with quite broad shoulders underneath the waterproof jacket, though it was difficult to discern her exact body shape.

'I can give you a lift somewhere, if you like,' Shell offered, instinctively. 'Where are you headed? There's the village about four miles around the coast, there – should be a place to stay. Or if you're going somewhere reasonably close…'

'Know what, I was headed out to some lodges, at the far end of the island. The uninhabited dark heart. In the forest, you know?' The girl's eyes bulged a little upon the word *forest* – the way you might say it to a child, if you were recounting a fairy story. 'They've got a weird name – Owl Tree Halt? Think it's an old military barracks, but they converted it into luxury cabins and what have you. I'm meeting a few friends up there. I don't think they've arrived yet – they're in transit. Seaplane from Glasgow, would you believe?'

'You're in luck!' Shell said. 'I'm heading to Owl Tree Halt, myself. Meeting some old schoolfriends there. Class reunion, you could call it.'

'No way!' The American girl beamed.

'Yeah. In fact, at least one of them's coming in by plane – your friends could be on the same flight!'

'You're kidding! That's awesome!'

Shell touched the control that unlocked the door. 'Get yourself in. Is your car secure over there?'

'Oh, it's totally fine,' the American girl said. 'I can turn off the hazards with the key, in fact… There we go. It's all locked up... Besides, I think you'd be hard-pressed to find any car thieves out here. I don't think anyone actually lives here, you know? Away from the harbour and the front? It's way too quiet.'

'Oh, you'd be surprised at the lengths people will go for some peace and quiet. There's a few houses and here and there, private houses, that is, not just holiday lets. It's not for me, though. I'm not sure I'd want to live here. There's quiet, and then there's too quiet, you know?'

The girl nodded at this, then said: 'I'll just go grab my bag. Then I'll be back. Thanks so much for doing this, you're a real sweetie.'

'No problem,' Shell said. Then, watching the woman scuttle towards her car, clamping her beanie hat tight against her head for fear of the wind running away with it, Shell felt a sudden... what? It was as indefinable as her feelings of separation from Ewan and the boys. Dread? Regret? Apprehension? She seemed harmless enough. *But you wouldn't have done this anywhere else, Shell*, she thought to herself. *Wouldn't have given it a second thought. You'd have driven on and forgotten about it in seconds. Getting soft, perhaps?*

The stricken hatchback car's hazards gave a final, stately all-out orange glare from the four corners, then were stilled. The American girl ran back towards The Wagon, with the loose straps of a backpack flailing at her back in the wind.

The Wagon's door was torn open in a gust of wind as the American girl opened it, surprising them both. 'Whoo! Almost turned into Mary Poppins, there. That breeze came out of nowhere. This place is wild!' She nimbly eased herself into the seat, placed the backpack at her feet, then clicked her seatbelt. 'Anyway, pleased to meet ya, my knight in shining armour. I'm Michelle.'

Shell took the girl's hand, grinning. 'Me too! Though everyone calls me Shell.'

'Shell! You know, I like it. I think I used to know a Shell, from way back… Anyway, thanks for helping me out there.'

'Not a problem. I'll take you all the way in. You want to put the backpack in the back seat, at least?'

'Oh no, it'll be fine at my feet.'

As she pulled back out into the A-road Shell said – just for something to say – 'You travelling light?'

'I've got all I need right here. Girl Scout – I know how to pack a bag, that's for sure!' Michelle took off her hat. For some reason, Shell had been primed to think long dark hair was going to flow out once the hat was off, but to her surprise she saw close-cropped short blonde hair, evidently dyed. It was a striking contrast with the dark, heavy eyebrows, but suited the pixie-type pointy chin and elfin nose.

'So how did you end up coming to a big weekend on a Scottish island? You're a long way from home, I'm guessing?'

'Uh, home is a relative term,' the girl said. 'I've been in the States a while. But I'm a Brit. Got the passport and everything.' And she saluted to Shell, eyes twinkling in that unsettling way. 'Have a few old friends from way back I'm going to see.'

An absurd thought struck Shell, but she went with it. 'Hey – you're not going to stay with Leah Louden, are you? Maybe a university friend, or something?' It was the sort of thing Leah would do, Shell thought, whether she'd been in charge of the trip or not. Invited someone she knew, out of kindness, that strange need to gather friends around her. She'd have done it for a work colleague who'd just been dumped, or someone who'd maybe just expressed an interest. She'd been famous for that. Mummy Leah. Shell smiled. She'd brought some right characters to nights out, over the years. All the deadbeats and misfits; one or two interesting men, too. Shell had thought this was a weakness of Leah's for years, before she'd seen the light. Out of the four, Leah was the one Shell was most looking forward to seeing.

'Leah what... Louden?' Michelle replied, a little harshly. 'What is that, a superhero? No, I'm not invited to that party.'

'Just a thought,' Shell said, dismissively. 'Anyway – this your first time in the Highlands?'

'Nah, been here loads of times.' Michelle sniffed. 'I scoped this place out a few weeks ago, in fact.'

'Seems a wild place. When I was at university, I went on a few hillwalking trips. Munro-bagging, you know? Fell in love with the place, though it was a total coincidence I ended up in the Borders. My husband's not from Scotland, either.'

'Yeah, that's not very interesting,' Michelle said. She bent down and unzipped her bag.

'What?' Shell gaped at her passenger. 'I missed that. Say that again, please?'

'I said that's very interesting.' Michelle unzipped something, then pulled a face as she rummaged inside the bag. 'I love Scotland. Wild place, everywhere. Great people. I suppose everyone says that. Sort of comment that might get you stabbed one day.'

'Well. That's a bit of a cliché,' Shell said. 'Village I come from, they're lovely.'

'The loveliest people can turn on you. I mean, take those four bitches you're on your way to see.' Michelle smiled, zipped up her bag smartly, and sat up straight. 'God, I can't wait to carve them. One by one.'

'Excuse me?' It came out as a croak, or a squeak.

'You heard me just fine,' the girl said.

She had a knife in her hand.

A long, thin one. Surgically sharp. In the turn of the light it shone weirdly, as if it was made of crystal rather than steel. Pristine.

Shell heard herself say, 'Oh my God.'

'Keep driving.' The girl lunged, grabbing Shell by the nape of the neck. Shell struggled, taking her feet off the pedals; the road and the sky and the mountains weaved and warped outside. Then the point of the blade touched Shell's cheek.

'I said, keep driving,' the passenger said, in a different accent. 'Nice and steady. Hands on the wheel.'

Shell whimpered. There was no doubting this feeling. This fear. This terror. 'Please,' she said, the words automatic, spilling out in a tremulous croak, 'I've got three boys. They need me. If you want the car, if you want money, my bank cards, anything...'

'I'll have those,' the passenger said, nodding enthusiastically. 'Thanks. But that's not what I *really* want, Shell.'

'Please...' It hadn't quite cleared her consciousness yet; hadn't broken through the surface of her waking mind, what was happening to her. Her legs knew, though; quivering, like they had after the time she'd nearly crashed into a jack-knifed lorry; and her hands, scrambling for purchase on the steering wheel as if it were a cliff face.

'Please,' the passenger said, mockingly. 'God, this is a disappointment. I kinda expected a fight. You've still got the build. Rugger buggerette, weren't you? Still got the look. The little fat face. Like a giant smashed your head down into your shoulders. Fucking boulder. Fancied yourself a bit, though, hey? Bit handy? Rough 'n' ready? Do you still fancy yourself, Shell?'

'Who are you?' Shell said. Again, that sense of recognition, but not identification.

'You'll see, Shell,' the passenger said. 'You'll know. Now – don't be thinking about trigging any in-car breakdown emergency controls, will you? This big old tank of yours is sure to have one of those. Face the front. Hold your head still… that's it.'

The tip of the knife touched the bottom of Shell's eyelid. She blinked, and tears spilled down her cheek. She was whimpering like a child. Like Karl did, in his sleep. 'Please,' she said again.

'Don't think about braking hard, either,' the passenger said. Her eyes were wide, now, and unblinking, the hard white laser gaze of a lunatic, surely a lunatic, *dear God, I've picked up a lunatic!* 'If you brake hard… just imagine what a knife like this would do to your eyeball, Shell. Just imagine.' The face darted forward, close enough for the lips to brush Shell's cheek; for spittle to momentarily wet her ear.

And the car carried on up the empty road towards Owl Tree Halt.

2

Leah Louden brandished her printed tickets at the man waiting on the end of the pier. He was tall, shabbily dressed but good-looking in ways only a surfer could get away with. The outsize shades were somewhat out of place, given the gloomy skies above, but still reflected the light with stark alpine purity. He had tight-cropped dark hair and a thin, reddish beard – unfashionably tidy, Leah thought.

This man had no business being, or looking like, a surfer in that part of Glasgow, a wharf in one of the roomier channels of the River Clyde. There were shiny concert venues and hotels on either side of the banks, and the new splendour made it difficult to imagine the old kind, the immense ships and saurian cranes of the place's industrial past.

Another modern factor was the banana yellow prop plane, bobbing gently at its berth. It had seemed small from a distance. Problem being, it still seemed small in close-up, which didn't do much to quell Leah's anxiety.

The surfer stuffed the last of a packaged sandwich into his mouth, and spoke as he was chewing. 'Got it on your phone?'

'I'm sorry?' Leah fumbled with the suitcase – far too small, bought online, and arriving fashionably late the day before at her house. Its titchy wheels squeaked in protest. 'I've got the form here, haven't I?'

'Yes, but it's a QR code I need,' the surfer said, with studied patience. 'One that I can scan, that is. You've folded over the code on your printout, here. Twice.'

'Oh,' Leah said, 'hold on, I think it's here...'

The surfer pushed his shades up on his nose and stared into the sky, as if willing the clouds to recede.

'Here you go,' she said, after struggling to tap in the name of the travel company in her online mailbox. 'I'll just minimise it, here...'

He passed a scanner over her phone screen, and it beeped after an agonising pause of a second or two. 'There you go!' the surfer said, a little too brightly. 'We're on. Just need to check some ID, and...'

'Here's my passport.' That, at least, she had to hand. Leah felt not unlike an underager having her fake ID checked at the door of a club. She beamed, the same way she had back then. It had its effect; the surfer beamed back.

'You're good to go. You're going to Eilean An Eich Dhubh, courtesy of Sgian Dubh Air.'

Leah blinked. 'I'm sorry? I think I'm going to Black Horse Island.'

He grinned, a more genuine, and yet more feral expression this time. 'Almost. It's Dark Horse Island you're going to. Eilean An Eich Dhubh is its Sabbath name. In Scots Gaelic. And I'm Captain Steve.'

He held out his hand; Leah, struggling to put away her passport, phone and dog-eared tickets in her bag, only shook his outstretched fingers, a little gingerly. 'You're... the pilot?'

'The very same.' He glanced. 'Do you need a hand on board?'

'The pilot,' Leah said again.

'Yep. And that's the plane.' He nodded towards the plane, swaying gently on the water. It had six seats, and two propellers, painted dark blue against the yellow of the fuselage. The aircraft was cute, but sometimes, Leah realised in that moment, you don't want a plane to look dinky. Sometimes in life you want power. The kind that comes with reclining seats and great big engines and stewardesses. A structure that could conceivably allow you to go for a walk. Not these things. These were the ones that crashed. The ones with manual turn-handle doors. The ones that appeared in news reports every summer.

I'm going to be flying in that thing. Actually up above head height. Dear God.

'Is it remote-control?' she asked, before she could stop herself.

Steve burst out laughing. 'I wish! I could take it easy, then. Enjoy the sights. Nah, it's all controlled by me.' In a gentler tone, he said: 'Nothing to worry about whatsoever. It's a new plane, fully serviced, strong as an ox. If an ox could fly. Nothing to be anxious about, at all. Promise.'

'I'm not really a nervous flier. Just haven't done it for a while,' Leah said.

'You'll hardly know you're up there,' he said. 'And when you are... Whoa.'

This last word was delivered not for Leah's benefit, it seemed, but for another person wheeling their suitcase down the smart, prim walkway leading from the dock down to the waterside. The newcomer was taller than Leah, slimmer, and not as obviously dressed for travel as she was. This figure was confident on her heels, and looked perfect in a pair of ochre trousers, black blouse and a reddish cotton jacket that flapped a little in the wind. She was as thin and wiry as she had been in school, with her hair just as long and chestnutty, an object of envy even as she'd become a friend: Toni Atherley, the second-best swimmer at St Martha's.

She, too, was wearing shades, just as large and ostentatious as Steve's. Maybe they were part of the same tribe.

'Oh, Leah's flown, all right,' Toni said, grinning. 'All the way to the moon, baby!'

Steve made some comment in response, but it was completely ignored as the two women embraced, Leah standing on her tiptoes to do so. 'Good God, have you actually grown in adulthood, or something?' she said.

'Ah, it's the heels. They keep growing, all right.' Toni nodded toward her shoes, grinning. This close, Leah could make out her eyes behind the shades; small, something she had always seen as a defect, but very kind. 'About time we got on board Toytown Air, isn't it?'

'At your service, ma'am,' Steve drawled, smiling.

It was just as dinky on board the seaplane, but cosy with it. The trappings of luxury were there: leather-upholstered seats, a shade or two up from beige with a consistency Leah wanted to call plush. In the twin holsters by her side were a bottle of tonic and a can of gin. Preloaded, she supposed.

'Fun-size plane, fun-size booze. Ha!' Toni hadn't lost her habit of laughing at her own jokes. 'I suppose they don't have hostesses?'

'Maybe they don't make them small enough?' Leah suggested.

'Oh! Little people serving drinks! That'd be awesome!' Toni looked around, perhaps for a reaction. The only other people who'd joined Toni and Leah for Sgian Dubh Air's flight to the islands were a thick-set elderly couple from Glasgow who looked as if they'd been formed from the same dollop of grey Plasticine, girthy and broad even after they'd removed their heavy overcoats and put them in the lockers overhead. The older lady, who had tight-cropped hair that had gone thin, had yelped when the plane moved in the water as she stood up. Leah moved a hand to steady her.

'Thanks hen,' the woman said. 'Some set-up this, eh?'

'It's a cracking little plane,' Leah agreed.

'Never been on one of these,' the lady said. She sat down beside her husband, who had not once glanced away from the silvery water at the port side window.

'Didn't think Shell was the type to organise a trip,' Toni said, studying her phone for a moment or two. 'I have to be honest, I thought we'd lost her forever.'

'Was it Shell? I thought Mouse had done it,' Leah said, clicking her seatbelt, allowing herself to sink into the cushioned, ergonomically designed seats.

Toni shook her head. 'No, definitely Shell. She was the driving force. That surprised me. I thought I wasn't going to be able to go, for a while. Too much on at work.' She slid her shades back on top of her head, another gesture that Leah recognised. She'd done this at school. Everyone had accepted her shades, at the time; there had been no ridicule for the taller, prettier girl. Leah still marvelled at this, remembering how she'd been slaughtered for coming into classes with a dollar-sign necklace, a lazy Christmas present from a drunken uncle. Were there any laugh lines on Toni's face, the way they'd crept into Leah's? Of course there weren't.

'How's work going?' Leah asked.

'Oh, you know… I'm at Patterson and Downey, now. Been there eighteen months. We're in turnaround. I'll give it another eighteen months to two years, then move on. It's doing well, all things considered. They needed to boost their online portfolio – simple to do, really. Few contacts, bit of outlay, you know how it goes. Happy shareholders, happy Toni.'

Leah, who didn't know what was meant by this, and didn't want to either, nodded enthusiastically. 'Sounds… exhausting, Toni.'

Toni sniggered. 'Too right! I get home on a Friday night and just collapse. Sometimes I'm even asleep before I've had a couple of cheeky ones.' Toni tapped a long red fingernail against the tiny can of gin, relishing the ting.

'And Roy?'

Toni flicked a lock of hair over her ear. 'Oh, Roy's Roy. Same deal, really. The company keeps him just as busy. Weekends away with the boys – still plays rugby. Still gets injured. I'm waiting on him breaking his nose again, any day now. I hope he does. It might mean it gets reset, at a normal angle. Apart from that, it's all work, from now until we're… about fifty.'

'He still with the same firm?'

'Oh yeah, he's the opposite of me – he won't ever leave Sutton-Pacey. Loves it. Loves being in with the bricks. They'll be giving him a grandfather clock when he leaves, never mind a carriage clock. If not a coffin. That's not for me, Leah. You know what I'm like.'

Leah did. 'Don't know if I could handle the pace in London. Never thought it was for me, really.'

Toni cocked an eyebrow. 'That's not the girl I used to know. You sure about that?'

'Positive. I was down for a training day a couple of years ago… My head was pounding by lunchtime. It's too late. The twenties are long gone.'

'You'd breeze it, even now. Hey… I like that top. Where'd you get it?'

'You know, I'm not sure of the brand,' Leah said, fingering the collar a little defensively. 'Just something I picked up online.'

'Look it up for me, would you? Looks nice and light, like a training top.'

Leah was telling the truth about the brand; she could, however, remember how much she'd paid for it. She was blindsided by the question. *Shouldn't be*, she thought, acidly. *That's the kind of question Toni used to ask, all the time.*

Then Toni's tone changed, as she said: 'How's everyone keeping?'

'We're all right,' Leah said, without pausing. 'We've got loads of support, now. There's a care centre near our new place, and my mum and dad have been a pair of geniuses. Always round to help. They moved, too, to be closer. To help us.'

'Oh my God, the pair of treasures. Just how I remember them! You'll have to tell them I said hello, won't you?'

'They said the same to me – they wanted to say hello to all the girls. When I said you were the House Party Four, they knew exactly who you were.'

Toni shrieked with laughter. 'The House Party Four! I

haven't thought about that in years! Your dad's poor koi carp...'

Leah smiled – although the memory was not quite a welcome one. 'Yeah... Koi carp, who couldn't fly, it turned out. Or breathe on land.'

'I swear to God, I don't know who did that... I'd tell you if I knew. So much water under the bridge since then, so to speak.' Toni giggled, and Leah joined her.

'And John?' Toni asked.

'Yeah, spot on,' Leah said. 'Surgeon's hours... surgeon's wages, I suppose... At least he gets to retire early.'

'Not long now, is it? He is a good bit older, isn't he?'

Leah smiled. 'He would say more mature. Distinguished. Geriatric.'

Toni laughed much too loudly at this. 'Like a good cheese!' she said, laying a hand on Leah's wrist.

'Ageing like a fine pint of milk,' Leah said, mock-ruefully.

'And David?'

Leah paused. 'He's fine. He has time at a residential centre... I haven't seen so much of him, the past few weeks. Difficult, you know.'

Toni's hand tightened on Leah's wrist. 'Must be. Must be. Poor David.'

The plane's door opened and Steve appeared. He had on a headset, and on top of that, an aviation captain's hat, which clashed unpleasantly with his tie-dyed shirt. 'All right, folks! Welcome to Sgian Dubh Air. I'm Steve, your pilot today.'

Glancing over her shoulder, Leah noticed that the older lady was wrapping a set of rosary beads around her hands, pale blue like a baby blanket, threaded tight through the gaps between her thick fingers. Her husband's head was still craned out of the window.

'Where's the co-pilot?' the lady asked, querulously.

'Oh, don't you worry, ma'am, he's outside, untying us. When you see him, you'll wish it was just me!' No one laughed at the joke. Steve took off his glasses and gave them the safety preamble. 'And for the two ladies sitting to the starboard side, I'd say, "No gins until we're in the air."'

Leah wasn't a fan of the delivery, here, but smiled anyway. Toni folded her arms, and said: 'Well, I'm not impressed.'

'No?' For the first time, Steve sounded uncertain.

'Absolutely not. I was expecting Bollinger, darling.' Toni looked around, hoping for a reaction. She got a smile from Steve, which was enough.

'I'll see what we can do on the ground,' Steve said, and he actually winked. Then he turned his head sharply, his attention caught out of the window. 'Right; I think we've got a green light – let's get this show on the road.'

The co-pilot entered the cockpit space, a small, dark-haired man with an arched nose and an almost comically hard expression shuttering his eyes. He had a moustache, which was just the right side of stylish, closely cropped. It had the curious effect of making him look younger than he was, the opposite of the usual scenario when it came to facial topiary. He closed the door and cranked the heavy handle, double-checking the locks, then spoke on a mobile phone. After receiving a response, he merely nodded to the passengers, then sat up front in the cockpit.

Steve sat to his right. The propellers started, one to Leah's immediate right, out the window.

'Jesus,' Leah said. 'This'll be like a bus ride. A bus ride, in space. This doesn't look big enough.'

Behind her, the older lady moaned, touching the rosary beads to her lips.

'It's a piece of cake, darling,' Toni said primly. 'I've been on a few of these things, before. Corporate freebies, that kind of thing. Better than being on an airliner. Well, unless you're going first class. Be a dream. Wait and see.'

Leah gripped the armrests as the plane seemed to recoil, as if preparatory to springing, then moved away. It soon gained momentum, the backwash surging up as far as the window. Leah thought: *We're not going to sink, are we?* She decided not to articulate this, even in jest, thinking of the woman in the seat beside her.

'Here goes, then. The highlands, here we come!' Toni actually punched the air and settled back as the plane sped up, the engine sound dominating everything, before it angled steeply and began to climb. The grey river fell away fast; drops of water elongated and disintegrated in thin broken lines; people waved by the dockside; a bridge came horribly close, then dropped away. Then came a blueprint view of the city grid, the trains crawling across the bridge, the cars. Then Leah remembered to breathe.

'Look at that!' said the old man, at the top of his voice. 'We're… flying!'

His wife whimpered, loud enough to hear over the engines. Instinctively, automatically, Leah reached over the seat, even as the plane angled, climbing into the clouds. The older lady's eyes flew open, on high alert to any sudden movement. Her husband still gazed out of the window, completely rapt, a sallow-faced man of about seventy, blue eyes gazing at the shrinking earth below.

Leah reached out further; the old lady clasped her hand, the rosary beads digging into Leah's palms.

'You'll be fine,' Leah said. 'This is amazing.'

'Not amazing, hen,' the older lady said, inches away from her husband. 'That is not the word.'

3

Leah drew some amusement from Toni's rapidly changing confidence once the descent began. Toni arranged things, by nature. That extended to speaking; speaking meant control. 'Well, this is the thing,' she said. 'Here's the deal. Here's how it usually goes. Plane goes down, right?'

Behind Leah's shoulder, the old lady moaned.

'Plane goes down,' Toni said again. 'It lands on a landing strip. OK? A landing strip. Most of the time. I mean, typically.'

'But it's a seaplane,' Leah said. With the popping of her ears and the slow, but unmistakable descent of the plane, she didn't like the change in atmosphere.

'Yes, Leah, it's a seaplane. It takes off on sea. Well, it took off on the river. But I didn't realise it actually *lands* on the water, too.'

'Same way it takes off, I guess. Or maybe it just drops an anchor?'

Toni arranged her phone and her e-reader, one on top of the other. 'That's not a very helpful suggestion.'

'OK. Hold my hand?'

Toni glanced out the window and swallowed. 'Maybe

when we get a bit nearer the water. Definitely not ruling out hand-holding.'

It had been close and grey on the way out of Glasgow, the clouds had disappeared as they'd travelled up the west coast. Steve the pilot had joked via the microphone on his headset that there was no avoiding the 'scenic route' – and it had been a sublime experience, the morning sun racing them into the sky as the towns and cities seemed to dissolve into undulating land and thrilling slashes of fresh water. They saw falls; they saw clusters of forest; they saw fast rivers threaded with gold, stoppered once or twice by anglers, hip-deep; and delightfully, they saw stags. Even the little old lady over Leah's shoulder cooed at one point, saying: 'Look – pylons!' Her husband's harsh laughter infected them all.

The flight was a little bumpy, but not as turbulent as Leah might have supposed. On occasion, the plane seemed to sail through the skies on a flattened, untroubled trajectory. It reminded her of a flight she'd taken to Iceland, near the start of her relationship with John. She had expected terrible weather, but the journey to the north had been blissful, almost surreal in its serenity.

The gin and tonic arrived at the right time. 'Not like Shell to arrange something like this,' Toni said, sipping her own drink. 'To be honest, I thought we'd lost her for good.'

'It's been a while… six years? Seven?'

'I've seen her once since the kids arrived,' Toni said. 'I think when the middle one was christened. You were there, weren't you?'

'I was at that one. Think I was pregnant, for that one.'

'No one was invited to the last christening. She came off

social media about the same time. I thought that was it for Shell, to be frank. Shame. She was a good laugh. What was it she used to drink, white wine spritzers? God, she almost converted me.'

'They're not bad. What did she call them? Liveners?'

Toni sniggered. 'Yeah. Liveners, for about two or three hours. Deadeners, after that.'

'Mind you,' Leah mused, 'I realised I haven't been out with you for, what? Three years, maybe?'

'Two,' Toni said. 'I saw you a few times, round about... round about the accident.' Toni paused. 'I guess time gets away from you.'

Leah stiffened. She had forgotten about that – how Toni had been there, in the immediate aftermath of the accident. With so much going on, she'd blocked out the memory. For all her faults – and friends know each other's faults, more intimately than family – Toni had rallied round after that awful day. Mouse and Debs too – they'd dropped everything. The only reason Shell hadn't was because she was in labour at the time.

'No joke,' Leah said. 'I always knew I'd turn into my parents. They started getting to forty-odd, and they didn't go out much. I thought they'd just got boring. Turns out they were knackered.'

'It does wear on you. I mean, we've not got kids, of course, but... Yeah. Some nights I go to more effort to plan a taxi home than I do to actually go out. And nightclubs...'

Leah sniggered. 'What are they? I think they'd transitioned into "late bars" by the time I gave up the ghost.'

'How about the rest – you see Mouse or Debs?'

'I haven't seen Mouse for years.'

'No way,' Toni gasped. 'I thought you two were really close.'

'Mostly to do with her, I guess... And she's lovely. She never misses a birthday, always sends presents for David... There are some weird postmarks on the parcels.'

'Oh, she's an international woman of mystery. She sent me loads of postcards, from all over – Goa, Switzerland, somewhere in the outback where they filmed the Mad Max movies. And Croatia... Peru... She's been all over. Mouse, eh?' Toni grinned. 'The quiet one. Who'd have thought it?'

'I don't know if she was quiet,' Leah said. 'She didn't lack confidence... She was deep, rather than quiet.'

'Debs always thought she was a moron,' Toni said. 'Reckoned it was a front. Say nothing, people think you know stuff, she used to say. Speaking of the devil... You see much of her?'

'I saw her six months ago – met her for lunch; she was in town.'

'She turn up drunk?'

'No,' Leah said, slightly discomfited by Toni's peremptory tone. 'She might have been a bit drunk by the end. You know what she's like.'

'I do,' Toni said. 'I invited her to a corporate do a while back. Stop me if I told you.'

Leah shook her head.

'Black tie, little black dresses, cocktails, that kind of thing. She blagged her way in, really – she's good at that. Forced me into an invite, once she heard about it. Anyway, she gets talking to Sid Mariner. Of Mariner and Porton.'

'I... have no idea who these people or companies are, but if I nod, like this, take it that I understand perfectly.'

'Yeah, he's a big deal. Anyway. She finds out that he has a hobby. Rock 'n' rolling.'

'You what?'

'It's like this style of dancing, popular in the Fifties. The man throws the woman around, to this horrible old man's music. That stringy bass, you know?'

Leah grinned. 'That rings a bell. I think I saw that on Record Breakers, a million years ago.'

'Which is almost exactly what Debs said. So anyway – bear in mind we've barely gone past the canapés stage, and she's already pissed – she challenges Sid Mariner to give a demonstration. Which he accepts, because she's gotten him pissed, too.'

Toni paused. The pause painted pictures in Leah's head – terrible pictures. She covered her eyes with her hands. 'This story isn't going to end well, is it?'

'Nope. He gets her up onto the table – we're talking, silver service still on the cloth, tuna and cucumber sandwiches and vol au vents still strewn around – and tries to rock 'n' roll with her. But Debs is, you know, she's been dieting, trying hard, but not doing very well with it, and he rock 'n' rolled her over his shoulder, and then the pair of them rock 'n' rolled onto their arses on the floor.'

Once Leah had stopped laughing, she asked: 'Did she win a contract?'

Toni blinked. 'Do you know, the bitch did?'

Captain Steve's voice cut over the intercom. 'Approximately ten minutes to landing, folks. Please make sure all your drinks containers are secured in the holders, your tables are upright and your seatbelts are fastened.'

'Oh God,' the little woman behind Leah said, tying up her fist with her rosaries again. 'Oh God, here we go.'

Her husband, his face red after two whiskies and ice, was still entranced by the rolling hills. The sea appeared, drawing gasps from everyone, and with it came sudden, menacing clouds.

'Looks stormy,' Leah remarked.

'Yeah. With luck we'll miss it.'

The plane banked towards a huge purple mountain, a vast cone upended into the earth, its lower reaches thronged with pine trees. There was a bright knife blade of water, through a decline in the hillsides. The plane pointed towards this, and the mountain scrolled underneath them – the water becoming detailed with sudden magnification, waves and ripples. Far too close for comfort.

'Oooh,' said the older lady. Leah instinctively reached out a hand, and the old lady took it again, tucking her head in like a blackbird hiding from the rain.

'It'll be fine,' Leah said, struggling to make herself heard over the din of the engine. Then she gasped herself, as the plane dropped sharply. There was the sea loch, a golden basin in the late morning sunlight. Houses appeared at sparse intervals through the trees; Leah wondered if one of these was Owl Tree Halt, and struggled to remember what it had looked like online. Leah had had little time to prepare for the trip.

Then the water came in fast, the engines took on the low burr of a wartime bomber. Leah's other hand was seized, tight. Toni sat up straight in her seat, chin thrust out, eyes tight shut.

'Maybe unclench your jaw?' Leah suggested. That worked. Toni laughed as the plane glided over the water, the surface close enough to touch, and then white plumes flared on either side of the plane and they felt the contact, right into their bones, as much as they heard it. Rills of water veined the windows; then the acceleration slowed, the tumult on either side ended, and then the plane came to a stop.

'Right then,' Captain Steve said, grinning underneath his aviator shades. 'Got you here in one piece – things can only get better! Welcome to Eilean An Eich Dhubh.'

4

There it was: sky, water, mountains, forest, and the wind hurled across all of it. Leah wasn't much of a mountaineer, and the absurd height and proximity of the Munro dominating the lochside was almost baffling. Wisps of sheep about three-quarters of the way up the path-seamed hillside gave it a sense of scale. It had a bigness about it that could not quite translate from a crisp image on a calendar or a watercolour at a car boot sale. It didn't feel real to be there, until she was off the plane and on solid ground.

'I think it's called Beinn cnoc an t-sealgair,' Toni said, confidently, noticing what Leah was looking at. 'The mountain. Hill of the Hunter.'

'Croc-and-what?'

'*An t-sealgair.*' Both women sniggered instinctively at the word – Leah as much at the curl of Toni's lips as the sound they made. 'I checked out the pronunciation and everything.'

'Beast of a hill.'

'Mmm, yep.' Upon the craft steadying itself on the water and then gently taxiing across the choppy surface to the pier, Toni had resumed her former self-confidence and poise. 'And if anyone suggests going up it over this weekend, I am going to suggest, "no".'

'I don't think it's on the cards,' Leah replied, 'but you never know. Mouse is into her outdoor pursuits, isn't she? The old sailing, climbing and camping business?'

'Is she?' Toni frowned. 'You know, it's ages since I had a proper conversation with her. What's she doing these days?'

'Still doing her art.'

'Art,' Toni scoffed. 'I remember. She had a thing about Batman, didn't she? Used to draw him all the time. And this was before Batman was cool. Gads, shouldn't she have grown out of that by now?'

'Well, no, she's doing all right. She draws a comic strip in France – some sci-fi thing.'

'Comics? Like the Beano, that kind of thing?'

'Not exactly. It's more like serious sci-fi... I remember the name, hang on...' Leah had switched her phone back on already, and she carried out a quick search. 'There you go. *Bloodline*.'

Toni's eyes narrowed, and then widened, at the images as she scrolled through Leah's handset – blood reds, starburst punches, impossible postures as characters performed their kicks and leaps. 'What's this... vampires? Good God, is that lesbian vampires? Snogging in a church? That stuff still turn people on?'

'Looks like it,' Leah agreed. 'And... I don't know.'

'You mean to say people buy these things? I mean, like, normal adults?'

'Still sells in France, I'm told. Italy and Spain, too. There's a big market for comics on the continent. It's a bestseller. She does well out of it. She's got *fans*. Think she sold the rights to a movie company, but nothing happened. Then the rights lapsed, and she sold them again. Does signings in bookshops, interviews on arts shows, festival appearances, the lot, over there. And hey… check out her pen name.'

Toni zoomed in on the screen, frowning again. '*Le Souris Bête*. That's what she calls herself! Ha! I had no idea. I thought she was painting friezes in nurseries and hospital wards.'

'I think she still does that, for free.' Leah held out her hand. Toni tapped and scrolled through Leah's phone again, then remembered herself, smiled, and handed the phone over.

'She did all that stuff for us, back in the day. Animal designs, and such. Remember?'

Leah didn't quite like the sly cast to Toni's smile. 'She did loads of stuff when she was a kid. Mouse was super-talented.'

'If you say so, hon. I remember her trying to sell bad caricatures of Take That down the market with her dad. Poor man. He probably bought most of them.'

Leah checked her phone. 'Had any messages from the others?'

'Just the one, from Shell. Saying she'd be late. Something's come up, she said. What's the betting she's the first drop-out?'

'You expecting more?' Leah heaved her luggage out of the locker.

Toni shrugged. 'That's how it is with you mummies these days. I get the drill. Something comes up, meaning Mummy stays home. Junior's had his first crap. Or lost a toenail. Something to do with the little ball and chains, anyway.' Then Toni caught herself. 'I didn't mean that, honey. Sorry.'

'Never mind,' Leah said, cheerfully. 'Let's get on the road. Hopefully they're not expecting us to walk across water, here?'

Steve the pilot had spun around in his seat, having removed his headset. 'I think you could fly across the water if you wanted, Angel,' he said, with an outrageous wink. 'But I wouldn't want you to accidentally dip your feet in the drink, so there's a car waiting for you at the bottom. We'll get you to the Halt, no worries. Oh – one other thing – from here, the mobile reception gets spotty. In fact, spotty is being kind. It's almost non-existent. You might get a bar or two on top of the Munro, but apart from that… if you've got any last requests, I'd send them now while you can.'

Then he spoke up, projecting to the older couple who were struggling to get into their overcoats in the enclosed space. 'Here we are, on Dark Horse Island! The Tail Wynd pub is right at the bottom of the jetty by the lochside, everyone – Alan and Maureen are probably still in their beds after the previous night's debauch. If not, they'll pour you a pint, and can order you a taxi as well, if you want to head straight to where you're going. Peter, my glamorous co-pilot, is going to give you a hand to get out and get organised.' Steve indicated the small, dark man with the stubble, who acknowledged this speech with a curt wave of the hand, his back still turned while he completed final checks on the instruments. Then he leapt out of his seat and opened the door.

A blast of cold air stirred Leah's face. She watched as the dark, wiry man waved to someone on the jetty. He caught a rope, then leapt an impressive distance from a standing start onto the boardwalk before tying down the plane. Leah caught sight of a woman in a wasp-yellow waterproof jacket, helping to secure the plane.

'Peter's more at home in the animal kingdom, as you can

see,' Steve drawled. 'A tree, or a spare tyre tied to a branch, either works just fine. Right, up on the pier, my lambs. Time for you to sample the delights of our humble island.'

The woman in the yellow waterproof coat and the baseball cap helped the elderly couple onto the pier, and offered a hand to Leah, who refused politely. Toni, however, handed over her bag, and then took a dainty step onto the pier.

'No messages from anyone?' she asked, taking her bag back with a nod and a big smile towards the woman in the yellow jacket.

Leah checked her phone. 'Nope. Not much of a signal here, either.'

'Disappointing. Guess it's part of the remit, though. The great outdoors.'

'God, look at it.' Leah gazed up at the mountains. 'Everything's kind of awesome. Epic, even.'

'So long as there's not an epic journey involved here, we're all good.' Then Toni simpered, her face becoming almost grotesque. Leah spun around, to see if she'd spotted someone she knew. And then there was an electronic click.

Leah flinched; Toni had taken a selfie. At that exact moment she was heaving her bag off the pier and onto the banks of the loch. 'You must have caught my best side, there.'

'Ah, every side's the best,' Steve said, at her back.

Leah straightened up, flustered, and couldn't quite think what to say.

Steve grinned and took her bag, stepping onto the

lochside. He extended a hand, which she took. 'So, what's the script for your weekend, girls?'

'We're just here for a day or so,' Leah said, evasively. Steve had delayed handing the bag back, just for a second or two.

'I know you're here until Monday morning, in fact. You're booked in at my lodge.'

'You're in charge of Owl Tree Halt?'

'That's right. Part of myself and Peter's expanding empire. Today, the island, tomorrow… maybe another island.' He grinned. 'Just two minutes, girls, and I'll sort out the car. Just need to hand over to Gwen, my relief pilot. She absolutely loves her job title.'

The girl in the yellow waterproof set her face in a mock scowl – a very convincing impersonation of a real one – then smiled.

Peter, whose expression had barely changed since the moment he'd got on the plane, said: 'Car's parked behind the pub, Steve.'

'Right,' Steve said. He jogged across the road, a somewhat ludicrous figure in his taupe-coloured board shorts.

'Bit frisky, that lad,' Toni remarked.

'Yeah. "Forward" may be the word. Hopefully not involved too closely in the weekend.'

Peter, who had been checking paperwork with Gwen, smiled at this exchange. He spoke confidently, for a man who seemed to scurry around a lot. 'Ah, Steve's a bit of a game show host, but you'll get used to him. We'll be looking after you for your activities tomorrow afternoon.'

'Activities?' Toni said, alarmed. 'What activities are these?'

'You've got a choice – anything you like. Hillwalking, sailing, spot of archery, horse riding... All sorts.'

'Not hillwalking,' Toni said.

Peter's true smile appeared – toothsome, a little goofy, but not unattractive. 'Or, you could just sit in the hot tub and drink fizz all day.'

'Now you're talking.'

Leah asked: 'How's the signal out at the Halt? Seems a bit spotty already. Is it any better up at there? It seemed quite high up, from what I read online. We don't know if our friends have arrived yet.'

'Ah, that's one thing we're up front about on the island – coverage isn't so good. We're working on it. All in hand. But I know that one of your friends is scheduled to meet you... Right about now.'

'Which one?'

'Lady Godiva – here she is, in fact.'

They heard the slow cadence of horses' hooves a few seconds before they saw her, emerging around a bend at the lochside road. She was clad in toxic yellow and wore a riding hat, but there was no mistaking Debs. It could only ever have been Debs.

'Hi-yo, motherfuckers,' she said, waving frantically with one hand, until she threatened to topple over.

5

Debs was helped off the horse by Steve, who seemed to have been teleported into exactly the right spot. For a second, Leah thought she was going to leap into his arms.

'Sir Steve! Thanks for the tip – this was great!'

'No problem at all, my queen. I think two of your ladies in waiting have arrived.'

'Yep, that'll be them.' Debs grinned, removing her riding gloves and helmet.

Even as she waved, Toni muttered: 'Changed her hair. About time.'

'Oh, it suits her,' Leah said.

Debs had been blonde since sixth form – but the length was gone in favour of a crop, in her natural light brown colouring, with a flicked-up fringe. It was shockingly boyish, but it suited her high cheekbones, rosebud chin and impish face.

'Looks like she'd suit a bow tie, now,' Toni said, barely moving her lips. 'Maybe some braces, too. Over her shoulders, I mean, not on her teeth. I can see a photo by-line on a crappy think piece in some broadsheet.'

'Be nice!' Leah said, in the middle of a laugh.

Debs' toxic yellow bib was removed, and underneath

was a low-cut spaghetti strap top that Leah would have regretted, and did, on her behalf. Keeping up alongside the horse had been an older man, with hair the colour of a damp cloth creeping out from beneath his helmet. He held Debs' jacket for her, and helped her put it back on.

'Whoa there! Thanks so much,' Debs said, reaching in to kiss the older man on the cheek. 'Maybe I'll get some of the girls over to join us tomorrow?'

'That'd be great!' the old man said, and sounded as if he meant it.

Debs ran over and threw her arms around Leah's neck, pulling her head down a little. Leah suppressed the urge to fight clear of this; it felt like an assault, no matter how many times Debs did it. Debs squealed into Leah's neck. 'I've missed you!' She looked up from the crook of Leah's neck, and reached out her spare arm towards Toni.

Toni dutifully came over and joined the other two. Leah caught a glimpse of Toni grimacing as Debs' hand closed round her neck.

'Look at the pair of you! It's like you've grown!' Debs said, standing back and appraising them both.

'Love your hair,' Leah said. 'Some change!'

'I took a mad notion one day... I know what you're saying. "That's not like you, Debs."'

Leah and Toni both laughed politely.

'So, yeah, I've gone for a new look. "Riding school teacher in a 1970s movie that all the surviving actors are still embarrassed about." And that gave me an idea – I got here far too early, so I checked out the riding lessons next door to our place.' Debs gestured towards the older man, who had gotten into the saddle Debs had vacated with surprising dexterity. 'His name's Keith. Very randy for a man his age. Nice enough, though. Wants us to come over and have cocoa later. I think he's got a hot tub in his garden. "Big enough to admit six," he told me.'

Steve, who had been watching this exchange while perched against a bollard, with his smile almost touching his sunglasses, sniggered.

'Didn't know you rode,' Toni said this without any apparent irony, but Debs laughed uproariously anyway.

'Ah, you know me, Tones. Anyway. I stayed sober specifically over the past week in order to get pissed with you two. So, what do you say? We on for it?'

'I'd say you're on,' Toni said.

Debs gestured towards Steve. 'I believe our coachman has our carriage prepared. Take us to Owl Tree Halt, my man. Don't spare the horses.'

'At your service, ma'am,' Steve said, standing up straight.

Leah's stomach lurched as the car struggled in second gear up a sharp incline. 'The lodge isn't at the top of the mountain, is it?' she asked. 'I'm not being funny, but I think I'm getting airsick.'

'Nah,' Steve said, one hand resting on the steering wheel. 'Carsick, is what you are, not airsick. Stare at the horizon – it'll help. I think.'

'I'll be fine,' Leah said, with more confidence than she felt.

'She just needs another G 'n' T,' Toni said, from the passenger seat. 'You don't have one of those little bottles from the plane here, do you?'

'Not in the car, I'm afraid. I think the temptation might be too great for some weak-minded drivers,' Steve said. 'But there's a few drinks waiting for you at the Halt.'

'Uh, I might have taken care of one or two of those,' Debs said. 'Apologies in advance.' She was sat in the seat to Leah's left.

'When did you get here?' Leah asked. 'I thought you weren't arriving until teatime?'

'Late booking popped up with Captain Steve, here, and his taciturn though still attractive side-man.'

Steve snorted. 'I am one hundred per cent telling Peter that. You get to live with the consequences.'

Debs shrugged. 'Anyway, I grabbed the early flight up to Glasgow, then swapped my seat on the plane... Isn't it something? A direct link to Brigadoon, it felt like. I think I might feature that in one of our tourism sites.'

'Yeah?' Steve turned his head to take in Debs in the rear-view mirror. 'What kind of travel stuff do you do?'

'Oh, it's not restricted to travel. I do PR.' A card appeared in her hand. She hitched forward in her seat, tucking the card into the well behind the handbrake. 'Sheldrake PR. You want it, you've got it. Infomercials, placements in the papers, all across the net, social media, take your pick. You might have heard of us. Might not. Look us up. See what we can do for you.'

'I will do that,' Steve said – perhaps the first unaffected statement Leah had heard from him.

'I can see some houses now,' Leah said.

'There are a few houses out here at this end of the island... Not many, but they stand out, you could say. Lifestyles of the rich and shameless, mainly,' Steve said. 'A lot of them lie empty for most of the year, though some are holiday rentals. There are a few permanent residents. But we're on the other side of the mountain, where it's more forested. The creepy part.'

'You're going to love it,' Debs said, with wide-eyed conviction. 'It's perfect. Thanks for setting it up, Mamma.' And she punched Leah on the leg – with some purchase.

'I didn't set it up,' Leah said, fighting the urge to rub where she'd been struck. 'I think it was Shell, wasn't it? Big reunion?'

'Was it? I thought it was more like something Mamma Louden would do,' Debs said.

Steve's eyes locked on to Leah's in the mirror. 'Why do they call you Mamma?'

'She gave birth to us and suckled us,' Debs said, cobra-quick. 'Still does, in fact, if we cry in the night. Nah. Leah here's always been the mummy of the group. We've ghosted the shit out of her for decades, now, but she's always there for us, no matter what. I bet you've got a meal plan all set out for us, haven't you?'

'I assumed we were eating out,' Leah said, a shade too quickly.

'Rubbish! I bet you brought place mats. Although, place mats and cutlery is more Toni's style, here. Toni's more likely to veto the place mats and provide her own.'

'Debs here is most likely to forgo the cutlery and tear the food apart with her bare hands,' Toni said, casually.

'We have a winner!' Debs said, thrilled. 'That reaction means Toni probably *has* brought her own cutlery.'

They bantered like this for a while, while a thick covering of conifers and pine closed in around them. The sudden shade of dark green speared through with mid-afternoon sunlight was slightly discomfiting to Leah, as if a veil had been drawn over the sun's face. The houses at the harbour had thinned out to the odd croft here and there. On the route to the mountain, there were no houses at all. Nearly every aspect was bleak as a result, and sometimes forbidding, but still beautiful. 'Nearly there,' Steve said. 'You'll get a good view of the sea loch, now, through a gap in the trees…'

They followed his gesture. Through a break in the forest, a sliver of water could be seen, pale blue threaded with gold in the sunlight.

'And directly ahead, your holiday home for this weekend: Owl Tree Halt.'

6

It was more imposing than it had looked in the online brochure. Owl Tree Halt could have been called a log cabin, but it was grander than the name implied. It was on two levels for a start, and Leah could now understand how it could 'comfortably sleep twelve people', as advertised. A steepled roof reached high into the pine treeline, and a front porch stretched the entire length of the structure.

Debs took off her sunglasses. 'I'll huff, and I'll puff, and I'll blow your house down,' she said. 'Don't think these three little pigs will have any trouble from the big bad wolf in this house, eh?'

'Speak for yourself, darling,' Toni said, tartly. 'It's a lot bigger than I thought. It's not a log cabin. More a log... castle.'

'You haven't even seen inside,' Steve said, getting out of the car. He moved to help Toni, whose suitcase was by far the biggest. 'Hot tubs around the back, patio, barbecue area...'

'No pool?' Toni asked.

Steve grinned. 'Bit too cold for an outdoor pool, at this latitude, I'm afraid... Toni, was it?'

Toni didn't affirm this. 'Disappointing. I was looking forward to some freshwater swimming.'

'You a swimmer? I might have guessed. They get a look about them.'

Toni blinked.

'Hey, Toni,' Debs said, 'if you fancy a swim, you just landed on a great big lake out there. Maybe we could have a rerun of the Great Shark Hunt of St Martha's?'

Leah's shoulders stiffened. She had a flashback at the very mention of swimming. Debs was being catty already. Out of them all, she usually missed Debs the most, and had the fondest memories of the girl – or at any rate, she produced better stories. But Debs had a turn on her, that was for sure.

Toni tutted at the remark and turned back to Steve. 'Aren't you going to show us into our rooms?'

'Be delighted to.' He walked up the path, trundling Toni's suitcase behind him. 'Don't worry,' he said, without turning around. 'I'll come back for everyone else's bags, too.'

Inside, the bottom floor was a massive open-plan lounge. Leather ottoman sofas with ancient brass studs and leather the colour of dried blood shone on every side; the kitchen equipment and the hanging utensils gleamed, and a patio door looked out onto a huge garden with hot tubs built into decking. The main room was dominated by a beautiful fireplace with green and white tiling that reminded Leah of an old tenement flat she'd seen in Glasgow.

Creatures glared at them from every corner. At the top of the fireplace, seemingly in pride of place, was a wolf's head – a comically benevolent-looking creature, more cartoon character than a prime example of taxidermy. Something that you might have cuddled in bed as a child. A bear snarled from the corner, reared up on its hind legs – a grizzly, almost comically large. Its fur looked in excellent condition, but its smell left a little to be desired as the three women posed for photos with it immediately.

'Please tell me we don't have to share the island with bears? Some rewilding insanity?' Toni asked, her head in the creature's armpit.

'You never know.' Steve smirked, snapping one photo after another.

'Wait a second,' Debs said. She stepped in front of the bear, then bent over in front of it, jamming her backside against its crotch. Debs looked up and bit a finger coquettishly; Leah and Toni looked from her expression to the bear's, and broke out laughing.

'Stop… you need to stop laughing,' Steve said, out of control himself. 'I can't keep it steady!'

'Barney Bear here doesn't have that problem,' Debs said, which made things worse.

'I'm so sorry, every one of those pictures is blurred,' Steve said.

'Probably just as well. Hey – is it true about the reception?' Debs had straightened up, and she stuck her tongue towards the bear's bared, yellowish teeth.

'It's bad, I'm afraid, as I told the others. But there are hotspots. First of all, if you go to the top of the mountain, you do get some coverage. Secondly, there's a landline. Now, I'm guessing you ladies are too young to remember landlines, but – lift phone, and press the buttons there.

That's if you actually remember phone numbers these days. That's something people used to do in the olden days.'

'So no Wi-Fi, then? Seriously?' Debs asked.

'No. Part of the service, here – isolation is what we promise. No internet.'

Leah felt the first stirrings of guilt. *That means I can't contact David.* She said: 'I was hoping for a telegraph service.'

'Fuck it, if we need to send any messages, we'll just tape it to Eddie's legs, here.' Debs gestured towards a stuffed golden eagle, wings splayed to their full preposterous span, claws akimbo, as if ready to seize a salmon, or a child. 'Hey – check that out,' she said, nudging Leah.

'What?'

Debs had indicated a painting, to the left of the fireplace. A huge figure of an owl, sat on a perch. It was a modern piece, quite crude in its way, white canvas with the figure of the bird slashed through in blue ink. The painting was rather too large for its surroundings, something that unjustifiably dominated the room.

'What does that remind you of?' Debs said, grinning.

Something flickered in Leah's mind – interference in a signal, somewhere. It wasn't as powerful a flashback as Debs' reference to the Great Shark Hunt of St Martha's, and God knew Toni might sulk about that. But there was something there, something from deeper childhood, something that made Leah uncomfortable. 'Not sure what you mean.'

'Bollocks you don't! Here, Toni... Look at that painting and tell me the first thing that springs to mind.'

Toni's face was blank for a moment as she studied the

canvas. Then a curious smile broke out on her face. It wasn't that she was uncomfortable or awkward… It was an innocent smile, Leah thought. One she rarely showed. 'The Owl Society,' Toni said.

'What Owl Society?' Leah asked.

'Don't tell me you don't remember the Owl Society?' Debs spluttered. 'It was only your bloody idea. Produced, directed and written by Leah Louden.'

'It kind of rings a bell… Is this some deep childhood stuff?' Leah felt her cheeks burning.

'Oh come on!' Debs clapped her hands. 'Is this something you've blocked out? Like trauma? You said we should start an Owl Society. We were… Twelve? Maybe less?'

'About ten,' Toni asserted.

'Yeah. And you were the owl – the leader.' Debs said this portentously, then tipped a wink towards Steve – had Leah blinked, she would have missed this. 'Then we all had other roles. Want to guess what they were, Steve?'

'Oh, you're the panther,' he said, without pause. 'Then…'

'I like it!' Debs said. 'I can see why you're in sales, mister! Go on…'

'And you…' he turned towards Toni '…I think you're a gazelle. That's how I'd put you.'

'Has someone got some money handy? I think I'd like to tip this man,' Toni said, taking the compliment with exaggerated poise.

'But you…' Steve frowned at Leah. 'You're not an owl. An osprey, maybe. A falcon.'

'He means you're a top bird,' Debs said. 'I'd go for mother hen, personally, but that's just me. But no… she was definitely an owl. Self-styled owl, at that, weren't you?'

Leah was so absurdly embarrassed, she turned away, lugging her suitcase towards the stairs. 'I remember something about that. Best the owl checks out her nest.'

She held the painted owl's stare as she climbed the steps. Even in the abstract sprays and splashes, its eyes seemed as glassy as those lodged in the skulls of the bear, the wolf and the eagle.

They came to a decision on who got which rooms. Or rather, the others had. Leah had been happy to take the smallest room, next to the shower room. Stags' heads appeared as she climbed the staircase leading up to the second level. She sighed as she hurled her suitcase onto the bed, glad to be rid of the weight. Then she grinned.

The others had been so busy scrapping over who got the biggest room, they'd missed out the fact that Leah had the best view. From this section of the lodge, she could see through the trees towards the sea in the distance – at that moment, a pale grey against the weird haze of the low clouds. Below, the garden area sprawled out, with space for a barbecue, a huge fire pit, the hot tubs and a number of well-appointed sheds at the back, unseasoned and suspiciously new.

Then she remembered the conversation about the owl, and the other animals. Leah had been the type of child who got embarrassed on characters' behalf on TV shows, and had to hide her face. What she'd felt wasn't embarrassment about a childhood game being exposed to ridicule – but something else. A sense of shame. Why in God's name would Debs bring that up? What was she playing at?

'Hey,' said a voice at her elbow.

Leah spun around. Debs was there, holding out a gin and tonic. 'Didn't even know you'd followed me.'

'Ninja skills. You never lose it. You all right, missus? You turned tail a bit, there. Hope we didn't scare you off?'

'Got to be honest, I needed to pee.'

'You always were a terrible liar, Leah. I think that's why we like you. Sorry to bring up the old Owl Society thing. I forget, you know, how it all turned out. Weird.'

'That painting reminds me of the logo. You remember?'

'Yep. That was the first thing that came into my head. Weird, eh?'

'Coincidence. One of those things.'

Debs sat down on the bed and folded her arms. 'I think Toni's enjoying the attention from our pilot friend. For all she's got a stick up her arse at the best of times, she always liked the attention part. Poor old Roy will be turning in his Bentley if he saw her behaving like that.'

'Usually she's more about control. I'm surprised she's not changed all the cutlery.'

Debs burst out laughing, then kept her voice low as she said: 'She has! While she was talking to Steve about wild swimming at the loch... she started getting out this case. I thought it was a frigging hunting rifle or something, but it's a full dinner service!'

'No way!'

'I was right! She did bring cutlery! There's so much weirdness to come this weekend...' Debs grinned and flicked her fringe up. 'I can't wait!'

'So, while I've got you to myself, tell me your news. I can't even remember the last time I emailed you...'

'Life's all right, I suppose.' Debs smiled, a little more diffidently. 'Company had a ropey couple of years, but we've weathered it. I got used to eating Pot Noodles again, but we're through it, now. It's the strangest thing, carrying your own can. Your name on the cheques, you know? Before, I'd just work at a place then move on. Now I've got my own... We're managing, though. I guess you could say we're all right.'

'And Eoghan?'

'Eoghan's Eoghan.' Debs shrugged. 'Enjoys doing the lecturing. Got tenure now; a PhD, or a professorship. I should know that. Somehow he has failed to have an affair with a student, unless he's absolutely brilliant at keeping things like that secret, which he isn't.'

'Ah, tell him I was asking for him.' Leah had met Eoghan the most out of all her friends' partners. He'd been there since Debs was about twenty-four, and he was twenty-six – though everyone assumed the age gap was significantly larger. He had been bald and socially maladjusted even then. Everyone had said Debs was mad to stick with Eoghan, and had marvelled that the self-styled Danger Girl had settled for someone so quiet and, it had to be said, dull.

But Leah knew Debs better. She knew that after having been courted by any number of princes from her mid-teens onwards, Debs had finally found her frog. Eoghan, with his curious half-baby, half-man face; dirty fair hair, badly receded, even in his twenties; and big blue eyes that were disconcerting rather than captivating. He had adored her from the very first, absurdly smitten. Debs had been delighted with the attention – the devotion – and from there, the control. She had once let it slip to Shell that despite their sometimes sickening couple-y behaviour among the group, things hadn't exactly caught fire in the bedroom. 'Smouldering might be pushing it,' Shell had said. They'd been seeing each other about a year by this point; Leah had always wondered about this. Debs had cheated on him, repeatedly, to begin with.

But they were together and seemed solid. They had that. It was becoming a rare commodity.

'How about the squirt?' Debs asked, kindly.

'He's fine. You know. He's at a residential place for a few days at a time – seems to thrive there.' Leah cleared her throat. 'He's back home with his dad while I'm away. Don't think he likes the idea of Mummy not being there.'

'And how about Dad?'

Leah shook her head. Then she covered her face, and turned away.

'Oh, Leah! I didn't know.' Debs' hand was on her shoulder. 'Poor lass. You split up?'

'God, no. Not split up. I don't think we could split up. But it's hard. Tough for us as a couple. Sometimes I think it's a miracle we got through. We've had a hard road with David, the accident. You think someone being a surgeon would mean they have some status, but John's grafting all the time. Especially trauma cases – you can imagine, the calls can come at any time,' Leah said, turning away to hide the tears. 'So it's been difficult. It's always going to be difficult. Difficult all our lives. And you know what's worse? There'll be a time when neither of us will be there to look after David. That's the worst, the absolute worst. Sometimes it feels too much… I feel like a failure.'

'Anything but! God, you've had to put up with so much shit…'

'I think with John, there was someone else, a colleague… I don't think it's still going on, and I never knew for sure. By that point I didn't even want to know. It's not something I want to talk about right now. Maybe later… This is the first time I've been away since then. It's ruining us – that's the truth. It'd ruin anyone. Imagine having it all, and thinking you've got it all, and then… I tried.'

Debs paused for a moment. 'It's a shit gig. I've told you before on an email. But not to your face. So I'm doing it now. You're a fucking warrior, Leah. You're a frigging Viking. I couldn't do it.'

'You could. Course you could.' Tears blurred Leah's eyes. She turned to the dresser, where Debs had lain the gin and tonic. 'Anyway, Viking you say? I think it's about time we started drinking like Vikings.'

'Yes!' Debs roared, lifting her own drink.

They clinked glasses.

And that's when the face appeared at the window.

7

'God in his righteous fucking chariot!'
Debs spoke for both of them. Leah grabbed her arm; Debs stepped forward, swiping back and forth, as if shooing away a pigeon.

It was not a pigeon. The shadowy figure etched against the sky took on detail. The face was upside down, and belonged to a slim, dark-haired figure, with sparkling green eyes. The newcomer smiled and waved.

'It's Mouse!' Leah gasped, in relief.

'What's she doing out there, for the love of all that's holy?'

Mouse gestured upwards, smiled, then disappeared.

'And how'd she get out on the balcony?' Debs shrieked. She had her phone held in her hand, braced behind her ear, as if she was ready to cast a spear. 'Come to think of it... *Why* did she get out on the balcony? Some sort of ninja shit?'

'I still can't be sure I actually saw it,' Leah said. She snorted, and nodded towards Debs' brandished phone. 'Hey, I hope that thing isn't loaded.'

They heard a window open; heading out into the hallway,

they saw Mouse stepping inside the bay window, grinning. 'Sorry – couldn't help it.'

'You scared the shit out of us!' Nonetheless, Debs was the first to throw her arms around the newcomer. 'Christ... I hope you weren't eavesdropping on any of the gossip.'

'Nothing I hadn't heard before, ladies,' Mouse replied, as Leah also closed in for a hug.

'Jeez, I know it's been a couple of years, but there's something different about you,' Leah said.

'You sure?' Mouse cocked an eyebrow. Sunlight glinted off a piercing, buried inside the dark, well-groomed line.

'Yeah, different – but she means "great" different,' Debs said, cutting off Leah's embarrassed stammer. 'How come you're the one who ends up looking younger?'

Leah hadn't seen Beatrice 'Mouse' Stewart for a while, now – it could have been years. But the effect was odd – her hair was the same length and colour, and she still had the same composed, angular features as when she was seventeen or eighteen, when the group had split for its university adventures. But there was something new about her that was difficult to put a finger on – posture, perhaps, demeanour, rather than looks. Mouse had been something of a tomboy in her younger years, football tops and tracksuits, but short of stature – hence the nickname among the rest of the girls. The boys had called her Sporty Spice, something she'd hated, but that had stopped the minute teenage years wrought their changes, and she'd grown tall and willowy – not as tall as Toni or Leah, but not far off it – with long black hair.

Mouse was the one who'd driven the boys particularly mad. What had made her seem timid when she was eleven had metamorphosed into cool, self-possessed confidence.

Mouse's eyes spoke the loudest, an unearthly green that might have studded the eyes of a feline idol unearthed in an Egyptian tomb. Looking at her now – she was clad in hiking trousers and a base layer top, and lumpen shoes – maybe there was an air of wildness to her, even though the black hair was tied back. This made another key feature, a large birthmark at the angle of her jaw, stand out all the more; brown and seemingly velvet-textured, it was like a comma on the side of her face; a natural pause, demanding more knowledge, even the touch of a fingertip.

The girls had all cried over Mouse's successes at one time, especially over that one boy.

Leah had a sudden flashback, to that particular boy's face. Owen Clancy, desideratum of St Martha's. The one they'd all wanted, and the one Mouse got.

For a while.

'Drinks!' Debs declared, as Mouse shut the bay window behind her. 'And for the love of God, tell us what you were doing out there?'

'Ah, I decided to explore,' Mouse said. 'It's an open walkway up on the roof, did you know?'

'You mean you can walk all the way around the roof? See in the windows?'

'No, that's just the entryway. I knew I could look in if I stuck my head over the side. Wouldn't recommend it, though. Steep drop down there, onto your head. Did you know there's another hot tub on the roof?'

'Our charming host is just taking us through the details.' Leah nodded towards the stairway. They could hear a conversation between Toni and Steve, down below – well, Toni's side of it, anyway. 'You met him?'

'Nah.' Mouse sniffed. 'Still to check in. Left my bags at the campsite.'

'Eh? Campsite?' Debs was genuinely shocked.

'Yeah. I got here a couple of days ago,' Mouse said. 'I decided to come over and check out the house.'

'What... you had a key?' Debs asked.

'Nah, just thought I'd scale the wall... There's a tree, makes it easy to climb as high as the roof... Quite dangerous I would think. I mean, in terms of security. Anyone could get in if they wanted to badly enough. QED.'

Leah burst out laughing. 'Just... why? That's all I want to know. Why do that?'

'Something I do.' Mouse shrugged. 'Anyway, we all here? You two, Toni and Shell?'

'Shell's not here – haven't heard much from her,' Leah said. 'You get any mobile reception on the mountain, incidentally?'

'Not really, since the ferry dropped me off... We're in a black spot for reception. No open-access Wi-Fi either. That's been nice, I have to say. No distractions. Way I like it.'

'And, sorry, let's scroll back a bit. You say you're doing what?' Debs gawped at Mouse the way someone might upon noticing they shared their salad with a snail. '*Camping?* Like, in a *tent*? *Outside?* How did this come about? Dear God, we've got things to talk about.'

Steve appeared at the head of the stairs – and his expression mimicked Debs' when he saw Mouse. 'Ah... I don't think I remember making your acquaintance?' he said.

Mouse gave her usual lightning-bolt smile. 'You must have missed me coming in. I was dropped off earlier.'

'That must have been Pete... He never mentioned anything, though.'

Toni squealed, and all but shoved Steve aside to get to Mouse. They embraced for a while, with Mouse's face peering out from among Toni's hair, as if behind a trellis. 'When did you arrive?'

'Just now.'

'I take it this is... Is this Michelle?' Steve said.

'No this is Mouse... I mean, Beatrice,' Toni said. 'Shell hasn't been in touch yet.'

'Ah – that was a thing I had to tell you all,' Steve said, a light blinking on behind his eyes. 'I knew there was something I meant to say. Pete told me – your friend Shell got in touch with head office. Said she had run into a delay and probably wouldn't arrive until Saturday.'

Sighs, and desperate sounds from the other four. 'She set this all up, didn't she?' Mouse said. 'Odd...'

'No, Leah set it up,' Debs said. 'Sure of it.'

'Hang on – I'm absolutely positive...' Leah began.

Steve cut her off. 'I think she mentioned something to do with her kids, or childcare... Pete'll tell you all about it. Right – I'll show you how to work the hot tubs and patio lights, then I'll leave you to it.'

'Hopefully we'll see you down at the pub?' Debs said. *And my God*, Leah thought, *she actually bit her lip*.

Steve grinned. 'You never know.' The front door opened, and Pete appeared. His face was flushed, and he was sweating heavily. He wasn't simply out of breath; he was agitated, even openly angry. Unconsciously, Leah backed away towards the wall.

Pete ground his teeth, clenching and unclenching his fists. 'What's going on here?' he said, huskily.

There was silence for a second. Steve showed no outward sign of discomfiture other than a tug of his earlobe. 'I'm getting our guests settled into the house, Pete. Showing them around.'

'You were just meant to leave them the key, not ferry them around on the island. We've got a schedule to sort out.'

'What's Gwen doing, then? She's meant to be on with you for the return to Glasgow.'

'Yes, but you need to sort out the paperwork after you land, and do a proper handover, don't you? And since when did we offer a taxi service?'

'Calm down, mate. We had plenty of time. I'll come down to the plane for you, chief. Not to worry.' Then he tittered, raising the tension a notch or two. 'God... did you run up the hill?'

For a moment, Leah was sure the smaller, but more imposing-looking man would barrel forward into Steve, perhaps skittling him right into the patio doors. But instead, he relaxed, and smiled. 'I challenged myself, you know. See how fast I could do it. I almost won.'

'You're almost dead, mate,' Debs said.

'Also,' Pete said, once the laughter had died down, 'I was counting on a return ticket in my car, which Steve so kindly borrowed.'

'Just providing a service, chief,' Steve said, saluting. 'Anyway, that'll be me for the day, girls. I'll hopefully see you down at the pub later on. Where I will be drinking only fizzy pop and the odd Virgin Mary,' he added, catching a look from Pete.

'Take care, ladies,' Pete said, ushering Steve out the door. 'Don't hesitate to get in touch if you have any problems. We'll see you tomorrow for the activities.'

Silence filled a few seconds after the front door closed behind them. Debs broke it. 'Was that some sort of... unresolved romantic tension, between those two? Because I have to admit – that was kinda hot.'

'Either that or they genuinely, openly hate each other,' Toni remarked. 'Which is a perfect fit for the two guys who'll be flying us back home on Monday.'

8

'Pub's calling,' Debs said, rubbing her hands, once the glasses were dry. 'No denying it.'

'She has a point,' Toni said. 'They never actually made it clear. Are they going to drive us back down?'

Debs and Mouse shared a look. 'No,' Debs said. 'Pete has to sort a return flight to Glasgow. We should see him pass us. Probably we'll be higher up than the plane.'

Toni frowned. 'Can we order a taxi then?'

'There's no one here to drive a taxi!' Debs' face was flushed already – a tell-tale sign when they'd been underage teenagers, stymied in their early attempts to get into clubs. All these years later, and she hadn't found a way to conceal it. 'There are alternatives, though.'

Mouse grinned. 'I have a feeling what this is going to involve.'

Debs got to her feet. She almost made it on the first attempt, but sank back into the sofa, and had to try again. 'There is a solution. Follow me!'

Toni watched her retreating back, muttering: 'She hasn't gotten any quieter, has she?'

As they followed Debs out of the patio door into the yard, Mouse took Leah's arm. 'Hey – you see the painting?'

She nodded towards the blue and white owl, with its

distinctive, though disturbingly distorted face. 'Yeah,' Leah said.

Mouse smiled. 'What does it remind you of?'

'I know, the Owl Society,' Leah said, a little irritably. 'They've already got stuck into me for that.'

'Oh… Sorry. Didn't realise it was a sore point.'

'It's not a sore point,' Leah said, carefully.

'I mean… It's how I got my name, after all!' Mouse rubbed Leah's arm.

Out on the patio, Debs gestured towards a rack hidden from view, tucked into an alcove. 'Behold!'

'Bikes?' Toni was aghast. 'No one said anything about bikes?'

'Come on, darling,' Debs said, grinning. 'Get your trainers on. We'll be down that hill in no time. They've got everything here – helmets, chain locks, you name it. We'll be down at the pub in no time.'

'That's all very well, but we've got to get back up the hill later on, when we're pissed,' Leah said.

'Ah, worry about it later, why don't you?' Debs said dismissively, and lifted a garish helmet off a hook. 'Check this out! The colours are giving me a hangover already. This is the ugliest helmet. I'll pick the ugliest bike, too.'

'Uh, I'll need to get changed,' Leah said, looking at her jeans.

Toni folded her arms and pursed her lips. 'I didn't sign up for this, really.'

'What do you mean?' Debs clipped the helmet underneath her chin. This compression lent a comical aspect to her full cheeks, and Leah chuckled. 'It's an outdoor activity weekend, Toni. You did sign up for it.'

'I'll have to change, too.' Toni sniffed.

Mouse peered over Debs' shoulder into the alcove.

'They've got canoes and trailers. We should take those out onto the water tomorrow.'

'You been canoeing before?' Debs asked. 'Bet it'll be absolutely Baltic in there. We'll freeze before we drown.'

Toni raised a finger. 'Um, can I just say, no one said anything about canoeing to me? I've never been canoeing before. Christ, I haven't been on a bike that wasn't anchored to the floor in years!'

'We all used to knock around on the bikes,' Mouse said, knocking on the orange hull of one of the canoes. 'Leah got us into that. We were the Biker Girls first, weren't we?'

'Oh yeah,' Debs said. 'That was before the Owl Society.'

'I remember the Biker Girls,' Leah said. She felt a little less embarrassed at these memories, with a gin inside her. 'That came after the Owl Society.'

'The Owl Society,' Mouse said. She turned and stared into Leah's eyes, with an odd intensity. 'It sounds so much more *mysterious* now. Maybe we should reconvene it?'

'You look a bit reluctant to talk about the Owl Society,' Debs said tartly, wheeling out a luminous green and black teenager's bike. 'As if you're embarrassed. Why should you be embarrassed, Mummy Owl?'

'You'll have to reconvene it for us. It's gone into the memory hole. I'm going to get changed into some exercise gear. I'm not really fussed if I look a fright down at the Slaughtered Lamb, or whatever the pub was called.'

'I'll join you,' Toni said.

'Don't be talking Leah out of it now, Tones,' Debs said. She perched in her saddle, wobbling horribly as she tried to maintain her balance.

'I'll head back to collect my gear,' Mouse said.

'You were serious?' Leah asked. 'You've been camping out here?'

Mouse nodded. 'Yep. It's how I got the lie of the land. Better bring my stuff back to the house. I'll see you down at the pub – don't wait for me.'

'You going to walk?' Debs asked, taking a very unsteady practice pedal around the stone slabs on the patio.

'I've got my own bike,' Mouse said. 'I'm in the room near the bathroom, I guess?'

'Yeah. That or the other really shitty one. Whatever's left goes to Shell, when she shows up.' After a few feet of wobbly progress, Debs hit the brakes to avoid the hot tub, and they shrieked.

Leah hated the way the helmet scrunched up her hair, and fully detested the way it seemed to bunch her cheeks and chin up, similar to Debs, as if in a fist. But the moment she kicked off down the curving road, her discomfort metamorphosed. Muscle memory kicked in. At the foot of the driveway, the road curved down a steep hill, and the moment that gravity took over she stood tall in the seat of the bike, shoulders and back braced. The breeze became a roar in her ears and she picked up speed, the bracken and mossy hillsides blurring as they scrolled past. Leah grinned.

'It's a bit steep!' Toni said, somewhere over her shoulder.

'Ah c'mon, let's kick into it.' This was Debs' goading voice. 'Quicker we go, quicker we have pints.'

'I think I'm drunk already! We're probably committing an offence.'

Leah ignored them. Below, the sea loch appeared as the

road corkscrewed down a mountain. A huge bird fluttered away at their approach, a suggestion of banked wings before it was gone. Leah allowed the bike to follow the curve, thrilled at the sensation. *The Freewheelin' Leah Louden!* She grinned. When was the last time she'd been on a bike? When was the last time she'd even thought about it? There had been a spin class, though that had hardly been the same thing. She'd enjoyed the camaraderie, though, and had made new friends out of it; a new Biker Girl Club, really. But that had been before John, and then of course, David. There had been new clubs once David came along – the NCT crew, which had turned surprisingly toxic, surprisingly fast, something that had taken John aback. 'There seem to be a lot of harpies pregnant at the same time as you, pet,' he'd said, in one less guarded moment. 'Something in the River Styx got them in the mood.' The breastfeeding group had been kinder, which had then morphed into a general support network.

Then there was the accident. The day her life stopped. The day she lost her husband and her son, she thought, with a sudden stab of regret and remorse. Though they were both still alive and still with her.

Leah shook her head and pushed on, calf muscles pumping. A glance over her shoulder confirmed Debs and then Toni following in train. Debs was the more comical of the two figures, hunched low over the handlebars, working hard at the pedals despite the favourable gradient. *She's trying to catch me up*, Leah realised, with an unpleasant start.

She ignored this, as well as the thought that followed on

from it: *Toni has a point. I don't fancy coming back up this way with a load of bikes when we're all drunk.*

But that was for later.

'Why do we have to be in a gang?' Toni asked.

'We are in a gang,' Debs said.

'I know, but why do we have to have a name and stuff? People might think we want to fight or something.'

'Then we get tooled up, guv'nah,' Debs said, in a more than decent impression of Bob Hoskins. 'We put the manners on 'em!'

'I just think we should have a name.'

'What about the Black Scorpions?' Shell said. She fit her helmet, prompting the others to do the same.

No one said anything. 'I mean… I saw it in a movie. Or maybe it was the Black Widows.'

'Nah,' Debs said, 'we'd sound like horrible, sweaty old geezers. Guys with their arses hanging out their leathers.'

'Ew,' Toni said.

'Big sweaty crack down the middle. After six hours on a motorbike. Take a deep breath, Toni.' Debs did so, a beatific smile on her face. 'Take it all in.'

'No!' Toni gagged.

'I think,' Leah said, peremptorily, 'we should be the Biker Girls.'

'Bit boring,' Debs said.

'Anyone got any better suggestions?'

'I thought we were the Damsels?'

'That's our band,' Leah explained. 'This is different. This is our biker gang. So we're the Biker Girls.'

'I like the Black Scorpions,' Shell protested.

'Scorpions don't go on bikes,' Leah said, archly. 'It'd be a bit awkward, wouldn't it?'

'I think it would be awesome to see a scorpion on a bike,' Debs countered. 'And you don't see black widow spiders on bikes, either, but that sounds awesome too.'

'Well, it's my club,' Leah said. 'I think we should be the Biker Girls.'

'Reckon we should get our own club, ladies?' Debs grinned at the others.

Beatrice, not yet Mouse – though she would be, by the time the summer was over – pushed off on her bike. 'Biker Girls is fine by me,' she said. 'We're wasting time. Let's go.'

As they all began to pedal, Leah spotted another figure, lurking up by the bollards at the canal path. It was someone she recognised – the new girl, who'd joined their class in the fortnight before school broke up. A sullen girl with a pale face and black hair cropped very short. She stood there, glaring at them, with a scooter in her hand, as the Biker Girls pedalled away.

Some change in the quality of the air startled Leah out of her reverie – an alteration in the pressure, as if some immense predator was bearing down on her. All it would have needed was the shadow.

That'll be Debs, overtaking.

Instead, Mouse zipped past her. Her personal bike was comical, an old lady's bicycle, coloured the grey of obsolete computer tech. It had a weird height to the saddle, and was undoubtedly foldable. But there was no denying the rider's speed and agility. 'Whoo!' Mouse yelled over her shoulder. And just for a second, Leah thought to pump the pedals and catch up. Then she remembered herself, and held back, enjoying the play of Mouse's ponytail, flailing in the slipstream.

9

The Tail Wynd was surprisingly busy, mainly with men. It was the sort of place that would have suited a gauzy fog of cigarette smoke, and indeed seemed to pine for it, judging by the brown and yellowed hue of the wood-stain panelling. The tables had been through a lot, and recently, too, judging by the stark flesh wounds on the pitted timber surfaces. Leah imagined feral teens, glittery teeth protruding over their bottom lips, even though there weren't any in evidence just yet.

The hubbub barely reduced when Leah, Mouse, Toni and Debs entered, though just about every pair of eyes followed them in.

Debs marched up to the bar. 'Hope you don't mind – we left our bikes tied up at your trough. They need to slake their thirst. And so do we. Four gin and tonics, please.'

The barman – what were the names Steve had given? Leah tried to remember. Alan and something? Maureen? – a thick-set man with pouchy eyes and saggy cheeks like a knackered old lapdog, grinned at her approach. His teeth were the same shade as the panelling that hemmed him in behind the bar. 'You'll be with Steve, I take it,' he said, in a heavy accent.

'Oh, with luck.' Debs beamed.

Leah took her drink to a table in the corner, a safe enough distance away from a party of four or five rough-looking men in their twenties who appeared as if they'd just stepped off a fishing boat, or a TV drama about a fishing boat. Debs remained at the bar, while Toni had disappeared to the ladies'. Mouse followed Leah to the table.

One man in a thick Aran sweater turned in his seat and addressed Leah. 'You signed up for Steve's activities tour?'

'Lambs to the slaughter,' Leah said, unconsciously hiding her face behind her glass.

'Ah, he's a pussycat, really. We'll sort him out if he gives you any cheek.'

'You think we need looking after, pet?' Debs thrust her chin upwards, mock-pugnacious.

Giving this exchange a wide berth, Mouse eased herself through a tiny space into the corner seat, with a curiously unsettling, sinuous move. She settled in beside Leah and leaned close, popping open a packet of crisps. A steel water bottle stood on the table beside her, and Leah realised: *She brought those with her.*

Mouse took a quick sip, and offered Leah the packet. 'Weird, isn't it?' she asked.

'How d'you mean?' Leah said, crunching a handful of crisps.

'We're all different, and all the same.'

'Guess so. I haven't really had time to think about it. I feel like I only just caught up with Toni, then, it felt like… clatter. There you all were.'

'Everyone's changed. You know what struck me? Age. We're ageing. Not old, but getting there.'

'Way to wet my towel!'

'Not in looks, or anything – and you do look fantastic, Leah. We're different. Wouldn't be right, otherwise, I suppose. I mean, Debs is the same, right? Bit too loud… bit too brash… But you have to admit, still quite funny.'

Leah saw the barman laugh along with Debs; most of the men were staring at her, now. She leaned on the bar top and stuck her backside out, and Leah almost choked. 'You could say that she's the same, yeah,' she said, finally, after Mouse thumped her on the back.

'And yet she's different, wouldn't you say?'

'Different haircut, for sure – not what I'd have chosen, but it kinda suits her.'

'Not just that.' Mouse took a sip of water. 'She's confident, now. You get that? She wasn't like that about five or six years ago. Or whenever we saw her. She still with that Eoghan?'

'I believe she is. Strongest partnership out of all of us, really. I mean, ignoring Roy.'

'I think Debs only ever wanted a guy to worship her. Mission accomplished. She still cheating on him?'

'I wouldn't know,' Leah said, uncomfortably. 'Did she cheat on him all that much?'

'Just about every time I saw her on a night out, when he wasn't around. Full-blown affairs, as well.'

'I heard that was just in the early days. I quite like him, you know. We used to be unkind about him, and that probably made him uncomfortable when he came out to meet us. But… he's nice, basically. Unthreatening. Clever. Sensitive.'

'And a little bit too good for her?' Mouse smiled, but not with her eyes. Leah felt goose pimples at this expression, the direct inquiry. This was the old Mouse; mysterious Mouse; inscrutable Mouse.

'No – I'd say maybe we got that the wrong way around. Maybe we underestimated Debs. Maybe she just made a good choice. A good match. As for the other stuff… Maybe she's having her cake and eating it. Lots of us would.'

'That true?'

Leah didn't have time to answer.

'Here you go, ladies,' Debs said, planting two large gins and two bottles of tonic down on the table. She saw Mouse's bottle of water and frowned. 'God's sake, don't tell me you're actually rehydrating? That won't do.'

'Definitely,' Mouse said, coolly. 'Not a good idea to get boozing after a cycle ride.'

Debs winked at Leah. 'She's after your job, Mummy Owl.' Then she sat down beside Toni, who had returned from the ladies' in time to collect the drinks for herself and Debs.

Leah sipped at her gin and winced. 'Oh Christ, that's a double.'

Mouse left hers, continuing to sip at the water. 'We could have an interesting trip back up the mountain.'

'Drunk or sober, we're going to struggle to get back up there. Didn't seem so far, going downhill. That might change.'

Mouse sniggered. 'Mummy Owl. You flinched, you know. When Debs said that. That takes me back.'

'It's kind of embarrassing, I guess. Kids' stuff.' Leah took another quick drink.

'You were Owl – I remember that. Had you been in the Brownies?'

'Yeah. But that wasn't the reason I wanted to start the Owl

Society.' The actual words – *the Owl Society* – hadn't come out of Leah's mouth in years. 'I watched a David Attenborough documentary, about an owl in the woods. All that cutaway camera trickery, infrared at night. Swallowing little mice whole. Bringing up pellets. I was fascinated... more fascinated than I'd have been had it been a show about, I don't know... tigers in Siberia, or monkeys in the jungle. I thought owls were amazing. My favourite animals.'

'So you do remember,' Debs said, slyly. 'You seemed to have amnesia about the Owl Society before. Little bit shy about our past, were we?'

'Well. Memory, you know,' Leah said, shrugging. 'Weird how it can come back.'

Mouse nodded. 'So, you like owls, I get that. And then... you named the rest of us after far inferior creatures.'

Leah held up her hands, a little more comfortable discussing it with the rush of the gin in her veins. 'True enough. You were the mouse. Debs was... Christ, what was she?'

'The mole!' Mouse spluttered. 'Oh, she loved that. "I want to be a tiger. Why can't I pick my own name?"'

Debs didn't respond – she had turned to Toni and started a new chat.

'Toni was the fox... Was Toni your best friend at the time?'

'That I can't remember,' Leah said, sincerely. 'I guess she must have been. That's a second-in-command name.'

'I dunno. Shell was Badger, wasn't she? The fruits of the forest. Hah. I hadn't thought about that in years.'

'You did some amazing artwork,' Leah said. 'That was your talent, for sure. Our club badges. The clubhouse poster, that went on my bedroom door... Oh God, that's embarrassing.' Leah covered her face in her hands, in not-one-hundred-per-cent-mock-horror.

But Mouse's face clouded. 'No. I didn't do the art. Lots of other stuff, but not that one. It wasn't me.'

'Wasn't it?'

'No. That was the other girl.'

Leah saw the moon face, the dark hair. Cut like a boy's. Then her own voice, from nearly thirty years before. *'Yeah, she's got a boy's arse as well.'*

The memory clutched at her, then; took her by the lapels and shook her. She wanted to flinch, to hide under the table. It was something that had grown and grown in her mind the whole day, her guts, her blood. It was a cancer. It had tendrils. It took root. Shame.

Leah remembered the name. She knew the face.

'Cheer up, you two,' Debs said, leaning closer. 'We've not even clinked glasses yet!'

They did – all four of them. Musketeers crossing swords. 'Absent friends,' Leah said.

'Oh Christ – Shell.' Debs took a long draught of her gin, winced, then spoke through gritted teeth. 'Forgot she hadn't turned up yet.'

'Specially as she set it up, I suppose,' Toni said, sulkily. 'What did she say – something turned up at home?'

'That's what she said,' Leah replied. 'Or, what Steve told us she said.'

'Forever crying off, wasn't she?' Debs said, in the middle of a burp. 'Since she had kids, that is. Always good for a laugh up until then. Even after she married Ewan. Popped those kids out fast enough, though. Bang-bang-bang, she's out the game.'

'You know, I think it started before that, when she

became a PE teacher,' Toni said. 'She was dedicated to that job. Wouldn't shut up about it on the phone. Back when we used to actually speak to each other.'

That remark lingered a little too long. 'Well – at least she gets to have a nice time tomorrow while we're all dying of a hangover,' Toni added, finally.

'That's the spirit!' Debs clinked glasses with Toni again, and the tonic sloshed over the side of the glass. 'Good grief, this stuff is moreish. I think it's the cheapest gin he had, too.'

'Hey, I think the guy with the Aran jumper's taking an interest, Debs,' Toni simpered, indicating the table with a none-too-discreet bob of the head.

There, indeed, the man in the Aran jumper with the bent nose had swivelled in his seat, and was openly gazing at the table. 'All right there?' he said.

'Yeah, not too bad,' Debs said. She moved her chair closer to the other table, and struck up a conversation. Toni joined her, a little too readily.

'Jesus,' Leah whispered. 'Already. Isn't it a bit too early to get drunk and flirt with the cast of *The Wicker Man*?'

'Might be a laugh,' Mouse said. 'Don't think I'll join in, though.'

Leah clocked the full glass of gin, untouched, at Mouse's elbow. 'Still not fancy it?'

'I don't drink so much now,' Mouse said, after a pause. She didn't meet Leah's gaze; instead, she fixed her fingertips on the edge of the table, like a solo pianist preparing for silence from the audience. 'I was going to try to hide it, you know… pour the glass into a plant pot. Or just top up Debs' glass for her, inch by inch. But there it is – I don't really drink. And there's no big reason, before you ask. Nothing dramatic. Nothing evangelical. No steps taken. I just got fed up with it. It wasn't so much the hangovers and stuff, it was the waste of time all around. And energy. I decided I didn't want to do stuff in my life that involved drinking. And recovering from drinking. I prefer other stuff. The outdoors, mainly. Although I was always going to make an exception for you guys.'

Leah felt she was being told something momentous, but couldn't quite grasp what it was. Perhaps it was one of their number making a leap into maturity which hadn't involved the tired dynamic of marriage and kids, but something more profound than that. This was a rejection. 'I remember seeing you in a tent in India, just before you dropped off social media for good. I thought... "I can't remember Mouse doing that stuff before." When did you get into it? The travel, the extreme sports, or whatever?'

'I kept most of that from you guys. I went away with my dad a lot – he took us to the Lake District and Scotland. Ireland once or twice; a few French campsites. We did Ben Nevis and that kind of stuff, but never anything hairy, to start with. He was a proper climber when he was young – took lots of risks. Crampons, ropes, vertical ascents, you name it. But he was gentler with me and Tommy when we got old enough to go with him. I caught the bug. But I never really told you guys about all that. I think I did, once, and you said something about tramps. Or... the Twits! That was it. You made a joke about my family being like the Twits. You know, Roald Dahl. I took it to heart, so I never told you about it again.'

There was nothing hostile in Mouse's demeanour. But Leah's eyes had filled with tears. She clutched at Mouse's arm. 'My… God. I don't remember that, Mouse. Are you sure? Are you sure that was me?'

Now Mouse laughed. 'Definitely you. Don't worry, Leah! Christ's sake, what age are we all? You were eleven, if that. Maybe even ten. Nowhere near St Martha's, yet. You said something daft that you didn't mean when you were a child. We all did it. I'm sure I did something similar to you.'

Fucking right you did, Leah thought. Then she shook her head, as if to clear it, and put down the gin. Too much already. Too much of a glow on her. 'I'm so sorry. If I did that… It wasn't me. I mean, I didn't mean it.'

'I'm serious, Leah. I have no feelings about that. It's long done, and it doesn't mean a thing. Even if it did, I'm at peace with it. You're a good person, Leah. You're the only one out of the five of us I really kept in touch with. You're the only one who doesn't spend an entire email or text message talking about yourself. Out of those two, anyway.' She nodded towards Debs and Toni, who had now transplanted to the table full of rowdy men, their conversation grown louder. A few of the men on the periphery glanced hopefully towards Leah and Mouse.

'They're good, in their way. Always good fun. Toni can seem a little cold, but I always liked that spiky side to her, if that makes sense. When I was a kid, I used to think she had a lot of class. Poise, you know?' Leah realised what she was saying, and stammered, 'Not that I'm saying she *doesn't* have class, but… All about appearances. She was always so beautifully turned out. She knew all the brands, the things to have, and her dad gave her them. I envied that.'

'She's beautiful, no doubt about it,' Mouse said, nodding. 'The Aran shirt guy? He was checking out Toni, not Debs.

Debs doesn't realise, or doesn't care. So desperate, that girl. After all this time. You can almost smell it off her. I know her qualities. I'd put a good chunk of money on her messing her man around again before we get off this island. I think maybe a weekend of her is my limit.'

Leah was sad to hear Mouse say this, although she could relate to a lot of what was being said. 'Debs' settings are on "a bit full-on" to start with, that's true.'

'I blame what happened to her dad. Even now, if anything happened to my dad...' Mouse shivered. 'Turned her into a bit of a party girl, almost overnight. She was so quiet, before that. Maybe it was her way of coping. Grade-A girl, I remember, up until then.'

'That's true. But I guess it was our age, too.'

'Oh yeah, I'll give you that. Plenty of good girls come off the rails the minute the dreaded hormones strike. You were kind to her, though, after her dad died. You really brought her into the circle.'

'The circle' was true enough – Leah, Toni and Mouse had been a trio before Debs was allowed in, and then Shell. But Leah, Toni and Mouse had been a good trio. They had looked good together; Leah with that beautiful smile and sweet face; Toni, statuesque and graceful; Mouse, ultimately the prettiest one, from a standing start, eventually offsetting a quiet nature.

'I remember one time,' Leah said, 'the boys called us The Corrs. You remember that? After the sisters in the band.'

'Yeah. I remember that. Owen Clancy and his mates. One of them turned around, pointed at Debs and said: "Yeah, you're The Corrs. And there's Jim."'

Leah's hands went to her mouth, but she could not

suppress the laugh. 'I remember that! Poor girl, she cried all lunchtime. I couldn't calm her down.'

'It was cruel,' Mouse said. 'Anyway. Tell me more about you. Tell me about John – he doing all right? Coping OK on his own this weekend?'

'Actually he took David to his mum's for the weekend. So, it means he effectively gets a weekend off out of it, too.'

'That sounds about right,' Mouse said, wryly.

'Other than that, he's good. Working hard. Busy hands.'

'I know this is a cliché about a surgeon, but he always seems so *confident*,' Mouse said, and actually puffed out her chest as she did so, like a strutting rooster. 'I hope you don't mind my saying it. He had that air about him. He could run out a spreadsheet and do a presentation with about five minutes' prep, you know those guys? They call it command presence, in the army.'

Leah nearly choked on her drink. 'God, you should write his business cards for him. What about you – not still seeing Ian, are you?'

'Nah, long gone,' Mouse said, without elaborating. 'Not much going on for me at the moment. Just chilling.'

'Don't let me stop you,' Leah said, gesturing towards the conjoined party. 'Feel free, pet. Bag yourself a farmer. Hey, farmer's wife would suit you down to the ground, wouldn't it? Be like camping, except in a big house with a proper roof and running water and a real toilet and lots of pets.'

Cutting over the top of their laughter, Debs announced: 'Yes! We shall play darts! I challenge you!' She drained her drink, raised both fists in the air, and then, to much cheering, she followed the man in the Aran jumper towards the dartboard.

10

'This vehicle smells of something,' Toni declared.

'Yeah... Sorry about that,' Debs said.

Steve was driving, with his shades folded into the neck of his T-shirt. He chuckled.

'No,' Toni slurred, 'I mean, it smells of an animal... something musky.'

'I think you mean Steve.' Debs, who was sat beside Steve on the broad front seat of the people carrier, nudged him in the ribs.

Leah, who was sat in the back with Mouse, studied Steve's face in profile from over his right shoulder. She couldn't tell in the dashboard-lit gloom whether or not he welcomed the attention.

'Sorry, ladies,' he said. 'The smell is my fault. I gave a sheep farmer a lift down the pub on the way to pick you up. I think he left a little something behind, off his boots.'

'Ew,' Toni said.

'I believe that is what they call the females, yes,' Debs said brightly.

Toni buzzed down the passenger-side window. Cold air surged in, and the four women shivered. Through the back of the people carrier window, the trailer containing their

83

bikes rattled and weaved on the steep road back up the mountain.

After a rain shower, the skies had cleared. Above them the dark was dusted with stars – more than Leah expected; more than she remembered ever seeing. Leah had started to talk about a winter holiday she'd taken with John, before David was born, somewhere in the mountains in Canada, when they'd seen the aurora. But the girls had quickly gotten bored, and Debs simply cut her off.

Leah had seethed for a moment or two, and looked out for a means of attack – only to come back to herself after a second or two's reflection. *Let her burn herself out. She does this because she's insecure. You're not a child any more. Laugh it off.*

Leah had laid off the gin after the first eye-watering double, finding herself too easily drawn into the noise, the silliness. It was when dancing had broken out, championed by Debs and Toni, that Leah had found herself toe to toe with a well-appointed young man with thick hair the colour of turmeric and a beard that she didn't find totally repulsive. After she had turned a pirouette under his hand and collided with the febrile lights of a fruit machine, an internal alarm had gone off, and she sat back down.

Steve had appeared not long after that. In fact it had been Mouse who'd sprung the idea of him giving them a lift back. He even had a trailer attached to a people carrier where they piled the bikes. He had acquiesced readily. Score one for Mouse, Leah had thought. And sobriety.

'Amazing you showed up,' Mouse said, leaning forward to place her chin between Steve's headrest and Debs'.

'Well, your friend here invited me down earlier, and I

thought it'd be rude not to show up for a soda water and lime,' he said, totally straight-faced.

'You can have something stronger back at the cabin, if you like,' Debs said.

'Oh yeah,' Toni said, leaning across Debs, 'we've got all sorts. Wine, mostly. You into your wine?'

'Yeah, I can do wine. But I have to keep a lid on it tonight. We're doing some outdoor activities tomorrow, remember? Plus I'm back in the air the day after that. Busy old time, now the restrictions are done.'

'You live here?' Mouse asked him.

'Yeah. Myself and Peter share a place down by the beach, on the south side.'

'Ah,' Debs said, pointedly. 'I get it, now.'

Steve burst out laughing. 'No, no – alluring as Peter is, it's not like that. We're more like lighthouse keepers – we swap around when we have to stay over. Me, Peter and Gwen, that is.'

'Thank goodness for that,' Toni said, placing her hand on her heart. She was the drunkest. Leah had noticed that Toni hadn't even finished the second gin Debs had slammed down in front of her, but she hadn't needed to. She'd fallen over twice, during an energetic performance to Dead Or Alive's 'You Spin Me Round', and that had been Steve's signal to judiciously steer her and Debs outside – to the chagrin of the rest of the pub's patrons. 'It would have broken me had you been on the other bus.'

'What's Gwen like?' Leah asked. 'I think we saw her briefly when the boat... sorry, plane, was moored.'

'Ah, great worker. I don't see too much of her. She's not a full partner, just drives the bus for us, when the other one's off. We'd be screwed without her. You might meet her, before the week's out – she could be flying you back on… When is it you go?'

'Monday,' Debs said, slapping her thigh. 'When we say it's going to be a long weekend, we mean it, God damn it!'

'So what have we got on tomorrow?' Leah asked. 'Archery? Clay pigeon shooting?'

'The works,' Debs said. 'Far too expensive not to be the works, frankly. Swimming and canoeing, too.'

'Great,' Toni muttered.

'Bit more cycling?' Steve grinned as he said this. 'I have to say, cycling downhill was fine… but considering cycling back up, after a few drinks… That's optimism, let me tell you. Hats off, ladies.'

'Nah, we'll skip the cycling, I think,' Debs said, wincing. 'It was OK coming downhill, and all that. Lovely to tick it off, but a wee bit uncomfortable. Like a sixty-nine.'

There was a fusillade of laughter. Looking out the windscreen, beyond the grinning wraith of her own reflected features, Leah focused on the lights illuminating the dark road as they corkscrewed back to the top. Occasionally, other bright points peeked out of the darkness, only to be wiped clear by the jagged darkness of the fir trees. Then, as they slowed for a tight bend, she saw a field of unblinking yellow eyes, gazing out at them.

'Jesus, what's that?' she shrieked, as something loped away from the car's path.

'Just one of our resident woolly jumpers,' Steve said. 'A sheep. Surprised they're out this late, in fact.'

'What a baaaaa-stard,' Debs said. 'Hey, I think we're nearly there. That's where the horsey guy lives. Look… I think he's out on his patio. He was lovely. Give him a beep for us.'

'I wouldn't, if I were you,' Steve said, quietly.

'You what? Don't be silly, give him a pump. So to speak.'

The headlights stole over a break in the trees. There, in among some burgundy-stained decking, two people sat in garden chairs, feet up, in front of a flickering fire pit. One of the figures stood up and waved heartily.

The car seemed to shriek, with the women's collective reactions amplified.

'Did you see that!' Toni said, at last. 'Completely naked!'

'I couldn't miss it,' Leah said.

'Yep. I tried to kind of warn you. Keith and Susan are a bit of a naked duo. They run an online newsletter. Tried to start a nudie colony out here, a while ago, but didn't get planning permission. Doesn't stop them getting involved in their own way.'

'That was full old man balls,' Debs said. 'I'd been warned about old man balls. I just never expected to see them out in the wild.'

'Was that actually balls? I thought he had a bum bag or something,' Toni said, shaking her head slowly.

'It was. Incredible distance from top to bottom – although I'd say the one on the left was a bit of a slouch.' Debs sighed.

'Was the other person his wife?'

'Probably,' Steve said. 'I can go back if you want a closer look?'

'Nah, you're fine,' Mouse said, and yawned. 'Think bed is calling, in fact.'

'What about the other person?' Leah asked.

'What other person?'

'There was another person, at the back of the garden. They weren't in the nude.' All she had seen was someone standing by the side of the building as the people carrier went past. The shadow had grown, disappeared, then lengthened in the other direction as they moved past the scene.

Steve frowned. 'Keith and Susan live on their own. They might have had a guest, all the same. They didn't mention anything, though. Anyway... here we are. Back at the Halt.'

He pulled up outside the lodge, and engaged the handbrake, hard. The people carrier seemed to sigh as it paused on the flat surface.

'Coming in?' Debs said, as Toni struggled to open the door.

Steve looked into her eyes and shook his head. 'Nah. As I said, working tomorrow. With you guys, in fact. I want to be fresh for it. But tomorrow night I could pop along. Only if it's all right with you.'

'We'll see,' Mouse said, somewhat peremptorily, as she opened the side door along its runners. 'We've got loads of catching up to do.'

Debs turned around and raised her eyebrows at Leah as Mouse got out. 'That was very tart of Mademoiselle Souris, wouldn't you say?'

'Think she's had a longer day than us,' Leah said, apologetically.

'Uh-huh. Don't think I didn't notice her giving her drinks away,' Debs said, sliding along the seat to follow Toni. 'Not up the duff, is she?'

'Not that I've noticed.'

'Take it easy, now,' Steve said, as the other doors were opened and everyone got out. 'Hey, wait a second – where are you all going? Don't forget the bikes!'

11

In the kitchen of the lodge, Debs put on the DAB radio and found an Eighties station – way before everyone's time, but they knew the tunes and danced for a while. Soon only Debs remained. She made full use of the kitchen space, moving from corner to corner with a Chuck-Berry-style duck walk to the guitar solo in ZZ Top's 'Gimme All Your Lovin''. A moment or two after this surge burned itself out, she sat down and completely crashed, sinking onto the kitchen table, chin tight against the slick wood-stained surface. She didn't seem to sleep, but she wasn't quite awake, either, Leah noted – she was breathing deeply, but seemed to be talking to herself, and grinning. *Maybe it's a party in her head*, Leah thought, crossing over to the tap and grabbing a glass of water.

'Such a cute child when she's asleep,' Mouse said, drily, from across the table.

'Mrrmfff, fuck off,' Debs muttered.

Toni was striding up and down the patio doors, tutting at a new out-of-service tone on her mobile. 'Wouldn't you bloody believe it? I go on holiday for the first time in years with the girls, and there's no signal. Last outpost on earth without it, this. Last message I got from Roy. He was asking me to call him. *Shit*.' She stabbed at the redial key.

'Hmmf. Roy,' Debs said, and then grinned, her eyes closed. 'Lovely Roy. He coming to take us away from here?'

Toni frowned at Debs, then tried again. 'Oh – hang on, there's a tone!' She stayed in the spot she was, frowning hard as if concentrating. Sipping at her water, Leah heard the phone. Then a rasping sound, sharp even at a distance. Toni winced. 'Roy?' she said. 'Are you there?'

The line was dead. Leah and Mouse shared a look, as Toni said: 'I thought he was catching up on some box sets? Hello?' Toni stared at the phone with a look of utter savagery for a second or two. Leah was sure she would smash it against the wall. 'Nice. I bet the bastard's only gone and headed out. Not sure who he's gone out with, all the same. He doesn't know anyone in the village. Well. I think I'll chase this hangover while I can then get to bed.' She held up a packet of paracetamol. 'Anything I can offer you ladies?'

'Not a bad idea,' Leah said, accepting the pack. She pushed out two of the tablets then gulped them down with water. 'I cannot... absolutely must not have hangovers this weekend. I can't deal with them any more. I've barely drunk since, you know... can't face it. And can't look after a kid when I'm in a bad mood and in pain. Plus, it's not just the pain, it's the horror. I can't believe I used to drink till three in the morning then roll out of bed to start a shift at Brightley's on a Sunday.'

'Guess the swimming will wake us up.' Toni winked. 'Anyone get the message from Shell? One came through. I just came into signal for a second or two.'

'I got a message,' Leah said. 'Just the one saying she was going to turn up tomorrow. She got caught up, had to turn back. Oh... hang on.' Briefly, her voicemail symbol flashed up on-screen. She clicked on it, and listened in. 'It's from Shell.'

After the tone, a shriek boomed out in her ear. Leah flinched. Then, as soon as it had cut in, the robotic voice cut the sound off with: 'End of message.'

Mouse sat up straight. 'The hell was that?'

'I don't know.' Leah listened to the message again, with the phone an inch or two away from her face. Again, the shriek came in – and it was a shriek made by a human. It must have lasted for a second, if that, before being truncated. 'Jesus. Sound like a scream, to you?'

'I don't think so. Can I have a listen?'

Leah handed the phone to Mouse. She flinched, too, when the message looped round again. 'It sounds like digital interference, to me. But there's a voice of some kind in there.'

'Oh my God... Are we saying Shell's screaming at us?'

Mouse laughed, but it was a nervous sound. 'No, not at all, it sounds like the sort of thing you hear just when the reception gets cut out. She's spoken to Ewan, hasn't she? And she spoke to Steve. He told us, earlier. It's fine.'

'Reckon I should call Ewan? There is the landline.'

'What time was this message?' Mouse peered at the screen. 'Look – it's timed 6.35. The text message came through ten minutes after that. Steve told us she'd called, and this was afterwards. So, it's all fine. I wouldn't disturb Ewan for that. It's just a daft bit of interference.'

Toni's hand was clutched to her heart. 'Oh Jesus. I might call him anyway... What if she's in trouble?'

'Here, listen for yourself,' Mouse said, handing over the phone.

Toni listened, biting her lip. 'It sounds like an old computer modem.'

'I suppose it does,' Leah said, taking her phone back. 'Probably nothing. Although I guess we won't be seeing Shell this weekend at all.'

'I'm off to bed,' Toni said. 'This is all getting too stressful and weird, now.'

After Toni had said goodnight and closed the kitchen door, Mouse leaned over to Leah and said quietly: 'You want to hear something weird?'

'Before I go to bed in this ancient lodge, in the middle of nowhere? How about no?'

'I think someone messed with my tent. After I left it on the hillside.'

'Are you serious?'

Mouse nodded. 'I always leave my tent zipped up a certain way when I'm camping alone – tags tucked in here and there, that kind of stuff. A sign, just for me. To make sure no one's unzipped the tent when I've been out. It couldn't be an accident; I leave it just so. Anyway. When I came down to scope out the house earlier, it looks like someone had unzipped the tent. Nothing was taken.'

'Why the fuck are you telling me this?' Leah said, incredulously. 'Why now, before I go to bed?'

'Probably nothing. I'm guessing it was the naked horseman just down the hill. Him and his wife are the only people around, this high up.'

Leah glanced at the garden, alien now in the bleachy light from the kitchen. The grass was bright, but not warm in that light, the furniture next to the hot tubs stunted into weird, irregular poses and awkward angles. 'I'm thinking we get every single door and window locked, regardless.'

'Roger that.'

From the table, Debs chuckled, her chin still on the table. 'They're gonna get you… They're gonna get you…' she said, in a creepy sing-song voice.

'Sleeping Beauty here might want to take a couple of paracetamol herself,' Mouse said. 'C'mon, Debs. Time to get your sweet ass to bed.'

'Steve?' she asked, blearily.

'Nah, not Steve,' Mouse said, taking one of Debs' arms. 'Not tonight, anyway.'

'Aw. Lookin' forward to that,' Debs said, as Mouse helped her to her feet.

In the cast of her eyes and their pinkish hue, Leah saw how truly drunk Debs was. She glanced at her phone, then, on a whim, redialled Shell's number.

But the signal symbol was gone. 'Damn it!'

Leah slept – eventually. She was comforted by the sound of the girls shifting in their beds across the way, the creaking in the beds, and their occasional trips to the toilet. On one occasion, she heard Debs vomit, noisily. Leah grimaced. *Thank God she got to the loo, at least.*

It was hard to shut down. Every time someone got up to go to the toilet, Leah wondered if the footsteps belonged to someone else, padding up the stairs. But eventually she did make it to sleep, flat on her back, swallowed up by the new mattress and fresh sheets, far cosier than her own bed back home, with the radiator ticking away against the wall.

In the dead of the night, Leah's door opened. Someone came in.

There you are... There you are... Oh, there you are...

A long, thin, blade glinted in what little light there was. The figure made no sound on its feet.

Shall you be first? Shall you? Shall you?

The blade moved towards Leah's nose as the delicate nostrils fluttered with each breath. The silvery tip paused an inch away. The hand that wielded it only trembled a little.

No, not yet. Not yet. Not yet. Can't spoil it just yet. Can't spoil my surprise.

'Some owl,' someone said, too low to hear.

The figure departed without a sound. Leah never stirred once.

I2

A fine rain more like mist had begun to fall over the dark mountains – the tail end of the storm earlier, Susan supposed. She gazed at it as it fell through the gloaming of her garden lamp, mesmerised by the yellowish halo. It reminded her of the streetlights of her home city, hundreds of miles away and a million years before. It was cold for this time of year, and she'd long gotten changed out of her bathing costume for her tartan jammies. Over the top of this, her treasured fleecy blanket, keeping her cosy on the outdoor settee, at the far side of the all-weather gazebo. A half-glass of wine was left by her side on the patio, and she wanted to savour it, for all that was left of Friday night.

Her husband was also fascinated with the slow caress of the water on the mountains, and he was still as naked as the day he was born. Steam rose from his body as he got out of the hot tub and switched it off, before allowing himself the dubious dignity of a pair of slip-on purple deck shoes. His spotlit penis bobbed like a will o' the wisp as he trotted down the path towards the gazebo.

'Gave them a bit of a start,' Keith leered, his tongue between his teeth. 'I asked that gobby one if she fancied coming on over tonight, when she was out for a ride on Derek. She didn't say no, either.'

'Fancy that,' Susan said, yawning. 'And how long has it been since you were successful with that pitch?'

'I dunno. Six, seven years? Maybe that charcoal artist from Ontario who came to sketch the mountains. But it kept raining and spoiling her drawings. I didn't know if she'd been crying or rubbing her hands on her face, but she looked a right clown. What do you call those artists? The ones who use the charcoal. There's a name for them, isn't there?'

'Dafties?'

'Jealous. Anyway, there's a whole squad of girls heading up to the Owl Tree Halt with Steve. He can't go through 'em all, surely.'

Susan drained her wine, appraising her husband's saggy buttocks as he put on his dressing gown then poured himself a glass of wine. 'You can't really behave like that, you know. Not any more. Do you actually read the papers?'

'No,' Keith said, grinning. 'What's the point? Unless they drop the big one down at Faslane, I don't give a flying one, pet.'

'Well, people are more sensitive to those kinds of things, now. You can't just proposition women. In future, maybe keep Keith Junior indoors when we know people are coming to stay at the lodges.'

'I know, I know,' he said, irritated. 'It comes to something when a man can't just get his John Thomas out. Political correctness. Or what is it nowadays – cancel culture?'

'I don't think you get cancelled – I think if you expose yourself to people, you just get arrested, Keith.'

'Ach, it's my property. I can't help it if they peer in on the way past. Anyway. You ever get around to chatting up Pete the Pilot?'

'Not my type,' Susan muttered. 'Bit too stubby. I like a bit of length to the bones.'

'You can say that again. Steve not budging, I take it?'

'Nah, Steve's not what I'm looking for.'

'You're a hard woman to please. I guess that's why you married me, eh?'

Susan sipped at her wine, making it last. Forty years ago, her hair had been short and stylish, like Sheena Easton's, and her blending technique with her emerald mascara had been the envy of most of her peers. She still had the short hair, but it wasn't so stylishly cut now, although she had dyed it a startlingly rich hazel. Keith had aged a little better, although she wished, if he was going to flaunt himself quite so much, he might do something about the white hair that covered his chest, like the head on a pint – not to mention the white sideboards down his thighs.

'I was hoping to get myself invited along to their shindig down at the loch tomorrow,' Keith said.

'What – that bunch of hen party women?'

'Yeah. Although I think it's a reunion – no one's getting married. I'll tell you, that Debs character's a total flirt, when I had her out on the horse. Frisky.'

'They all seem frisky to you, dear. It's because you're old. You're safe.'

'Old and safe does the job sometimes, sweetheart. Don't you worry about it.' He winked.

'I was kind of hoping that you'd ignore them for the night,' Susan said, quietly.

'Yeah?'

'Yeah.' She peered up at him as she drank. 'I was hoping maybe I could be your fantasy date, on a Friday.'

'Why didn't you say?' Keith threw back the rest of the wine. 'For you, anything, m'darling.'

She grinned at him, finished her drink, and walked to the patio. She heard him scramble across the paving stones at her back, his shoes slapping on the wet concrete.

He took the glasses into the kitchen while Susan headed up the stairs. He was just rinsing the first glass when there was a sound like two bottles clinking, and the lights went out.

A little drunk, a little stupefied, Keith swayed in the dark of the kitchen. The glow from the LCD lights, staked into the corners of the lawn, gave only the faintest glow.

'Fuses,' he said, on a belch. 'Dammit. That's not happened for a while. Hold on, sweetheart,' he yelled, 'I'll just head out and sort them.'

Susan padded down the stairs. She already had on a headtorch, which cast haphazard blue beams through the banister and railings as she descended. 'No, you won't,' she said, peremptorily. 'You're pissed, love. I can see you putting your finger somewhere you shouldn't and getting fried.'

'Sorry. I thought you liked it when I did that.'

She could sense, rather than see, his buck-toothed grin. 'Just stay there and I'll flick the switch. I know where the key to the box is. And don't make any jokes about my box.'

'As if I would!'

The patio door slid shut, and Keith poured a glass of water. He paced the kitchen while he drank, enjoying the squelchy, slappy suction of his shoes on the kitchen tiling, even though he knew he was probably leaving some footprints for his wife to go apeshit about the next morning.

Out of the patio doors, he saw the blue headtorch beam cut through the falling rain – strong, that light, like a death ray in foggy conditions – and heading towards the fuse box on the outside wall, etching the house's L-shape in fairy blue. Keith looked away for a moment, still a little excited at the prospect of a naughty Friday with Susan, after all these years.

'Been a while,' he said, somewhat ruefully.

Then his head snapped up.

The beam of light described a high parabola in the smirr, spinning as it fell before sparking out on the decking.

'Susan,' he said, in a tremulous voice. Then he tugged open the patio door and was out in the cool air.

'Susan,' he said again, running now. 'Christ's sake, Susan! You all right, girl?'

There was no sign of her. In the stables just over the dividing fence, he heard Derek the horse whinny.

'Are you there? What's going on?'

There was a bang against the side of the house. It was the door to the fuse box, in the wind, striking the end of the wall.

It banged again, and Keith closed it against the wind. 'If you're out there, where did you…'

Then someone was screaming in his face, with a demon's eyes and a demon's mouth, wide open, shrieking, and Keith was stabbed six times in the chest, stomach and abdomen before he could exhale properly. When he did, he emitted red arcs, dulled to black in the gloom. He managed to make an old man sound, the sound of someone losing control of their legs as they climbed the stairs on a bus, and then he did lose control of them, sinking to his knees, as the long thin blade came in again and again. His clavicle shorn, splitting his voice box, three times in the chest, white hot and stinging between his ribs, and he was on his side and fading by the time she knelt down and then it was his neck, the edges of his mouth, an eyeball.

'Fucking dirty old pervert,' the demon screamed, 'I saw you, I heard you. That's the end, that's you. Can you fade? Are you gone yet? Are you gone yet?'

SATURDAY

13

*M*iss Tarrant was probably only in her early thirties, but with her hair scraped back and pinned and her eyes scrunched up behind tiny glasses seemingly fastened all the way around her head, she might have passed for ten years older. This meant that she could have been anything between forty and eighty to the swimming class at St Martha's.

They lined up on either side of the pool, and they shivered; the girls aged thirteen, all shapes and sizes, but all wearing the same black one-piece as per regulations. Only one person deviated slightly – Debs, of course, her costume cut far too low. Miss Tarrant wanted to say something about it, but she knew Debs well enough by then, and knew this was precisely what she wanted.

'Now,' Miss Tarrant said, her voice ricocheting off the high roof, 'we're going to see the front crawl demonstrated by the two best among you. First of all, that's Antonia.'

Toni got up – already tall, already elegant and confident as she stepped towards the deep end of the pool. She moved with the poise of a cat on top of a fence. Even the quick tug she gave at the back of her costume for more comfort had grace and insouciance to it.

'And Leah, please.'

Leah had wondered if it might be her – perhaps Lori McLean might have been chosen, a barrel of a girl who played rugby with a team at weekends and had shoulder muscles like cable car cords. When the name was called out, she blinked, and brushed her hair back off her head.

'That's right, I mean you, Louden. Come on. Now, everyone, watch the form, and the poise.'

Toni's eyes met Leah's just for a second as she picked her way out towards the top of the pool. Much more diffident, Leah kept her head down. She was only aware of Debs' eyes, glittering like those of a fox in headlights.

Diffident, but not unconfident.

She focused on the pool, its earlier tumult from the lengths and breadths workout subsided, and close to smooth. The reflection from the lights had coalesced from broken white spears and splinters into a facsimile of the circular lamps on the ceiling.

'I'll blow my whistle. You'll both dive. And you'll both compete.' She looked at Leah as she said this, and this kindled something in Leah's breast.

'On your marks... Get set...'

Both girls' toes on the very edge of the pool, knees and elbows bent, muscles braced.

The whistle shrieked.

'Look out, shark!' Debs screamed.

The water drowned out the laughter with its gurgling thunder.

'Trimmed her, didn't you?' Mouse said. 'An absolute whooping. I remember it well.'

'I don't remember a thing about it,' Leah said. She sipped from a Thermos flask full of tea. They were stood by the shore; Leah in her bare feet, uncomfortable on the shingle beach; Mouse, of course, having packed soft-soled canvas shoes among her rucksack.

'Bullshit,' Mouse said. 'It was always a sore point. Which Debs exploited to the full.'

'She bloody would.'

'I remember the look on your face when you came out of the water,' Mouse said. 'You looked absolutely shocked that you'd won. I don't think anyone expected it. Toni was still swimming. When she got to the end and pulled herself out, she couldn't believe it, either. She looked like she wanted to cry right there.'

Leah remembered comforting Toni afterwards. She'd made excuses for her opponent – she'd been up late studying for a science test; it had been unfair to spring the race on them; she'd tired herself out, pushing it hard during the lengths and breadths. 'Kids' stuff. Just a game.'

'Yeah, but these things have an effect. She thought she was queen bee, and then suddenly she wasn't. Me and Debs spotted it. Things had changed.'

'Over some swimming contest, set up by a sadist?'

Mouse laughed. 'Miss Tarrant wasn't so bad, compared to some of the others. She was quite fair. And she liked her subject, even if she didn't like teaching it.'

'True of most teachers, I gather. I'll tell you one thing, though.' Leah lowered her voice, and scanned the beach for any sign of Toni.

'Yeah?'

'You said I looked as if I couldn't believe I won? I was

putting it on. I knew I could beat her. I knew she didn't go swimming as much as she said she did.' This long-buried enmity was like putting on an old coat for Leah – long forgotten, but surprisingly comfortable. To her liking, in fact.

'You sly old devil.'

'Every week she said she went to practice, on a Saturday morning... I did, too. But I never said so. That meant I knew she was lying. Not sure why she did that. To be fair, she was getting into boys at that time, make-up, clothes... She'd lost interest. About six months earlier she probably would have beaten me. Just... not that day. Anyway. You definitely not coming in?' Leah knew the answer. Mouse wasn't dressed for the water, wearing nondescript training gear with a zip-up training top. Leah, however, was wearing an outdoor swimming bodysuit, that felt more comfortable than she'd imagined.

Mouse shook her head. 'Not my arena, so to speak. Prefer my kicks on solid ground. I do swim at the local pool now and again; it's cracking exercise. Not a fan of water deep enough to swallow the light. It's a no. Canoeing – definitely out. I can paddle, though.'

'Someone's enjoying it, I suppose,' Leah said.

She shivered as a breeze ruffled the surface of the loch. Out on the water, maybe one hundred yards away, two orange-hulled canoes splashed through the water. Debs was in one; in the sudden quiet from Leah and Mouse, her voice carried across the water, a sudden shriek that caused the person in the second canoe to paddle closer. They were heading for a floating target, not too far away from the two canoes, a decked platform that moved with the water, but never too far from the one spot. Leah supposed it was anchored, but the water was surely too deep for that.

'What were we saying?' Leah asked. 'Is Debs putting on the screaming fits for his benefit?'

'Oh yeah. He'll be carrying her out of the water like Tarzan any minute.'

Toni strode out from behind some trees, where she'd gotten changed into her own bodysuit. Leah had a sudden flashback to that day in the pool. Toni was measured and confident as she walked down the beach. She had a pair of flip-flops on, which she kicked off when she got to the shore.

'How much wild swimming have you done?' Toni asked, pinning her hair back.

'I wouldn't call swimming at a lido "wild swimming", exactly,' Leah said, laughing. 'There are a few wild creatures who swim in there, mind you. Older men and women, buzzing around all day.'

'Wild enough, I suppose.'

'How about you, Toni?' Mouse asked. 'You done much wild swimming?'

'Oh yeah. We did the Loch Awe Challenge not so long ago. Middle of October.'

'Ouchy. It doesn't freeze over or anything?'

'Nah—' Toni sniffed '—thermocline.' Without explaining any further, she took in Mouse's clothes. 'You not going in?'

'Nah, I don't generally do deep water.'

'I thought you were a decent swimmer?'

'I was. I am. I just don't fancy it today.'

'Ah, suit yourself. So. Leah.' Toni pointed to the float. 'To the platform. First one to get there is the champ. What do you say?'

Mouse turned away to hide a smile.

'You're on,' Leah said.

I don't quite feel so sure about this one, she thought, wincing as the tiny stones found ways to jab in between her toes and the delicate flesh of her instep.

'It'll feel quite cold,' Toni explained. 'I mean... even colder than it looks. So I wouldn't dive in, or anything.'

'Fancy giving me a head start?' Leah started shivering. *Psychosomatic, they call that.*

Toni didn't respond. She fit her swimming cap; Leah, of course, didn't have one. 'Want to call it, Mouse?'

'Sure. Shall I make the starter pistol noise? On three?'

'Perfect.' The goggles went on. Toni was transformed. A tall figure with her features compressed behind her goggles like an octopus squeezing itself into a bottle on a sunken galleon, Leah reflected that she looked a bit like Miss Tarrant, from all those years ago.

'OK, girls,' Mouse said. 'Good clean contest, now. On your marks... get set... Poow!'

Toni splashed into the water so quickly, and with such confidence, Leah expected to see her skip over the surface on her tiptoes, like one of those supercharged but faintly ridiculous salamanders. By contrast, Leah was ponderous. By the time Toni had gotten in up to her thighs, her competitor gave a gasp, which turned into a full moan, as the water covered her bare feet.

'Oh Jesus...' Leah started forward, and the stones dropped away so fast that she did instinctively half-dive into the water after a couple of steps. Her whole body jolted; she took a mouthful of earthy water. She kicked off, took a couple of strokes through the dark water.

Toni was already streaking away in a burst of white water, her shiny cap bobbing to the side as she swam with perfect, concentrated strokes towards the float in the middle of the loch.

Leah put her face in the water and pumped her arms, trying to build speed.

That's when it happened.

For an absurd moment, she thought something had grabbed her from below. The feeling of something tightening around her calf muscles was specific – not like a shark bite or a groping hand, but as if she'd been snared around her lower leg. That something pulled tight, and Leah couldn't move. She'd barely moved more than a few yards off the water's edge. She tried to right herself in the water, and the whiplash feeling attached itself to her other leg.

'Oh,' she said, instinctively throwing an arm up.

Cramp. Her legs had cramped. She could not move them. She swallowed water. She thrashed, not in panic, more in disbelief. She jerked her head to the side.

Mouse, then, Mouse at her back, her hand cupped gently underneath Leah's chin; Mouse, taking her back towards the shore.

'That's all right, you muppet,' Mouse said, her legs flailing out on either side of Leah. 'Don't drown on us, will you? Not the best girls' weekend scenario, that one.'

'I...' Leah could barely speak.

'Silly question – can you breathe, sweetheart?'

'Yes.' Leah spat water. The stones were back, her useless

feet digging furrows in them, heels first, as Mouse dragged her onto the bank of the loch. 'Cramp. Can't…'

'Ah, gotcha. Hang on.' Mouse laid Leah on her back, then raised her legs, one after the other. 'You know the drill… That's it, point your toes. Come on…'

'We're back. We're fine. It's gone… God.' Leah struggled onto her elbows, breathing hard. 'What an absolute embarrassment.'

Shouts came from across the loch. Steve and Debs were paddling hard towards the shore, Steve struggling to make himself heard over his pupil. Debs, Leah noted, was paddling well enough, now.

Toni was still pummelling the water, a slick dark torpedo streaking towards the float. When she reached the transom she pulled herself out of the water and stood, shining, in absolute triumph, head and arms held in the pose of a gymnast at the end of their routine. Then she opened her eyes, saw what was happening on the beach, squeaked aloud and then dived straight back into the water.

'I'm so sorry… And thank you.' Leah took Mouse's hand, and got back to her feet, unsteadily. 'I knew this was a bad idea on a half-hangover.'

'Don't worry about it. I probably caused a drama over nothing. You're grand,' Mouse said, clapping her on the back. 'Maybe you should join me for a paddle?'

'I didn't warm up. That's the thing. I haven't been swimming for months, either.'

Then something caught Leah's eye – over Mouse's shoulder, one of the branches of the trees swayed against the breeze. There was a suggestion of an arm among the dense, almost glowing green.

'Hey...' Leah said. 'D'you see that?'

'Our fan? Yeah. I saw that.'

'But Toni was getting changed over there... You reckon it's that nudie old bloke who got his kit off in the hot tub last night?'

'No, it was quite a short figure. A boy, I thought. Anyway, look out – here comes the coastguard.'

Steve leapt out of the canoe and beached it, springing onto the shingle in his bare feet. Water dripped off his face and his cannonball-thick helmet. 'All OK?' he said.

'Just a bit of cramp. I was daft. I should have warmed up,' Leah said, embarrassed.

'Gads, don't die on me,' Steve said, shivering. 'It's really awkward when I have to put a death in the accident book.'

14

Leah downed the tea, feeling the warmth seep into her. She was in her pyjamas and dressing gown, sat in the kitchen of Owl Tree Halt Lodge. Fluffy on the outside, cosy on the inside, thanks to a hot shower, and of course, the cup that was uncomfortably close to burning her hands.

Steve had thankfully removed the helmet, but his Neoprene suit was still on. His nipples were poking out, disconcertingly thick and stubby, and Leah wished he would put them away.

His eyes were bloodshot, and he could have passed for someone on a spa break, left outside after the fire alarm sounded. 'Now, you sure you're feeling all right? Has the feeling come back into your arms? Does your chest feel cold?'

'She might need her chest rubbed,' Debs said, crossing over to the fridge.

'I'm absolutely fine. It was cramp,' Leah said. 'Thanks very much for getting us back up here. I'm only sorry that it cut short the day on the water.'

'It was cold and bollocks anyway,' Debs said. Then she added quickly: 'Not that it was anything to do with our host.'

Steve scratched the whiskers on his chin, probably to disguise the fact his cheeks had coloured. 'Just making sure. It's going to have to go into the accident book, I'm afraid. Got procedure and all that.'

'If you have to.' Leah finished her tea. 'I'll be back out for the archery this afternoon.'

'If you get cramp, do let us know, Leah,' Toni said, sitting across from them both. She had on her dressing gown, but it wasn't clear to Leah if there were pyjamas, or anything at all underneath. Toni pulled away a towel she had wrapped tightly about her hair and let her long, damp tresses fall over her shoulders. 'I wouldn't want you to fire an arrow if you fell over.'

'Honestly, it's nothing. I was silly to get involved in the exercise. And hey – let's hear it for the champion, in the Wild Swimming Championships!'

Leah raised her mug at Toni – and this time it was the latter's turn to blush. She grinned, all the same. 'Well, you know, bookies' favourite, and all.'

'You won by default,' Debs drawled. She had cracked open a craft beer, a dinky little drink with a fancy can that Leah suspected was just repurposed supermarket own-brand stuff. It had been in the fridge when they got there. 'I think Leah might have whipped you, had it been a fair contest.'

'Well, "might have" doesn't cut it,' Toni said, smartly. She crossed her legs savagely – never quite upping her certification into fifteen or eighteen territory, but almost certainly forgetting that Steve was stood directly in front of her. 'Anyway. Maybe we'll have an archery champion this afternoon, too?'

'She's very competitive,' Debs mock-whispered to Steve. 'Thinks she can beat us all at everything. Hey – want a beer?'

'No, absolutely not,' Steve said. 'I need to head down and make some final preparations for the archery range. It's over the other side of the mountain, so I'll have to make sure it's ready to go before I come back. Please relax for a couple of hours – or dry off, whatever comes first.'

'See ya soon, Robin of the Hood,' Debs said. Once he was out the front door, and his sealskin-wet frame had gone past the side window towards the gate to the front, Debs said: 'Tell you what – he can't half move a canoe through the water. Forearms like a Greek god.'

Toni smiled, but only out of one side of her mouth. 'Your Eoghan would be chuffed at you making a new friend, I bet?'

'Maybe. Maybe not. Who cares?' Debs had finished the can already. 'I don't complain about all his little work trips for conferences over in Germany and Stockholm, or wherever. He's got a trainee he emails all the time. PhD student. Her name's Jessica. She leaves him kisses at the bottom. Now, he doesn't leave *her* kisses, but, get this – he always emails her first.'

'How do you know this?' Leah frowned. 'Do I want to know?'

'Ah, I know his mobile phone passcode. Same year his football team was founded. Ipswich Town, or whatever. I don't know. Men and their fucking football teams.'

'So, you're spying on your husband. That seems like a solid foundation for a relationship.' Toni nodded thoughtfully at her own supposition.

'Aw give over,' Debs said. 'None of you ever felt the itch? We're all long servers, here.'

'No, not particularly,' Toni said. 'You, Leah?'

'Nope. Nowadays, even if I wanted to, I'd never get the time.'

'And do you want to?' Debs' eyes narrowed. 'I saw how fast our Steve moved when it looked like you were in trouble.'

'That was just professional courtesy,' Leah said. 'Or, you know… being a human.'

'Yeah, whatever. You always did fill out a swimming costume, sweetheart. Anyway. It's time you put your knickers on and we thought about some more drinking.'

Before anyone could respond, the landline rang.

'Jesus Christ. What's that strange sound?' Debs said, after a second. 'Fire alarm? Someone got something in the microwave? Are we being invaded? When was the last time anyone actually used a landline for anything other than clobbering your man?'

'Shut up,' Toni said, irritated. She crossed over to the phone on the table. 'Uh, hi, this is Owl Tree Halt. Who's… Sorry, I can't quite…' Her eyes widened. 'Ewan! I can hardly hear you. Are you on a mobile? Wait… Yes, that's better. That's not so bad.'

'What's going on?' Debs said. 'Can you hear?'

'Shh,' Leah said, leaning forward in her seat.

'Oh, that's… No,' Toni said, firmly, 'she texted us last night, saying she'd got held up. Shell said she might be along today, but that she'd keep in touch and let us know. She had to stay on the mainland apparently… Are you absolutely sure? Oh…'

'This is trouble,' Debs said, the irony leaving her voice, for once.

'No, of course, we'll let you know, the minute she shows. That must be worrying. Sure, I would ring the ferry company, just to be sure. Maybe call down at the pub here; it's near the terminal. They might have seen her get off... I'm sorry, Ewan. I'm sure it's nothing. She'll turn up. Yes. Of course.'

Toni put the phone down, then, before being asked said: 'It was Ewan. Shell apparently said she'd get in touch last night to say goodnight to the boys. Made a promise to them. She texted Ewan to let him know she was stuck and couldn't get over, something to do with the storm causing a problem with the ferry. She'd gone to a B and B – same thing she told us. When she didn't call to say goodnight to the boys, he called her number – got a dead dial tone.'

'Weird,' Debs said. 'Same thing we got, early on. Anyone tried to get in touch with her since this morning?'

'I gave her a try in the car on the way back in,' Leah said. 'I got a couple of bars of reception when we came around the side of the mountain. Nothing now.'

'I tried it too, but I don't think it connected,' Toni added.

'Could be a boring, obvious explanation,' Debs said. 'I mean, the reception is crap over here. They weren't joking about that. Crap would be an improvement, actually, on non-existent. What did Ewan say he was going to do?'

'He's driving up if he can't get in touch.'

'Drama mama,' Debs scoffed. 'It's not worth panicking over, surely to God?'

'I don't know,' Toni said, 'maybe it is.'

Mouse came into the room, munching on a protein bar. 'What's up?'

Leah told her.

'I took a walk up to the summit, to get a reception. Shell called me when I was up there,' Mouse said.

'Oh thank God,' Leah said. 'We should call Ewan back and let him know.'

Mouse nodded. 'Terrible reception, where she is – she says she's on the mainland. Stayed at a B and B. She's trying to get the ferry over. There aren't many sailings – she says she might be over early evening. The line was awful. It cut off, eventually.'

'The storm wasn't that bad, yesterday,' Debs said. 'I mean… far as they go. Bit blowy, some lightning, a heavy shower, then nothing. It's not like it was terror on the high seas, you know. Hokusai painting, whatever.'

'Well, she just about got the story out. She said she'd had trouble with the car, too. Had to get someone over to check it.' Mouse flipped open the pedal bin and dropped in an empty wrapper. 'Poor Shell. Sounds like she'll be lucky to get Saturday night out of it.'

15

Concentric rings; black, white, red, blue, yellow.

A single arrow thudded into the white ring. Leah flinched at the sound.

'Three,' said Steve. He was a more than respectful distance away from the target, and he had to peer closely to be sure of the score.

Mouse, poised beside a blackboard, changed Toni's points total. 'You got it closer, that time.'

'Yeah, but no cigar,' Toni muttered, lowering the bow. Her face was flushed, and she blew a stray lock of her hair.

Good God, she's annoyed, Leah thought. She's genuinely irritated that she's losing a daft game.

Leah took up her bow and nocked an arrow.

'Back it up a bit,' Steve said, grinning. 'That's it.'

Leah saw what he meant. In aiming the dangerous end away from Toni, her bow was angled towards Mouse and Debs, who were sat beside the scoreboard. 'Whoops. That would have been a capper on the day, if I'd shot anyone.'

'All the same, please stop what you're doing, and don't nock the arrow just yet,' Steve said, hurriedly.

'Uh, sure.' Leah let the arrow come away from the string, then came up to the mark. The range was on a flat, springy lawn, underpinned by mesh that kept the worst of the moisture and mud sealed away. As she'd been taught, Leah braced her feet, took the strain on her left hand, which held the bow, nocked the arrow and then pulled back. It was tough; she didn't like this effort and neither did her back. The hidden cables and connections back there seemed to thrum and vibrate in much the same way as the bowstring. She wondered if this was the inevitable retribution of her body after yesterday's bike trip, followed by the morning's stress in the water.

'That's it... now sight along the line... Focus on that bullseye, Leah,' Steve said, in a firmer tone. 'When you're ready – release. Kill it!'

Leah let the string go. As before, her shoulder jerked, and the arrow went high over the target, embedding itself in the rubber-faced wall behind the target. 'Every time,' she said, exasperated. 'Every single time...'

'It's like you're afraid of hitting something,' Steve said, and Leah bristled at the condescending tone. 'C'mon, there's a killer in you. You've got some points on the board. You get a big number, you can move off the bottom. Let's have it, come on.'

Leah picked out another arrow, and nocked it as before. Brace; arm muscles sore; strange, twanging pain in back. Like the cables on a suspension bridge failing, maybe.

'C'mon, Leah,' Debs said, somewhere over her shoulder. 'Think of someone you hate. Wait, that's not easy. Leah's a saint. She doesn't hate anyone! OK, think of yourself. Use your self-loathing. Come on, now.'

Leah thought about Debs' wide open gob. Then she released the string.

The arrow flew into the black. Seven points.

Leah bowed at the applause as she turned away from the target – with Steve joining in.

'What do you know?' Steve said. 'Up to third, past Toni. There *is* a killer in you.'

Leah shrugged, and joined Mouse and Toni by the side of the board as the former upgraded the scores.

Debs pushed off the bench and strode forward. 'Now make way for the talent, lads 'n' lasses.' She picked up the bow and slung it over her shoulder, then nonchalantly picked out an arrow. She sighted along the arrow, one eye screwed shut, then grinned at Steve. 'Point out where you want Robina Hood to put this one, then.'

'Bullseye will do me. Right down the middle.'

'I like a man who knows what he wants. Nice and direct. OK then, hold on to your knickers.' She loosed the first arrow. It hit the ring, which immediately surrounded the bull – plumb inside the line, a fine contact, but Debs tutted. 'God damn it, I'm losing my touch, here.'

'Nine points,' Steve said neutrally. 'I don't think you can be caught. You're queen of the ring.'

'What do I win?' Debs said, resting on the bow.

'Undying fealty, m'lady.' Steve mock-bowed.

There was a sudden silence at this display. Toni, clearly as uncomfortable and incredulous as the others, broke it. 'Have you been practising, Debs?'

'Nope. I've played darts, plenty of times. You might remember from last night, though I lost heavily. I was pissed then, of course. Same principles, isn't it? Line up your shot, take it.'

'But you have practised archery?' Toni asked.

'I did it once at a team bonding exercise. Two or three jobs ago. We certainly bonded. Half the team were dying in their beds with a hangover. But the activities were a joke.'

'And did you win?' Toni asked.

'That's right.' Debs gazed towards the target.

'Guess we're all good at something.'

Debs stared at her, a slight frown underneath the flicked-up fringe. 'I'm good at lots of things.'

Toni said nothing, but took a drink of her gin and tonic. Leah saw that she was hiding a smile; Toni had hit the target with something, at least.

'I don't remember you being so competitive at sports, Debs,' Mouse said. 'I could be wrong, though. Memory plays tricks, sometimes.'

'Sports? Well, I'll have a go. Even if I'm no good at it. Thing is, it wasn't that I didn't like sports. I just didn't like school,' Debs replied. 'And I especially didn't like sports at school. Some of those fuckers at St Martha's, you wonder what was going on in their minds. Making you do cross-country running in December. Screaming at you if you got it wrong. What was that bitch's name? Glasses, with us all the way through that dump?'

'Tarrant,' Leah said. 'Miss Tarrant.'

'Gads, how could I forget. Yeah, Miss Tarrant. You ever wonder what the screaming and vindictiveness was about in these people? Like… "Miss Tarrant, I am fucking *twelve*."'

'You were quite cutting, as I recall,' Toni said. 'Disruptive.'

'What you call disruptive, I call having a laugh.'

'Most people would call it disruptive,' Toni said, peremptorily. 'You can't have a laugh all the time. Said the funeral director to the airline pilot.'

'Oh, my salary's serious enough,' Debs said. She nocked up an arrow, and fired.

Bullseye.

'And that's the win,' Debs said. She stared at Toni as she plucked out the arrow. 'The *win*. The final victory.'

'You're superb at this,' Steve said, applauding. 'If this is only your second go, you should get onto the Olympics selectors.'

'I just might.' Debs came to join them.

'So, that's victory to...' Steve squinted at the chalk message on the board. 'The mole? That's you? The mole? I don't see it, myself.'

'I never could, either.' Debs grinned and swigged at her gin. 'I'll own it, though. I kinda like it now. Mouse, here – she loved it so much, that's what we call her.'

'You're never a Mouse in your life!' Steve spluttered.

'Oh. What is she then?' Debs asked.

'She's a puma. Or a lioness. Something lithe and majestic,' Steve said.

Mouse cracked up laughing. 'A lioness! I'm having that.'

'What's the story, anyway?' Steve asked. 'The animal names, I mean.'

'Mummy Owl will explain,' Debs said.

Leah took a breath. 'When we were kids, we had a gang...'

'No, no, that won't do,' Debs scoffed. 'Come on. Own it. Why are you embarrassed?'

'As I said, we had a... club, called the Owl Society. We all had animal names. And...'

'Ah, you're deviating!' Debs hooted. 'Come on, tell the truth. Who came up with it all?'

'I did,' Leah answered, trying not to bite back at Debs. 'It was all my idea. And I got Mouse to do some of the artwork, and we all had an ID and a role. With me as the leader. The owl.'

'What age was this, then?' Steve asked.

'Nineteen or twenty,' Leah said, then laughed. 'No, eight or nine. I was going through a phase. Animal stories. Animal clubs. BBC documentaries. David Attenborough was my pin-up, for a while.'

'I'd do it,' Debs mused. 'David Attenborough. Young or old. No question. The top rank.'

'In his khaki jungle outfit?' Toni's eyes had lost focus.

'Oh, babe, he's got to arrive in his jungle onesie. British colonial khaki all the way. It's a dealbreaker if he doesn't wear it.'

'So what did the Owl Society get up to?' Steve asked.

'Well, nothing really,' Leah said. 'I think we were meant to be a community help group or something.'

'She's pretending she doesn't remember,' Debs scoffed. 'We had a pledge of allegiance. I think I can remember it! "I promise to do right by the natural world, to help small animals, to do no harm to the living creatures of the world, and to champion the cause of animals everywhere." She made us *say* it. Every time we met. We slagged her black 'n' blue, of course. Behind her back.'

'Yeah, as I was saying… We didn't really do anything. I think I just liked the idea of a club and a logo and everything ranked and co-ordinated. I wish I was that organised in my life just now.'

'I loved the Owl Society,' Mouse said. 'I didn't even mind being a mouse. It suited me at the time.'

'I'd like to have been a tiger,' Debs said. 'That would have suited me.'

'Oh you were never a tiger,' Toni said, in a neutral tone. 'Not back then.'

'Well, you know… life wasn't easy for me, Toni,' Debs said, seriously. 'I acted up a bit, but things were hard.' She turned to Steve, and said: 'My dad died, you see, when I was quite young. Not to put a downer on things – these guys here, they picked me up. They gave me something to belong to. That included the Owl Society. And Mummy Owl, here. She was kind to me. They all were, but Leah made us feel included.'

Leah had tears in her eyes. She looked to the ground, suddenly more embarrassed than when she'd been in conversation about the Owl Society. Steve smiled kindly at her.

'But that didn't stop me making up a Dirty Birds Society, later on.' Debs beamed, as the others broke out laughing.

'Do I even want to know?' Steve asked.

'I was the Tits Tiger. It's true. This is because… Well, I'm sure you can see why this was what I was called. This is what we called ourselves. Toni was the Constrictor, because she could crush a man with her thighs.'

Steve raised an eyebrow, and said nothing.

'Mouse was the Spanish Widow, because she has the sexiest eyes, you must admit. And Leah was… what were you, again?'

'No idea,' Leah spluttered.

'Oh my God!' Toni clamped a hand to her mouth. 'You were the Hair Trigger!'

'Now this, I do want to know,' Steve said, folding his arms.

'Eh, it was because one of my first boyfriends…' Leah began.

'Logan Blackmuir,' Debs said. 'Looked him up on Facebook. Seen him on Instagram. Stalked him thoroughly. Sorry, carry on.'

'Yeah, Logan, when we were necking, he had an unfortunate problem, you know. Things happened a bit too fast for him. Hence: Hair Trigger.'

'Now I'm embarrassed.' Steve turned towards the board. 'Hey – we forgot Mouse, you've still got a turn. You were in second. Fancy a go?'

'Sure, I'll take a turn.'

'I'm heading back to the car. I think it's time we got ready for the return journey from Narnia.' Debs drained her drink, then placed the empty glass in the cool box Steve had provided. 'C'mon, Constrictor. Let's plan the food.'

Toni followed Debs out of the enclosure and towards the people carrier. Steve began packing up. 'I don't have to tell you not to shoot anyone, do I?' Steve asked Mouse.

'This could be the fatal moment,' Mouse said, darkly. Then she smiled. 'You don't have to worry about me.'

All the same, Steve stood by as Mouse lined up a shot. Leah stood close to her.

'I don't follow those two,' Mouse said, sighting along the arrow. 'One minute they hate each other, the next it's all big bezzie mates.'

'That's a friendship, I suppose,' Leah said.

'It was nice what she said about you.' Mouse let the arrow go.

Bullseye.

'I thought she was getting the knife in,' Leah said. 'Like she did before. I'm not going to respond, but… sometimes I think she wants to destroy me. She used to be worse, when we were out and about. Eighteen, nineteen… she wanted to bury me. I'm sure she made up all sorts of stuff about me and Eric Glynn.'

'Eric Glynn.' Mouse's face went slack as she picked up her second arrow. 'You know, I haven't thought about him in, God…'

'Yeah. Anyway, I'm sure she spread that rumour about us. Absolutely untrue.'

'You know what it is, don't you?' Mouse said. 'Those two… they want to win. I'm not saying that's wrong. Look at Debs, now. The business, the money. Look at Toni, the house she's got, the car she drives. That's how it goes. But they still want something they'll never get. A status they'll never achieve. It goes back to school. It goes back to the way things were.'

'I don't follow,' Leah said, genuinely baffled.

'They weren't *you*. You were luminous – the one they all turned to. Mummy Owl is used as a piss-take, but it was you, all right. You led the group. Didn't always stay like that – we all had our phases, with boyfriends, exam results, what courses we went on, what friends we made. But you were the one they all wanted to be. There was just something about you.'

'What about you?' Leah said. 'You were the cool one. Everyone wanted to be you. Especially when you had boys trailing after you.'

'They'd have trailed after you. But you settled. Quicker than the rest of us.' Mouse let the second arrow go. 'You weren't really much of a player. More of a homebody. I don't say that to belittle you in any way. I wish I'd been like that.'

'You got Owen Clancy, love,' Leah said, wryly. 'You won the crown. I think we all cried about that.'

'Oh yeah. So I did.'

The second arrow was buried in the bullseye.

Steve whistled through his teeth. 'You've finished second, by... just one point! Unlucky.'

'I was just seeing the lie of the land,' Mouse said, coolly.

A phone rang, startling them. It was Leah's unchanged stock ringtone from the day she opened the box of her phone. 'Shit, it's Shell.' She turned away, the phone stuck to her ear.

'Hello!' The interference was terrible. 'It's me... Is that you, Leah?'

'Yeah... Are you on a boat? What's going on? We're waiting here for you.'

'Just to... Won't be able to... Really, really sorry.'

'You can't make it, was that?' Leah and Mouse shared a disappointed look. 'You all right? I guess if it's a hassle... Sorry, I can't hear you, Shell love.'

'...tomorrow or Monday. I think I'll just head...'

'You're breaking up. Hey – Ewan was on the phone, looking for you, I guess you must have spoken to him? He was very worried when you didn't call. Something you'd agreed.'

'No, that's all fine,' Shell said. 'I spoke... Better... Speak soon, all right? You there, Leah?'

The line went dead.

'And then there were four,' Leah sighed. 'Yep, you guessed it. Shell's out.'

16

Debs whipped the pan, her face a study in comic determination. A smell of burning wafted through the kitchen; Leah gave a fearful glance towards the smoke detector.

'Nope,' Debs said, flinging the spoon aside and turning off the heat. 'I've definitely failed the béchamel test.'

'Ah just pile it on anyway,' Toni said. 'It'll be all right when it comes out the oven.' She didn't exactly muscle Debs out of the way; Debs moved willingly, but she still frowned at Toni's back, and even buried a remark in her fresh gin. Toni scraped the sauce on top of the tray of lasagne. After that, she layered on a variety of cheeses with the skill of someone who knows she's being watched, and enjoys it – ovals of mozzarella, flakes of cheddar, and something that might either have been ricotta or cottage cheese.

'Maximum overcheese,' Debs said. 'And I mean that as the most sincere compliment.'

'It'll look better once it gets bubbly.' Toni slid the tray into the oven – Leah felt a comforting blast of heat from the door before it slammed shut again. 'Now – I think it might be time for the main event.'

She took out a bottle of Chablis from the fridge, and placed the dewy glass against her cheek. Leah wondered if this was some sort of affectation, something seen on a cookery programme that everyone would have to do now. 'Lovely and cool,' she said. 'It's the good stuff – anyone joining me for a glass?'

'I think I will,' Leah said. 'Did you have that in your luggage?'

'Yep, this and some pinot noir. Thought I'd save it for the big Saturday blowout. Though the stuff they've got in here isn't bad.'

'More gin to go around,' Debs said. 'Suits me.'

Leah poured herself half a glass of the Chablis and took a sip. 'Thought you were Mrs Wine Fiend? I remember you having some kind of membership.'

'These allegations are true. However, I've had to come off the stuff. I'm happier with a gin and tonic. Less of a hangover, less depression, less… deep need to refill a glass once it's empty. Plus, you can kind of cheat on yourself. I pour myself more and more tonic, less and less gin. It's a good trick. You can stay topped up, and not get plastered.'

'Like you were last night?' Toni asked, mildly.

'Yep, exactly like that, in fact. I was drinking stout. Who drinks stout? Untrustworthy old men who have laundry days marked on the calendar. Guys with jumpers a foot thick. Beards not much better. Stout's barely evolved from molasses. It's not even really a liquid. Still, it does the job; I'll say that much.'

Toni staked her claim for a spot in the lounge, sitting on the corner of the long couch, legs curled up underneath. Leah had secretly hoped they might get changed into pyjamas, or at least something comfortable; Toni had opted for a blouse and skinny jeans, so Leah had followed her lead. Debs had changed into a sunflower-print dress, the squares of material occasionally sneaking in a smiling sunshine face in among the flowers. It was cut quite low in front, a little bit much, but very eye-catching. In short, quintessential Debs. She had moaned a little when it turned out they were not going to the pub 'for a couple of liveners' – Toni, and then, more surprisingly, Mouse, had been against it.

Leah had been a little disappointed. Pub trips were a thing of the past, and she'd known a fugitive glee the previous night among the raised voices, noxious music and, eventually, the crackling fire in the corner. A part of her felt like she'd come home. She'd always been a pub girl rather than a clubber. But she supposed that she owed the rest of them tonight, and the closeness they'd lacked for most of a decade.

She felt a sudden pang at Shell's absence. Shell was the most sentimental of them all – the one in the centre of the group photos, arms clamped around shoulders. *What a shame.*

Leah sat diametrically opposite Toni on one of the armchairs, resting her wine glass on the table. The glass beneath was polished to a high sheen, and reflected Toni's face. Debs sat beside Toni, and then Mouse padded past Leah, startling her. Mouse had on a jumper that matched Debs' description of a stout drinker's Saturday night pulling gear. The hem sat quite low on her hip. Underneath, black leggings, and bare feet.

'I'm kinda jealous,' Debs said, eyeing up Mouse as she sat down. 'Wish I'd gone for the cosy option.'

'Ah, it's all academic, we'll be naked and partying before we know it.' Mouse took a sip from a tumbler.

'That looks suspiciously like a soda water and lime, to me,' Debs said.

'Correct. So – let's touch the glasses. Here's to absent friends, first.'

'Poor old Shell,' Toni said, as they all came forward to touch glasses. 'Imagine going to the trouble to set it up... Jeez.'

'We can always sort another one out,' Leah said. The wine had warmed her tummy and struck sparks in her head, already. 'We can make it an annual event. Nothing stopping us, I guess.'

'Spot on,' Debs said. 'I'm bang up for that.'

'Here's to us, as well,' Leah said. The glasses clinked again.

Before they could sit down, Debs blurted out: 'And... here's to me! For finally having an excuse to wear this ridiculous dress!'

Leah caught Toni's eye. The latter's face fell, blatantly. 'To you,' Leah said, and they all clinked glasses, less obviously.

'So,' Debs said, perched back on the sofa beside Toni, 'tell us, Mouse... Lumpy jumper... Not a drop of booze has passed your lips... Give us the exclusive. Give us the inside scoop.'

'Nothing to tell you,' Mouse said, evenly, without a hint of discomfort – a contrast to Leah, who felt a sympathy pang of embarrassment. 'I've stopped drinking. That's all.'

'Nothing serious I hope?' Toni said.

'Of course it's serious. I loved a drop. Up until kind of recently. I came to a decision not to poison my body.'

'No twelve steps?' Debs asked, serious for once. 'I know some people who do that. You'd never believe it, either. Steadiest people I knew. Management, twenty-four-hour people, squash three days a week. I don't know how they ever fit in the drinking – maybe they just topped themselves up. Even so...'

'When did you decide this?' Toni cut in, returning the conversation to Mouse.

'After I temporarily split up with Sophia,' Mouse replied. 'I...'

'What?' All three of the others said this in perfect harmony. Debs slammed down her shot glass.

'Sophia?' Debs said. 'Meaning, like... a girl, Sophia?'

'Oh yeah,' Mouse said, unperturbed. 'You might even have met her. I think she came to the pub, when I was working for the agency. Again – no Damascene conversion. I'd split up with Ian Farsley, guy I'd been seeing for about eighteen months... He was too keen. Think he wanted a dress on me and a big day with his family, but it's not me and never has been me. He was devastated...' Here, she blinked. 'Anyway. It happened. Sophia was a good mate. Got me into yoga, park runs, half-marathons, that kind of thing. It's true what they say, you know – you do love the person. I can tell you that for a fact, now. It works pretty well. We both have to disappear, now and again. I have to take off, find other places to do my work; she takes two months off every year to go travelling. We travelled together once, but it didn't work – we were close to splitting up again halfway through a tour of Vietnam. So now, we both hit the road, once a year, we come back, and everything falls back into place. I'm...' She paused. 'Happy.'

'Good for you!' Leah said. 'Jeez Louise, I'm glad you've found someone. You should have brought her along!'

'Gads, no, she counted herself out. Didn't want to cramp my style. She said this with a straight face.' Mouse sipped at her soda.

'I had no idea you drinketh from the furry cup. No idea at all,' Debs said. 'And you had Owen Clancy at school, too!'

'All part of life's rich tapestry,' Mouse said. 'Anyone stalked Owen Clancy on social media, lately?'

Toni took a deep breath. 'Yep, still looks great, married to a charity worker called Sara, no H, and has two children who look like what they are: the products of the loins of a seraph.'

'Bitch,' Debs said, bitterly. 'But never mind that shit. Level with us, Mousie Mouse: Is it, like... you know...?' There was a terrible silence. 'Better?'

'Better, lasts longer, full marks across the board,' Mouse said, an impish expression on her face.

'God. The great divide,' Debs said, shaking her head with a kind of awe. 'Imagine that. I mean, I'm not saying you have a great divide, down, you know... But hey. That's great! More carpet for Mouse. Jeez! I think the only time I got down with that was when I practised kissing with Toni.'

She had expected a thunderstruck silence, but instead Leah and Mouse tittered. 'Oh, we all know about that, love,' Leah said. 'That's no secret. Was the talk of the school.'

'I didn't know we were practising kissing,' Toni said, sitting up straight. 'I thought we were doing it to wind the boys up.'

'It was a twofer. Actually, it was really nice. You must

have eaten so many mints before it – no boy ever went to that effort for me.'

'You weren't bad,' Toni conceded. 'Anyway. Here was me thinking you were Keith Cheggers, Mouse.'

'Pregnant? Interesting scenario if you were,' Debs said. 'Is there a significant other in the shape of a male still lurking, or did you head down the wank bank?'

'Sorry to disappoint you,' Mouse said. 'Anyway. Haven't we got some games or something on the go?'

'We do,' Debs said. 'It's nothing fancy. We have Monopoly, or... good old spin the bottle.'

'God, Monopoly's boring,' Toni said. 'I'm sorry if there are any fans, but it bores me rigid. It's the favourite game of all my least favourite people.'

Leah, who loved Monopoly, said: 'What's the score with spin the bottle, then? I don't think we ever did that, as teenagers.'

'That's why it's so exciting!' Debs said, setting her tumbler down with a sharp report. 'When the bottle moves towards you, you have to fulfil the category. Or, in forfeit, you have to down a Jägerbomb.'

'Jägerbomb? Category? We didn't agree to this on the itinerary,' Toni said.

'Don't worry, it's all set up,' Debs said. 'By me.' She reached behind the sofa, and pulled up a backpack. Inside there was an old Wheel of Fortune board game. A presenter Leah could only vaguely remember grinned from the faded box-top, his haircut and sports jacket ancient relics. The box was dog-eared, and fixed down along some battle scarring and splits with duct tape, which in itself had begun to peel and unravel with advancing years. 'I've converted it. Here we go…'

Debs took out the plastic wheel and its casing from the box, then set it up on the table. There were several categories, which Leah couldn't quite make out. After an experimental spin – the wheel made a satisfying roulette sound – she took out an empty bottle of beer.

'Right then. It's all very simple – I'll spin the bottle, and whoever it picks out must spin the wheel. Then you answer the questions that come up. Nothing for two in a bed, of course – if it picks you out twice in a row, play moves to the next player. Same for categories – if you've already answered the question, then you spin again until you get one you haven't answered.'

Mouse peered at the wheel. 'Not too many questions… And among the ones I can see…'

'I'm uncomfortable with this,' Toni said.

'You're supposed to be.' Debs grinned. 'Drink up – you'll get in the swing of things. We're all friends here. We know all the answers already. Or do we?'

'All the same, if I get a question I'm not comfortable with, I'm not answering.' Toni folded her arms and sat back. One leg swung against the sofa, nervously.

'Suit yourself,' Debs said. 'I'll ask the spirits if they'll answer for you.' She stood up, shut her eyes and raised her hands, palms outwards. 'Mighty spirits, if you're here, make yourself known! Give us a sign!'

The landline rang. Everyone screamed.

17

L eah was closest, and she lifted the receiver.
'Hello?'

There was a moment of complete silence. Then something that might have been a breath – an inhalation – then the connection was cut.

'Did someone drop the phone?' Toni asked.

'Pretty much.' Leah put down the receiver and returned to her seat.

'Heavy breather? Wrong number? Jealous husband?' Debs asked.

'I think... no, it was nothing. Silence. I'm not even sure I heard a breath. Just cut the connection.'

'A silent call isn't nothing,' Mouse said, frowning. 'Probably just a wrong number. But, it's weird that they got in touch at that particular moment, whoever they were.'

Debs grinned. 'Not weird at all, if they're listening to us and watching our every move. It has a ring to it. A masked killer... four hot babes, out in the middle of nowhere... watching, as they have pillow fights in their jammies... showering together – totally as friends, nothing dodgy at all... And all the while, out there among the trees...' She gave a corny, horror movie laugh, starting at the back of her throat. No one else was amused.

Leah turned to Mouse. 'There is someone out there, though. Isn't there?'

'What do you mean?' Toni asked. She was sat up straight now, her wiry shoulders bunched with tension. 'Are you messing with me?'

'She's not,' Mouse said. 'It's probably nothing. This place is very isolated. But yesterday, just after I met up with you, when I went to collect my camping gear... someone had messed with it. Nothing was stolen. They just had a quick look. I would imagine it was something to do with Mr Nude Hot Tub UK who runs the stables, just down the hill. Nothing sinister about it...'

'But then, there was this afternoon, out at the loch.' Leah's heart beat faster at the recollection. 'There was someone watching us, from among the trees. Just a shadow, really. I couldn't make anything out. But there was someone there, close to us, when I was pulled out of the water.'

'I didn't make much out, either. Whoever was there didn't hang around. Once we'd made sure you were OK, Leah, I took a quick look around. There was no sign of anyone there.'

Toni's voice had a shrill note to it. 'And you're only telling us this now? God almighty, there could be someone from a 1980s slasher movie out there. Machetes and stuff. Why didn't you mention this before?'

'Because it's bullshit,' Debs said, peremptorily. 'Eh, not that I don't believe either of you, because I do. Just because it's not a problem. Someone had a poke around your sweaty cycling shorts and decided not to pursue matters further,

Mouse – I mean God knows, that's a fool. They missed out. But it's no problem, really. There are other people living on this island. Including dear old St Keith of de Dangly Balls. It was probably him. Or Steve. Or Pete. Nothing to worry about. If you started freaking out about one daft phone call or wondering if someone's watching your house, you'd never go anywhere on holiday again. So. Stow that talk. All right?'

Debs' demeanour had utterly changed. Even when she was sincere, her smile wasn't. But now there wasn't a trace of humour on her features, and her grey-blue eyes focused on them, one after the other. 'So... as I was saying. We're spinning the bottle.'

Debs placed the brown beer bottle on its side on the glass table, then spun it. Leah flinched, expecting froth to spit out, but the inside was dry and the sound of glass against glass was strangely pleasing, like a skate slicing across ice or a glazier drawing a diamond cutter down a window.

The bottle stopped at Mouse, who covered her face. 'Aw, Christ. Can I forfeit? I'll sing, do a dance. Striptease. Whatever you like.'

'There are no forfeits in this game,' Debs said, still very serious. 'You must answer the questions.'

'If I don't want to, I'm not answering any questions,' Toni said.

'...Or, indeed, you can be a pussy your whole life, and not answer any questions,' Debs said, recovering her old tone.

'Don't be disrespectful,' Toni snapped.

'OK, ladies, I'll spin the wheel, now. Hang on... How does this thing?'

'Grab it by the nubbin, and give it a good old yank. Like you did with Owen Clancy. According to sources.'

Mouse sighed. 'The triumph of my teenage life. And only now, is it an occasion for shame. OK. Here we go.'

Mouse spun the wheel. It ticked through each little segment, the marker pattering through each section, growing slower and slower. With the exception of Toni, they gave a rising moan as the sections spun more slowly, and the needle finally rested on: 'THE WORST THING YOU EVER DID'.

'Blimey. That's a tough one.' Mouse bit her lip. 'I'll have to think about that.'

'Bullshit,' Debs said. 'Everyone has that one thing. It flashed in front of your eyes, right then. Go with it. Tell us. You can tell us anything. Christ, it's probably something we already know.'

Mouse sat down. 'Well now. That's a weird thing…'

'Don't answer it if you don't want to,' Toni said. 'See, what Debs is doing here, is… collecting information. I kind of remember you doing it at school. You asked us all who we fancied. Next thing you know, it's all round the school that I fancied Owen Clancy.'

'That was one of life's harsh lessons, it's true,' Debs said. She swirled her gin and tonic, watching the ice shards collide. 'But a vital one. Trust no one. Present company excepted.' Debs grinned. 'It was that weird little girl who spread that around. The one, you know…' Debs' eyes met Leah's, briefly, then looked away. 'Not guilty, is what I'm saying. You want it to be me, but it wasn't me, and that's the truth of it. Anyway. It's not about you. Or at least, not yet. This is about Mouse.'

'I can tell you. It's not a... Well. It is a big thing. It is something that I regret, and something I don't really like thinking about.' Mouse's posture was rigid, and she folded her arms across her chest. 'But I'll talk about it. It's something I wanted to say to one of you... or all of you... anyway.'

'This is a bit heavy. Don't you think this is heavy?' Toni entreated Leah, particularly.

'It's... I guess we can talk. I'm OK with it if Mouse is OK with it?' Leah wasn't OK with it, though. She racked her brains for something else, some alternative. A replacement shame.

'I said I'm OK with it,' Mouse said. 'It happened recently, about four years ago. I was hiking in the Hindu Kush. Nothing hairy, nothing requiring oxygen, but the terrain was mental; it was a commitment. I had a few moments where I was looking down the wrong gradient, and regretting my life choices. I had gone alone, but I fell into talking with a few walkers from Canada, and one guy from America called Jonah.'

Leah expected a snort or some other contribution from Debs at the mention of a man's name, but everyone had fallen silent.

'We were a close-knit little group, but the numbers whittled down. There were only three people tackling the peak, our final trip before we had all decided to head back. One of these was Jonah, the other was a Canadian climber called Richard. Both younger than me, both of them in their mid-twenties, I'd say. Good condition. Experienced. Rich kids, I hate to say. Trustafarians. But both nice men.'

'Which one did you have?' Debs said.

'Neither,' Mouse said, with a touch of Toni's hauteur. 'Wasn't in my mind. I'd just come out of a relationship and wasn't even in the mood for a bit of a laugh. I needed the peace. But it was clear that it was in Jonah and Richard's minds. This irritated me. I dropped all the hints; you know the score. One night, when the weather got really bad, I said something like, "I'm not in this for anything other than mind-clearing." I didn't tell them where to go, to stop probing. They didn't hassle me or anything, but it was obvious they were both interested. The inevitable happened.'

'They ignored you and copped off with each other?' Debs finished her drink.

'Not in this movie, sweetheart. No – they started competing with each other. Jonah was more aggressive with it – not outwardly aggressive; assertive might be the word. He wasn't a pleasant character – he'd seemed nice at first, but what he thought was competition brought out a nasty side to him. If I had been interested, I wouldn't have had anything to do with him, that's for sure. He belittled Richard, belittled Canada, found out where Richard had gone to study, belittled that, belittled his gear, his climbing... Richard started hitting back, and once or twice it got heated. No violence. But not far off it. Shouting and bawling. I calmed it down, but I still didn't tell them to pack it in and forget about it. A silly thing to say, but it would have seemed presumptuous of me to tell them to calm down, that I wasn't interested in boys, just then.

'That night the weather got really bad, and some snow came down. Richard came into my tent, and started to apologise for the row with Jonah. Then he made his play. He didn't come on to me in any forward way – just had a go, said he really liked me, asked if I fancied going to dinner with him once we got back to civilisation.

'That's when I lost my rag. I was tired, cold and stressed. I told him to behave – asked him if he wasn't very good at picking up hints, or if he was born different. The shame of saying that… All I had to do was to let him down easy. But I was exhausted, it had been a long day, the climb was less and less fun the longer I spent with these two guys, and the weather might make a bad situation actively dangerous. I gave him short shrift, told him to get out of my tent, and get lost. Which he did.'

Mouse paused – not through any obvious discomfort, but because she was choosing her next words carefully.

'When Jonah and I got up the next morning, there was a foot and a half of snow outside. Not as bad as it might have been. Richard's tent was open. He had left a note inside, sticking out from inside a guidebook – left for someone to find easily. He wrote that he was glad that I'd said what I had, and that he would follow my advice. All his gear was stowed inside, backpack, equipment, food, water – all that was missing was his boots and whatever he was wearing. The snow had stopped during the night and Richard's footprints were clear, leading away from the camp towards the edge of a gorge, dropping into a river. That's where the footprints stopped.'

'Jesus,' Toni said.

'His body was found six weeks later, somewhere down-river. We'd moved on, of course. We had to. We wanted to complete the climb, and we did. We had no one to contact. We had to tell the authorities as soon as we got back to civilisation, a day or so later. The secret hung heavy on us, while we kept walking. Jonah kept telling me it wasn't my fault, it couldn't have been my fault. He was speaking the truth, but... I knew I could have handled it better. What made it worse was that there was an inquiry and it established that Richard had been a depressive, long history of it, and he'd actually come out there to get out of a cycle of toxic friendships and to meet new people who shared his interests.'

Mouse looked away for a moment; both Toni and Leah put their arms around her.

'No, it's fine,' Mouse said, 'totally fine. It's just something that happened. It's not like I pushed him. But that's it, I think. That's the single worst thing I ever did. I dismissed some guy who probably didn't know anything about relationships and women, even at that age, and he's dead because of it.'

'Not your fault, and you know it,' Debs said. And she actually showed her teeth, as she said: 'Know what irritates me here, Mouse? And I mean no offence... The worst thing about that story is that you actually blame yourself for something. What are you meant to do? "Yes, sir; please, sir?" Bend over, take one for the team? Even if you'd known he was a depressive? That word right there tells you it wasn't your fault and couldn't have been your fault. What I'm picking up from this story is that the guy was bullied by this Jonah character. So blame him. Worst thing you've ever done? It's not on the radar. Not in the same continent. So put it out of your mind. Now... on that delightful note, it's time to eat.'

18

'I don't think I can eat any more.' Debs sighed, leaning back and cradling her tummy. 'I think if I have any more I might... You know what, I'm going back in.' She broke off a segment of garlic bread, and mopped up some stray mince and tomato sauce from the tray.

She spoke mainly to herself, with the other three women having retired from the dining table to the sofas in the corner of the main room.

Toni had resumed her seat on the couch, and cuddled into a cushion with a bizarre patterning effect that reminded Leah of red wine spilled on a carpet. 'Maybe we should do what the men do, now – sit around farting.'

'You forgot the porn and hookers. Definitely got the ballast, with all this food, mind you,' Debs said.

'Please let us know if you do,' Toni said. 'I think I'm downwind.'

There was silence for a moment, then Debs giggled. 'I am so, so sorry, I promise I did not time that release...'

'For God's sake! That's awful!' Toni shrieked, and went over to open up the patio window.

'Well, you know, you always process me as kind of the disgusting one – I thought it'd be an idea to revert to type. You know, meeting audience expectations. Which is important in my line of work, I can tell you. That is what they call a value-add.' Debs took another sip of gin, and winked at Leah and Mouse.

Leah sipped at her own wine. On the corner of the table, the Wheel of Fortune remained, its ticker still stuck at 'WORST THING YOU'VE EVER DONE'. She hoped that was the end of it; that they'd move on from that. Even better, that someone would put on the television, in the hope that this would draw attention away from it.

Toni sat down with a full glass of Chablis, its troubled surface meeting the lip of the glass perfectly. Leah was reminded of an infinity pool she'd been too afraid to go into on a holiday long, long before David arrived. Toni sipped at it, almost too quick to process properly. 'Anyway. We've listened to Mouse. Maybe it's Debs' turn.'

Mouse raised a hand. 'No – I told you guys that because I wanted to. It was a sober decision. Maybe it's best if we just leave it. Dodgy game, anyway, if I'm being honest.'

'Oh, I disagree,' Toni demurred. 'I think if we're going to play this game, then Debs should tell us all about the worst thing she's ever done.'

'That isn't quite how the game works,' Debs said. 'You let the bottle decide.'

'Not a cowardy custard, are you?' Toni's eyes were bright in the lamplight.

'Hm. A dare. I never could resist a dare. All right then.' Debs cleared her throat, and began without hesitation or preamble. 'When I started my company, I was partnered with a man called Rundle. Gay as they come. Nice bloke. Good fun. We were a bit of a double act for a while, had both worked for Fitch and Arrowby; hated it, hated everyone else in it, drunkenly talked about opening our own place. It was easier than you might imagine. Debs & Rundle was the name of the company. We had a very good first year. Then someone at – you'll be amazed at this – Fitch and Arrowby found out that we had been scraping clients off them. So they scraped us back. The second year was difficult and we went into the red. We had a lease on an office we couldn't afford, and they really fucked us for it... That's when I discovered that Rundle's party lifestyle was kind of a 24-7 thing, and not just when he was out and about in Soho with me. He crashed, hard. He had been running up an expense account, on God knows what... I had it out with him, and he promised to level out. But he didn't.'

Debs took a drink. Her face had barely changed during this conversation. She hadn't looked at anyone else's face, preferring to stare at a point on the back wall, over the shoulder of the blue owl painting.

'He fell into depression... Or maybe he'd always been depressed. Started not showing up for work. One night, he called me from somewhere outdoors. Windy night, bit of rain. Like tonight, in fact.' She gestured towards the patio door, where a light rain had begun to rattle against the glass. 'He told me that he was thinking of taking care of our problems. He wanted to leave. He would pass over full control of the business to me. He was staying at his parents' – they had money – and he gave me a laughably low offer to buy him out. I accepted.'

'How could you afford that?' Toni asked.

A single tear dripped from Debs' eye. She didn't wipe it away. 'Well. This is the thing. I had been cosying up to someone in the video games industry. Twenty-one, bit of a hotshot, bit green... in many areas. He thought the sun shone out of my bottom. But I could see the sun shining out of his bottom line. He told me he had an idea for a mobile video game. Just when they started taking off. He showed me demos of it, one night... I practically had him signed up to a contract that night. I knew this game would work.'

'What was it called? Would I know it?' Leah asked.

Debs told them. Eyebrows were raised; drinks were sipped. Mouse whistled, softly.

'Yeah. You'd know it, all right. So, Rundle has his breakdown, without knowing I had this coming up. And I never told him. Just let him go, with his share of the business in my pocket. A few months later, our advertising campaign's up and running. It doesn't win any big awards, but it gets nominated for all of them. You might even remember the tune we commissioned for it. Another rip-off – a student on a retro synthesiser. Eight-bit video game sounds. He didn't make anything like what he should have, either. But I did. It put me on the map. I was back in business. And it could have been the shot in the arm that Debs & Rundle needed. It just turned out to be a shot in the arm for Debs. That put me right back on the board. Work flooded in after that.'

She took a drink. They listened to the rain patter off the windows.

'Thing is,' she continued, 'the night of the big kiss-off, Rundle said I had fifteen minutes to change his mind. I said, thanks, give me fourteen minutes to think about it – and I hung up. Once the fifteen was up, I didn't call him, and that was that. I was drunk, of course. Like I'm drunk now. It's never an excuse, really, is it? They say *in vino veritas*, but that's nonsense. It distorts. Drink's a liar. Drink makes you liable to say and do things. But we're not puppets. We're not programmable robots. And it is never an excuse. I didn't call him back. All the same, I knew.

'Several PR industry awards later and a client list that people might actually murder me for, here I am. I knew all this. I knew the video game contract would set me free. And I sat there that night, after Rundle got off the phone, and I listened to the clock tick. Then I poured myself another drink. And I don't think I even feel too bad about it. I can probably even guess what you're going to say to me now, to make me feel better, or justify it. It won't work. I've betrayed people in life, particularly men. Some I care about, some I don't. But Rundle didn't deserve that. I... I smelled the money, and I took it, at his expense. It's the worst thing. The most disgusting thing.'

Mouse cleared her throat, began: 'As you said to me...'

'Oh, I know, love. I've been through it many times. Mainly I think: Rundle was off the rails. Any other business would have binned him long before I did. Any other boss. But that's just it – it wasn't that kind of situation. For one thing we were partners. For another, we were mates. The best of mates, really. And then I also know that turning the cards in was his decision. Not mine. So in that respect I guess our two situations are close. Not the same. Similar. But the fact is he was asking for help – asking *me* for help. And I didn't give it to him when he needed it. I took advantage. I'm still taking advantage. So there it is. The worst thing I ever did. And I don't even think I feel bad about it. It worked out for me. I don't even think I miss Rundle. Do you know, I heard he was driving Ubers nowadays? The person who told me that might have been winding me up... Or maybe they knew what I'd done. Word gets around, I suppose.'

Toni shook her head. 'You're speaking with hindsight, here. As far as you knew, the guy was a liability. He was causing you a problem, and if you'd both felt the benefit of the new contract, he might have screwed that up as well. It was a tough decision, but it turned out to be the right one. You're not responsible for his actions, ultimately. Any more than Mouse is over the guy on the mountain. I think you're beating yourself up for nothing.'

Debs shook her head, and shivered. 'No. Here's what should have happened. That night, when he called me, I should have told him to sit tight until I got there. That we'd figure this out. That we'd stick together. That I wouldn't let him fall. But I did.'

'You had no agency there,' Mouse said. 'It sounds like you want to have it, some kind of guilt trip, but you didn't have an active hand. It's no more ludicrous than me blaming myself for what happened to Richard.'

'Ah, spooky Mousie,' Debs said. Her eyes were moist and red, but she was not weeping – as if her very tears were grudged. 'You're very zen – you know that? In a lot of ways you always were. People thought you were shy. "The quiet one". We all treated you the way the Beatles treated George Harrison. We made a similar mistake. You're just a sly old boots, aren't you?'

Debs' tone was sneery as ever, and Leah's shoulders stiffened to hear it. Mouse's smile was pleasant, but her eyes were cold. She got up from her seat, and Leah's discomfort turned into something like fear. But Mouse sat beside Debs, then folded her in her arms. Debs sobbed, and allowed her head to rest on Mouse's shoulder.

'Sorry,' she finally croaked, as Mouse stroked her hair. 'This is what always happens when people are nice to me. Had to go and ruin it all with your cuddliness, didn't you?'

'Silly old mole,' Mouse said softly. By then, Toni and Leah had joined them. Debs, her cheeks bunched up against Mouse's bony shoulder, had the absurd look of a child who'd fallen asleep at a wedding, about to be carried off to bed.

'I think this isn't a crying issue,' Toni said, her hand on Debs' back. 'Really, I don't. If you need to get it out, get it out, sweetheart. But it's not on you, that one. You were smart. You didn't betray him. He betrayed himself. He was dragging you down. And no one drags our Debs down.'

Debs sobbed again. 'Even more of the nice!'

'She's right,' Leah said. 'It's the truth. Don't blame yourself for that. You were playing for high stakes. He lost, and... why am I talking like a voice-over for a movie trailer?'

Debs laughed. 'One starring Bruce Willis.'

'Or Steven Seagal,' Mouse ventured.

'Point is, don't blame yourself,' Leah said. 'You did nothing wrong. He did you wrong, it sounds like. Why do this...' Leah frowned suddenly. 'Why do we do this, in fact? Two stories now, and it's stuff you shouldn't have been blaming yourselves for! Why don't we quit this kind of thing?'

'You're right,' Debs said. 'We'll quit this. But obviously not before we've heard your story, Mummy Owl. You don't get out of it that easily because I cried. Who had me as the first crier, in fact? I wouldn't have bet on that.'

'I think it was evens on all four of us,' Mouse said. She still hadn't let Debs go.

'You know, thank God for this... For the four of you. Thank God we've all still got this. I couldn't say this to anyone else, any other time. Thank God for it. Owl Society for life, I say.'

'Amen,' Toni said, and raised a glass. Debs finally broke away from Mouse's embrace, and took another gulp of her gin.

'Thanks... Thanks for... Well. All of it,' Debs said. 'I thought that would be easier, to be honest. Thought I'd tell you it and I could sit here and be cool. Fat chance!'

Toni gulped down her own drink. Her eyes brimmed with emotion, and some glee, too. 'I can tell you mine. If you want.'

'I think we've had enough of this game,' Mouse said. 'Let's do something else, maybe?'

'I'm happy to play,' Toni said. 'I want to know what you think. Here's my thing. When I first met Roy...'

There was a high 'Whoooa...' from everyone.

'Oh don't tell me,' Debs said. 'Roy's not the one? Did you finally hook up with Owen Clancy?'

'No I did not,' Toni said. 'And it is not what you think. I didn't cheat on Roy. Even when we had our break. But there was another girl in the picture when I made my move for Roy. Her name was Elsie, Elsie Fremont. She didn't look like an Elsie. Beautiful pixie face, incredible body. She was a rival. That's for sure.'

'Where did you bury her?' Debs said. Her eyes were bright pink from crying, but the sobbing had subsided, and some of the old swagger was back in her voice. 'Was she in one piece, or a few?'

'I don't think Elsie and Roy got together. If they did, I didn't know about it. And… it's one of the things you can't ever ask. After a certain amount of time, no answer will be enough, you know?'

'Now that can play one of two ways,' Debs said. 'That means they definitely, definitely didn't get together, because I can see you stalking her pixie-featured face all over town. Or, they did, and you just can't handle it. Like you struggled a bit with Mouse and Owen Clancy, at school.'

Malice lit up Toni's features like a jack-o'-lantern. Leah flinched, and the expression wasn't even aimed at her. 'As I said, they didn't get together. So far as I know. But I was determined to get Roy. We were a good match, and we both knew it. But this interfering bitch got in the way. So, I made a plan.'

She smiled at Leah and Mouse in turn. Leah felt the same way as a school pupil making a presentation, swallowed by panic, only the muscles of her mouth resisting.

'I knew this guy called Matt. He was what was called a mature student, but in reality he was only about twenty-five or so. He pretended he was dodgy, so I called his bluff on it. Asked him to do me a favour. He agreed. It cost me money, cash in hand, you know, but he was as good as his word. It was exciting… It was a conspiracy.' She gulped down half of her Chablis. 'Anyway, it was set up for a night after the hockey club player of the year dance. This bitch Elsie had been going on about it for ages. Girls on tour, blah blah. She was mad about her rugby team. Closet fucking lesbian.' Toni's eyes fluttered, and she glanced at Mouse, startled. 'I'm sorry.'

Mouse waved a hand. 'I've got your drift.'

'Right. Sorry. Anyway, I got Matt to show up. At this player of the year party. It was on pretence of him getting them all some toot. In fact, Elsie was too much of a goody two shoes to take any of that. But it turned out she was a slapper. Matt got her pissed, took her back to his flat. They did it. He filmed her, took pictures of her, and sent them to me.'

'That's... wicked,' Debs said. 'No denying it.'

Leah raised her eyebrows and said nothing. 'Hard core,' Mouse said. 'In a bad way, I have to tell you. That's... agency. That's actually doing something.'

'I know that,' Toni said. 'And it got results. Don't worry, though. I know what you're thinking, but I didn't send the pics on anywhere... Matt wasn't quite so scrupulous. He told me that the video might have ended up on a website. Viewed fifty squillion times. You can't really tell it was her. Or so he said. And I knew that I'd have the law on my hands if I leaked them or sent them on...'

'So you never blackmailed her?' Debs asked.

'Not exactly. That's the beauty of it. I just told the story. About how Matt had got her stinking drunk and made her pose for photos. Took a video. No one had to see it, and Matt denied doing it, of course. But the story reached Roy's ears. And he wasn't bothered about Elsie after that. She fronted it out, but after that term ended, she never came back. Transferred somewhere else. Took her credits and ran. Nice girl, really. Has a family of her own, now. Lives in Ghent. Roy wouldn't go near her after he heard she'd been with Matt. Well, who would? Damaged goods, and all that. Matt's one of these guys who sounds like a newsreader but looks like he slept in a skip. It's a dealbreaker. So the way was clear. I made my play for Roy. And I got him.'

Leah knew Toni had been determined. And as soon as Roy had become a possibility, determination had turned into something else. She'd talked about Roy, non-stop, whenever they'd got together. Leah had to admit he was a handsome man – tall, not too slender, wore a knee-length grey woollen jacket and Italian-style scarf like a pro. With his babyish cheeks and clear blue eyes, Roy's appearance spoke of money, privilege and confidence. Toni had met her match. But my God... to do something like that... Brutal didn't cover it. It was criminal. She thought about how it would be to be Elsie. To know something like that had happened. To know her privacy, the most intimate moments, could be violated like that, by a two-bit no-mark, a braying jackass she had the misfortune to encounter one drunken night. And behind it all, was Toni.

She wondered at the shock, experienced at the precise moment she found out that had happened to her. Happened every day, to someone. Every day on the planet. And people like Toni could be guilty of it. She could go to prison for it, Leah realised. Actual culpability in something criminal, and utterly repugnant.

'I don't think we've learned too much we didn't already know, or suspect,' Debs said. 'Shit, Tone, fair play to you. It's not like you accidentally killed someone. Or deliberately killed someone. But Jesus, it's bad.' She burst out laughing, but it was mirthless. 'I have to hand it to you... you've made me feel better.'

'You asked for it, and I've told you my worst thing. And it is the worst thing. I admit it. I do feel bad. I wish I'd thought of something else, some other way to win. Or maybe I could have trusted to fate and won him fair and square. But that was my choice. I wasn't in my right mind at the time. I was in love. It was a big risk, for a big reward. So I feel bad, but I'm not sure I regret it.'

Mouse cleared her throat. 'They do say something about all things being fair in love and war.'

There was a silence, then. Toni's poise wavered, and her lip trembled. 'If there's a hell, I'm going to it, aren't I?' Then, like a ripple across a cool clear pool, she snivelled.

It was Leah who comforted her first, clasping her head into the crook of her neck. 'You confessed it, you feel bad about it... And like you said, you didn't do the worst element. You didn't actually send the stuff out anywhere.'

'I planned it though,' she said, voice muffled. 'I had the idea. I knew someone who would do it. It's wicked. No question.'

Debs said: 'Truth be told... you're right. It's terrible. But... you had something you wanted and you got it.'

Mouse spluttered. 'Oh come on! Said every psychopath in the world!'

This time the silence was deep. Leah felt horror-struck. It *was* worse than the other two. Pure wickedness.

'She's not trying to conquer a country, or open a concentration camp,' Debs said. 'She was trying to get some bitch to stay away from her man. A bitch who, by your own admission, got stinking drunk and bounced with some guy who, I'm quoting here, "looked as if he slept in a skip". Not saying she deserved what happened to her, but she didn't deserve Roy, either. You did. You made your play, and you succeeded. This is whole-life stuff, here, Toni. This is your whole future. You staked everything on it. Not many people would have had your courage. Not saying what you did was pretty, but you got your result. I say, you're the baddest bitch in the lodge.' Debs raised a glass.

'It'll never go away,' Toni said. 'That sickening feeling whenever I think about her.'

'You've confessed it; it was years ago. Love made you a maniac, and that's how it travels, sometimes,' Debs said. 'We don't get tough enough, sometimes. I'm not saying we should be thinking about blackmailing people or getting into fist fights like the meathead boys, but... You got tough and got results. Hang on to that.'

Toni nodded, disengaging herself from Leah. 'I'll try. I'm glad I mentioned it. It's a terrible secret. I couldn't tell it to anyone else.'

'Owl Society rules,' Debs said. 'It travels no further. Agreed?'

'Agreed,' Mouse and Leah said, together, before Toni joined the chorus.

Now Leah felt dread. *I can't not say anything here. And there is a worst thing, all right. More than one, in fact.*

So it would have to be the one that everyone practically knew about. The one she didn't really have to hide. The worst thing Mummy Owl did. The worst thing the Owl Society did.

'Anyway,' Debs said. 'Without further ado, there's one story yet to hear.' She grinned at Leah.

Mouse said: 'This is really where I want to call a halt to this, now. Leah doesn't have to talk about, you know, anything she doesn't want to.'

Leah's pulse was wild. She felt sweat prickle her armpits, the greasy kind that came with fear. 'It's OK... I know what you're thinking. I wouldn't label what happened to David as something I did. It was just an accident. It was no one's fault. You don't expect a car to mount a pavement, after all. So that's fine – don't worry about that. I won't go over it again. You've all shared something. I'll share something. Fair's fair. There is something worse than that. Something I did.'

'What have you done, then, that qualifies for this?' Toni scoffed. 'Ten Hail Marys if you swear, or something. Good old Mummy Owl. Actually, I'm intrigued – I want to know what you're going to say. It might just be bland enough to be funny.'

'Isn't it staring you all in the face?' Leah asked, a note of tension in her voice. 'What else would I talk about? The absolute worst thing I ever did?'

She was met with blank stares.

Leah gestured towards the owl painting, with its huge, blank eyes. 'You've only been talking about it for a whole fucking day! The Owl Society! That girl Halfpenny, for Christ's sake! What else was it going to be about?'

19

Leah began to cry. She felt as if someone had taken her by the scruff of the neck. The drink, the tension in the atmosphere, and a mild case of indigestion from a slice of lasagne as thick as a kerbstone had combined.

She wasn't sure who reached her first. It didn't matter. They clung to her. She sagged against them.

Debs was the first one to make a coherent sentence. 'Hey up, Leah, you've got snot on my frock! Ease up, horsey.'

Leah laughed, causing a bubble to blossom in one nostril like the throat of a bullfrog. 'I guess it washes out... I have absolutely no idea why I did that, sorry. I've gone soft.'

Someone's hand stroked her hair. Another was laid across her shoulder. 'You aren't soft,' Toni said. 'No way. Here. Let's get you another glass.'

'Ah, I'm not sure.' Leah actually sleeved away some tears, like a child.

'Here y'go, you muppet. You've got a silver sleeve on you.' Debs handed her some tissues from a box. 'And, also, here you go.' She handed Leah a glass of white wine.

'Um, she did say she didn't want any,' Mouse said, sharply.

'She didn't – she said, "Ah, I'm not sure." Not projecting, are you?'

Mouse made no response. She patted Leah on the shoulder then returned to her seat.

'It's fine,' Leah said, taking a sip of the wine. 'I'll tell the story. Christ, you all know it.'

'You don't have to say shit,' Mouse said. 'And I'll tell you something else – whatever deep dark secrets you might think about spilling, it won't change our opinion of you. You can take that to the bank, Leah.'

Debs sat back down in her own seat, and smirked. 'What if, though… she had eaten someone? In a casserole, I mean, not sexually.'

'Yeah, good point,' Toni said, raising her eyebrows. 'If someone said Leah was a multiple murderer or something, I guess that'd change my opinion of her. I would definitely visit her in prison, if she ended up there. Otherwise I might be a bit wary of meeting her in a house in the middle of nowhere.'

'Maybe if she was an evil genius… yeah, that'd change my opinion, I suppose,' Mouse said, in a lighter tone. 'Plotting, planning world domination. It'd be cool, all the same.'

'Evil genius, plotting and planning… that's kind of the problem. That's what I don't like, about the Owl Society,' Leah said. 'I know worse things have happened in my life. I know what happened to David… God knows, that'd change anyone. But there's something about the Owl Society, how it all turned out. It haunts me. I think I forgot about it, or I was in denial, for years. It's always in the back of my mind. It's something that I think about when I wake up in the middle of the night. Not something I dream about, exactly… But it's there, under the surface. I think it's the worst thing I ever did. I'm sure of it.'

Debs raised her hand. 'Uh, point of order here… Am I alone in thinking that I don't know what the fuck you're talking about? The Owl Society? Some stupid little club we made up when we were what… eleven? Twelve? It was the equivalent of playing with dollies! What's there to be embarrassed about?'

Leah cleared her throat. The glass trembled a little in her fist, until she relaxed it a little. 'You all know what the problem was. You all know what we did. What *I* did.'

Debs tutted. 'For Christ's sake. You mean the freak, don't you? The crazy chick? Let's say it. This is what it's about, isn't it? I can't even remember her name, that's how meaningless it is.'

Mouse said, quietly: 'Halfpenny. That was her name. Fiona Halfpenny.'

'Fiona Halfwittery. That's the one!' Debs whooped. 'What a fucking muppet. Seriously, Leah – you're feeling guilty about that? You're feeling guilty about some stupid prank, which happens ten times to the dozen…'

'I am feeling guilty because it was horrendous, a horrible thing to do. It was my fault.'

'Put it out your mind, Leah. You've got bigger fish to fry in this life. I'm serious,' Debs said. 'Mouse was right, absolutely spot on. I agree with you, Mouse. You don't even have to talk about it because it's not even a problem.'

'It is,' Leah said. 'And it's my story. I had to listen to yours. I need to put it out there. You know it, probably. Discussed it to death. It haunts me. And it's something I definitely did. Like Toni's. I don't think I could stop it, now.'

'I only want to listen to this if you are absolutely sure you want to tell it,' Mouse said. 'Sometimes therapy... isn't the best thing for people. But if you're sure, I'll listen. Maybe then we can make a better judgement, and help you process it.'

'Good for blackmail, too,' Toni said. She laughed, nervously. 'Sorry. I never did know when to drop in a joke.'

'I remember she was friendly with Mouse,' Leah said. 'That was how it all started with Fiona Halfpenny. She was brought into the class at registration. Mr Dougan. Computer science teacher. Clodding halfwit with his oatmeal trousers.'

'I remember,' Debs said. 'You get some teachers who you suspect were bullied as schoolchildren. They come back to school as teachers and it's *all started again...*' She said this in her horror movie voice, and again, Leah didn't like it.

'Dougan just said something like, "This is Fiona; now be nice, everyone." And they made that girl wander down the rows of desks to the very end. All those eyes watching her. I remember that silence. If she'd fronted it out, sat next to someone, had a chat, she might have been all right, but she looked... With hindsight I'd say she was crippled. Crippled with anxiety. Someone sniggered at her. Then everyone did.'

'That was me,' Debs said. There was no trace of the usual glee or sarcasm in her voice or her expression. It had gone blank. She was, briefly, no longer in the room. She was obviously remembering.

'Might have known,' Toni muttered.

Debs shrugged. 'Hey, it's what happens. And you've got to remember, we were *children*.' This sounded defensive, and Debs clearly knew it. 'You start regretting daft things you did as a kid... My God, where do you stop?'

'You saying you would have laughed at her today?' Toni asked.

Debs merely smiled. And took another drink.

'She drifted through classes,' Leah continued. 'I remember Mouse was paired with her in art. That was a kind thing to do, really. Mrs Mawdsley. Mad old clown, sharp tongue on her. But she had a heart. She had a kindness to her. I think... I'm speaking out of turn here, maybe, but she saw Mouse's quiet nature and thought there was someone there who could help, who could give her a route in.'

Mouse nodded. 'Mrs Mawdsley took us both aside, and she put it beautifully: "Mouse here can spot a talent, and I saw the way you used charcoal for that sketch last time. Why don't you pair up with Mouse and see what you can come up with in still life?" She was good, Mrs Mawdsley. We slagged her black and blue, but she was decent. Kind soul. Good heart, as you said.'

'She wore it on her sleeve,' Debs noted, 'as well as about half a tonne of crappy costume jewellery. You could hear her walking down the corridors from the other side of the building. Bloody Noddy with bells on. She was married, wasn't she? Imagine living with that. Someone rattling everywhere they go.'

'So,' Leah continued, 'Mouse being Mouse, you introduced us, and... Well, I don't know what happened to me. I thought I was kind. I thought I was a nice person. But something about that kid freaked me out a bit. I saw her hanging around my house one day. She must have followed me. I remember calling you guys up, watching her mooch around my street. I made a big drama out of it.'

'I remember that,' Toni said. 'You thought she was going to break in and murder you!'

Although she smiled at this, Leah said: 'I know. And that breaks my heart, too, because she obviously thought we were going to hang out. You know. She just wanted to come around and be friends. But she never actually knocked my door. And I didn't go out to see her. I was... I was a snob, basically. Someone weak had joined the group. Maybe I thought I was establishing a pecking order. I don't know.' She shook her head, suddenly.

'Here it is again,' Debs said. 'You're too nice. I reckon maybe you lost something since those days. You were the queen bee, all right. The one we all looked up to. What happened since then? Now you're all tears and snot because you rejected the local weirdo. Man, remember her face? That thick brow. And the hair, like a boy's. Someone gave her a short back and sides... It wasn't a stylistic thing, either. No Bowie-style androgyny.' She touched her cowlick fringe, surely unconsciously. 'And so fucking pale, too. Sickly. Shine a studio light on that face and it'll be pale blue.'

'I don't want to think about her face,' Leah said.

There was silence for a moment. They all thought about the same thing.

Leah felt nauseous, and held her breath for a moment. This was an effort, this admission. It was costing her physically as well as mentally. She felt sweat prickle at her armpits, the small of her back. She waited a second or two for the sick feeling to pass.

'And then she followed us on her bike,' Leah continued, 'and we kind of let her tag along. She was like an annoying kid sister, even though she was the same age. She just looked so young, a tiny little kid. Even her bike was weird, like an old lady's. One of those fold-up numbers that can fit in the back of a car.'

'Nothing wrong with those,' Mouse muttered.

'I... bullied her is the truth. Took the piss out of her clothes, but I did it behind her back. Pretended to support her in class, then tore her to shreds outside it...'

'This is kids' stuff,' Mouse said. 'Debs is right. Think about it – everyone did stuff like this as kids. Everyone was a little bit nasty to friends. It was school, Leah – you'd think you were running around knifing people or mugging old ladies. This kind of stuff happened. You were a good kid. If you made a few mistakes along the way, they were only little ones. And, with the best will in the world... Fiona Halfpenny didn't fit in.'

'Fiona Halfpenny – not the full shilling,' Toni said. 'That one was pretty good, you have to admit.'

'That was my fault,' Leah said. 'I thought that up. I thought I was being clever. Then there was that time we ditched her at the shopping centre when she went to the toilets... we hid in the café of the bowling alley on the top floor and watched her wandering around, trying to find us. That was fucking nasty. And the thing is, even at the time, we knew it was nasty. Why did we do it? Why were we such bitches? I wish I'd been nice. I wish I'd been kind. Even if it meant she was sitting here with us, right now.'

'You don't know your own mind at that age,' Debs said. 'It's not an excuse, really... except it kind of is. The hormonal bomb goes off, sending you all over the place, mentally, physically, sexually... You do weird things. No doubts about it.'

'And we all did that, not just you,' Mouse countered. 'It's embarrassing, but it's not all on you. You weren't guiding us, in that. No, I'm not proud of what we did. But you have to be honest with yourself and look at your own life. How you turned out. You can't go on beating yourself up about cruel things when you're young. It's a learning experience. At least you have the decency to admit that it wasn't the best thing to have done.'

'And let's not forget, she was a lunatic. Absolutely howling mad.' Debs rubbed her eyes. 'She started screaming that time in class, telling something or someone to "Shut up shut up shut up!" This was in Religious Education with Miss Cramer. Mildest-mannered woman you ever met. She didn't know what to do; her face was a picture. Even when she began hitting her head on the desk...'

'She might have been hearing voices,' Mouse said. 'We joked about it at the time, but that's what she really heard, I am guessing. And that type of illness... you can't really fix that just by being nice to someone in class.'

'No, but you can make it worse by being a bitch,' Leah asserted, 'which I was. I remember Shell once telling me to calm it down. That I should be ashamed of myself. I was... But not right away. What it took to trigger the shame was the thing I want to confess.'

'The prank wasn't your fault,' Debs said. 'We all take a share of that. And anyway... wasn't much of a prank, was it?'

'This is what I want to say. What I want to confess.' Leah took a deep breath. 'Something I never told anyone about the prank. That night. That Halloween.'

20

Make the circle, make the circle,
Witches mean to fly
Make the circle, make the circle,
Bite the baby's eye
Take the knife, take the knife,
Make the crimson flood
Take the knife, take the knife,
Drink the baby's blood

'So, like, what's the magic ritual?' the otter said. Someone had gone to time and trouble to create her face paint. Brown smears around the forehead – and Fiona had a big forehead, they'd all decided – and a black dot on the nose, and white greasepaint around the cheeks and chin, with black mascara lines radiating outward in what Leah had supposed were whiskers.

Leah had told her they were appearing in their Owl Society guises. Then they hadn't, of course. Leah was a witch, with livid green skin and a long fake nose that her mother had worked hard to blend in with her make-up, and cereal flakes stuck to her skin that made for queasily convincing warts.

Debs was a werewolf, whose grafted sideburns, hairy hands, claws and especially the yellow teeth – an expensive purchase from a joke shop – were initially meant to be silly but were genuinely frightening in a certain light.

Toni was a ghost, of course – but a scary one, with what looked like barbed wire transfers around her neck, black eye make-up blended into a porcelain-white face, and a gauzy white gown that showed how long her legs had grown.

Mouse was a pirate, but looked more like a troubadour, and everything she wore looked expensive – all the girls had felt the quality of the silken red jacket she'd worn, slightly too big for her, reaching down to the hip where her frilly white chemise bloomed.

Shell was a vampire, with a little bit of greasepaint and some glutinous red corn syrup... but her costume might have been the scariest, with some yellow fox eye contact lenses that she insisted on wearing throughout. A little bit like an optical illusion that seemed to shimmer and move on the periphery. Leah didn't like looking at Shell's vampire eyes for too long.

And of course, there was the otter. 'I love these costumes,' she'd said, realising that she'd been duped; realising that they'd been cruel. Leah most of all.

Leah's room was lit only by a star projector that cast shimmering shoals of planets and stars across the face of her boy-band posters, her study chart, and her own watercolours. Its engine whirred, a counterpoint to the girls' silence.

'The magic ritual,' Leah said, 'is that you have to get in the box.'

And Leah tapped a cardboard box. It had contained

their new washing machine, which rattled against the wall downstairs at that moment. 'We all have to take a turn.' She looked at the girls, one after the other.

'And there's a spell,' Debs said.

'Cool,' Fiona said. She swallowed, looking from one to the other. 'So what's in the box?'

'First we have to make the spell of summoning,' Leah said. She reached into a drawer by her bedside, and pulled out scraps of paper. 'We have to banish all fear.'

She passed out pens and pencils. The scraps of paper had been cut into even squares.

Then she pulled out her brass wastepaper bucket, putting it in the centre of the floor. It was empty, and glinted when the revolving lights struck it.

'What we have to do, is write down the thing we're most afraid of, fold it up, and throw it into the magic circle.' Leah nodded towards the wastepaper bin. 'Then we'll burn it. With that, our fear will vanish. After that, we'll chant the magic spell.'

No one said anything. They all scratched something onto the paper. Even Debs fell silent at this point, her wit deserting her for once.

Otter began to fidget. She chewed the end of the pen Leah had passed her. She made sure the other girls were writing something down. Then she made her mark on the paper, and glanced up at Leah once as she did so.

Leah smiled, her straight white teeth splitting open the witch's face. And Fiona grinned back. Then she folded up her paper and dropped it in the bin.

The other girls quickly finished up their own notes, and then hurled them into the wastepaper basket.

Leah struck a match. 'Now we banish all fear. Say after me: "I reject fear."'

They all did it. Otter fidgeted again, her hands juddering at her sides, her fingers disappearing inside her mouth occasionally.

The flame of the match danced in Leah's eyes. 'And there goes the fear.'

She dropped the match into the basket. The paper caught light quickly; once the flames had leapt high enough, she poured a glass of water, quickly dousing them. There was smoke, but Leah had the window open.

Toni coughed, but the atmosphere soon cleared.

'And now, we say the spell. Chant after me... Make the circle, make the circle, witches mean to fly...'

They linked hands above each other's heads, all sat in a circle around the brass basket. Leah had borrowed the weird cadence from the soundtrack of a horror film she claimed to have watched, but she had in fact only heard the music through the walls. The tune was off-kilter, but catchy, and despite knowing exactly what was coming, Leah felt a kind of dread. Her pulse seemed to follow the chant.

'...drink the baby's blood.'

Leah clapped her hands; the chain being broken, the others stopped chanting, and all bowed their heads. It took the otter a second or two to realise what the others were doing, and to follow their example.

'And now, who goes first in the box?' Leah asked.

The others kept their heads down, elbows on knees, perfectly matched in form if not appearance.

Otter glanced around nervously, until she noticed Leah was staring right at her, unblinking.

'I suppose… I suppose I'll go. All right.' She shrugged. 'I'm up for it.'

'Be aware that the box contains many things. It can contain delight, or it can contain misery. It all depends what demon we summoned. If it's benevolent – if it looks into you and sees you are at one with it – then you will be rewarded. If not…'

'The demon's in the box?' Otter asked.

'It's from another dimension. "In the box" doesn't matter. It might manifest itself in the air outside, and you'll never know. It might manifest in our hearts, or in our blood. It might never take material shape, but transmit as sound waves… Many things are possible.'

'If you do it,' Debs said, 'you're braver than any of us.'

'Unless you're chicken,' Toni added, blinking her black-frosted eyelashes. 'Not a chicken, are you? Maybe we should make you the chicken in future.'

'Pock-pock,' Debs said, flapping her arms, elbows bent. 'Pock-pock says Mrs Chicken.'

'I'll do it.'

'Good.' Leah gestured to a clear space on the floor. 'Make your way over and be seated.'

The otter sat down. 'Should I close my eyes, or something?'

'Well, no, you don't have to. Not in a box.' Leah tutted. 'Think about it. OK… If my assistants could help?'

Shell and Toni helped Leah lift the box. They placed it over the otter. She dipped her head a little to make sure her head did not strike the top of the box. She was completely covered, the four edges of the open box splayed out on the carpet.

The other girls grinned at each other, suppressing laughter.

'And now we sound the gong...' Leah said.

She punched the brass wastepaper bin; it emitted the desired sound effect.

Then Leah shrieked: 'Oh my God! There's spiders! Spiders, coming out of the bottom! The box is full of spiders!'

A scream pierced the box; the carboard rose as the otter struggled to get to her feet.

The other girls grabbed the box and held it down.

'You must stay!' Leah cried. 'Stay and face the gift of the demon!'

'Let me out, let me out, there's spiders, let me out!' The pitch of the voice inside the box distorted at its top note, fit to break the glass. But not the cardboard box. A foot shot out, colliding with Shell's leg; she cried out and hopped away. The box twitched, crashed, bulged.

'Spiders, all over your face!' Debs yelled, then burst out laughing. 'In your hair and down your top! And up your bum!'

The otter's screams were beyond comprehension now, on the outer reaches of human range. The box burst open at a weak point and a fist emerged, flailing.

That's when Leah's mother appeared among them – not dressed up as anything, but aghast, all the same. 'What is going on here? What are you all doing?'

The girls flinched. The box fell onto its side, legs pinwheeling. Then it righted itself, comically. On the carpet, the spiders emerged; all different sizes, many different colours, some with jewelled eyes, some with slavering fangs, some hairy... and all plastic.

Leah's mother tore off the box and the struggling figure

beneath was revealed. Leah would never forget the face and its expression; the otter make-up a stained ruin, criss-crossing the features, and those eyes, officially now the scariest eyes, even scarier than Shell's. She shrieked, drew in breath, shrieked again.

'It's all right!' *Leah's mother said, a jocular note that failed to disguise a rising sense of panic.* 'They're just messing about... having fun.'

She reached out to the otter. The otter snarled, and drew her fingernails down Leah's mother's face. She sprung back, clutching her cheek. Leah was thunderstruck at the blood, blackish in the star projector's punch-drunk orbit. Incredibly, Leah's mother remained calm. She raised her other hand, as she might to a mean dog. 'It's OK, sweetheart. It's all right...'

The otter got to her feet and ran. There was the door. Closed. But she kept running, as if spring-loaded, or as if she was still inside the box, and rebounded off the woodwork with a nauseatingly dull sound.

The otter lay flat out on the floor. Those eyes again, but not as panicked, not as feral. Revolving in their sockets. The otter spreadeagled, as if its pelt was laid out to dry.

'Oh my God!' *Leah's mother said, getting to her knees beside the girl.* 'Fiona, are you all right, sweetheart? Someone turn that fucking light on, right now!'

21

Debs broke the silence with a barbed little titter. 'If I am being honest, when the otter totalled herself on the door... it was extremely funny.'

'Shut up,' Leah snapped. Spittle flew from her mouth on the closing plosive. 'You've got too much to say for yourself, at times, Debs. We don't need your jokes and stupid comments every minute of the day. Is it a form of Tourette's or something?'

Debs was open-mouthed. Then she chuckled. 'Now that's the real Leah. There she is! That's more like it. Come on, tell us all what to do. I like it. I like having a boss.'

'She said, "shut up",' Mouse replied, curtly. 'Give it a try, for five minutes.'

Debs mimed drawing a zip across her lips, and reached for a drink.

Leah took a breath. 'I'm sorry. That was stress... It wasn't easy to talk about.'

Debs waved her away. 'Forget about it.'

'I'm trying to say that all of this was my fault. What happened to that girl. It all stemmed from that. When she sat up and started talking in that little girl's voice, like she was a baby... That still makes me shudder. My mum said she'd never seen or heard anything like it. It's like she was hearing voices. Then it was like she was trying to pluck things out of the air.'

'You still had your star projector on,' Mouse said. 'I think that might have been it. Or maybe she was seeing stars.'

'Could be. But she started talking about the spiders who lived in her room... She'd lost her mind. She had totally snapped. And I planned it all out.'

'You helped to plan it all out,' Mouse said. 'There were five of us in that room. We were all delighted with it. We all contributed, we all went along with it, and not one of us raised any objections or said that it might have been out of order. So if there's any blame to be attached, it should be on all of us.'

'I did say that we shouldn't do it,' Toni said. 'For the record. I did say that. I thought it was mean.'

'Nah, you got cold feet at the last minute,' Debs said. 'Not for the first time in your life.'

Toni frowned. Before she could think of a response, Leah continued: 'Good God, my mother, after she'd cleared out the house and called Fiona's mother...' She closed her eyes for a moment. 'That's the last time she lifted her hands to me. My ears were ringing for days. They might still be ringing, now. "You disgrace, you absolute disgrace. You're a bully. Bullies are the worst of the worst. They change lives." And it was the first time I realised that I *had* been a bully. That I wasn't the heroine of my own little story. That I should have been looking after the weak one. Instead, I just pretended to look after the weak one. To boost my own status. My ego. So if she's still around, I'd want her to know that it changed my life, too. I learned a lesson from that. I followed my good nature, from then on.'

'Ever think you lost something as a result?' Debs muttered.

'Maybe so,' Leah said. 'But it's for the best. It's not a quality I like in myself. As far as the plan for the box goes… It was conceived by me and executed by me. You could say I was the boss. So it's my responsibility. And then it got worse. She didn't show up at school the next day. You remember that? Or the day after that. The registration teacher told the class that she wouldn't be coming back, and left it at that. But we found out, of course. Because Fiona's mother came around to my mother's house and had a screaming match.'

'I'd actually forgotten about that,' Toni said. 'You told us, though. Good God. Nightmare.'

'That was when I heard the word "sectioned" for the first time,' Leah continued. 'I remember that woman's face. Demoniacal, is the word. I cowered behind my mother. My dad wanted nothing to do with it. Stayed upstairs with the curtains shut. The whole street must have heard. "You've killed her," the woman said. I thought she meant it literally. I thought I was going to jail. "She thinks the spiders are everywhere."'

'That girl, and her mother, had mental health problems,' Mouse said. 'It was a bunch of twelve- and thirteen-year-olds playing a prank. If it had been any of the rest of us, we might have screamed a bit, but we'd have taken it for what it was – a joke. But, yes, if I'm being honest, we knew how vulnerable she was, or we sensed it. We didn't understand the consequences, but we had an idea. So we shouldn't have done it. But the emphasis is on "we", here. You might have felt like you were the boss, and we might have treated you like one, but we were all culpable, there. We all knew better – even if we didn't understand the consequences, and what it means when someone has those kind of issues, the devastation it can cause. What I would also say is, you didn't know what the exact consequences would be. None of us did. For all you knew, she'd have screamed a bit, then taken the joke, not had a complete psychotic break. You're only thinking that way because of how it all turned out.'

Toni cleared her throat. 'I agree with Mouse. You weren't to blame. We all had a hand in that, but... she had big problems. You forget that time she had to be fished out the swimming pool.'

'If that's not too sore a topic for you,' Debs simpered.

Toni ignored her. 'Then there's the time she rode her bike after us, screaming... She never explained what she was doing. Said she wanted to scare us. She did scare us. So that probably fed into why we did what we did on the Halloween party. She wasn't right, Leah. If she got sectioned, we probably did her a favour, long-term. Better she was caught early, than going into teenage years, or early adulthood.'

'Then we're all in agreement, in fact,' Debs said. 'Consider yourself absolved, oh head girl of St Martha's. Now get that goblet down you, and forget about it, before this party turns into a fucking morgue.'

'I wonder how she turned out, all the same,' Leah said. 'Married? Kids? Still sectioned? I wonder what the problem was. Schizophrenia, or something?'

Mouse drummed her fingers on the end of the chair. Then she said: 'Fiona Halfpenny wasn't schizophrenic. I think she had some sort of personality disorder. Something there's a term for, but not one you'd know.'

'Nutter, is the term,' Debs said.

'"Nutter" is the term used by insensitive people,' Mouse said. 'There are all sorts of psychological issues that can't be diagnosed, or cured. Lack of sympathy and empathy are part of that.'

'God you're fierce tonight,' Debs purred, rolling her tongue along the R in 'fierce'. 'You really found your voice, I suppose. The mouse that roared.'

'That's right,' Mouse said.

'Wait a minute...' Leah turned to Mouse. 'How do you know what she was and wasn't diagnosed with?'

'This is the thing. I hesitated to mention it, but... a few years ago, I had the same sort of memories and feelings about Fiona Halfpenny as you.'

The ensuing silence was broken by the continued percussion of light rain on the windows.

'And?' Leah asked.

'And... Well, it played on my memory. The night she melted down, the Halloween party where we were all kicked out of your mum's house. I felt guilt. Maybe a bit different from yours. Just that I let it happen. I felt I should have stopped it at the time, too. So, I looked her up.'

'When was this?' Leah felt her guts writhe like a fish on a line. She regretted the Chablis.

'About six, seven years ago. It wasn't easy to find her. She's not on social media. So, I made a couple of inquiries through people with a similar name. I found her mother, and an older cousin. There was a coincidence, too, as the cousin was an art teacher. That let me in. I happened to mention the name, said I'd known a Fiona Halfpenny. Mentioned the town. It was her. I made inquiries then was put in touch with her. She's a graffiti artist. Well known in her field. There's a rumour she knows who Banksy is. Mentioned in those circles. Goes by the name of... you'll never guess?'

'Otter?' Leah whispered.

'Yep, you're there – OtterDotter. Not a household name, exactly, but getting there. You might have seen her bombs on the side of trains, in and out of stations. And, if you're still beating yourself up, I can tell you – she seemed happy with her life. She didn't bear any ill will towards us. Asked how we were all doing. Mentioned that she'd had mental health issues, which she related to her mother, funnily enough. She'd moved from school to school. She'd done it before she came to St Martha's, too. She's OK basically, Leah. What happened was bad. It should never have happened. We should have...' She took a deep breath, and her lips trembled for a moment. 'I should have stopped it, and I didn't. But it's important to know that she's fine. She got over her problems, she moved on, and she's a success in her own way, on her own terms. If you were ever to meet her again, she'd tell you that.'

'I never want to see that girl's face again so long as I live,' Leah said. 'Please tell me you didn't pass on our details?'

Mouse raised a hand. "Course not – God, I'd never do that. I was curious. I did it off my own back. I didn't mention it to you or anyone else because... Sleeping dogs, and all that. It was just for me. It was just to be sure.'

Debs pulled out her phone. 'Show me. Otter... Daughter, was that?'

Mouse spelled it out. 'All one word. You'll get a hit right away. You won't see her face, though.'

Debs threw her phone onto the sofa and tutted. 'Forgot. Can't get a signal here. Last place on earth for it. And no Wi-Fi. I'll thank Shell for that when I see her next.'

'Emergency calls will work, though,' Toni said. 'Just in case we need them... Don't they?'

'Let's hope we don't have to put that to the test. Would be nice to have some contact with the planet, though,' Debs muttered. 'Or even just to see the mysterious Fiona Halfpenny. Artist, you say? Famous? You meet her in person?'

Mouse shook her head. 'I wasn't quite prepared to do that. But I spoke to her, online. Messaging system. I put my mind at rest. And I apologised, on our behalf. She said she understood the need for... expiation. I think that's the word she used. I know I should have said something. I held back from contacting you all – especially you, Leah. I knew I should have done it eventually. But life gets in the way. You just forget.'

Leah blinked. 'I'm struggling with this... You're telling me this now? It's taken you this long to tell me about it?'

Mouse licked her lips. 'It's just something I thought about. It would have been weird... I wanted to find out for myself. I guess I felt guilty in my own right. And I wasn't sure if opening up old wounds was the best thing to do, for anyone else.'

'You're struggling a bit, Mouse,' Debs said. 'You seem a bit confused about this.'

Mouse sat back. 'All I'm saying is – if you're beating yourself over that girl, don't worry. Fiona Halfpenny is doing fine. She had her problems, but she's over them, now. She's thriving. She's made something of herself.'

'I suppose that's... sort of reassuring.' Leah rubbed her eyes. 'God almighty. What a night. Whose idea was this game, again?'

'It was mine,' Debs said. 'Maybe we should change the topic? I think we've all had a go, by now.'

'We've not all had a go,' Toni said. 'We're forgetting someone.'

Debs glanced over her shoulder, to where the rain was trickling down the glass. 'The bogey man?'

'No – Shell. She's not here, but we could do her entry for her.'

'You know Shell's deepest darkest secrets?' Debs said. 'She was all action, I suppose. But she was a bit of a closed book, as well. I reckon folk at university got the best out of her. She got a bit of a personality transplant within her first year. Straight shooter, I thought. Next thing you know she's downing pints with the rugger buggers.'

Toni and Leah shared a look.

'I can think of one moment Shell might say was the worst thing she ever did.'

Debs' jaw tensed. 'What was that, then?'

Toni grinned. 'You remember, I'm sure. Or maybe you blanked it out? Might have gotten a concussion.'

'Oh. That.' Debs chuckled. 'Yeah. I think I know the incident you're referring to.'

'Kapow!' Toni yelled. 'The time you beat her at pool and you just used it as an excuse to pick on her. Remember that?'

'Hard to forget.' Debs laughed – perhaps a little too loudly; a little too quickly.

'You made some sort of reference to… what was it?' Toni placed a finger to her lips. 'Ah yes, hang on. You made some crack about her body shape and the figure of 8, on the eight ball. You riffed on it for ages and ages. You thought you'd said something very clever. What were we, seventeen?'

'About seventeen. Summer before upper sixth,' Mouse agreed. There was something in her sly expression then that Leah didn't quite recognise; didn't quite like. 'All of us out for a pint and a burger. A few of the boys from sixth form college were there. Can't remember half of their names, now.'

'Owen Clancy being one of them,' Toni said. 'Yeah, and you had an audience, Debs, and the guys were enjoying it. "Victimise the fat girl" night, I think you called it, and that got even more laughs. So Shell said…' Suddenly Toni leapt to her feet, legs apart, hands on hips, and growled: '"You say another thing that I don't like, and you'll wish you hadn't." Big comedy pantomime noise from the audience. That whooooooa thing. And then you said…' Toni burst out laughing, head bowed for a moment. 'Then you said… I'll remember this until my dying day…'

She broke up laughing. Mouse completed the line: '"I'd like to see you try it. Most exercise you'll have had in years."'

Toni nodded, eyes screwed tight shut, laughing at the top of her voice.

Leah's shoulder muscles tensed on Debs' behalf. This was mean. That night had been horrible, awful, something that was never spoken of, even quite soon after the event. They had made up, and Shell had apologised, and Debs had half-apologised, but still…

'And then, whack!' Toni said, slapping her fist into her palm. 'The noise. It was exactly like you hear on the movies. Plumb in your cheek. If it had been your teeth they'd have ended up in your spine. If it had been your nose, she would have turned it inside out. And you went *flying*...'

'It was hilarious,' Debs said. 'Truly was. A funny night.'

'And then you got up.' With elastic suppleness, Toni got onto her knees, cradling her chin. '"I think my jaw's bwoken!"' she said, in a pathetic falsetto.

'That'll do, I think,' Leah said. 'I'm bored of this.' She got to her feet. Something beyond the patio door shifted, and she frowned for a second. The pale blue LCD lights seemed to flicker; or something moved across them for a second or two. Then the wind changed again, and the fine rain grew heavier. Just the rain. 'I'll get another bottle. Then I think we should put the telly on, and have a good grumble about music we don't listen to.'

'Oh, no,' Debs said, all mirth gone from her face and voice. 'I want to carry on with the bottle. It's been interesting, don't you think? I'll give it another go. Wait a second.'

With some difficulty, Debs got to her feet, and lurched over to the table. She spun the bottle, again with some effort. 'Oh look – it's come up as me, again. Let's spin the wheel, see what comes up.' She spun the wheel, scrutinising the blend of lettering closely. When it slowed, she openly gave it a nudge, to push it on to where she wanted it to go. 'Here we are!' And she grinned.

Leah peered closely at the wheel.

FIRST AND BEST SHAGS.

Oh.

22

The rain began to flow in torrents the closer he got to the top of the hill. Rills of it ran over his hiking boots – an awkward pair, perhaps too big, and so well insulated that he was barely aware of the impact of his feet on the tarmac, let alone outside moisture. Moving at a stiff angle up the mountainside with an ungainly clod, he felt a bit like a Victorian aquanaut, or maybe Frankenstein's monster.

Ewan hadn't long crossed into his forties, but he was feeling every minute of them. Ever since the ferry had dropped him off, things had gone wrong. No taxis available. The pub had been rammed with drunks, unfriendly locals for the most part, and no one had been prepared to give him a lift to the lodge. One of them had even taken issue with his accent – a hint of menace in among the supposed jocularity, even when he'd explained his family on his father's side was originally from Edinburgh.

'Close enough,' the man had told Ewan, nose about a quarter inch from the tip of his own.

He'd only had one message to go on from Shell, one single crackly communication. The message had been clear enough. And he'd obeyed, leaving the three boys with his mother before making the trip.

In a way, the mountains had been a tonic for him, even if the rain made the journey north more difficult. He had started the walk up the road to the lodge in high spirits. He'd even enjoyed the early part of the walk, as the road snaked around the mountains and the tableaux of the loch, the sea and the other mountains dropped away below him. But this feeling soon faded.

He bypassed one house with a sign outside saying 'Keith and Susan's Riding School'. Ewan could barely make it out as the rain got heavier, the sign creaking in the poor conditions. The noise was irritating, rather than spooky, although Ewan did get a chill when he saw that the lights were out in the property with the exception of one single point of illumination in the kitchen – a readout on a fancy fridge, a console on a heating system, or similar. The owners must be out for the day, he decided.

Ewan made a few more attempts to get through to Shell, but there was no response, and seemingly no reception on the island, even higher up the hill. All Ewan could do was grit his teeth, and hope that the route to the Halt was as simple as the online gazetteers had suggested.

The darkness grew oppressive. There were no lights on the road, and the gloaming from the village at the lochside had all but disappeared. The moon was obscured by the clouds, and the rain absorbed what light might have filtered through. Ewan had that thin-ice feeling that he was on the wrong path, and that it was possible he might step right off the roadside and take a tumble down the ferns and bracken, all the way to the bottom. Perhaps he might even leave his boots planted there.

Silly bitch, he thought to himself, knuckling his

waterlogged eyebrows. Whole thing was a disaster from the start. Should never have gone. She only did so she could catch up with Leah. The only one she truly liked, out of them all. Possibly that Mouse girl, too, but as for the other two...

As the road crept higher to the summit; the trees grew thicker. A detail from one of the travel blogs he'd skimmed on the ferry stood out – something about trees having been planted thirty years ago, an early rewilding scheme of some kind, having led to these immense conifers.

A house appeared through the trees – with shouts and laughter filtering through over the air. Someone passed by one of the windows. Ewan considered going there and knocking the door, as the house took on more definition through some gaps in the trees and the steadily increasing rain. It looked a likely venue for the girls' weekend. But out there in the dark, with the rain dripping off his chin and the end of his nose, Ewan didn't go with instinct. He knew that this was Owl Tree Halt Lodge, exactly where his maps had placed it, the first place visible from the roadside once he was past the mountain trail riding school. It was a guideline; but it wasn't where he'd been told to go.

Foxbar Fort, close to the summit, was what he was looking for.

Ewan came to the place unexpectedly – the turreted tower looming through a thick cordon of trees, slick and silvery in the dark. As in the riding school he had passed first, there was a single light on in the kitchen.

Ewan knew what his first line was going to be. It ricocheted around his mind. *The boys have been worried sick.* In his years together with Shell, he knew that a reference to the kids would find a gap between her ribs, close to the heart. He would be speaking the truth, though. He remembered the boys' faces, reflecting his own panic as he dialled her number again and again.

'Is Mum all right?' asked Gordon. 'Is she coming home?' Questions he had asked himself in those awful incommunicado hours. The transition from a slight worry, to a horrid doubt, to a fear that was difficult to conceal.

He felt curiously out of place as he found a gate and pushed it, then started up the concrete-slabbed driveway. His knees hurt, and his underwear chafed, and he badly wanted a cup of tea, a hot shower, and a great big row.

'Come out here, it'll be great... I need you out here. It's a couples' thing, I must have made a mistake... I am on my own out here... Foxbar Fort, come out and have fun.' This entreaty came in an absolute mess of text messages, dolloped onto his phone in a rush. So unlike Shell.

A light blinked on at the top floor of the tepee-styled building, and he saw Shell briefly appear at a window. Then a hallway light came on further down, illuminating the abstract stained-glass window over the top of the front door. Warm amber, bright orange, dull red. Here he was, at last.

Seemed quiet for a party. Maybe they had all decanted to the lodge further down the hill. Owl Tree Halt? That looked more like the party house, all right. He'd even seen disco lights stabbing through at one point, that curious starship effect lancing through the trees.

No one arrived at the door. No one appeared at the windows. Ewan frowned. He checked his phone – futile, he knew – and then he tried the door handle.

The door was open. He flicked on a light, and moved into a vestibule that hadn't been long decorated, with a shoe rack similar to the one he and Shell owned, but devoid of mud spatters. There were no boots resting there.

Instinctively, he took off his own sodden pair, and felt the prickly mat through his thick hiking socks.

'Shell? It's me. Come down,' he called out.

There was a shifting sound from above, then silence.

'Shell?'

Ewan felt uneasy, doubting himself. Common sense told him that the venue for the get-together was the raucous house just down the hill. Perhaps he was right. Perhaps he'd intruded upon someone? He wondered what it might be like, if you were alone in a house in the middle of nowhere, and a strange man blundered in.

'Hello? It's Ewan. I'm here for Shell Michaels. Is Shell Michaels up here?'

He opened the door into an expansive circular space, not unlike a lighthouse or oast house. There was a table at the far wall, but only a bucket seat against the natural curve of the wall. The floors were bare and spattered with paint – old paint, not new. A sink near the back door was crammed with pots and brushes, and there was a smell of turpentine in the air. That wasn't what immediately drew his attention, though.

In the centre of the room, seemingly suspended by some hidden force, were four immense cardboard sheets, stretching from floor to ceiling. As he moved closer, the illusory effect changed as he saw that they were hung with clear string, like fishing line, as if they were marionettes. The sheets were slashed through in an odd, wave-like pattern.

Ewan could make no sense of it. It was painful to look at; as you moved closer, or sideways, or backwards, the irregular slashes showed through and appeared to take on a strange movement. It was similar in effect to 3D puzzles he remembered from about thirty years ago. Every single movement created a simulation of motion among the images you were looking at, as the slashes and gaps intersected. Nothing stayed the same; every perspective was different. It was strange, and entrancing, and Ewan wondered what it all meant, even as he knew on the instant that he had indeed come to the wrong place.

'I'm so sorry... hello? Is anyone there?'

He didn't want to touch the canvas... He'd thought they were sheets at first. Or were they sheets? But he had no choice, if he wanted to get to the door. He moved among the corrupted white surfaces. Tiger stripes shifted in front of him. Spewing gases. Liquid pressed under glass, as if on a microscope slide. The setting sun through the sparse leaves of an autumn tree. A kaleidoscope in blood.

'All right?' said a voice from beyond the door to the left.

'Yes, it's me, it's Ewan!'

It sounded like Shell. He brushed the canvas aside, cursed the flapping intrusion, and opened the door.

The staircase curved around the turret, lit in stages by candles. Ewan came up the stairs, grasping the banister. 'Shell? Are you OK? Come on down; it's me.'

He thought he heard someone giggle. He stopped for a moment, then got annoyed. He stomped up the last few steps, not caring how intimidating it might have sounded.

He came upon a narrow corridor, with rooms on the left-hand side. Light filtered through the bottom of one single door, and through an aperture that Ewan assumed was a keyhole.

'Shell?' He made towards it.

He knocked on the door. Someone gasped inside. Sweating freely, his hand and voice shaking in tandem, Ewan said: 'Look, my name's Ewan. Shell told me to come here. I don't know if I have the wrong address… She was quite specific it was Foxbar Fort.'

No response.

'I'm sorry, is anyone there? I'll leave if there's no response.'

Someone was breathing through the other side. Looking down, now, he saw that it wasn't a keyhole emitting the beam of light, but a genuine hole in the door. He thought he saw something move, changing the quality of the light inside. He knocked again, hard.

'Hello? This is your last chance. If this is a trick of some kind, I don't appreciate it.'

He bent down towards the yellow globe.

Someone was whispering.

'…Bite the baby's eye…'

The light vanished. He had time to blink, once, before the blade punched through his eyeball.

He screamed, but there seemed no volume to it in his pain and shock, no sound of note. It blended in with the roaring of his pulse in his ears and temples and chest. Ewan staggered back, a hand clamped to his eye, everything drowned out. He felt warm wetness pulsing through his fingers, over the back of his hand. He fell.

The door opened and the light from within the room froze him, a death ray perhaps. A shadow flew out like cinders torn away from a fire in the wind. It started cutting him, splitting the back of the hand clamped to his face, then his forehead, then across the neck.

'...Drink the baby's blood!'

Ewan might still have been screaming. He threw both hands up as he hit the floor, but the darting shadow pierced that defence and slid the long, thin blade through his other eye, right to the quick, and that was all.

23

Leah wrinkled her nose as the viscous liqueur punched her in the palate. 'Jägerbombs. Yeah, I remember now,' she said, coughing. 'I've had these before. Last works night out I went on. My opinion has not changed.'

She laid the shot glass down on the table and pinched her nose. There was still most of the shot left. *No chance*, Leah thought. *No more of that. If I do, snap of the fingers and it'll be tomorrow morning.*

Toni sniffed at her own drink, then drained most of it, smartly. She didn't wince as Leah had, but smacked her lips, then said: 'I'm getting tones of shame and lairiness, with just a hint of fuck-you.'

'Yeah, that'll be about right,' said Debs, downing her own. She was steaming drunk now, playing pinball with the edge of the couch, the table, and any other vertical plane within her vicinity. The sly look on her face that usually foretold some malicious comment was now a constant on her flushed face, her rounded corners and soft edges puffy and bloated. *She never was a good drunk*, Leah thought. Not that she knew many who qualified for that status. 'They have a bit of a belt to them. Hey. Mousie, you're a bit down in the dumps. Fancy a livener?'

Mouse shook her head. 'I think I might head to bed soon, you know.'

'Look, if you're up the duff, just tell us,' Debs said. 'Never mind the suspense. Out with it.'

'I'm not up the duff,' Mouse said, calmly.

'She's blushing! You've actually blossomed into a terrible liar.' Debs hiccupped. 'I like that, though. It's very becoming. Better to play the cherry-cheeked ingenue, than... than... What's the word?'

'An arsehole,' Toni said.

Debs winked at her. 'If you're in the family way, Mouse, that just leaves me and Toni as the only free citizens left in the group. Fair play to Shell – dearly departed – she popped those three out fast enough with old Ewan. Kapow. I lost count; I couldn't keep up. I always need to ask one of you guys what I need to put on the Christmas cards. Hughey, Smoothie and Phooey. Huey, Dewey and Louie. Eggsy, Oestrie, Flappsy. Epidurus, Suture and Queefie. She must've taken to it... Being Keith Cheggers. Some birds do that, I guess. Then Leah, of course.' She paused. 'Anyway, Toni, not fancy it?'

'I think you've had enough to drink, Debs,' Toni said.

'That's a fair shout. But... why so defensive? Your man firing blanks, then? Or have you got your fallopian tubes in a twist?'

Leah opened her mouth to speak, but Mouse stood up. The way she started forward, it looked for an instant as if she was actually going to hit Debs. 'I know you like a laugh,' Mouse said, 'and I know you like to shock people. But I think you need to be dialling it down, now.'

'Jesus. I'm intrigued. When did you become a tough guy, Mouse?'

'About the same time you became a comedian.' Mouse returned to her seat and folded her arms.

Debs took in the expressions of the other three, and raised a hand. She was drunk, though, the extra alcohol having pushed her way past the threshold of reason. The girl who'd cracked earlier on, in the story about Rundle, had gone. 'I'm sorry. Sore points, these. Y'know, I only do these things to exorcise them, if that makes sense. These thoughts. I don't really mean to hurt anyone. Bit like when my old man croaked, you know? Motor neurone disease. I mean, it's a funny way to go, let's face it. Everything else fucks up, but your mind's fine. It's proof there's no God, no heaven, no justice. All you can do is joke about it. You have to, don't you?'

'Think you're about twenty-five years too late for that excuse,' Leah said, in a cold tone. 'Let's talk about something else.'

Debs clicked her fingers. 'I know what we were doing – the wheel of shame! Come on. First shags, best shags. You can all say your recent partners, if you like. But if you lie, I'll know.'

'Why's that – do you have secret powers?' Toni asked. 'You've kept these well hidden, if so.'

'Nah, I just work in advertising. Everything we do is a lie. Hey ho, and ho hum, before I cause a full-on riot here...' Debs lurched to the table and grabbed the empty bottle. It almost slithered out of her hands, but she steadied it with her free hand just in time. She spun it on the table, and it threatened to fly off, only just stopping short of the edge as it completed its revolutions. The tip of the bottle went to Mouse.

'Go Mouse! First shag first. Then best shag.'

'You know who my first shag was,' Mouse said. 'I'm sure I've been interrogated about this before. It was Owen Clancy, leavers' ball.'

'Seniors balled, more like. Owen Clancy, in a tuxedo, you in an evening dress. Virginities turned to confetti. Your own *Dawson's Creek* moment! You lucky, lucky bitch. I'll never get over that.'

Leah pictured Owen Clancy's face, the chiselled jaw, the dimples at the corners of his mouth, the dirty fair hair, cropped close, a good match for his slim build and long face. And his blue eyes, chips of cobalt that might have been intimidating had he not been so quick to smile. Leah remembered her knees almost giving way, when he used to smile at her. She'd been sure Owen Clancy was going to work his way towards her, over time, but had backed off when Toni staked her claim. Toni had been sure they'd be together, too. *But ah, life isn't like that, Toni. Bit like the swimming*, she added to herself, sourly.

Debs had also been obsessed with Owen since the age of eleven; and Mouse… Mouse had said nothing. She'd blossomed at just the right time. And she'd asked Owen Clancy to the prom, and he'd said yes. And she'd said nothing at all about sleeping with him, nothing about the where or the when. Rumours had started to trickle in from the rest of the boys. No one could believe it. Toni had been distraught, Leah simply stunned. Mouse? It hadn't seemed possible. But it had happened. She'd confirmed it years later. Looking at her face, her fantastic figure, it was obvious why he'd gone for her, of course, but not openly admitted.

'I'd never thought he would want me,' Mouse said.

'Maybe that's how it came about. I relaxed. We had a laugh. We studied together at the library – he lived quite near my house. We got talking and swapped notes. He was kind, when he was away from the football boys. Polite. Maybe even a touch shy, once you got past the front. It took me a long, long time to realise he fancied me.'

'You've never given us marks out of ten,' Debs said.

'It wouldn't be fair to do that. No one's a prodigy in bed. He did have some experience. I didn't have any. But it was still lovely to have done it. I was mad about him, but then three weeks later... he was gone. St Andrews university. Hardly saw him, after that. Hardly even a text.'

'You still sad about that?' Leah said. 'I was kind of sad for you.'

'Emphasis on "kind of",' Debs said.

'Maybe. It's one of those things. Experience. It was never meant to last. Your good times don't. Nothing does. It happens in your teenage years, that's your lift-off time. You're open to the world, and it's open to you. New beginnings and experiences are exciting, but sooner or later you're going to have to... settle. We all know about that, I suppose.'

'You never quite settled though,' Leah said. She surprised herself; it was the kind of aside she made to herself, rather than out loud. 'Even now, you'd rather take off than build a nest. Isn't that true?'

Mouse nodded. 'Spot on, I suppose. But I'm in a good place now. If you must know.'

'We're deviating,' Debs said. 'Who was your best? Think fast.'

'My current partner,' Mouse said, and gazed into Debs' eyes.

Debs held the stare for a moment, then laughed. 'You win. You're serious. Spot on. Now how about Toni?'

'I don't really want to talk about my first,' Toni said. 'Not for any sinister or weird reason, just… it had to be done. I had to get it out of the way. Fresher's week. Nobody knew what they were doing. The poor lad was terrified. Sweated pints before he even did it. Turned out he talked the talk, rather than walked the walk. I'm not even sure you could count it as having had proper, full sex.'

'In 'n' out?' Debs asked.

'Yep. Pretty much. Round pegs, round holes, but just… First-year effort. I'm not ashamed – it's just reality. You think it's going to be true romance. Fireworks and fanfares. You think it's going to be Owen fucking Clancy.'

They laughed.

'But, at the end of the day, it's something you have to get out of the way. Best is Roy, always was Roy, and always has been Roy. From the first to last.'

'Soup to nuts?'

'Absolutely.' Toni took a sip of what remained of her Jägerbomb. 'Sorry to be boring.'

'Never been tempted?' Debs asked. 'With anyone else?'

'If I said I had never found any other men attractive, I'd be lying. If I said that they hadn't shown some sort of interest in me, I'd also be lying. But I've never acted on anything, and never will.'

'And what about Le Roi?' Debs asked.

Toni frowned. 'What about him?'

Leah said: 'She's answered the question. It's your turn now, Debs.'

'Yeah, in a minute, Mummy Owl. What about Roy, Toni? Has he ever strayed?'

'I will answer it,' Toni said. 'Not sure why you're asking, apart from the usual reason. Which is winding people up. But the answer is, "as far as I know, no". That's all anyone can say about their partner. Anything else is fantasy. And if you try too hard to find out, spying, snooping... you're a wrong 'un, basically. But he's with me, it's all secure, and that's all there is to say about that.'

'Didn't you guys have a break?' Debs asked. 'After your first year or something?'

'We did. There weren't any other people involved. We made a mistake, and got back together.'

'Just asking. Sorry to pry.' Debs grinned. 'I'm thinking things didn't work out for him in Bassetton?'

'What?' Toni frowned. 'What did you say about Bassetton?'

'Just something I heard. It's fine. Yeah, you were asking, who's next? It's me or Mummy Owl. An intriguing duo, to be sure...'

'No, hold on,' Toni said, growing agitated. 'Bassetton? That's where Roy moved with his job, that year... What do you know about Bassetton?'

'Nothing. Maybe you told me... I'm sure you did.'

'I'm sure I fucking didn't.'

'Someone told me, at some point. Maybe he did, at one of the weddings. Yeah, I should shut up really, shouldn't I?' Debs fidgeted with the bottle, staring down at the table.

Leah's heart had gone into overdrive. She felt it thudding in her eardrums. 'Yeah, let's move on.'

Toni turned to Leah, and was about to say something. She thought better of it. Her eyebrows actually twitched, and she bit the side of her mouth, savagely.

The bottle needed a nudge away from settling at Mouse, for the second time, to take it to Debs.

'Me? Well, my first is a bit of a strange one.'

Eager to see the topic of conversation moved on, Leah said: 'I don't think you ever told us about that.'

'There's a reason, y'see.'

'Was it someone embarrassing?' Toni asked. 'Lucas Murphy? He was bloody keen.'

'Oh Jesus! Who in their right mind would do that? Man's eyebrows were like gorse. He had the forearms of a Turkish prison officer. Imagine what his pubes are like! Frigging treasure hunt, to find a dick in there. No, nothing like that.'

'Please don't say it was one of our dads,' Mouse said.

'Nah. It's kind of worse than that. It was…' Debs paused, and belched. 'It was Mr Haggerty.'

There was silence for at least two full seconds.

'You fucking… What?' Toni thundered. 'Mr Haggerty? The chemistry teacher?'

Debs nodded.

'Mr Haggerty… 1980s slip-on shoes… grey suit out of *Miami Vice*… moustache in our first year at St Martha's, wisely ditched after that… Looked a bit like Jean-Claude Van Damme, or so he liked to think… *That* Mr Haggerty?'

Debs nodded again.

'When did this happen?' Mouse asked, quietly.

'Not at school, before you ask. The summer after we finished. And I know, it was still totally wrong. I know. But I regret nothing.'

'But... how?' Toni asked. 'I mean, I thought he was quite a handsome man. I think we all suspected he was gay, though. There were some rumours doing the rounds among the lads. Hanging around the showers after a football game. Sounded like the usual homophobic rubbish, though. That weird fear they get. Or projection. Or denial. Or something.'

'Oh, Mr Haggerty is straight, I can confirm. An absolute stallion. It was kind of wasted on me, at the time. We met in The Right Plaice, as in, the chippie. Right Plaice, Wrong Guy, you could call it. Boundary Lane; 11pm. I'd been at Carter's with the works team from Videodome. Seventeen, the Saturday girl, trying to act older. Always really pissed me off, that, incidentally. The name of the place, I mean. Looks like a letter missing. Like it should have been Videodrome.'

'Yeah, you cracked those jokes twenty-odd years ago,' Toni said. 'So, you met in a chippie, and, what? Sparks flew over the saveloys?'

'It's even grubbier than that. He gave me a lift home, which was extra naughty as he'd had a couple of pints himself, in town. Said that it would be really awkward, if the police breathalysed him, and then asked why an eighteen-year-old former pupil was in his car. I didn't tell him I was only seventeen, but I got the reason why he said "eighteen" right away. That led to a bit of a naughty conversation. I was totally into it. Exciting. He went to a place he knew – somewhere he'd been loads of times. I don't know where it was, but I remembered a pond, black water. We did it right there. In the car. Seats pulled back. He nearly rammed me into the fucking boot. Not a euphemism.'

That must have hurt, Leah thought. *Must have.* But she said nothing. There was an almost rapt expression on Debs' face, nothing to do with the act she was recalling, merely the act of recalling it. What was the truth in these stories, really? When the telling of the tale becomes an act in itself?

'And he came back for more. I moved away a few months later, but he was still texting me as recently as ten years ago. Some nights I'm tempted to look him up.'

'Dirty bastard,' Toni breathed. 'He must have been what, mid-thirties?'

'He was thirty-eight, in fact. Now I'm not saying it was right. And he's probably broken every rule going. Criminal offence, now, isn't it? Breaching a position of trust. It might have got him put in jail, if I was to complain about it. Shit, now there's a thing – I could blackmail him!' She snapped her fingers.

'Why did you never tell us before?' Leah asked.

Debs thought for a moment. 'It was embarrassing. He wasn't cool, was he? Not a fantasy figure or anything. I've got a brass neck, but not that much of one. Not then, anyway. It was a secret I found it easy to keep, for once.'

'Still totally wrong,' Toni said. 'Jesus, what a sleazebag. How many times do you reckon he got away with that?'

'Loads. It looked like a bit of a tried 'n' tested strategy. And I don't feel bad about it. Gave me a load of confidence. Moved me on to the next stage.'

'Was he the best?'

'Nah. Wasn't tuned in to my needs, you could say. But Jesus Christ, he could give you a seeing to. Arse like a Singer sewing machine. I can tell you the man who *might* have been the best was – a guy from Amsterdam who I met at a convention, down in Brighton. Looked like that football player, Ronaldo.'

'Does he have buck teeth and play for Brazil?' Toni asked, seriously.

'What? Fuck, I dunno. Nah, tall and lean. Thoroughbred. And he knew it. He could do everything, extremely well, and wanted me to know it, but... I ruined it. I kept laughing at him. I thought he was going to strangle me, at one point. His ego couldn't handle it. It was his fucking *face*, literally, it was too serious. You'd think he was scaling the Eiger or something. Wrestling with the helm on a ship in the middle of a hurricane. Bit like Rocky, at the end of *Rocky*. This was like... round three, four... maybe even five. I was more fascinated than turned on. Soon it got funny. It's a shame. I spoiled it. That might have been the best, but fell short. We didn't close that deal, strangely enough. I mean, the deal to represent his firm.'

'So...' Toni pressed. 'If he's your second-best, who's your best, then?'

Debs' expression lost shape, then. She looked sad. 'It's Eoghan. Guy fucking adores me. I'm not sure if I quite adore him back, but... He's kind and loving. Whenever I take my clothes off in front of him, his eyes pop out like something from an old cartoon. It's been like that since day one. He can't get enough. He's the guy who's always there. He's my man. There it is.'

Leah felt herself tearing up, absurdly. She took a drink of the Jägerbomb.

'Now,' Debs said, 'with that out of the way, what about Mummy Owl?'

She considered a moment. 'First was Howard Lansing. American student. For about seven days, he was my entire world. I thought: Owen Clancy's mid-tier compared to this guy. I couldn't think straight. I wouldn't say Eighties Pop at the union on a Thursday was quite fireworks and fanfares, like you said, Toni, but it was getting there. It felt like it, at the time. I had a pull-out bed that doubled as a sofa in my room at the halls. I still felt like a Disney princess, pulling her prince. It was that ridiculous. I wonder if that's how marriage happened, in the old days. There was a proposal, and people just got married as kids. But then he started saying things like, he wasn't into normal relationships. He wanted things to be open, if we were going to be together. He said he was an unconventional person... fucker was eighteen years old! Open relationships!'

'Oh, you're angry about it. I like an angry Mummy Owl,' Debs spluttered. 'Did you take your revenge?'

'Like what? Knife in the back?'

'I was thinking more like fucking one of his friends. That's how you find out how open your relationship really is.'

'No. Didn't cross my mind. I was hurt, I'll be honest. My mum spotted it right away. Called up, heard something in my voice. She took a day off work and came to collect me for lunch. We talked about it, without talking directly about it. This'll pass, she said. It'll pass quicker than school ever did. One day you'll wonder what you were upset about. This is the shallows, the rest of your life's an ocean. She said that. I never forgot it. And she was right. So, that was Howard Lansing.'

'What's he doing now?' Toni asked.

'I've no idea. Not into the cyber stalking thing.'

Debs' tongue flickered at her lips. 'There's lie number one.'

'It's true. I've no idea. It's the past. I barely know what

you guys are doing, any given day, let alone someone from a long time ago.'

'Crunch question. The best?' Debs asked.

'It's John, obviously.' Leah took care to make eye contact with Debs, but she must have blinked, because Debs creased up laughing.

'Come on, love, you can do better than that!'

'It's true. John's the best. That's why I'm still with him.'

'We believe you,' Debs said. 'Wasn't there another one, pre-John, that you really liked, though?'

'Don't think so.' Leah folded her arms.

Debs laughed. 'Spilling tells like playing cards out the sleeve of a crap conjuror,' she said, in a quick voice; a dark voice; a sober voice.

'I didn't have a go at you guys when you were all gushing about your present partners.'

'Yeah, because we were telling the truth.'

'Game's over,' Leah said. 'I'm going to grab a glass of water. This Jager stuff is rank.'

'Don't be huffy,' Debs said. 'Just tell the truth. You'll feel better for it. Wasn't there some guy, about ten... eleven years ago? When you were in your first job, on secondment to that weird place with all the roundabouts in the Midlands?'

'No. I've already given my answer.' Leah took up the bottle by her fingertips.

'The Midlands? Where was this?' Toni asked. She was chewing the side of her mouth.

'Nowhere.'

'Come on, tell us. Jesus Christ, we've all shared stuff. Don't go cold on us now. Take your turn. It'll go no further.'

Whereabouts was this? I'm intrigued.' Debs sat back, smiling, folding her hands over her knees.

'I don't even remember. I had a bit of a fling with someone. When I was single. It was good fun.'

'It's not like you really, Mummy Owl,' Debs said. 'Bit out of character, it sounded.'

'I probably embellished the story a bit.'

'Whereabouts, though?' Toni pressed.

'Brankholme... somewhere like that? Real middle-of-nowhere place. Offices were in an industrial estate, next to a cinema, or a bowling alley.'

'You did it behind a bowling alley,' Debs said, nodding. 'We've all been there.'

'No...' Leah laughed, in spite of herself. 'It was some guy who knew some guy from work. That's all.'

'And he was your best?' Toni asked.

'No, John's my best.'

'Why does Debs keep bringing it up, then?'

'Because she's a shit-stirrer,' Mouse said.

Toni frowned. 'Brankholme... I know that name, from something.'

'You don't,' Leah said. 'It's the middle of nowhere. Industrial estate. It was already struggling, back then.' She gathered her glass, and got up to leave.

Mouse said: 'I'll give you a hand, Leah,' and followed her out.

They both went into the kitchen area, where the special beer fridge was kept. 'I think she needs reeling in,' Mouse said.

'That's been true since the day she was born,' Leah said.

'The stuff about kids, God almighty... She's one of these people, you can't be sure if she's said something in total innocence, or if she's trying to needle you. She's one of these fucking people.'

'She is,' Mouse agreed. 'I'll be honest with you, there's a reason I don't bother with Toni or Debs. No harm to them – live your life, you know? But I think I'm going to pull out of this shortly.'

'What... You turning in?'

'No, I mean out... of this place. Tonight.'

'Where are you going to go, at this time of night?'

'Not sure. I'll set up the tent maybe. I just don't want to be here. I'll warn you, though... don't engage with Debs on this true confessions bullshit. Ignore her from now on. It's going to lead you into trouble.'

Leah felt a surge of panic. She couldn't think of a response, or a deflection.

'I don't know where Debs was going with it, but she's damned right about your responses. And I don't know what your response means, but if this was a quiz show, and the star prize rested on it, I'd know what I would guess.' She held up a hand, as Leah began to protest. 'Don't say anything; it's fine. All I'll say is, get away from those two. They're insecure. Could be a million reasons behind that, things we'll never know, and things we don't want to know. But I can only go by their behaviour, and I think if it came down to it, those two would eat you *alive*. That aside... I don't think I'll be seeing much of anyone in future. For reasons that have already been guessed.'

Leah nodded to Mouse's stomach. She was stroking it, unconsciously. 'Been feeling sick much?' she asked, quietly.

'Not especially,' Mouse said, neutrally. 'Anyway. Don't tell the others. I don't think I'll be seeing the weekend out. Not here, anyway. I'd got a bit of island-hopping planned, anyway, before I get too big. I'll keep in touch, don't worry. You always were my favourite Owl Society member.'

'You're leaving now?' Leah said. She didn't like the idea of... *of being left with those two.*

'In a little bit. Maybe tomorrow morning. I'll see how it goes. I am tired, I have to say. Been a long one. Getting old, I think.'

'Can I ask you a question?' Leah asked.

'I'll give you the answer, before you do: sperm donation, off the books, a poet called Ranald from Denmark. Beautiful blue eyes, six feet three inches, his dad's an architect and his mother played cello professionally.'

'Good Lord,' Leah whispered. 'The appliance of science. With a turkey baster.'

They both laughed.

Then light flared, igniting the patio, startling them.

'Security light?' Leah said.

'Yep.' Mouse shaded her eyes, peering out into the wet, blustery scene outside. 'Hasn't gone on once, since the sun went down.'

'The door locked?' Leah nodded towards the wooden door, which led out into the alley along the side of the house.

'Best check,' Mouse said.

Leah reached her hand towards the doorknob. Before it got there, the door was wrenched open.

24

The man in the doorway shrieked louder than anyone. He dropped the plastic bag he was carrying, with a dull, glassy crash.

Mouse recovered first. 'Steve, you silly twat!'

He raised his hands, mouth open to display a furry tongue that made Leah itch. 'I am so, sorry.'

'You should be!' Leah said, clutching her chest. 'We could all have been in the nude, or something.'

'Then I'd have been mortally offended,' he said, recovering a little of his swagger. He grimaced as he lifted the dripping plastic bag. A shard of glass poked through the blue material. 'This was, at one point, a bottle of vodka. The good news is that the six pack of beers and the mixer is available.'

The effluent stung Leah's eyes, and she had a flashbulb memory of downing screwdrivers in nightclubs, long ago. She had not drunk vodka since. 'I wasn't aware we'd made a final decision on you joining us tonight, Steve?'

Debs squawked, providing Leah's second big fright in a matter of moments. The newcomer shouldered her way in between Mouse and Leah and clutched at Steve – who had to look lively with the punctured carry-out bag, lest

Debs should impale herself on it. 'Ah my man! I must have forgotten to tell you, Leah – I invited Steve over tonight. I invited Pete, too, in fact... Is he coming?'

'Ah, Pete can't make it. Doing some maintenance with Gwen on the plane. He passes on his regards.' He scratched his chin while he said this. *What was it Debs said about tells?* Leah thought.

'Never mind, old son, you'll do for us,' Debs said, linking arms with Steve. 'Set your drinkie down there... in fact, don't, honey, that looks a real mess. Set it on the floor, we can come back for it later. That's it. Now... follow me. I think it's time we made full use of the facilities out in the patio.'

They made their way out of the kitchen into the main living room. Through the open door, Leah glimpsed Toni's face, a picture of confusion – then turning into a beaming smile. 'Steve!' she cried, leaping forward. 'You've saved my night!'

The door closed over, sparing Leah the sight of Toni grappling with Steve while he was still attached to Debs' arm.

Mouse pointed towards the door. 'That there is a liberty. I didn't know about this, I'm assuming you didn't, and judging by her smacked poodle face, I don't think Toni did, either.'

'I'm more disturbed by the patio comment... God, she doesn't mean the hot tub, does she?' Leah nodded towards a window, dotted with rain. 'The weather's not the best for it.'

Mouse sighed. '*Existence* isn't well suited to it. I suppose it might be fun. If you're the sort of person who likes online videos of people banging their heads. I'm making a cup of herbal tea before I split. One for the road.'

Once he was seated, Steve seemed unusually tense. He looked as if he was attending a job interview, and Leah supposed that he was, in a way.

He appeared defensive on the armchair, clutching a can of pilsner patterned like the front of a rebellious teenager's school jotter. He had taken off his jacket, revealing a tie-dyed T-shirt, over the top of what Leah had once seen described as 'board shorts'. In his slightly bedraggled state, he looked less like a surfer and more like a tramp, making do with whatever garments he could pick up. He had clearly not shaved since Leah and Toni had met him on the dockside in Glasgow on Friday.

'So,' Mouse said, sipping on her tea, 'can I ask how you got here, Steve?'

'Car's parked round the front.'

'Surprised I didn't see the lights,' Mouse said. 'Guess the weather's really bad.'

Steve gulped at his can. 'I heard a lot of shouting and stuff when I got out the car. Maybe you were distracted?'

Mouse nodded. 'I guess we were. Party games, you know? So, seeing as you're drinking, you won't be driving your car back, then? Maybe you've planned on staying somewhere around here?'

'We have an empty unit up at the top of the hill, in fact. No one's there, this weekend. Foxbar Fort. I was going to bunk up there for the night. It's very nice of you to invite me.'

'I didn't.' Mouse could do playful all night. But her look was hard, now, an unflinching quality that Leah would never have attached to her friend. 'But I suppose Debs did.'

Debs, who had been trying to pour a fresh Jägerbomb so long, and so carefully, that there could be no doubting how drunk she was, said: 'Mouse is trying to wind you up, Steve. Don't you worry, puddin'. We'll get over to the hot tub soon. I'm not sure how it works – could you show me?'

'Absolutely, it's a doddle. Pretty much brand new, those things. Hardly been tested.'

'That's reassuring,' Debs said, 'because usually these things are simply a filthy reservoir of sex.'

'We wouldn't want any of that going on here,' Steve said, as he got up to join her.

Toni got to her feet, and said, 'Guess I'd better get into my cossie, if we're going to have a dip.' She nodded to Steve, who was watching her cross the living room floor.

Debs slid open the patio door. A gust of cold wind blew in, causing everyone to shiver. The rain was heavier outside, pale blue bolts moving through the LED lights.

'Now, I think this is the control panel?' Debs said, before Mouse slid the door shut.

'I'm not getting into the hot tub. Absolute and final,' Mouse said.

'Me neither. We going to watch this horrendous occasion play out?' Leah asked.

'Oh yeah, definitely.'

Leah reached for the bottle of carbonated water and refilled her glass. 'I'm going to look out a jumper, then. Save me a seat.'

*

Wisely, the hot tub had been placed underneath the balcony, set deep into a patch of false turf covering the decking. The cauldron bubbled, steam rising into the air. It would have been big enough for all of them.

'Nice and warm now,' Steve said. 'I'll head back in for a beer, if you don't mind. Uh… I'll leave you to it.'

Toni had appeared in a one-piece, which had been strategically cut in sections at the sides. Debs had muttered something about a kid cutting out paper dolls, but the joke hadn't gained much traction. The costume was blood red, and Toni looked amazing. Pilates, park runs and Peloton had given her enviable muscle tone and a flat stomach, with the shoulders and neck muscles of an Olympic swimmer.

'Shit, I forgot about that tattoo,' Leah said. There it was; lurking just at Toni's hip, a curly bluish gecko with a tail like a question mark.

'Tattoo?' Mouse narrowed her eyes. 'Oh wait, hang on a second. When did she get that again, a holiday?'

'Her and Shell went to Magaluf for a summer,' Debs said. 'Bar work. We were meant to head over but I think it all fell through, for lots of reasons. Money reasons, for me, I'll be honest. They got tattoos near the end. Absolutely mental.'

'It is quite cool.'

'It's cool, but it isn't Toni. I didn't think so, anyway.'

Toni went into the water first, giggling a little. 'It's lovely!' she said, using the rail to guide herself in, before sitting down. 'Even better when it's a bit chilly outside.'

'Steve doesn't know where to look,' Mouse said, under her breath.

'I think he knows exactly where to look,' Leah replied. She looked away from the steaming pool towards Mouse's mug. 'Herbal teas – they any good?'

'Yeah. Get all sort of flavours, now.'

'I only ask because I had a go at green tea, years ago, and I nearly chucked up.'

'I've heard some folk have that reaction. Tonight I'm packing good old ginger, sourced from a shady dealer somewhere in Soho.'

Debs still wore the same dress. She had moved on to Steve's beers, ostensibly in an effort to sober up, and she belched as she said: 'Well, it's time to get wet, Steve.'

Leah cringed. 'Surely she isn't,' she muttered.

But she was. Debs started taking her clothes off. She kicked off her shoes, smiled and slid off the straps on her dress. A quick shimmy, and it was off. She flicked the dress on the end of her toe with no little skill onto the patio furniture in the L-shaped corner.

'Debs,' Leah said, almost aghast. 'You need to think this through, honey.'

'Oh, when did you turn into such a granny pants?' Debs said. She stood with her hands on her hips. Her strapless black bra and matching knickers were sheer, expensive, see-through, and surely amounted to a great big stock cube of disaster with the addition of water. She had gone thick in the hips as she got older, but Debs carried a little bit of timber well – always had. It always sounded like a cliché when both men and women referred to pot bellies as cute, but in Debs' case it was true. Her breasts were of course monumental – they had been since she was about fifteen. The best word to use about her now, stripped of pejorative connotations, was shameless.

Steve looked properly embarrassed. 'Uh, I'll leave you to it, ladies.'

'Not at all. Get in.' Debs turned, smiling at him over her shoulder, and stepped into the water.

'I don't have my swimming trunks.'

'You want to be excused from games? Then I hope you've brought a note from Mother?' Debs barked. *My God*, Leah realised, *that voice... that was the PE teacher. Tarrant. Perfect mimicry*. 'Got kecks, haven't you? Or you could slip them off and come in. We won't look, will we?'

Mouse tutted. 'Ridiculous. What a total embarrassment. Not to mention abusive. Imagine the situation was reversed? We'd get jailed.'

'Not if it's what he wants,' Leah said.

Steve caught her eye, perhaps having heard the conversation. Then he smiled, and that's when Leah felt a note of dread. Had the shy guy act been simple pretence?

Steve pulled the T-shirt over his head. He was skinny underneath, something Leah had never liked in a man, wiry rather than muscular with a sunken chest that did no favours for how his flesh draped across it. Off came the shorts, revealing a pair of rather tatty tartan boxer shorts, which complemented his earlier vagrant aspect. When he moved, the golden hairs on his legs seemed to catch the light, the red fleck in among the blond.

Both Toni and Debs gazed at him from the pool, with blank expressions.

'You're going to wet your pants,' Debs said.

'You'll find these can go on land and water. Amphibious leisurewear.'

'Amphibious?' Debs said. 'You think you're special because you can write with your left hand?'

'Standard issue for a man my age, if you please,' Steve said, sniffily.

'Whatever. In you get, then. Scaredy-cat.' Debs grinned, spreading her arms to grip the circular edge of the tub, allowing her legs to float.

'This is all right, isn't it?' Steve said, a little more uncertainly, as he immersed himself up to his ankles. 'Please tell me if not – I don't want to make anyone uncomfortable.'

Mouse, who'd actually covered her face with her hands, said: 'For the record, you are making me very uncomfortable.'

'Then you can head indoors, adventure girl,' Debs sneered. 'No one's stopping you. There'll be a nice BBC4 documentary on about sheep farming, or growing your own kumquats, or crampons. You can watch that. Or you can stay outside and have a look. We're easy, aren't we, Toni?'

'Oh, I think you'll find we take a little bit of effort,' Toni replied.

Steve sat down in the tub opposite Debs and Toni, stretching out his arms, sighing as the warm water surged over his shoulders. 'Oh – we forgot the drinks.'

'One of these two dears can go in and get it for us. Unless they're coming in as well?'

'Don't think I'll bother,' Leah said. 'I reckon I'll see if there's something on BBC4. About cracked pottery.'

Debs laughed. Her make-up had begun to run, black trails at the corners of her eyes. 'Look at the pair of them! You know if this was in Germany or Sweden, we'd all be butt naked and no one would care. Or if they did, no one would bother. The British curse. I've got a theory, you know. Most of our problems in life come from how we think about our bodies. "She's too fat... she's too thin... look at her tits."' Debs locked eyes with Steve. 'So, it feeds into social anxiety, phobias, all that kind of stuff. Not saying you don't get that in continental Europe, but their attitudes to bodies are totally different. Much healthier. There's not that tabloid taboo.'

'I guess you're right.' Steve grimaced as the bubbles tickled his chin. 'Never thought about it like that before.'

One of Toni's feet breached the surface, a sudden flicker like a shark's fin in the surf. She wiggled her toes right at Steve, and Leah noticed even from that distance that her nails were perfectly manicured and painted purple. Then the foot disappeared.

Steve shrieked, as something touched him beneath the surface.

Mouse sighed, and turned to Leah. 'Milk, no sugar for you – is that right?'

'I think I'm done,' Mouse said, sipping at a hot tea in the kitchen. 'Though I have to admit there's a part of me that wants to see the rest of this car crash actually happening.'

Leah sipped from her own cup and glanced through to the patio. The rain was coming down heavier, partly obscuring what was going on outside, but she could make out that Debs had shifted position and stood in the middle of the tub, facing Steve. Toni hadn't moved, still sat opposite, and must have been slightly obscured by Debs. 'I feel as if I've been caught watching a dirty film by my parents, or something. I expected that sort of behaviour from Debs, though fair play – getting into a hot tub in her kecks was bold, even for her. Toni, though… she's playing a dangerous game.'

'Bit competitive, is Toni,' Mouse mused. 'Speaking of dangerous games… I wanted to smack Debs. Her mouth was running away with her brain.'

'She's devious. Gets herself into trouble, and makes sure you get into it, too. That's why I'm having a cuppa tea, sobering up, and not going near any hot tubs.'

'Quite right,' Mouse said. 'All the same… dodgy territory. This is why I'm done with them, really. Toni's got colder, if that's possible.' Although Toni was behind glass, Mouse lowered her voice. 'You know, when I was upstairs grabbing something earlier on… I caught her having a look through my backpack.'

'You're joking.'

Mouse shook her head. 'Gospel. I heard a zip, and you know that way, I thought – "Oh, she's gone into my room to get changed. How embarrassing." Your brain fills in the blanks, even when there's no logic to it. Maybe you avoid the confrontation. Then I saw she had the same clothes on. The only reason she could be in my room, and zipping a bag up, is because she was rooting around in my stuff.'

'Jesus… What did she say?'

'She had an excuse – I was so shocked I forgot what it was, she said something like, she wandered into the wrong room. "Oh! It's this one!" I didn't tackle her, it took me so long to process what was happening that she was long gone, and I lost the chance. She'd have denied it anyway.

I suppose I could have chased it, but I didn't strictly speaking see anything untoward.'

'That's weird. What would she have to gain from going through your stuff?'

'Controlling mindset. Some people see a bag lying unattended, or a computer screen left unlocked, and they just can't help themselves. Maybe it's cunning. Maybe it's how we evolved. Maybe it's to get an advantage. Maybe it's just a compulsion.'

'That's really, really odd.'

'Yep. I wouldn't want to be married to her, that's for sure. With that knowledge in mind... you sure you can handle those two on your own?'

'You're going right now? In this weather?'

Mouse nodded. 'For the best. Those two are about as distracted as you can get. If I went in the morning or after breakfast, I'd just get grief from the pair of them.'

'But where are you going to sleep? Don't tell me you're taking your frigging tent out. It's pouring with rain. There's meant to be a storm tomorrow.'

'There was a storm the other day, just when you and Toni arrived. It was ace. You ever slept in a tent when lightning's been in the sky outside?'

'No, and let me tell you I don't intend to, either. Lightning? You'll get fried!'

'Nah, I've got little caps for the tent, plus a thick rubber mat. I'll be fine. If not, follow the smell of fried chicken.'

'That's not funny. Is it really safe for you to be doing that?'

''Course. I'm only sorry I'm leaving you to it. Make sure

you take notes and get back to me, though. I want to find out how this story ends.'

'Ah, you take care, now.' Leah felt her lip tremble as she gave Mouse a hug. *Good old Mouse*, she used to say, patronising the girl. Once she'd even ruffled Mouse's hair. She'd cringed many times over this, but now the phrase was in her mind, stripped of any negatives, and she uttered it against her friend's cheek. 'Good old Mouse.'

'You'll be fine. Any nonsense, there's a tactic I've got for dealing with difficult people that's never let me down yet.'

'What's that?'

'Tell them to fuck off, turn on your heel, and walk away. Don't hesitate. Don't listen to any crap. And don't stop. "Fuck off." Short 'n' sweet. Does the job. Works for me.'

Mouse was used to packing quickly and moving fast; her belongings were cinched tight into the backpack and ready to go. She peered out of the window – she'd left the light off specifically in order to make out the details outside, without being seen herself – and saw that Debs was sitting on Steve's knee. Mouse remembered Steve was just about naked, and shivered. The ribcage, the ultra slim hips, the sunken chest that looked like it contained neither heart nor lungs... Mouse wasn't an entirely closed door when it came to men, but the guy had repulsed her. The scenario had repulsed her. Worse still, her friends had repulsed her.

And this was what happened with friends, she mused. Your shared history becomes a burden. Your antic tales become an embarrassment. The old you, the one you don't like any more, makes a reappearance, like a butterfly regressing back into a puffy, slothful grub. You're reminded of things you'd rather forget. Your teenage triumphs become a scourge. And the friends remember every utterance you made, every error of judgement, every inch you moved out of line during your most sensitive, awkward, ignorant years.

Mouse's instinct had been to forget all about it. Shouldn't have done this. She did have one friend, though. The one who was worth the effort. One who made an effort in return. One who never forgot your birthday, and wanted nothing in return. The one who was always there. The one you'd phone first with any news. The only one you wouldn't hesitate to invite to a party. Mouse wished she'd said as much to Leah, before she'd left.

Fuck it, she might still do it.

'Poor old Leah,' she whispered, watching as Debs slipped, flapping at the water. The resultant shriek carried through the double glazing. Luckily, Steve was on hand. He put his hand on Debs' slick shoulder. Mouse wondered if Debs had taken her bra off, then remembered that she'd been wearing a strapless number. Not much to it, such as it was. Not much point wearing it, now, really. Good God, Debs deserved all she got, sometimes.

'You absolute tramp,' Mouse said, enunciating every word, as she watched Debs flailing to the other side of the tub. 'How desperate can you get?'

Leah reappeared in the patio space, bearing the bottle of Jager and some mixer. Debs and Toni cheered. Leah had a tumbler of what looked like water in her hand; she ignored the others' entreaties to join them, before disappearing into the alcove where there was a set of robust outdoor furniture. 'So much for the tea,' Mouse sniffed.

Then her chin dropped, and her eyes widened.

She let the backpack drop to the floor. Then she backed away from the rain-blistered window.

'Christ,' Mouse said. Then she opened the door and darted out.

Mouse tried the door opposite – Toni's door. It was open. She opened the window, gently, giving the mechanism a couple of twists before it fully opened. Mouse pulled herself onto the sill, then eased out onto the outside, legs dangling.

A couple of feet down below was the walkway, leading to the balustraded outer edge of the Halt. Mouse tested it with one foot, before easing herself down.

The rain had grown fine again, misty when it moved through the spotlights. Mouse crept through it, bent double, moving on the balls of her feet. It didn't quite negate the sound, as she'd hoped.

When she rounded the corner, Mouse gasped.

So did the shadowy figure crouched low at the balustrade – the one she'd spotted through the window. There was only a suggestion of a face, there, before the figure scuttled off.

Below, Debs, Toni and Steve were singing Billy Joel's 'Uptown Girl', as the song played on his phone. If they'd seen anything, they made no indication of it.

Mouse gave chase. 'Hey!' she said. But the figure was gone – disappeared. Impossible, unless it had jumped to the ground level and run off?

No – Debs' window was open.

25

Mouse poked her head in the window. Debs' room was dark. There was no one to be seen, but Mouse knew there was an en suite in there. She shook her head. Then she walked past the window to the balcony area.

That was empty, too. This area trapped the wind, rustling the azaleas and other sturdy potted plants on the balcony floor. There was something forbidding about this, and although there was clearly no one hidden behind the wicker-woven furniture or crouching behind the bolted-down table out there, Mouse felt trapped.

She moved onto the slated roof, picking her steps carefully, then lowered herself back down to the walkway outside Leah's room, where she'd appeared earlier.

The window was on a latch. Mouse pushed, and it gave easily. There was a child lock preventing it from opening fully, but there was enough of a gap for Mouse to ease herself through.

She did this quietly, until her boot slithered across the top sheet of Leah's bed.

A floorboard creaked outside the room. Mouse tore the door open, triggering the light.

There was someone standing in the doorway of Debs' room. Their face was hooded, and partly hidden.

Fully exposed in the light, Mouse relaxed. 'Look… I don't know what you're doing here, or what your game is,' she said, raising a hand. 'But you have to leave, now.'

'I'm sorry,' said the intruder, brightly. 'I thought I'd lost something here.'

'Look. I've been polite, but you have to leave, right now. Or I'll call the police, and we'll say no more about it. You looking for money? Something to sell?'

'Oh no,' the figure said, snorting. 'Nothing like that. But I have come to steal something.'

Mouse had been acting on autopilot, barely believing the evidence of her own eyes, her voice surprisingly strong and calm. Now, fear kicked in. There was something about the face and the eyes staring at her across the hallway, something ultra-focused. Something decided, and decisive.

'Just get out. The front door isn't locked. Be on your way, and we'll say no more about it.'

The figure nodded. Then raised her hand.

She was holding a crossbow.

'Oh,' Mouse said, in one long, drawn-out sound. She tried to duck; then she felt the bolt punch through her shoulder. Strange that the chief sound was fabric ripping, and not flesh being struck and violated.

Mouse fell into that surreal buffer zone where nothing hurt. It didn't sting but she felt something of a shockwave, twisting her entire body, forcing her to her knees.

Mouse twisted a hand around the bolt jammed in the meat of her shoulder. Blood seeped over her fingers. She turned towards the open window, gearing up to shout – *but her friends were at the other side of the house.*

A hand gripped the bolt that had shattered her collarbone and punched through the muscle on the other side. The intruder's skin was next to Mouse's; then the bolt was wrenched, and she was heaved to her feet, providing no resistance, going with the direction of travel. Then she cried out.

The intruder kneed Mouse in the groin and then shoved her into the open door of the en suite bathroom in Debs' room.

Mouse cried out, falling to her side.

Before she'd even lifted her head off the tiled white floor, something swiped her across the face, a single, confident blow. The line opened in her cheek burned, a clear sensation of her flesh being split. Then another cut cleanly traversed the gristle of her ear, bisecting her downy birthmark. Then another cat's claw crossed her brow, transverse to the fine black hairs, intruding into her upper eyelid.

The long, thin blade was a blur, now, back and forth. Mouse's forehead. Her hand. Her fingers. Her mouth. More than one mouth, now.

Mouse squeaked. And Mouse begged.

'Please… please,' she said, her own blood surging into her mouth. 'I'm… I'm having a baby.'

The other voice giggled, high and shrill.

'Let's see it, then!'

26

Leah snapped awake. A massive figure stood in front of her, and she gasped, throwing up a hand.

'Hey, relax!' Steve's features came into view. He was towelling himself dry, at the far end of the patio sofa.

Leah didn't remember doing so, but she must have lain flat on it, her head cushioned on her forearm. The wickerwork all-weather furniture had left deep impressions on her arms. She blinked once or twice; Toni and Debs were still in the hot tub. The rain had stopped, but the entire scene was still slick in the LED lights. Tinny music played from a phone – possibly 'Africa', by Toto. Debs laughed at something, then wolf-whistled. Leah couldn't quite make out what Debs was saying, but she got the main points from the smutty tone and cadence.

'I know,' Steve said, 'half-naked man, popping up in front of you. I left my top over here.' He pulled his appalling tie-dyed T-shirt over his long, skinny frame. Then he sat down on the edge of the couch.

Still groggy, Leah retreated to her default position – polite. 'You got a day off tomorrow?'

Steve seemed to literally chew over his reply, his jaw working. 'Tomorrow afternoon, got a couple of flights. In fact, it's not you guys, is it?'

'No, we're off on Monday morning.'

'Ah – Gwen and Peter will sort that out.'

Leah sat upright. There was half a glass of water by her side. She took a drink. Steve had a glass of wine in hand, and he sipped at it, staring at the two other women in the hot tub.

'You all go to school together, is that right?' he asked.

'Yep. Known each other since we were at junior school.'

'That Debs is a handful, eh?'

'More than a handful, these days. As you can clearly see.'

'Frightens the life out of me,' he said, puffing out his cheeks.

Bollocks she does, Leah thought. But she said: 'Yeah, she's a bit forward.'

'She got a husband?'

'Long-term partner, yes. His name's Eoghan. He's a good, kind man.'

'I think he'd need to be.' Leah wasn't too polite to hide a frown at this. Catching this, Steve said hurriedly, 'I mean, she's a bit forward.'

'You came here, didn't you?' Leah said. 'She invited you over. Not me.'

He didn't have any answer to that. 'I don't have any pals left from school,' he said, at length. 'I envy women that, you know? I think guys just fall out of touch. I can't remember the last time I went for a pint with Peter. I don't keep in touch with anyone from school or college, or even flight lessons. Just social media, you know? I only log in to say happy birthday. Or perve up the wives' holiday photos.' Remembering himself, he shut his eyes. 'I'm… not really selling myself here, am I?'

'What are you selling, exactly?' Leah regretted this immediately, but he took it in his stride, raising a placatory hand.

'Absolutely nothing. I just came here because I was at a loose end. Honestly. I'm thinking I'll go soon. So, was Debs the live wire in the group?'

'Kind of. Your identities change. Or your status, maybe. I think Debs made herself into a live wire, if that makes sense. Give a dog a bad name, and all that. I think at heart, she's shy. There's something missing in her life. Dad died when she was very young. She had it quite rough. She did a lot of things for attention. Still does a lot of things for attention. Eoghan is a lovely man. She's lucky to have him. But identities swap around. In a group of friends, one week you're Pollyanna. Next week you're the cock of the walk. Eh, so to speak.' She blushed.

'Same with blokes,' Steve said, nodding. 'You get guys who think they're the hard case. Or the genius. Or the ladies' man. It's a mask they put on. I had one mate who thought he was John Lennon. I mean, down to the haircut, the glasses. He wanted to be a songwriter. Couldn't play a note. Voice like a rat with emphysema. Exercise books full of poetry. He took it really seriously. Then one guy says to him in the pub: "Who the fuck are you supposed to be – Yoko Ono?"' Steve cackled at this.

'Debs has her talents and strengths,' Leah went on, ignoring his joke. 'But we all do; she maybe felt she had something to prove in the group. She goes the extra mile. Maybe a bit like what you said, about how some lads act the tough nut. Somewhere along the line it can become a reality, if you want it to. Debs is the tough nut, really. She'd fight you about anything. But she covers it up by being a clown. Personality's… weird.'

'She got any kids?'

Strange question. But Leah answered; there was a confessional aspect to the conversation, and maybe the scenario, which made her less guarded than she would normally have been. 'Debs doesn't, no. Neither does Toni.'

'Career women, then?'

'You could say that. I think Debs doesn't want them, and never has. She reckons it wouldn't be in her skill set. On top of that, she enjoys her life too much.'

'Selfish, you mean?'

'No,' Leah said, sharply. 'I mean she's realistic. Until you have kids, your life isn't serious. After you have kids, your life is never your own. Never. Debs is intelligent enough to understand that. She knows what she'd give up. She doesn't want to, and Eoghan is happy enough with that. That's a mature decision. I can think of people who had kids, then realised they didn't want them, really. Marriages have gone out the window; people have ended up miserable... That's ignoring the effect on the kids.'

'How about Toni?'

'I'm not sure,' Leah said, and looked away.

'She has a husband?'

'That's right. Roy. Six foot four. And about as wide again across the shoulders.'

Steve smiled. 'Of course he is.'

'Just making sure you're informed.' Leah blinked. 'I've just assumed you were single. You might be sitting on your second wife and five kids, here, for all I know. Top of the leader board.'

'Hey, for all I know, I might be.' He flashed a ghastly grin. 'Nah, sorry, that's a bad joke. No, no kids for me. Free rein. Libero role in midfield. How about you?'

'I've got a little boy, David. He's seven.'

'Ah. Bit of a handful, then?'

'Something like that. Actually, he's severely disabled.'

'I am so sorry,' Steve said quickly. He shifted forward in his seat, agitated.

Leah shrugged. 'It's just part of life, now. It's my normality. Maybe it's the role I was meant for. I used to think the idea of predestination was a bad joke, that everything's a matter of coincidence. So many people have told me, "I couldn't do what you do. I don't know how you survived, never mind David."'

'And how did you survive?'

Subtle, you ain't, she thought. Then Leah said, without hesitation: 'I'm not sure myself. There was an accident. It was the worst day of my life, but I get a weird comfort from it. It was the worst day there'll ever be. Nothing could top it. You remember every little detail, when that happens to you. The stuff that happened before the bad thing; the "before". It's a funny kind of torture. I remember having a row with someone about our broadband. I was really pushy about it, threatening to leave, comparing other deals, all kinds of thing. Poor guy on the other end, probably on less than our minimum wage, just to listen to me being stroppy. What a life. I remember feeling happy because I got a good deal. I'd spent twenty minutes on hold, listening to a muzak version of "We Don't Need Another Hero". It sounded as if it was played through the one remaining speaker of an Eighties ghetto blaster down the phone. And I think, if I'd been given just *one* of those twenty minutes back, it would have made the difference. Or just half of one of those minutes. Maybe even ten seconds? You torture yourself. Or... I did.'

It surged out of her, all of it. She had never recounted this detail in front of any of her friends before – only her husband and her mother. And here she was, recounting it to this scruffy chancer in his board shorts and his stupid tie-dyed T-shirt.

'I was walking down the high street with David in his buggy. It had rained that morning, but the sun had come through. I remember he was wearing his blue and red waterproof coat. I had bought him a sausage roll. He threw a tantrum, because he'd seen a cake and would have preferred that, but he soon ate the sausage roll and enjoyed it. I remember the main street was busy, and the pavement was narrow, so I took a shortcut through to the back of the high street, down a lane, to the entrance of the park. I was going to walk there with the buggy until David fell asleep. Then I thought I would sit on a bench and catch up on emails, or read an ebook, or... maybe just enjoy the peace.

'I heard the sound of the engine. Cars don't go down here, I thought. It's an alley. But it wasn't a car. It was a quad bike. I turned the pushchair and was going to head back to the high street, on instinct. I tell myself that I never had a chance of dodging it. The quad bike was going far too fast. I never saw the face of the boy riding it. Not the details, anyway. He wasn't wearing a helmet. He clattered the pushchair while I was turning it. It wrenched out of my hands. The boy on the quad bike came off, and broke his wrists. David was...'

Suddenly Leah blinked back to reality. Toni was getting out of the water. There was a towel handy as she approached the wicker chair, but she didn't use it. She didn't even look for her flip-flops. Steve stared at her, brazenly.

Dripping wet, she didn't say a word to him, or to Leah. Didn't even look at Steve's face as she came straight towards them.

She just tapped him on the shoulder. One single movement, with her forefinger. She barely even paused.

Steve didn't say a word. He didn't bid Leah farewell. He simply got to his feet and followed Toni through the garden patio door.

Leah was alone, and open-mouthed. For a moment, she was too shocked to even think anything. Then she burst out laughing at the audacity, the effrontery of it. Then she noticed that Debs was unconscious, half out of the hot tub with the waters reaching her knees, head resting on her hands as she lay on the edge of the pool.

'Jesus Christ!' she shrieked. She started to run through the rain.

Debs turned her head and was resting it on the upper edge of the hot tub, her hands folded underneath as some sort of pillow. Her mouth was open slightly, and there was a peaceful aspect to her face.

'Debs, what...? Mate. Come on. You can't lie here, you daft mare! You'll bloody drown.'

There was a short farce as Leah heaved her out of the water. One of Debs' breasts escaped as she pulled her out of the water by the armpits. Swearing freestyle, Leah stuffed it back into the sheer bra like a watermelon that had popped out of a bag of shopping. Debs flopped; her flesh had a sentience of its own. She escaped, she oozed, she bulged, she could hardly be held or handled, she flailed, quailed, her body recalcitrant while her mind was docile.

Hooking an arm under her shoulders, Leah thought of an octopus trying to squeeze itself into a pint glass. 'Not sure why I'm bothering. For God's sake, Debs, snap out of it.'

Debs' eyes fluttered. 'Did you just feel me up?'

'Oh fuck off, Fleabag. Get up, you daft tart!'

'No need to be rude,' Debs said. It looked as if she'd gained some purchase, her knees on the edge of the hot tub, her underwear having slipped, buttocks bared to the world. Then she yawned, and tried to get back in the water.

After more swearing, Debs came back to mission control – or at least, partially. She leaned on Leah as she led her towards the patio door, shivering. Debs gazed in stupefaction at her sodden underwear. Then she burped, ominously.

'Get this on, Debs,' Leah said, grabbing a towel. 'And for God's sake, get upstairs.'

'Where's Mouse and Shell? I mean, where's Toni?' Debs said, glancing around the empty kitchen.

'Same place you're going. Bed.'

'Best idea,' Debs said. 'Lame party if it's just you and me. No offence.'

'Next time, I think I'll let you drown.'

There wasn't a sound from the upstairs rooms as Leah steered Debs upstairs, taking her full weight on occasion.

Leah was aware of the chill even before she opened the door to Debs' room. 'You've left the window open, you berk,' Leah said. 'It's freezing in here.'

She shut the window, staring out into the slanting rain briefly as she did so. She wondered if Mouse was out there, beyond the trees.

The en suite bathroom door was closed. 'You going to be all right here?'

Debs nodded, and belched again, which suggested that very soon, she was not going to be all right. With some difficulty she peeled off her underpants, and unhooked her bra. Then she collapsed on the duvet, sighing.

Leah looked around for pyjamas; finding none, she pulled out the duvet from underneath Debs, and covered her up. Then she plumped up some pillows, and eased Debs' head onto them.

'G'night, Mummy,' Debs murmured, and smiled.

As an afterthought, Leah picked up the wastepaper basket and placed it at the side of Debs' bed. Then she left, closing the door behind her.

Still no sound from Toni's room across the corridor. Were they lying there, silent, waiting for her to cross the corridor into her room?

Good God. Poor Roy.

Leah put it from her mind. *Mummy is right. I'm practically a crone. Putting grown adults to their bloody beds.* She shook her head, went back downstairs to tidy up.

Leah had a brief moment of unease when she switched off the hot tub – not remembering Steve's tutorial from earlier, but trusting to the big red zero symbol on the dial as well as the I/O binary choice. The mechanism gave a reassuring click, and the steam and the bubbles reduced immediately.

As she picked up the glasses left by the water's edge, she thought she saw some movement on the roof. *Isn't there that seated area up above?*

Nothing, of course. Just the trees up above, swaying in the wind and rain.

Leah headed back inside, tired now, and loaded the dishwasher. 'Don't envy you, Mouse,' she said, yawning, as she made sure the patio door was locked. 'Balls to staying out in that.'

SUNDAY

27

*I*t wasn't a banner birthday – just nineteen. Hilariously, all the girls of St Martha's had worried about the slow turn of the digits towards twenty, as if this marked a final station on the journey to adulthood. Scarcely understanding that it was one of the first. Leah had marked the date on the calendar with a groaning cartoon skull, the segmented fingers clutching the actual cheekbones, the eye sockets a total ocular eclipse – carefully shaded in to admit not even a single point of light.

Having a birthday in mid-August meant she could get together with friends from in town. Her mother and father had put on a do at the rugby club. Debs, Toni, Mouse and Shell all appeared, sans boyfriends at the time. Leah was secretly relieved; she'd had fun with friends at university, but was looking forward to partying back home – even, for the first time since she was in single digits, with family members present. It was the first time she'd recognised that she was homesick.

Leah was supposed to act surprised when she was taken, not to a meal as advertised, but to a function suite complete with balloons, banners, and badly printed, embarrassing childhood photos. In these, the girls were present – appearing *almost pixelated in some, like video footage taken at a crime scene played on the news, a sure marker that Leah's ham-fisted dad had creative control of this material. The bad hairdos, the goth phases, the band T-shirts, the piercings – it was all there. Fortunately the girls were there in person, too, laughing over the images. Leah's eighteenth the year before had been a complete and utter maelstrom of booze, sickness and a two-day hangover in which she thought she might actually perish. She'd shunned her family's plans for a party, preferring her own friends, choosing her own venue and company, and her dad's clear disappointment in this had led her to this party now, complete with sandwich and sausage rolls buffet.*

And she'd been enjoying the event, catching up with the girls, until the gatecrashers arrived. Colin Nicholson and Hugo Royle, plus one or two others. Invited by Debs, as it turned out. They'd been too loud, a brazen contrast to the aunties and little cousins in shorts and fairy dresses who ran around the dance floor, oblivious. They helped themselves to handfuls of the food, they swore, they were clearly off their faces. The word 'lines' began to be passed around – and Leah believed it. She'd already seen one or two of the more affluent students on cocaine, and it would not have surprised her if Colin, Hugo and the others had chosen this status signifier, on top of the expensive block-graphic trainers.

Leah had shrunk from them. She'd never liked them at school – they were the football lads, clubbish and unpleasant – but this was a new level of obnoxiousness. Although still trim in his late teens, Colin's face poured with sweat despite little evidence of physical exertion. His jaw muscles reared and flexed like horses preparing to bolt, and his eyes radiated a cool, cocksure confidence that Leah didn't like one bit. Hugo Royle – seen as Colin's sidekick, but easily the worst of the two – had gone to seed in the years since PE was not part of his routine in life, a firm jawline swallowed by fat and the beginnings of a receding hairline already apparent. He'd been openly unpleasant when Leah's dad had asked them to tone it down a little, after some comment was made about Leah's great-aunt Marion's pearl necklace. Her dad had simply walked away after making the warning. It looked as if Hugo would pelt him with half a tuna, mayo and onion sandwich as he retreated, but fortunately it was all for show.

Debs tackled them at this point. 'Hey – I didn't realise I hired the clowns for the evening. Maybe it's best if you went home now?'

'You didn't hire us,' Colin Nicholson said, standing far too close to Debs, just off the dance floor. 'You invited us.'

'I'm revoking the invitation. This is a family do, guys. Maybe you're better off heading somewhere else?'

'A girl has the right to change her mind,' said one of the other lads.

'Not what I've heard,' Hugo Royle said. He had strange eyes, an odd heterochromatic yellow/hazel, that might have looked better on a jackal. Leah had gone right through her schooling with Hugo Royle, and even at primary level he had been one of those kids who might have graduated onto a mass shooting or serial murder. She'd never liked him. He had asked Debs out six or seven times since his hormonal advent, all without success. God may have liked a trier, but none of the girls did in this instance.

Toni appeared then – taller than Hugo, though. not entirely fearless, judging by her crossed arms. 'I don't think that's a very kind thing to say.'

'No?' Colin said. 'And who made you the justice of the peace?'

'I think what everyone's saying is, you need to go,' Shell said. Shell was handy and she looked it; she clenched and unclenched her fists, chutzpah and pinot grigio fizzing through her blood.

'It's my party,' Leah said. 'I think you have to go.'

'I think we'll stay,' Hugo said. He stuffed another sandwich into his mouth, chewing openly, performatively, disgustingly. 'This is my kind of place. My kind of people.' He tipped a wink. 'I'll get a round in. Some shots? Anyone want shots?'

'I don't think you're taking the hint. You've already left. You just don't know it.' She gestured towards a side door, where someone in a high-vis jacket and a peaked cap was making his way towards the function room through a long corridor. 'I called them five minutes ago. Not got anything on you, have you?'

They made no further comment; took no further part in the proceedings. Colin and Hugo and whoever else was in their entourage took flight out of the door at the opposite side of the hall, a row of malign scarecrows picking their way through the dance floor in the middle of Black Lace's 'Superman'. There was some ironic applause as they vanished.

Then even more ironic applause as the man in uniform appeared, timed for the end of the track.

'Good evening,' the officer declared, in a voice higher and

reedier than his build and stature would have suggested. 'I'm Officer Chippendale, and I've come to take down Leah's particulars!'

More laughter, more cheers, and so many memories. Dancing alongside a grandmother who only had nine months left of life, though no one had any idea at that time; teaching a star-struck younger cousin how to do The Time Warp; posing for photos with her lovely dad and mum, the latter looking better than she had in years. And the girls, of course. Dancing in a circle, arm in arm, yelling along to Supergrass's 'Alright', to the rafters. Leah and her crew. The Owl Society reconvened.

Leah blinked, and said 'Blaah,' and when she had decided she was awake, turned to the bedside cabinet, where she'd left her glass of water. Despite remembering to brush her teeth and drink a lot of water, and having sobered herself up to a reasonable extent, the inside of her mouth was foul and dry. She gulped down water, blinking at the grey light filtering through the blinds, and tried to shake the feeling that something had been banging on the walls. Remnants of a dream, she thought.

She was just thinking about emptying her bladder when she realised the banging was real.

The front door.

Throwing on a dressing gown, she passed through the hallway and padded down the stairs.

Steve was there. He looked hungover, and he was struggling to fit his arm in the balled-up sleeve of his tie-dyed T-shirt. He paused when he saw Leah, completely confused and unsure what to do next. 'Fuck is this on a Sunday morning?' he whispered.

'The front door, I guess,' Leah said. 'Expecting anyone?'

'No, 'course not. I don't live here or anything. I was on my way down when they started knocking.'

Leah frowned. 'I'll go and get it.'

The front room was tidy, but the patio furniture seemed to be in disarray, and here and there were the signs of the night before, in spite of Leah's efforts. The angle of the chairs, thrown back under the table in some haste; the sag on one end of the sofa. And a wet footprint on the kitchen floor that still hadn't quite evaporated. *It grows cold down here, before the summer arrives*, Leah thought.

Through the pane of frosted glass set into the door, Leah made out a shadowy square head like a graven idol. Whoever was behind the door was tall – and impatient. A series of thumps rattled the door, and she gasped in fright.

'Hold on, for goodness' sake!' she cried, cinching her dressing gown tighter.

She unlocked the door and pulled it open.

He carried on speaking, whoever he'd been speaking to. '...Absolute disgrace, this. No phone calls, no contact, nothing, for all we know they're lying in a bloody ditch...'

'Roy?' There he was, big as life, six foot four of him, a goalframe that walked. He looked like the poster boy for a countryside publication you might only see in a GP's reception, something with a surprisingly large circulation; green wax jacket, gaiters, burgundy boots surely on their first proper campaign, a plaid shirt tucked into commando green trousers and, naturally, a hat. He was a little chunkier than Leah recalled, but still a handsome man in a bovine way. Big shoulders, big hands, hams that wouldn't have looked out of place in a butcher's window. He looked like he might have been a farmer only weeks away from taking over his father's estate, as he'd always known he would.

Oh God… Toni…

Leah blushed, the way a cuttlefish might redden upon the intrusion of a frogman's facemask at the bottom of the sea.

'…'Sake, Leah, what's going on here at all?'

He didn't hesitate, just stepped into the living room. 'I half-expected to see body parts in here. What's the score with the phones?'

'Didn't Toni tell you? There's no reception here. We all made calls through the landline.'

'No one made any calls to me! No one made any calls to Eoghan, either, or your John… We've all been worried sick.' He stood with his hands on his hips and his thick bottom lip protruding, a gesture that would have been comical, if not for…

Toni.

Leah glanced over her shoulder. Steve wasn't there. She felt a surge of relief. Then she hoped this wasn't because he'd sneaked back into bed.

'We're all fine, here. Well, Mouse has headed off… It's just me, your other half and Debs.'

'Where the bloody hell's Michelle got to, then?' He stomped into the kitchen, taking in the glasses shining in the rack, the furniture wiped clean… drawn to the points of order in the room, whereas Leah had been more attuned to the signifiers of chaos.

'Shell never arrived. Roy, I don't know why you're here – what's going on?'

'Shell asked Ewan to come over here... He told me. He mentioned some sort of mix-up, or bust-up. Man was nearly hysterical. He left the kids with his mother and drove up here from the Borders himself.'

'What... he's here?' Leah had a sudden flashback to the incident by the lake; the darting figure in the undergrowth.

'Said he was coming here. Gave the address as the one up the road. But the pilot, girl called Gwen, told me you were staying here.'

Leah shook her head. 'I don't understand this – we spoke to Shell. She said she was going back home...'

'You seem quite flustered.'

'Yeah, I would do when my friend's husband bursts into my holiday house, unannounced, on our weekend away. It is a bit odd, Roy.'

She regretted this; would he pick up on something in her tone?

There was a creak on the stairs. Roy pointed, and his eyes locked with Leah. He didn't say anything. After a moment, he started up the steps. He hadn't taken off his boots; they left dark patches on the oatmeal carpeting as he ascended the spiral, bypassing the stuffed red squirrel, a carved wooden nut clutched before its mouth forever.

'Roy,' Leah said, loudly, following him up the stairs, 'just hold on a minute.'

'You seem a bit frit.' He said this mildly, but there was a dark expression on his face. 'Maybe I'll give Toni a tap and see that she's up.'

'She'll have a massive hangover,' Leah said, with a feeling of helplessness. Short of grabbing his arm, there was no way to prevent Roy going up there. And if she did grab his arm, she didn't stand a chance. She might as well push at an elephant's leg to get it to bend a knee.

Steve darted away from the corridor's edge, but not fast enough. He looked startled as Roy closed on him.

'Who the fuck's this?' Roy said. 'This a youth hostel? You got house guests?'

Before either Leah or Steve could reply, a door opened. Debs appeared – her face had that smudged look that denoted either an interrupted sleep, or, in her case, a huge hangover. Although she had a blanket wrapped tight around her something in the fashion of a yogic master and showed nothing more than bare arms and her legs from the calf muscles down, she was undoubtedly naked.

'Steve!' she croaked, darting forward. She embraced Steve, whose pose had not changed since Roy had bellowed at him from the stairs. 'Coming back in?'

'Ah, Debs,' Roy said, face falling.

Debs waved. Then she wrapped her arms around Steve, the contact between their bodies stopping the quilt from falling and completing the indignity of the scene, and she kissed him. Steve didn't resist, taking the escape route that was offered to him – and maybe a little bit more.

'C'mon love, back in with you,' Debs said. 'Don't hover around out here, keeping Roy waiting.'

Before anyone could retreat anywhere, or say another word, another sound seemed to pierce Leah between the shoulder blades, an unearthly squawk that might have been heard in an aviary, or a dinosaur movie. Everyone flinched; everyone turned; everyone knew pure shock. Except Roy. He had a smirk on his face.

'Eoghan!'

The name emanating from Debs' vocal cords was unlike any human utterance. She detached herself from Steve and rebounded with the back wall, cinching the quilt tight around her. 'What? What's going on here?'

Her partner's eyes were red, his skin pale, his teeth white. His hairline had receded even further since Leah had last seen him, only a few golden curls and tufts remaining. He couldn't say anything, he only blinked, glared at Steve and Debs, then Roy and Leah, then back again.

There was a dreadful silence, broken by a sigh from Eoghan. He had on a thick brown woollen jersey, waterproof trousers tucked into yellow and navy-blue wellington boots. He might have been dressed for a day at sea, rather than a day's hiking.

'I...' He just sighed, once more. He stared at the carpet. 'I'm off,' he said, nodding. His eyes brimmed over with tears. 'I'm just going. That's it. Bye, everyone.'

Just as suddenly as he had appeared, he was gone. The slammed door's percussion shook the house. Leah closed her eyes. Her face and hands felt cold; no blood. *Can I be anywhere but here?* she thought. *Anywhere but here.*

Steve shook his head, incredulously. 'I'm going to see myself out,' he said.

'I'd recommend the back door, son,' Roy said, not without a trace of sympathy. 'And be quick about it. On your way.'

Steve seemed to think about a rebuttal, then simply nodded. He took the stairs quickly, with an anxious glance towards the vestibule, before he made his way out of the patio door.

'Well, Debs, that was an interesting minute or two,' Roy commented. 'You got some knickers to put on?'

Debs' shock gave way to fury. 'You're a fine one to talk, you fucking drip!'

He laughed in her face. 'Where's my wife? Which door?'

'Never you fucking mind.'

He pushed past her. 'I'll try them all, one by one.'

'You've got no fucking right, none of you…' Debs jabbed a finger at the cliff face of his retreating back.

Toni appeared at her door. She had a pair of pristine pyjamas on – black, with pink cats curled up and shedding zeds. Her slippers matched. She sighed and rested against the doorframe. The door opened out to reveal a tidy room, the bedspread tucked in tight, hotel-room neat. 'I need this explanation to be very, very good, sweetie,' she said, in a bored tone. 'Why are you here?'

28

Debs swigged at a bottle of prosecco. It flowed far too fast, and she ended up coughing. From somewhere among the mossy green that surrounded them, a bird took fright, rustling the branches.

'On a scale of one to bollocks,' Debs said, once her final cough subsided, 'where would you put this weekend?'

'Oh, I don't know,' Leah said, drily. 'I think *some of us* had a good weekend.'

Toni said nothing. She stared straight ahead, only a slight movement at the side of her jaw betraying any tension.

They wore hillwalking clothes – Toni's were as fine and fancy as Roy's had been, but Leah and Debs wore waterproofs, bright jackets and sturdy shoes. They had traversed the mountain and crossed into the valley on the other side, a heavily wooded area with a road bordered by drystone walls that threatened to collapse into them. The afternoon was cloudy but not cold, although a sharp breeze could cut through every now and then. Their aim was to reach a place called The Spindling and have a picnic, and there was one major problem with this: none of them could be even remotely arsed.

'Has Eoghan been in touch?' Leah asked, gently.

Debs shook her head. 'We've kind of been in this situation before… Last time was maybe four years ago. I got a bit daft at a wedding reception… Too many drinks, just about everyone's dancing, Irish best man's wife didn't show up for some reason… We got a bit frisky during "Born Slippy".' She shrugged. 'Thing was, Eoghan was there, watching it. I promised him I wouldn't do anything like that ever again, and I sort of haven't. By and large.'

'By and large,' Leah echoed.

'Yeah. The thing is, this morning, I was doing our Toni a favour. A bloody big one. But who's going to believe that?' Debs took another swig.

'Bit of a radical step, all the same,' Leah said. 'Throwing yourself at the guy?'

'I was thinking on my feet. What would you have done, like?'

'Left the gormless bastard to his own devices?'

'It was a kind thing to do,' Toni said, solemnly, looking down at her boots. 'It's what a mate would do. So… thanks.'

Debs mock-saluted. 'I'm there for my pals. What can I tell you? I'm not some sort of country vicar getting my knickers in a twist. No pointing elbows, like.' She scratched the back of her head, angling an elbow towards Leah.

'Yeah. Mummy Owl swoops in,' Toni said, grinning at Debs.

'Not sure why you're aiming a kick at me,' Leah said. 'You'd think it was me who'd made a royal arse of it in front of my partner.'

'Oh, you never do anything wrong, do you?' Debs said. 'You've got some dignity – I'll give you that. And because

of that, it's really funny when you fall on your arse. Hey...
Remember the 34C incident?'

Toni sniggered. 'Oh God. I was thinking about that just
the other day. The storm in a C cup. Weird, the things you
remember.'

'Remember when Danny Ferguson found it underneath
all the coats... Poor old Leah, sitting there with your ears
burning. You couldn't say it was yours, could you? Danny
Ferguson managed to get that bra hooked and ran around
with it for the rest of the night. Fucking hilarious. And
Leah never cracked a light that it was hers, because Stuart
Lenehan managed to get it unhooked, earlier on, and she
forgot to put it back on. Never said a word.'

'You wouldn't have expected it to be hanging off that
road sign on the way to school the following Monday –
right after you admitted it had been yours.' Toni shook her
head. 'It was awful, too, Leah. Cerise and yellow, like bad
ice cream. My God.'

'The whole school,' Debs shrieked. 'You're lucky your
old mum didn't sew your name into it.'

'I had forgotten about that, until you reminded me,' Leah
said. 'Now that I think on it, public relations was always
your thing. The whole school knew it was mine before the
first break. A couple of the teachers even mentioned it, later
on. I had to deny everything – badly. So, thanks, once again.
But never mind my underwear from decades ago. How
about your swimsuit, Toni? Left that stuffed in any cracks
back in your room?'

'Never mind about my swimsuit, hon. It's packed nice
and neat. All dried out.'

'Think Roy bought the story?' Debs asked.

'Course he has. Mainly thanks to you. But in any case, Roy'll buy anything I tell him. That's how we work. I tell him what to think, I let him think he came up with it first, then I agree with him, and he believes that he's clever. It's tried and tested. But fair play, you did distract him with all the drama. So that's a pint I owe you, once we get back to this terrible pub.'

'Smooth work.' Debs offered Toni a swig of the prosecco, which she accepted.

'Where is Roy now?' Leah asked.

'On his way back, I expect, if he's not gone already. He'd seen enough. He's gone to sulk somewhere around the island. Plus, a text message sneaked through from Shell and Ewan – they're on their way home. Big drama's over.' Toni turned to Leah, and said, in a withering tone: 'Next time we do this, let's do it somewhere civilised, yeah? A place where there's buildings, and people, and roads.'

'No sign of your John?' Debs asked.

Leah shook her head. 'I think he might be out and about himself... left David to be looked after by his mother... There's no reason for him to come out here. I got a couple of text messages away on Friday.' All the same... she wondered at the absence, given Roy and Eoghan had showed up, presumably following Ewan's lead in trying to trace Shell. What a farce. If it had been somewhere civilised, as Toni put it, then Leah would have taken a cab to the train station and gone home by now.

'Roy looked like he was going to pop an aneurysm,' Debs said.

'Worse luck that he didn't,' Toni muttered. She offered the bottle to Leah; Leah declined.

'Thought you and ol' Roy of the Range Rovers were quite tight,' Debs ventured, taking the bottle back. 'Bit like Leah and John. Not sure I envied either of you, if I can say that without it seeming like a deadly insult. You're both a wee bit "IKEA catalogue", as couples. Some days I'd like to be "IKEA catalogue", it's true. I suppose the older you get, the more you want a dull life.'

Leah spluttered. 'You cheeky bitch!'

'But, yeah, I thought, you and Roy, Leah and John... didn't see any troubles looming, there. But you don't seem too bothered about hooking up with Captain Steve. So what's the story?'

Toni sighed. 'No story, really. You've hit the nail on the head. Life's boring. I gave up a lot of good years to be boring. Nice house, big holidays, car with a badge that teenagers keep trying to steal... It's dull. And I say that with all due respect to people who don't have those things.' She held out a placatory hand towards Leah, a gesture so pungent that Leah blinked at it, twice, stupefied, before her brain remembered she should have been angry.

'You what?' she barked.

Toni continued: 'But you just get sucked into a dull life, and it's not for me. Your bedroom insulated with farts first thing in the morning and late at night. He buys the same clothes, year in, year out. The same styles. Same shoes, same jackets, same jeans. He's even talked about going to the same places on holiday. Places we've been before. I mean, my God. I'm a bit old for a fixer-upper.'

'Maybe you should have adopted,' Debs said. 'If you are really, really determined to fuck up your life.'

She laughed at her own joke, but Toni and Leah were

silent. It echoed off the stone walls on either side of them as the road angled downwards through some overhanging trees.

'This is like an enchanted forest, or something,' Debs said, running her fingers over the mossy surface of the drystone wall. 'When I say "something", I mean something awful. What is this stuff? Lichen? Flesh-eating acid?'

'Just moss, I think,' Leah said. 'Shouldn't think there'd have been too much of it.'

Debs sighed. 'And on cue, Mummy Owl appears with the answer.'

'You asked a question. Maybe you'd prefer it if I didn't speak? Or should I only say what you want me to? Maybe you could give me my lines in advance, then I can learn them?'

'Touchy,' Debs said. 'Anyway, riddle me this: how far away are we from the Spindling?'

'Dunno, I don't have accurate figures,' Leah said. 'I'd say we have another two miles. We've barely got going. Sorry, was that a rhetorical question, or did you actually want an answer?'

Debs marvelled at this response. 'My God, were you always this angry, Leah? Did I just forget it?'

'I don't know about angry, but she was always disdainful,' Toni said. 'Right little miss smart arse, back in the day. Time goes on, obviously, and the accomplished people stood out, of course.'

'Is that right? What accomplished people were these?' The words came out bright and hot, but inside, Leah was sour ashes and dust. She didn't look or sound like it, but she was close to tears. What was wrong with them? Was it hangovers? Was it shame? A need to lash out? One of them had just had a possibly relationship-ending disaster, and the other had come very close to it. So why were they unloading on her now?

Same reason they did as teenagers, she thought, savagely.

'Can you tell me a time I was disdainful?' Leah said. 'I'm serious. Tell me when I was disdainful.'

'Just in general,' Toni said. 'I think you'll find lots of us thought that about you.'

'Who exactly? You and Debs?'

'Oh, you're a treasure now,' Toni said. 'You didn't stay snarky. We all change.'

'Funny, I don't remember being disdainful, Toni. I do remember laughing at you for some of your bizarre tantrums. Like that time I kicked your ass in the swimming face-off. Or when I got any number of boys who you had your eye on. Or the exams, where I got better marks than you. I wasn't disdainful, Toni. I was just better.'

'Not the case, in the end, though,' Debs said. 'You didn't get the best exam results.'

'True. That was me,' Toni said. She smiled and winked. It was then that Leah felt a compulsion welling within her to hit Toni; to grab that chestnut mane and dash her head against the paving stones.

'I think you'll find it wasn't,' Debs said. 'You said you got, I forget... six As, a B, something like that?'

'Yeah, something like that.'

'Well I got seven As and a B.' Debs stared unblinkingly into Toni's eyes, until she laughed.

'Complete bollocks, Debs. You didn't even show up to get your results.'

'The reason I didn't show up to get my results is because my mum lost her mind the night before. Tried to go for the paracetamol record. She got damned close to it, too. I managed to get her stomach pumped at hospital. Then I had to go home and clean up after it. I'd kind of forgot about the exam results. But I did do better than you, Toni.'

'Bullshit,' Toni said, dismissively. 'If I'd said seven As, you'd have topped that, too.'

'Kind of what I was thinking,' Leah said, struggling to keep a note of triumph from her voice. 'Strange thing is, I can top that, Toni. I got eight As for my GCSEs. Sorry if that pisses on your fire, a bit.'

'Oh, you didn't, Leah. I was there when you got your results.'

'I didn't tell the truth, Toni, because I knew it would upset you. You were so happy. I was happy to let you think you'd won. I think I'd already beaten you at netball, or something... No, wait, I'd been necking with Jack Plomley outside the under-18s at CJs. I think that bothered you.'

Toni threw back her head and laughed. 'Oh, love. You expect me to believe that? You pull that one out now? Those results came out of a Christmas cracker. Or your backside.'

'You can believe it or not believe it – it doesn't matter. I've got the receipts, somewhere in a box. I'll happily prove it to you. I'll make a point of it. Sounds like you were third place. In your imaginary league table.' Leah's orbit stabilised. She didn't even recognise her own voice, as she spoke. Perhaps it had regressed; risen an octave, maybe. How silly it was to speak like this – to dredge this stuff up. Wasn't there anything new to talk about?

'Still, Leah,' Debs said, 'if you were top dog with the

GCSEs – congratulations. You really made it count, didn't you?'

'What's that supposed to mean?'

'Meaning, you had a great career. What was it you did? Worked in magazines, for a while? Hoping to get a breakthrough in the glossies, just as the print market died on its arse. You wanted to be a little *NME* hack, didn't you? Who was it you wanted to be, again? Jo Whiley? She's quite cool, all the same. Hell of a job trying to emulate her. No wonder you gave it up and retreated to the bosom of the civil service.'

Why was it coming to this? Leah wondered. Were they all just hungover and stressed? Or was it a fundamental set of differences that would never be resolved? Character traits that didn't mesh, frayed edges that soon became ragged, then serrated. Debs, seeing herself as the underdog who wins, except she didn't. Toni, ultra-competitive, every defeat a deadly insult, every victory a deadly weapon. And Leah...

'I had a cracking career, thanks,' she said. 'I moved up the promotion chain there, without hesitation. I had to drop my hours because of... after what happened with David. I'm proud of what I've done and where I've gone in my life. I'm sorry if it doesn't measure up to your glamorous, 24-7, always-on-the-go, skinny-latte life. You can keep it, frankly.'

'Wasn't offering it to you,' Debs returned. 'It'd be cheap at double your price.'

'Cheap's relative when it comes to you, sweetheart.'

Debs had been midway through taking a draught of prosecco. She choked on it, doubled over, coughing. 'Point to you! Ha! That's a good one.' She wiped her mouth and took a step forward.

Leah felt her anger turn, in an instant, to fear.

'Don't put "cheap" in the same sentence as me, Leah,' Debs said, quietly. 'Not now, not ever.'

Leah folded her arms, defensively, and swallowed. 'You're the one getting shirty, not me. The pair of you are. I remember you did this the last time we all got together. Started braying and laughing at the table at a wedding. The same stories. I think the "bra" one got aired then, too. I was too pissed to care. You know how many stories there'd be about you, if I was to start pulling those out? Dozens of them. But I wouldn't do that, because I don't really have a problem with either of you. Maybe you could try getting over whatever your problem is with me?'

'No problem here. You're a very well-respected member of the community, Leah. Fine, upstanding, hard-working. Never do anything wrong. Never, ever.' Debs sniffed, snorted then spat like a teenage boy, and took another swig.

Toni frowned.

'Yeah,' Debs continued, 'I mean, we all have a stage in our careers, don't we? There's a beginning... there's an ending... and right now, we're about in the Midlands? Aren't we, Leah?'

'If there's something you're trying to say, or feel you need to get off your chest, go for it,' Leah said. Holding her gaze. Daring her. 'That goes for you, too, Toni. Because I'll tell you now – I've had it with you. I thought you might have grown up over the past few years. Being adults, and all. Instead I'm getting grief, for no reason – from the chippy snark, and the rampant climber.' It had been an expression Leah had used in an email, probably to Mouse, terms that had pleased her and remained on the tip of her tongue, ready to strike. At that moment.

'Insults, now! You better watch yourself, Mummy Owl.' Debs' gaze was steady.

'Or what? You know your trouble, Debs – and I'll say this. We're friends. Behind this act you've got... the daredevil, the comedian, the edgy chick... you're about as insecure as they come. You can't get anywhere in life without dragging someone down. You don't seem to have a good word to say about anyone. God almighty, I don't want to think about what life is like for Eoghan. Poor bastard. What must it be like, every night, knowing he's tied to you? The things you've said about the guy this weekend alone. "He puts up with me." That's the best you've got? He *puts up* with you? He knows what you're *like*? I fucking know what you're like. And if I was him, I'd kick you so far out the door you'd leave a vapour trail. You'd go so fast you'd catch fucking fire.'

'Maybe you'll get your shot.'

'You want to have a go, go for it, tough girl. We all remember that time you got tough with Shell. She didn't fucking miss you. I should take a leaf out of her book.'

Toni broke in with: 'Debs. Put that bottle down, love.'

Debs blinked. She was holding the bottle in her fist, tight. She blinked. Her hand did drop, a fraction. 'Don't get excited, Toni. We're having a discussion. That's all.'

'I think we're all a bit tired, and a bit stressed, and definitely hungover, and maybe we should drop it,' Toni asserted.

'I'm not tired or stressed,' Leah continued. 'I went to bed at a reasonable time. I'm just a bit sick of you two getting on my case every two minutes. All because, at one or two points in my life, I might have been better than you.'

'You know what? Game's over. I won't listen to this delusional housewife any more. It's been nice knowing you.' Debs took another drink, and then simply dropped the bottle. It chimed, but did not break; it rolled a few feet, then made a haphazard left turn and lodged underneath an overhanging flat shelf on the drystone wall. It had still been half-full, and the contents gasped out, mingling with the wet paving.

'Pick that up,' Leah snarled. 'What are you, fourteen years old? Mentally, you probably are.'

'Make me, Mummy Owl.' Debs flipped her the finger, and gave her a sneer of such utter disgust, Leah flinched from it as if from a slap.

'That's you in a nutshell, isn't it?' Leah said, picking up the bottle and sliding it into a compartment in her backpack. 'That's you, right there.'

'I probably won't be here when you get back to the Halt,' Debs said. 'It's not really a shame or a matter of regret. I'll leave you two to catch up. On the long hot summer of 2006.' Debs clenched her teeth, the grin of a political prisoner with a gun at their back on a news bulletin, and waved gaily. Then she started back up the path.

Leah gave a long, slow breath. 'She got to me. I'm sorry… I…'

'You're not used to being spoken to like that, and you don't like it,' Toni said, smiling. 'Never mind. You had a point. About her, and me. I've been a bit of a bitch. I'm sorry.'

'It… don't worry.' Leah did cry, now. A sob racked her

chest. She wanted to cover her face. 'I didn't want that to happen. I don't remember being cruel to people, I honestly don't. I was a bit silly. I might have been a bit patronising, conceited... We were kids, for God's sake.'

Toni offered no comfort. She took a sip of water. 'Well, what's done is done. Let's get down this path. The Spindling, is it? Sounds like somewhere a witch lives.'

'It is, I think.'

'Where did you read that?'

'The guidebook that nobody else read.' Leah saluted. 'Mummy Owl, right?'

'Oh yeah.' Toni laughed. She hadn't looked in Leah's face, had barely reacted when she cried. Even for Toni, this seemed cold. 'Now, before we do that, want to talk me through this stuff about the Midlands?'

Leah blinked. 'I'm sorry?'

'She's been tilting at it all weekend. I've half an idea what it's about. No details. Nothing I could sue for. Just my instincts. Which are never wrong. So, talk me through it, please. I'll find out, one way or another. The Midlands, 2006. What happened? What is it Debs is trying to tell me?'

29

He hadn't planned to come to the cliff's edge. His feet knew where they were going, though.

He was at a slab that protruded over the edge of the water. Below him was the sea, at a drop of maybe sixty feet. His feet dangled, one loose shoelace swaying slightly in the wind. He kicked his legs, though not in any mirth. The sea was sprinkled with gold in a patch of sunlight, as if a rill of glitter was poured in from heaven.

The sea below was relatively calm, but Eoghan's mind was turbid. Moments of rage that had him clenching his fists, twin cables of tension travelling up both his arms and shaking him by the shoulders. Moments of sadness that had him weeping openly, bitterly, barely feeling the rain against his forehead or the tears that found their way through his beard, to drop into the sea. A listener might have discerned odd phrases, twisted utterances that would never have been intended for another human being. The excoriations that were only ever aimed to thin air, without an audience, whether the intended target was internal or external.

'Bitch... fraud... knew it... told her, I told her, I told you!'

There had been times of happiness for Eoghan. Friday nights at home with wine and pizza, mostly. Trips to the movies, with her by his side. Talking about the film over a drink or two afterwards. Otherwise, he had been alone to focus on his interests. He'd tried to get involved in her social scene, but had quickly backed away from that. Eoghan had not lacked in self-awareness. But he'd believed... No. That was the wrong word. He'd had faith in her. He'd trusted what she said, her every utterance. He had suspected, knew she was a bit wild with a drink in her. But if you did not have faith in a relationship, what was the use in pursuing it?

What was the use in anything when you knew it was all a lie, and the person you had given your youth to was a...

'*Whore*. Worthless, scheming bitch... How dare she do that to me...'

There was the water. The space between him and the surface seemed to shimmer and vibrate. A curious sensation of excitement set his legs quivering.

He'd read about this before – seen a Reddit thread on it, in fact. The call of the void, was the technical term. He'd once stood on the edge of Beachy Head, a strange ticklish sensation in some unpleasant corner of the mind, a thrill when he considered what it might be like to jump... the rushing wind, the gathering speed. Silvery scales of light dappling the dark green sea, gaining definition with each millisecond. What might it be like to pierce them?

Whether he was merely pondering the matter, or considering taking his own life, or simply playing with himself, he would never know. Footsteps scraping off hard rock alerted him to the presence of another.

He had expected to see Debs. He was pitiable, weak, even in that moment. Still in her thrall, after all that. *After I caught her doing that.*

Eoghan didn't move aside as the newcomer got to her haunches, then sat beside him. She nudged him, her proximity crude, brusque. She was more assured in her movements than he'd been, this close to the drop, even given his dark design. He was annoyed. He hadn't wanted to fall by *accident.*

She hitched up her trouser legs and took a deep breath.

'Want to hold hands and go?'

'What?' He turned to look at her. She was gazing at him frankly, but her composure dissolved into laughter.

'Sorry. Didn't mean to be dramatic. Look, I was passing by, I saw you sitting there, and I thought: doesn't look good. I mean. Step outside yourself. Look at it in the third person. It doesn't look good, does it? You sitting there. Looking sad.'

'Suppose not.' He was thirsty, he realised. As if on command, she raised a metal-shelled water bottle and took a drink.

She wiped a rill from her mouth. 'Want some?'

'I guess.' He accepted the bottle and took a drink. It was freezing. Vacuum flask, he supposed. His hand shook as he handed it back. 'Thanks.'

They sat for a while. They listened to the water. Then she said: 'You know, I don't know what's going on in your head. And I'm not here to judge. I'm not some earthy, hippy-dippy all-mother type. Regardless of what my friends say. But think about this. Take the worst-case scenario, here. Do you really want to do it?'

'I wasn't planning anything,' Eoghan said.

'Sure. You didn't have a grand plan. But that's true of a lot of people, isn't it? Think about it. There are some husbands and fathers out there, brothers and sons… They didn't really think it through, either. It's short-termism. It's a lack of planning, in fact. They didn't have a big grand plan or scheme. They didn't have a big game that they were in control of. Christ. No, that's my bag. They probably just took a notion. They followed a whim. Are you following me?'

'I guess so.' He put his weight on his hands, on either side of his thighs. He was less calm about being here, now. And for all that, the distance between him and the subtle undulations below took on a new, dreadful urgency.

'OK. We're part of the way there. Relax. Now, you don't want to be going down there. Look down there. They say you shouldn't. But have a look.'

He did look. He saw the distance. It did something to his head, something that couldn't be properly defined. An acceptance in his head of the space between that one dangling bootlace and the face of the water. Where there is, and where there wouldn't be.

Eoghan drew back a little.

'That's it,' she said. 'That's right. No problem. Hey. You all right?'

She took his hand. It was subtle but it felt right, in there. Like he had gained power. Such a simple gesture.

'I'm all right,' he said. 'I think I'm all right. I was thinking…'

'What it might be like to jump?'

'Yes. I don't know. Maybe.'

'Please don't jump. It would be a waste.'

'You don't know anything about me.'

'I know enough. Listen, when you get to the bottom of

this, everything will be in the right place. That's a promise.' Her thumb flicked across his knuckles. 'Me and you. All right?'

'I suppose so.' He swallowed.

'OK. Now, just relax, don't worry. We're staying here. Remember, if you fell… or you jumped… no one would find you. You need to take that into account. That's not fair. And if you jumped, rather than fell, then… I wouldn't be passing any notes on. I can tell you that for a fact.'

He laughed. 'That's fair enough.'

'OK. We're all good?'

'We're all fine.' He wasn't, though. There would be no 'all good', and certainly no 'all fine'. All he had was a promise made. Which he knew was worthless.

'Excellent.' Her breath tickled the fold in between his jaw and neck. She bent towards him, and how could he do anything else? Their lips touched. Their lips relaxed. She exhaled into him, and this was exciting. His tongue flickered on the end of hers. And then she drew back.

'Whoa there,' she said, smiling at him.

'What?'

'It's not that kind of a kiss.'

He frowned. 'Then what kind of kiss is it?'

'Goodbye.'

Faster than anyone would have believed, and faster than Eoghan could properly process, she had him opened. A shark-bite semicircle following his ribcage. His guts slick and raw red and tumbling down over his knees and into the void and dangling towards the thick green sea. She pushed him after them, wet tendrils slapping his face before the sea punched it, roaring its derision, and he was gone.

30

*It all started in that weird town in the Midlands, a place
surrounded by roundabouts, anchored by US-style
shopping malls that had already started going to seed.*

*For three weeks that summer, Leah the trainee had
been sent out on a series of courses, based at a scrubby
late-Brutalist tower block that must have seemed stylish at
one point. An early experiment in controlled conditions,
everything beige, the view out of the windows tinted a dusty
brown colour even after cleaning. Nothing about it shone.*

*Leah hadn't wanted to go. Her and John's nascent careers
had pulled them in different directions, towards different
locations. They had seriously discussed splitting up, without
much rancour and certainly without any tears or hysterics,
though Leah's terrible, overwhelming dread at the idea of
life without John told her all she needed to know about that
idea. John had seemed a little too relaxed about it. She had
always wondered if someone else had appeared, another
medic at the hospital he'd worked in as a junior doctor for
those six months. A pretty little nurse, maybe. In awe of the
superman in scrubs. She'd always wondered, but never, ever
asked. Because of what happened next.*

The courses — team skills, management, role-play

scenarios, outward-bound trips, games involving Lego and cardboard cut-outs – were, on paper and in practice, execrable. But something weird had happened. She had gotten along well with some of the people who had also been sent there from various departments of the civil service all around the country. They were mainly young people like herself, newly hatched fry from university – one girl, Francesca, had been very close to Leah for a long time, but had faded away once she got married. And, yes, there were one or two single men who Leah had found attractive. Edward, from Liverpool, quiet, soft-spoken but almost brutally handsome, and Ryan, a second-generation Irishman with the charm and the patter straight out of the most hackneyed play, but all the more effective for it.

The first social event was organised quickly: a night at the pub – meaning the bar of a local restaurant – which had gone on very late, and had led to a couple of scandalous couplings among the delegates straight away, and left just about everyone in the training room the next day trying to deal with an appalling hangover. It brought them closer together. It was a good bunch of mainly young people, getting through the course and having a nice time.

Something even stranger happened. Leah had a renaissance, of sorts. Away from John, away from her family, away from the sudden, drab curtain of bureaucracy that had dropped on her stage after she'd decided to leave publishing for a less haphazard, more responsible way of living, she loosened up. In a way, she let herself go – preferring jeans, trainers and band T-shirts which she'd brought along as slouch wear to smart suits, skirts and blouses. She wore her hair differently – spending less time on looking like Jennifer Aniston, and *becoming more like Phoebe. The transformation did not trouble her. She enjoyed people's company – she sought it out. She made friends easily, both in the weird community in that odd concrete outpost and among her fellow trainees. She was funny. And she was attractive. But it was the band T-shirt that caused the big issue.*

'Hey,' called a familiar voice, across the bar. 'I thought it was you. Biggest Supergrass fan I know! What the hell are you doing out here?'

His handshake had been warm. It became a hug, all too easily.

Leah had always liked Roy. He'd been a comical figure, for the most part. John had often referred to him as 'The Farmer' because that's what he most resembled, from his rural background somewhere in the south-west, even down to the hairy ears and the slightly rubicund complexion. Perhaps a better fit would have been a rugby hooker just, just on the right side of travelling to fat. 'Big-boned' was such a stinging pejorative in many respects, but it fit Roy quite well. He was a big man, well over six feet tall, muscular without being dynamic, with a big, open face and a blunt, though not unfriendly manner. He could be authoritative when the situation demanded, and quite fearless – he had defused a confrontation between baseball-hatted teenagers at a picnic all the girls had gone on with their partners during a rare meet-up between them all. He'd displayed enviable confidence and none-too-subtle hints that he would snap their scrotes like kindling should things travel much past the pointed fingers and spitting on the ground stage.

But he was sensitive, too – she always remembered that Roy had been a big fan of dogs and would stop whatever he was doing to pet one, or make friends with it, whenever he encountered one, whether that was a skittish Lhasa Apso cringing between its owner's ankles, or a Tyrannosaur on a chain-link lead. No matter if it, or the owner, bit him.

Roy was also extremely rich, in terms of his family background and his property portfolio, both of which suited Toni to the ground.

He had been out for a meal, having taken part in a convention in the next town, helping to set up his company's stall, meeting and greeting and forming alliances with contractors. He had been in for a drink with a senior partner, an old man with sectioned trousers like Toad of Toad Hall and a face like a haunted Rupert the Bear doll. Leah couldn't remember this other man speaking to her once, even when he was directly introduced to her. She did speak to Roy, though. In the middle of this strange interregnum in their lives. She knew, of course, that Roy and Toni were on a break, and of course the idea never once entered her head, not for at least half an hour, at any rate, that a few pints in the brightly lit corner of an ersatz Frankie and Benny's plonked twenty yards off a roundabout in a town with no personality would lead to...

Toni could barely look at Leah. She was shivering, on the verge of some cataclysmic event, an eruption that might sweep them both away. Through gritted teeth, she said: 'The town Debs mentioned that you stayed in that summer is very close to the place Roy went with his firm, that summer we split up. She's mentioned it a few times, and she's probably done that for a reason. Did you meet Roy?'

Leah paused. She'd discussed it only once with Debs, when the dust had settled, and both she and Toni had reunited with their respective units again. '*Not a word*,' Roy said. '*No matter what*.' She had completely agreed. Technically speaking, no one had done anything wrong. It had been indelicate. It had been bad form, morally dubious. But everyone had been young, free and single, at exactly the wrong time.

'You met him,' Toni stated. 'Didn't you?'

'I did.'

'He never said a thing about it. And neither did you. Strange, that.'

'I'm sure it was mentioned at some point.'

'You're lying,' Toni said.

Leah's face started to twitch. She resisted the urge to mask this by scratching herself, or fixing her fringe. 'Well, either way, yes. I met him. We had a drink one night.'

'I see. And how long were you shagging, then?'

How quickly the mind gropes for deception, at this point, Leah thought. How readily we will seek a rhetorical escape hatch, how quickly we feed out a tangle of lies.

It was pointless to continue, though.

Leah took a deep breath. 'Toni…'

Toni sobbed. She held a hand to her mouth, as if to suppress it. She shook a finger at Leah. 'No. Don't patronise me. Not on this one. You slept with him, didn't you?'

'Yes.'

'Once? A couple of times?' Tears spilled down those razor-stropped cheekbones. 'More than that?'

'A handful of times, over two weeks. It was… It was just one of those things. You had split from him. I didn't advertise it, but John and I were in trouble. He was working away on his elective. We were living apart and thinking of finishing it... I know it doesn't make it any easier. I know how much it will hurt, and I've lived with the guilt for years and years. Dreading seeing you both together. Dreading it coming out.'

'Except it must have come out. Because Debs knew about it. Goading me all weekend, dropping her stupid hints. When did you tell her?'

'It slipped out one night, when we were drunk. She pumped me full of shots, cocktails and God knows what else. I could barely remember it – I would have forgotten I'd told her. But she reminded me the next day. "Our secret's safe, love," she said. Except it clearly wasn't. I'm sorry, Toni.'

'I'm sorry, too. You know, for all the joking and piss-taking, I really admired you. Always looked up to you. Despite what you think, I didn't want to beat you at everything, all the time. We were rivals, and I did want to win – that's only natural. But I never thought the less of you for it. I never wanted to see you down in the dirt, or totally beaten. I thought you were awesome. I modelled part of my life on you, the way you carried yourself, your attitude, the way you applied yourself to things. And I never thought you were capable of this. "On a break". "Everyone was single". Absolute bullshit. You do not do that with your mate's ex! You just don't! He's off-limits, forever!'

'I can only say I'm sorry, Toni. And I am.'

'You will be sorry if I decide to wipe that stupid expression off your face. Bitch.' She fumbled in her pockets for a tissue.

'Toni, don't... It was a long time ago. You can't blame Roy for it. If you want to blame someone, blame me.'

'I do blame you! I always will blame you! How can I go home and face him now? How can I sleep in the same bed, knowing that you... Of all people, *you*...'

'I don't know what else to say. I wish it had never happened.'

'I wish you had never happened. I wish I had cut you loose, after school. You became a liability. Always trying to get your "girls" back together. Your little gang. Needy little Leah.'

'That's not fair, Toni.'

'I thought about it. I got closer to Debs. We used to laugh at you, love. The queen bee, turned civil servant. The big dog, down in the kennels. All that early promise come to nothing. All the top marks, the head girl, the senior prefect, the clubs and societies... And after all that you just got a shit mid-level job. And you've got the nerve to blame your brain-damaged child for that.'

'Don't be disrespectful.' Leah blinked. A sudden surge of anger threatened to choke her. She wondered what it might be like to unleash it, and instead choke Toni. The idea was dangerous and intoxicating. It made the idea of her flesh, her bones, her weight, its posture, its gravitational anchor to the slippery paving stones, curiously light and insubstantial. Leah wondered if she could spring. If she could take off. If her foot could connect with Toni's chest. If she might send her flying into the drystone wall. And from there, she wondered if she could ever stop hitting her. 'You mention David to me in any context apart from one of complete and utter respect, I will pull your fucking tongue out by the roots, Toni.'

'Tough girl. You're not really that tough, though, are you?

Bragged a little bit about being a fighter. I never remember you being in a fight. Not once. I'd bet you're a pipsqueak, really.'

'You don't want to find out.' Leah softened her tone, unclenched her jaw. 'Neither of us do. I think we should walk away.'

'You can do that if you want, but don't think I'll make it easy for you. I'll make life difficult. Maybe I'll let John know. A problem shared, and all that. Maybe John and I will have a get-together, in fact. In private. See how you like that. I've seen how he looks at me, Leah. Sometimes you get a look, and you just know. Who could blame him? I mean, look at what you wear. On a surgeon's salary, can't you do any better? What's the score with your hair? Did you even wash it this morning?'

'Even for you, that's petty. So, so petty. I'd drop it now, if I was you.'

'In a lot of ways, John's a good fit for me. And Roy, well, he's been middle-aged since he was about twenty-seven. A good prospect, at one point, but I think I've outgrown him. I might take half his money, then... A surgeon might be just the job for me.'

'Goodbye, Toni. I'm going to keep walking. Catch up if you want.'

'What I don't see is you both *fitting* together. In any way. The most boring boyfriend, and the most boring female of our whole crew. Even Mouse has a bit of mystery to her – you think she's quiet and dull, and then she surprises you. This is probably the most exciting thing you've ever done, both of you. It's funny, really. A joke.'

'It wasn't funny when... as I said, cheerio.'

'When what? Don't tell me it was good, Leah. I know the man inside out. I know every little corner, every little thing he likes. And he's a bore, let me tell you. Maybe some of you rubbed off on him?'

'If you have to know, it was bed-breakingly good, the best I ever had, hour after hour of it. The sun came up, and we didn't notice. Better than he ever had with you. He told me. He told me you've got problems with intimacy. That you treated him like some kind of freak, that he always did it wrong, that his body was disgusting. His body wasn't disgusting. You want my opinion, it was control. You had a fucking thoroughbred, but you wanted a gelding. Poor man, he fell for it.'

'This is hilarious! You, trying to tell me about my man? You?'

'And the funny thing was… You had cut-outs of every sex position going out of the magazines, stuck to your fridge. When you were a student. He told me you wouldn't actually try any of them. That you thought it was disgusting.' There was no mirth in these terrible stings, no humour, however bleak or feral. Leah said it all with a straight face.

Toni emitted a shriek like a blast of interference on an old radio set. 'I'll fucking kill you! Kill you!' Her hands hooked into claws. But she did not attack, her face set in a scowl of impotent fury that Leah hadn't seen since primary school.

'You won't kill me, though,' Leah said. 'You won't even try it. I don't think you're up to it. True of most areas of your life. You fall just short. As you do everywhere else. All ambition, but no talent, despite all the good cards you were dealt. The support. The luxury of choices. That's you. All the advantages, none of the substance. None of the right stuff. I didn't plan it that way, but I've put one over you in every single respect. Every single one. Even with your man. And I want you to remember that. I feel no remorse about it. You know why? You're a bad person, Toni. You're a shit mate. You were lucky to have me as a friend. You all were. I've a feeling we won't be friends any longer. That's a shame. I'm going to finish this walk, now, to the Spindling. They say a witch lives there. I'll pass on your regards.'

Leah walked away. She did hear footsteps behind her, a sudden rush; she cringed, braced for fingertips punching through the back of her neck – but they stopped short. No shadow fell over her, no blow landed, no hands clawed or clutched her. Leah simply walked on. Her face crumpled within about twenty yards. She passed a hand over her eyes, already wet with tears. What had she done? Why had she said those things?

She stopped. She turned around. She might have gone back. After all that, she might have tried to apologise, to make it right, to fix it, to soothe and console. But Toni was nowhere to be seen.

31

Steve threw his keys on the kitchen table, sat down in one of the seats, and allowed himself a laugh at long last.

'Bonkers. Absolutely batty,' he said to himself, running a hand through his hair. 'Met some messed-up bunches before, but man...' He crossed over to the kettle, filled it, switched it on, plucked a teabag from the tin, and flicked it expertly into a mug from a distance. Then he sat and pinched the bridge of his nose, allowing weariness to descend. The kettle was a big, powerful one, and its rising roar drowned out the sound of the patio door opening.

Steve literally fell off his seat when he opened his eyes, with a dark figure stood in front of him, blocking the light. 'What are you playing at?' he bellowed, getting up off his knees.

'I might ask you the same thing,' Pete said, folding his arms.

'Well, you can knock the door and ask me, or cough, or make some kind of noise! Jesus.'

'Worried someone was after you?'

Steve clutched his own throat. 'Not especially, no.'

'I'm worried someone *is* after you.' Pete's hands were loose by his sides, but they twitched, as if eager to make fists. His expression was darker than usual.

'Like who?' Steve feigned nonchalance and poured the hot water into his mug. He didn't offer to make Pete one.

'Oh, like the walking battlecruiser who came into the office, asking about you. Said he recognised you from the online link his wife had passed him... and he also saw you running around at Owl Tree Halt with, and I quote, "a look of guilt on his face and his dick in his hand".'

'Was this a big guy... Type that looks as if like he'd suit a hat... Kind of like a bouncer at a barn dance? Yeah, I bumped into him earlier on. Excitable lad.'

'Bumped into him where? You were at Owl Tree Halt?'

Steve shrugged, and watched the teabag bleed into the hot water in his mug. 'Sure. I was up there.'

'Doing what, exactly?'

'If you must know, I went back there last night, for a few drinks, and... What's the matter?'

Pete had turned away, his face in his hands. 'Are you serious?' he hissed. 'Why in God's name were you up there? Don't tell me the big guy had the *right* end of the stick. You were with one of them?'

'Shagging one of them, if you must know. And it was the big guy's wife.' Steve grinned. 'She's well kept, I'll say that. He's a lucky man. Fit as a fiddle. Swimmer. Tennis player, I'd say, looking at her thighs. She had a lot to get off her chest. Don't think the big guy was looking after her, really. Hey... he's not lurking around at the patio door, is he? I don't think I can handle any more dramas, today.'

Pete took a couple of deep breaths. 'First things first... We don't mix with the guests. Not for a drink. Not for a meal. And definitely not for any shenanigans. If word gets out... If it makes it onto one of these review sites, then we are sunk, mate. People will stop flying with us and staying with us. This is not the first time you've done it, either, according to the boys down the pub.'

'They can talk all they like. Doesn't mean it's true.'

'Second thing… you can't drink the night before you fly.'

'Pete, we've got hours before we're back in the air…'

'You know the rules. You can't break them. We could lose our licence and be out of business in two seconds flat! It'll be over, Steve.'

'Look, I know you're angry.' Steve crossed to the fridge and pulled out a two-pint carton of milk. 'But think of it as a value-added service. They enjoy it, they come back. As for reviews on the internet… There's no such thing as bad publicity. You go viral, more people will want to fly with us. It could be part of the service! Hey, we could cater exclusively for hen dos. Or stag parties, if you prefer. No judgement, boss.'

A vein throbbed on Pete's temple like a worm on a hook. 'I'm getting tired of this behaviour. Every weekend off you get here, it's the same. Out at the pub. Hassling some of the female guests.'

'They asked me up there, Pete. You can talk to them about it, if you don't believe me. They invite me up for a party, it's on them.'

'They invite you up for a party, you say *no*. It's off limits. And I don't like the smart-arsed attitude, either.'

Steve stirred the tea. 'You don't own me, Pete.'

'I don't, but I can sack you.'

Steve let the teaspoon clatter against the worktop. 'You'd do that? Two years up in the air, business taking off, bookings coming in, and you'd do that? You'd sack me? Over a frisky housewife?'

'Believe it,' Pete said. 'Consider this a warning. I'll even write it down for you, if you like.'

'Write whatever you like, Pete. I can get another job.'

'That might save us both a lot of trouble. Sharpen up, Steve. I liked it when we were friends. I liked it when I could trust you.'

'And I liked it when you were a laugh. I liked it when you seemed like a normal bloke. Is this cracking you up? Is there something wrong at home with Gwen?'

'Shut your mouth, Steve. Or we'll fall out.'

'Point taken,' Steve said quietly. 'I'll rein in the horses. I hope the big scary farmer type wasn't rude to you.'

'He wasn't friendly,' Pete said. 'I took an earbashing. But that's what you do for a workmate. I calmed him down, and sent him away. But that's the last.' He stabbed a finger at Steve. For a moment, he looked as if he might cry. 'The *last*.'

Pete slammed the patio door behind him, and Steve exhaled. He sipped at his tea, then, on a whim, started taking his clothes off.

Out in the garden, he flicked a switch on the hot tub. Soon the water bubbled and steamed. Steve slipped off the cover and then took off his clothes, leaving them in a pile by the staircase. Shivering, he ran up to the rail and then slipped into the water, sighing as he sank up to his neck.

His heart had only just calmed down. Pete was only pint-sized but looked a handy customer – one of these disgusting people who ran decent distances or worked out. Steve was listed as the outdoor activities expert, and he had the badges to prove it, but he only ever did enough to take his charges through their archery, kayaking or bodyboarding. He'd had the fright of his life when that Leah character had taken a funny turn in the water. God knew how he'd have got on had she needed resus. *I should really retake those first aid courses*, he thought. *One day I might actually have to do that shit.*

But he really would have to move on, soon, fun though this was. Steve would happily have stuck it out. The wages weren't brilliant but the perks were obvious. A man of talent but with no sense of stability, he'd forgotten how many aviation jobs he'd had over the past eight years since qualifying – moving around every eighteen months or so. Pete had needed a partner who could help get his business up and running. There was talk of a percentage at some point, and Steve had taken Pete at his word, but nothing more had materialised.

Gwen intrigued him, his co-pilot on some shifts or other. She was an enigma; at first Steve had assumed she was Pete's other half, or maybe even his business partner. There was something proprietorial about his attitude to her. It turned out this wasn't the case, but even so, Pete didn't like Steve talking about Gwen – that was when he'd come closest to losing his rag, earlier on. That was for the watching, no question. And, for other reasons, maybe one to note down, for future reference. Maybe he could engineer her a little stay here on her own? Maybe he could pop in... Steve smiled and rested his head against the rim of the tub, feeling the champagne surge of bubbles surround his neck. *Enjoy it while it lasts*, he thought. This was something he'd understood since he was a boy. *Enjoy everything. Key to life.*

Steve's knees rose as he lay back; he stretched out his spindly legs and they made contact with something soft on the other side of the circular tub. Something that shouldn't have been there.

Something that was weighed down like the base of one of the parasols, utterly hidden by the foam. Steve took a handhold, and pulled the weight aside.

He sat upright, flinching, peering into the water. Something dark lunged – for an absurd moment he thought that the head of a shark was about to burst through the foam, with black eyes and a razor-tipped smile.

What bobbed up was a body. It was huge, and clad in a long dark coat. A face appeared, strangely calm in death, the fair hair flowing across the brow. Steve recognised the face. It was the farmer type; the husband who'd accosted him at Owl Tree Halt. The big, bellowing man.

Steve gagged, thrashed, and totally lost control for a moment. The hot tub might have turned into an oceanic trench; he flailed, grabbed the rail, righted himself. There was the face again; there were the eyes, staring. His feet slipped and he fell back into the water, his back slithering off the seating. The dead man's hair billowed in Steve's nostrils for a moment. He surfaced, half gasping, half gagging, and got to his feet, water pouring from his nose and mouth. He turned to get out, dripping wet, suddenly freezing in the air.

He could barely credit that there was someone else in front of him; his systems overloaded, he simply stopped dead, his hand on the silvery rail.

That's when the long, thin blade sliced deep across Steve's Adam's apple, opening his neck up.

Steve couldn't even gasp. He pitched back into surging heat, his blood turning pink in the foam.

He didn't hear the voice say: 'You pig. You absolute, filthy, disgusting pig.'

32

Leah stopped about fifty yards from the Spindling, which turned out to be a squat, ancient cottage at the very end of the road, hemmed in by trees. There was no roof, and only a suggestion of a glassless window that hinted that the place had been any kind of dwelling at all. It was suffused with that same weird greenish tint that seemed to surround her. With spring proper a matter of weeks away, and a bite to the air, it gave the place an uncanny atmosphere, and the green tone felt sickly rather than verdant.

'I need to call her... Christ, what a mess,' she said aloud. Leah hadn't been crying, exactly, but the tears had cascaded down her face. She hadn't ever been through a prolonged, horrifying break-up in her adult life – curiously, only Mouse seemed to suffer from those – but this surely couldn't have felt much different.

There is no going back, a stronger voice said. *Even if there is, it won't happen today. There's nothing you can do.*

She picked up her phone, and checked for a signal. The screen wouldn't light up; even when Leah held the button down, nothing happened. Odd. She had charged it up in the morning.

She trooped down to the Spindling and read the laminated sign about old Aggie, the witch who had supposedly lived there. The sign was covered in pitted Perspex, and the font was an eyesore. Leah would have guessed at a push that the artist was local – surely they would have struggled to commission someone so bad at drawing even a cartoon witch, otherwise. There was a story about a woman and a spinning wheel, a curse, and the wailing woman who haunted the valley who had fallen victim to it. Leah wondered if she'd heard something similar in the tales of the Greek myths. It was amateurish and badly spelled and irritated her far beyond reason.

There was a wooden hut or shed at the bottom of the slabbed stone road, which ended at the entrance to thick, dark woodland, not so much shadowed as cast in the night, even at this time of the afternoon. A natural path appeared to continue through the middle before the darkness swallowed it, but Leah didn't want to go near that place – there was something primevally foreboding about it.

She prepared to go back. She hoped they had all left; perhaps Mouse was still around on the island. Hopefully she'd pop her head back round and see if anyone was still there. Perhaps she'd stay over until Monday, with the other two having cleared out. An evening of chat with Mouse seemed like the tonic she needed. Leah was cold and lonely and wanted to be back with John and David.

Even in propinquity, she felt stained and ashamed by her friends' infidelities of the night before – even slightly culpable, in having been an observer. *I should have sent that Steve character packing*, she thought. *Bad lot. Didn't like the look of him, or his patter. Womaniser. Nothing to recommend in it. All pejorative.*

'I'm too Catholic for this,' she declared. Out of curiosity, she made her way to the shed. It had once been stained dark brown or red, but was large, flat-roofed and spacious. A sign above the doorway read: 'The Bothy – Come on in, take a load off'.

Leah peered in the window. She'd read about these places, and actually quite fancied staying in them, in a way. Remote outposts in Scotland where walkers could stay the night, free, with the only rules being that they had to clean up after themselves after they'd bunked down for the night. There were dozens of them dotted around the Highlands. Something romantic about that, she thought. *And I might have to stay in it, tonight.*

She tried the handle and the door swung open. There was the smell of coal or charcoal, as if the wood burner set into the far corner had been used recently, though the grate looked clean. No sign of footprints, either. The place could have been a showroom; almost spotless.

Then she heard the buzzing sound. Was it a motorbike? Leah frowned, and closed the shed door, somewhat alarmed. She wanted to crouch low and hide, some craven instinct, which she resisted.

Something flashed past the window – it *was* a motorbike, by God, or a dirt bike.

Leah caught her breath. The figure on the top had been a blur, a wraith. She had imagined the arms outstretched, but surely her imagination had filled in that detail. Leah had taken David on walks in farmland where she lived – sometimes lonely, but idyllic in springtime... Until some young people had discovered that the tracks were perfect for quad bikes. Rather than taking David along the flat paths in his chair and showing him the miracle of life, rebirth and growth, Leah had listened to that same malevolent, insectoid buzzing across the fields, intruding over her garden fence that whole summer long.

The sound of the engine faded, and Leah got back to her feet. *Cowering, there, just about on your knees,* she thought. *Probably Debs. She probably conned Mr and Mrs Flasher into giving her a loan of their bike for the day, to eat up the time.*

Break her bloody neck.

Debs. She'd been unpleasant to Debs, too. Her problems and her behaviour were her own – and they were bigger than Debs herself realised – but she'd been a good friend, and good fun, if you ignored the needling.

Yes. That was true. But you couldn't quite ignore the needling. Whatever traumas Debs had come through, and whatever sympathy you naturally felt for her as a result, the fact was they had curdled her personality. She was dynamic and eye-catching, but the dark side of that was that she could be unpleasant, cruel and socially destructive. And she sucked up attention like fucking *oxygen*. In her way, she'd been just as competitive and snarky as Toni. Sometimes she seemed more like a mortal enemy than your closest friend.

And if there was a fuck-up to be made, Debs would make it – with some glee, you suspected. Debs got you thrown out of pubs and clubs. Debs caused fights. Debs would make a fool of your other friends, or your workmates. Debs would make a scene at your birthday, your hen do, your wedding, probably your funeral. Debs was, let's face it, a nasty piece of work. Leah sometimes suspected she put time and effort into it. She'd probably arrived with a fucking dossier, a checklist of sensitive topics and pre-scripted lines. This was no idle conjecture – Leah remembered her actually doing this as a child. Debs had tried to put the others up to bullying Fiona Halfpenny – not Leah. '*When the silly bitch says this, then you say this... then I'll say...*'

The engine drone got louder again. Was it coming back? Or another motorbike? Just a couple of kids, charging up and down the road. To be fair, there couldn't be much to do on this island unless you liked hillwalking or... hillwalking.

Leah peered out of the window. Now she was concerned about making a sudden movement and startling a fourteen-year-old on a dirt bike zooming up the uneven pathway.

She stopped with her hand on the door.

A dirt bike was on its kickstand, against the far stone wall.

But the engine sound was still there. And growing louder, and deeper. It could have been a higher-spec engine, a proper motorbike.

Someone was singing, too. High, and jolly. It was hard to make out over the snort and burr of the engine, but the singer did their best.

'...the baby, bite the baby, bite the baby's eye...'

The engine rose to a shriek, as Leah gasped.

Then the entire hut shook, the buzz of the engine transfixing every solid surface, reverberating in Leah's brain. It was as if a combine harvester approached, preparing to churn and obliterate the timber in its revolving blades.

'Stop! Stop!' Leah shouted, clutching her ears. 'There's someone here... *I'm* in here!'

The engine rose to a shriek.

There was a shower of sawdust on Leah's forehead; a sliver of light intruded like a death ray.

Then the chainsaw blade burst through the wall, six inches from Leah's face.

33

Leah screamed. Her brain strived for something rational, something that led down the path of normal, polite interactions. For those few concussed moments, she could not, or would not, see the reality of what was happening.

'Stop! There's someone here! I'm in here!'

It was lost in the sound as the chainsaw began to make a long, vertical slit in the woodwork. Shavings bit into the side of her face and she jammed her eyes shut tight against them, just in time.

Leah lunged for the door. The chainsaw withdrew, but the sound continued.

A figure in black appeared behind the window that took up the upper portion of the door. It was a slight figure, wearing a shiny black biker's helmet with the visor down. The chainsaw, long as a medieval skirmish weapon, braced on that slight frame, still roared and trembled. The figure brandished it at Leah and she dropped the latch on the door, springing back.

The helmeted figure disappeared. The chainsaw's whine rose in pitch and intensity as it bit through the wall, cutting another vertical slice.

Leah clutched her face, sobbing, wailing and shaking

her head. The effect stripped her of all reason; she couldn't think, couldn't attune herself to what was going on. All she could do was gibber, wail and plead.

The blade cut out as it withdrew. In the sudden silence a muffled voice said: 'Going to make it interesting for you, Leah. Especially for you. Ready?'

Leah flinched as the planks at the side of the hut split under a heavy blow. Two of the panels fell out upon this blow, the grain of the wood clean and bright where they'd been cut.

The helmeted head peered through; then another blow brought another plank. A fourth had been relying on the one underneath to keep it in place, and that fell too.

The helmeted figure slid through, the chainsaw following, held low.

'Drink the baby, drink the baby, drink the baby's blood!' the intruder shrieked, and cranked up the blade again.

Leah didn't exactly formulate a plan – a series of connections lit up somewhere on her circuit board, a streamer of lights that led her to a firm course of action. She raised a chair and the blade met it. It punched through the pitted wooden seat with alarming ease, and the spinning gold-stream blade got within an inch of her nose. Leah saw her open mouth and bulging eyes reflected in the visor of the helmet.

She did exactly the right thing by sheer luck, or pure instinct – bracing her feet, crossing her wrists and twisting the chair. The blade coughed, stuttered and died, then it felt to the floor as the chair split in two.

The figure in black staggered a little as it groped for the chainsaw. Leah hurled both ends of the chair at her. One leg bounced off the helmet; the other hit her in the shoulder, and checked any progress she might have made.

The table between them was hurled, almost as an afterthought, its weight a minor consideration for Leah in that state. Then she thought – wood burner – basket – full of logs – and then she was hurling thick, heavy cuts of timber at the newcomer. One missed completely and clattered against the far wall. The second found its mark on her attacker's back. She fell to one knee. A third log hit a gloved, outstretched hand.

Leah took off. Her finger slithered off the latch. The attacker snarled, got to her feet and lifted the chainsaw.

Leah was outside, walking boots thudding on the path, inclining back towards Owl Tree Halt.

The chainsaw didn't start behind her, but the helmeted figure laughed. 'That's good! Keep going! Be right there, darling!'

Leah turned her head. Her attacker was already on the back of the bike, already revving it up. Then the chainsaw started. The awful harmony of the two machines reached an unbearable pitch as the bike skipped and then leapt towards her.

She raised her hands. The blade rose, held horizontal, neck high. It seemed to snort at her as the bike sped up, coming straight towards her.

'Make a wish, bright eyes!' screamed the figure on the bike – unmistakably a woman's voice.

Leah dropped to the side, her backpack taking a lot of the weight, punching her between the shoulders.

The blade swiped at her. She felt a finger prod at her

uppermost shoulder. It parted some of her hair from her head; Leah felt the ends tickle her forehead.

Then the bike was past, bouncing along the path.

Leah felt at her shoulder; the material had ripped and split under the blow, but it hadn't cut her. She got to her knees, then onto her feet.

The bike slowed, turned, pivoted on the rider's left foot, and then came back towards her.

This time the blade was held low, towards the paving stones. Leah swung the backpack off her back, and braced to throw it.

'No going back, now,' gurgled the figure on the bike.

Leah feinted once; the bike slowed and tracked her. There was nowhere to go; she couldn't climb over the drystone wall, or take refuge in the forest. The bike was too fast.

Her fingernail tinged on something solid inside the bag. Another connection was made. Green glass; Debs' empty prosecco bottle, cool in her hand; darted towards the front wheel of the bike as it got close.

The chainsaw was raised high overhead; ready to come down, the killing stroke.

The bottle went under the front wheel, detonating with a crunch. Then the bike took off.

The effect was astonishing. The bike, and its rider, screamed. The chainsaw clattered, spun and bounced away; the front wheel of the bike buckled like a drunk trying to put its trousers on; the figure in black was catapulted way over Leah's head. The bike skidded and stalled, its back wheel spinning, turning an almost full circumference.

The rider in black tucked in and rolled, three or four times, limbs flying, then came to a halt.

The silence was sudden, and shocking.

Leah got running. She dropped her backpack and ran, feeling the incline get harder. She was not aware of being out of breath, or of her lungs hurting, even as they wheezed like an old man's.

She dared a look back.

The bike and the rider were gone.

Can't go back. Keep going. For God's sake, keep going!

Leah heard a distant, familiar buzzing, and cried out. But the sound was nowhere near; it was travelling away from her. She kept running, knowing that the path would empty her out into another winding around the main road towards Owl Tree Halt.

There was no choice. There was no other road to take.

34

Leah expected the jump-scare moment; that as soon as she got to the mouth of the drystone wall channel, she would be faced with a cat's paw swipe from the side across her neck, a sudden bite, a surreal detachment, and it would be over before she knew it. Or maybe she would simply be run over, the rider in black eschewing the theatricalities, mowing her down and finishing her at leisure. None came.

She reached the top of the road, sweat pouring off her, knees, calves and feet aching. No one met her at the road. When she darted across, no one came back down it to meet her.

Leah sucked in air. If anyone was hiding, waiting for her to come near as she got to the leafy alleyway, she was making straight for them, unconcealed.

She darted up the pathway. It was narrower, more claustrophobic, with budding branches reaching out for her. But at least there were options if she had to escape, with a covering of pines and conifers she could dodge around, or even hide among. Again, no one followed her, and there was no sound of bike, or chainsaw. Her heart was still pumping but the adrenaline and raw fear had burned off somewhat.

I know who that was, Leah thought. *I know.*

She considered simply disappearing into the undergrowth,

and taking the direct route off the mountainside, down the side of the hills. It was unorthodox, but it would have got her to the bottom, and a chance at raising the alarm, or escaping.

Not that this was her preferred choice. Even now, even after someone had tried to kill her.

It's probably a trap, but I've got no choice. I have to warn them.

She saw the back of the naturists' house, a sudden surge of dull red. *Dutch-style house*, she thought, her internal tone the kind of lulling, *Watch With Mother* voice she used to distract herself, like holding music. *As if a windmill should be on top.* She got back onto the road, following the curve upwards, expecting to be intercepted by that dark-clad wraith at any point...

Then all of a sudden there was the front of the lodge, with a light on. She saw someone pass by the windows as she pulled the keys from her pocket. Her hand shook, the keys rattling comically loudly, as the internal *Watch With Mother* voice said, *Of course the most dangerous time for a diver is when they are preparing to surface...*

Someone was moving through the window at the door into the vestibule.

What if it was her?

The panic set in again. She glanced around, expecting to see a figure in black flying for her round every corner.

She reached out for the door; it wrenched open before her fingers could curl around the handle.

It was Debs. She tutted and looked down her nose at Leah. 'Well, I have to say I've been looking forward to this, Mummy Owl.'

'Shut up,' Leah wheezed. 'Let me in.'

Debs' eyes were slightly bloodshot, most likely from drinking. They widened as they took in Leah's stricken, sweaty face. 'What in God's name's going on?'

'Let me in, please…' The world swam for a moment. Leah flashed back to that time in the water when her legs seized up, and the water's cold fingers interlinked over her face.

'What's wrong?' Debs started forward and placed a hand on Leah's shoulder.

'I said, let me fucking in!' Leah shoved her aside, and slammed the door. Debs staggered back into a shelf against the side wall, knocking over a couple of yellowed paperbacks.

Toni appeared, a glass of wine in her hand. 'Oh, look. She's come back in tears. That's a fiver you owe me, Debs.'

'Shut up,' Leah said, scrambling to put her key in the lock. 'There's a maniac out there. Someone tried to kill me with a chainsaw. They were on a motorbike.'

Toni snorted. 'You what? That's your big excuse, for some of the things that came out of your mouth? It's a pretty good one.'

'We need to lock every single door and window, and call the police. Right fucking now.'

'Wait a second.' Debs came forward and prodded at the torn material at Leah's shoulder. 'Are you serious?'

'I am deadly fucking serious! Give me that.' Leah snatched the glass of wine from Toni's hand. Toni gaped as Leah gulped it down, then hurled the glass away.

Leah tried the door; locked tight. She removed the key from the lock. 'It was a woman. I'm sure of it. She sang our rhyme. The baby song. The night we shut her in the box.'

'Is this a joke?' Debs asked.

'It's Fiona Halfpenny. She's *here*. She tried to kill me.'

'Wait a minute – you saw her?' Toni said.

'No, she had a motorcycle helmet on. But who else could it be?'

Toni blanched, a hand to her mouth. 'A fucking chainsaw? Are you serious?'

'The patio door's open,' Debs said. 'And I think, my window... Jesus.'

'Get them closed, set the locks if you can... She's got a chainsaw. There's a bothy down there, near the Spindling... She cut through the wall, while I was in there. She tried to run me down...' Leah began to hyperventilate, and sank to her knees at last. 'Oh God... what about *Mouse*?'

Debs pulled her up, and Toni's hand was at her shoulder. 'She won't get through that door, easily, whoever it is. Come on through, Leah. Take it easy.'

'We have to close everything up. Call the police, now. Use the emergency setting, it should still give us a connection. Or, wait! There's a landline!'

'That's the thing...' Toni said, her voice suddenly high with fright. 'There's something weird going on with our phones... we wondered if there was a system failure, but... someone's taken out the SIM cards and damaged the phones. We only just found out ten minutes ago.'

'And the landline cord's been cut, too.'

'What? She's been here?'

'I thought Steve, maybe,' Debs said. 'We did invite him in... Although... Eoghan was here.'

'And Roy.' Tears bulged and fell down Toni's face.

'This was a woman. I'm sure of it. It's Halfpenny. We've got to think.' Leah took deep breaths, steadying herself against the wall. 'We've got to seal this place up, get weapons. And check every corner. Maybe she's been here already...'

'Fiona Halfpenny? From school? Leah, that can't be right,' Debs said.

'Who else would know that rhyme?'

'Mouse,' Toni said. 'Maybe it's Mouse?'

'Don't be stupid,' Leah snapped. But... maybe it was Mouse. She shook her head, dismissing her own treacherous suspicion. 'It might have been anyone... There was someone creeping around, all the time we've been here. Remember that? Someone up at the naturist couple's house, the folk who hire out the horses... Mouse saw her too, at the loch. She said someone had broken into her tent.'

'I didn't see anyone,' Debs said. She clutched at her own arm. 'Did you?'

Toni shook her head. 'No. What are we saying, a female?'

'The person who attacked me was female; I'm sure of it.'

'OK,' Debs said. 'I think Leah's right. What happened with the phones is weird. Maybe we should barricade ourselves somewhere...'

'The roof,' Toni said. 'There's that roof garden. No one can get the drop on us. Then we shout for help... make some kind of signal...' Her voice trailed off as she considered the futility of this, in such a remote place.

'Steve and Pete are the only people who might see us, from the air. And... they might not.' Leah shook her head. 'No, I think we should get some weapons, and either stay here, barricade ourselves in a room, maybe... Or get into one of the other houses. There's got to be an option.'

'I don't believe this,' Toni said.

Then they all froze.

The door handle rattled.

Leah had never had the experience of her hair standing on end, but now it did, an electric wave that rolled across her scalp. She sprang back from the door. Debs and Toni stood behind her.

There was a shadow at the side window.

Then the door banged, hard. They flinched. Toni cowered, both hands on Leah's shoulders.

'Help!' someone cried outside. A woman. 'For God's sake, let me in! Let me in! Help! Please!'

'Get a knife,' Leah said. 'Biggest one you can find.'

'Wait a minute,' Debs said. 'Hang on...'

She darted forward and ducked down, peering at the side window.

Leah gasped: 'You idiot! Don't go near that window!'

'Is someone there?' The door was banged repeatedly, frenziedly. 'Help me! She's out here! Help me!'

Debs' face grew slack. 'I don't believe it!' She pulled her own key out of her pocket and slid it into the lock.

Leah grabbed her. 'What the fuck are you doing? I said...'

Debs wrenched her arm clear and unlocked the door.

A short, but broad figure fell in the door. The face was streaked with blood, worm-lengths of it matted through the short blonde hair. The newcomer was sobbing, hands clamped over her mouth. 'Leah? Debs?' She looked around, face crumpling, sobbing in relief and amazement.

As Debs gathered her up in her arms, Leah said, almost in a whisper: 'Shell?'

35

The door was shut, and a chair was wedged under the handle. Shell was taken into the kitchen, where she sat at the table, drinking a glass of water. Her hands shook so badly that a lot of the drink cascaded over her arms and chin. Her fingers were filthy, the nails cracked, and she seemed to have been wounded several times on the face and scalp. One particular abrasion at her temple seemed to have bled freely.

Leah found a cloth under the sink, while Toni and Debs locked all the doors and windows.

They took knives from the block over by the toaster. Slate-effect handles, marbled through with lighter grey; glaringly ugly, Leah thought.

'Here,' she said, handing Shell a damp cloth. 'Your temple's been bleeding. It'll sting...'

Shell sucked through her teeth. Her nose looked broken, Leah thought. Two black eyes were in the process of forming, too. 'Thanks,' she said.

Debs sat on the other side, with her arm around Shell's shoulder. Leah noticed, with no little amazement, that Debs had changed into her gym gear, with her waterproof jacket over the top. 'Shell, love, it's not the kind of thing for someone to say at a reunion, but… you've not weathered the best.'

Shell spluttered laughter, then buried her face in her hands. The other three crowded round her as sobs seemed to pierce her body. 'I'm sorry,' she kept saying, 'I'm so sorry…'

'What happened?' Leah said.

'There was a maniac, out on the road… A woman. She told me she was that freak from school, Fiona Halfpenny. The girl who got locked up. She's come to take us all out. She said she wanted to save me until later…'

'How did it happen?' Toni asked. 'Did she jump you, or…?'

'She flagged me down from the road. I took the ferry over. I just saw a woman with car trouble. She had a knife… She told me what she was going to do to me. What she was going to do with all of us. She made me give her my phone password, made me call home… I thought she was going to cut my throat. She had this long, thin knife, like a scalpel, something surgical. She was out of her mind… The things she was saying. Said that after she kills us, she's going to come for our families. She's going to keep going until someone stops her.'

'She'll do nothing,' Leah said, fiercely, gripping her by the shoulder.

'She tied me up and left me in her house. The one at the top of the hill. Foxbar Fort, it's called. But she left me in a room with a sharp edge on a fireplace. A place where the tile was broken. I managed to keep sawing on the cable tie until it snapped. Then I got out and came down here.'

'How long's she been gone?' Leah asked.

'A good hour. I think she's got a motorbike… She's crazy. She said she'd killed people this weekend. I didn't believe her but she came back to the house last night. She was covered in blood. So was the knife, caked in it. She said: "Your mousy friend got caught in the trap."' Shell covered her face at this last.

Leah flinched, touching her mouth. 'No. No, surely not. Mouse was here until last night.'

Then she thought about it. The open windows. *Surely not*, she thought.

'Mouse was planning on leaving,' Leah murmured. 'She couldn't be bothered with the partying... She was actually having a baby. She told me. She just wanted to bunk down in her tent out in the trees, then move on tomorrow. She'll be fine. No one could get the drop on her.'

'We don't have time to be worrying about Mouse right now.' Debs started to pace, biting at a thumbnail. 'Fiona Halfpenny? How did she end up here? How did she know that we were coming?'

'Maybe she brought us,' Leah said. She turned to Toni. 'Didn't you both say you thought different people had set up the event?'

'I thought it was you,' Toni said.

'So did I,' said Shell.

Debs said: 'I thought it was Mouse...'

Leah shook her head, and pointed at Shell. 'I thought it was you. In fact I'm sure it was you, I know it for a fact. I got an email through. I had a chat with you.'

Toni placed her own butcher knife on the table and ran her fingers through her hair. 'What we're saying is – she lured us here? To kill us? For something that we did years ago, when we were little kids?'

'Whatever the reason, we need to think up a plan for

getting out of here. Where did you say you came from, Shell? Another house?'

'She's based up at the top of the hill.' Shell pointed out towards the patio. 'It's a lodge, like this one. She said she's been watching... spying.'

'She might not be in much shape for doing anything at the moment.' Leah told Shell about what had happened at the Spindling.

'A chainsaw?' Shell said, her jaw slack. 'Is this for real?'

'I think I heard it,' Toni said, in a voice close to a squeak. 'I remember thinking, someone's got a motorbike, or something...'

'I knocked her off her bike,' Leah said. 'I don't know where she went after that – she took a hell of a tumble.'

'She's crazy,' Shell said. 'She... she hurt me. She kept telling me all these bizarre plans. None of it made sense. She said stuff about how we behaved, what we did...' Shell shook her head. 'I don't think we did half those things. I think she was making it up, or deluded, or... God almighty, I didn't think I was going to see the kids again!'

Leah took her hand. 'You will. You've given me an idea. If she's around, she can't get us all. We stick together. I thought we might hold out on the roof, but it's too much of a gamble. I think we need to move on.'

Debs held out her phone. 'She's been in here, for sure. She messed with our phones. Can't dial out, can't receive a call. Nothing.'

'Mine's with my backpack – I had to dump it and run.' Leah chewed at the side of her mouth. 'She probably got to mine, too. I remember trying to make a call. I think she was here. Last night.'

When she got Mouse.

'The pushbikes are gone, too,' Toni said. 'Someone must have come around with bolt cutters. The chains were left behind; they'd been cut.'

'I say we head over to Mr and Mrs Nude UK across the way,' Debs said. 'See if they can help, give us a ride back to town, and call the police.'

'She'll have thought of that,' Shell said. 'She'll have covered all the angles. It's best we stay here. Try to call for help… There must be a way.'

'I think Leah's right,' Debs said. 'We're sitting ducks – we'd best get on the move. Unless she's got a machine gun or something, if we stick together and don't go down into the basement to investigate a funny noise, we'll be fine. And if she shows up…' Debs mimed a sudden stabbing motion, startling Leah. '…shish kebab.'

'Easier said than done.' Toni had gone almost translucent; the capillaries, muscles and tendons might have become apparent if she lost any more colour. 'Easier said than done. Leah, you mentioned the roof? Isn't it secure? She'd struggle to get up there?'

'Surely that's all we need to do,' Shell said. 'Pull up the ladder, wait for help. Aren't we supposed to be leaving?'

'Not till tomorrow morning. They're sending a car… It's a long while to wait.' Leah shook her head. 'No. I'm with Debs. I think we should arm ourselves, and get over to the house over the hill. The old couple, they've got a car, surely. You'd need a car, out here.'

'Worst comes to the worst, they've got a horse,' Debs murmured. 'Get us down to the harbour. One of us, anyway. Raise the alarm. Or – what about the sea loch?'

'The company has a workstation,' Leah explained to Shell. 'We were down there, just yesterday. We went swimming.'

'Steve's got all sorts there, in the storeroom. I saw it. We could kayak it,' Toni said. 'We could head out to the water. I mean, no one's going to get the drop on us there. Unless the bitch has a submarine.'

'I wouldn't put it past her,' Shell said, shivering.

'You mentioned that she had a plan,' Leah asked. 'What did she say?'

'Not a plan, as in, a set of steps to follow,' Shell said. 'Just a plan as in, what she's going to do to you all individually.' She shivered. 'You don't want to know.'

Leah shook her head. 'We can't think too much about that. Just accept that she might try something. So, what's the thing she'll be expecting us to do? As in, expecting the unexpected?'

Debs drummed her fingers. 'I think the sneakiest way out of here is the Captain Steve route. That's where we head out through the patio, go through the gate, go down the ginnel that runs onto the woods at the back, and emerge onto the road.'

'That's a killing floor, if ever I've seen one,' Leah said. 'Go down the ginnel, one of us can end up trapped. Though… it is the best way to get in and out.'

'You're assuming that she knows that you know about that,' Shell said.

'True. But I think our best chance is if we just walk out the front door,' Leah said, firmly. 'It's out in the open. It's not like she can sneak up on us. If she does, there are four of us.'

'She's got a motorbike,' Toni said. 'That's what you said, wasn't it? A motorbike, a dirt bike?'

'Yes – nothing high-spec, the kind of thing you'd see a teenager charging around on. But quick enough to run us down. Just not all of us. And I'm pretty sure I damaged it.'

'There's something else we're assuming.' Toni looked around to everyone, in turn. 'We're assuming there's only one of them out there.'

'We could sit here and talk about it all day. Let's get onto this.' Debs clapped her hands. Everyone jumped. 'I'm with Leah. Head over to the house across the way. See what help we can find. I don't think we should stay here. If someone's hunting us, that's what they'd prefer. That we all stay somewhere she can invade. And she's gotten in here already, don't forget, assuming she messed with the phones. If we move, we have a chance.'

Shell shook her head. 'Believe me, this bitch is clever. And she's unhinged. If we can secure ourselves in this house, we should do it. I don't want to go out there again!' She began to sob.

Leah hugged her. 'We are going to have to decide, and soon. If she's out there, she's going to find out you escaped. Meaning she'll be here soon. If she's not outside already.' She turned to Toni. 'How about you?'

'Let's do it,' Toni whispered, nodding. 'Right now. Majority vote. It's decided. Let's get out of here.'

36

'Worst commandos ever...' Debs mumbled, as they edged their way down the front path.

'Quiet,' Leah said.

'I'm only saying... If this bitch has us on a video camera somewhere, people will be laughing at this for ages.'

'I need you to stop talking so we can listen out for anyone sneaking up on us,' Leah said, tersely. 'Speak if you need to. Otherwise, keep it zipped.'

'*Ja, mein kapitan*,' Debs said.

They moved as a single unit – badly arrayed, poorly equipped, but with a plan of sorts. Leah and Toni were at the front, Debs and Shell were at the rear. They had a stock of knives with them, some from the block by the sink, some taken from the kitchen drawer. It wasn't quite the same as a set of hoplites advancing with their spears poking from beneath their shields, but it would have been difficult, indeed, for anyone to sneak up on them.

Plan B, if Fiona Halfpenny should try something – split up in four directions, and take their chances.

The mid-afternoon sun had broken through, and though it still wasn't exactly warm, the rain had held off and the wind wasn't quite so sharp. Every sound set them on edge; every gust of wind, the distant call of the seabirds.

Leah remembered her own words, before they'd braved the chilling open space beyond the front door: *She's planned out every single bit of this. We have to go against the grain, wherever we can... sometimes take the weird option; sometimes take the most obvious one.*

And after this, she remembered Toni's warning from earlier. *We're assuming there's only one of them.*

Once they were past the gate and onto the road, now it became obvious how exposed they were.

'If she's got a gun...' Shell whispered. 'If she has a target on us, right now...'

'She'd have opened fire by now,' Leah said. 'Through those trees, right there – I'd head over to that couple's house from there, rather than the driveway. It's a footpath; it must run alongside the road.'

'We'll be sitting ducks there, as much as anywhere.'

'We have to try. I don't know of any other way into that property. Jesus!'

After two or three thunderstruck seconds, Debs clutched her arm. 'Well, don't keep us in suspense! What is it?'

Leah rubbed at her forehead. 'It's... It's fine. I think it was her I saw, you know. When we drove over here, first night. Remember? I thought I saw someone by the wall, at that couple's garden. I wrote it off at the time.' She shook her head. 'Come on. This is as good a chance as any of getting help.'

'Maybe she's been there already,' Shell whispered.

'And killed everyone inside? I doubt it,' Leah said. 'She's just one woman.'

'You've already met her – when she tried to run you over with a chainsaw in her hands. I was in her company for a few hours. She's capable, all right. She's capable of anything. And she crept into the house you were in without anyone noticing!'

'Let's get in and see what's what. If there's no one here, I say we break in. Use the landline – if there is one. If we set off an alarm, that's fine by us. See if there's bikes we can use. At least one of us can head off down the hill, and get help from there.'

'And what if there's nothing of any use at all?' Debs asked.

'We'll go down on foot. Take the most awkward route. She's not taking a dirt bike down those trails and through the trees. Too steep, for a start. Going on foot will be treacherous enough.'

Leah pushed through some loose ferns and branches at the entrance to the old couple's property. In full summer she guessed this natural archway would be overgrown. Perhaps it would become a natural garland, with blooms of all colours waiting to explode across the green frieze. For now, though, it was winter-bare, and bleak. Leah took a deep breath and walked through, crouching low, looking this way and that as she emerged onto the shady wooded path.

No one. And the pine trees beyond were surely too thin to conceal anyone.

'Let's do it on the double,' Leah said.

There were no arguments. Breathing heavily, they ran down the path, carpeted with pine needles, until they reached the fence that marked off the whitewashed little cottage.

'No sign of life,' Debs said. 'I can't see through the windows for the glare, though.'

'I don't think any lights are on.' Leah squinted hard at the windows. There was nothing to suggest anyone was there. A narrow path ran round the side of the house towards a garden area, where the gentleman in question had seen fit to greet them in his Sunday best.

'OK,' Leah said, wiping her palms on her trousers. 'Let's try knocking, first. Best we keep an eye out. Debs and Toni, watch out on either side for anyone coming in. Shell, stay with me.'

'Not sure I like being stuck on the outside, here. Where some maniac could come around and cut my throat.' Toni's voice ululated on the final word, a querulous, aquiline sound.

'You don't have to hide around corners. Just keep an eye open. You see anything, shout.'

Debs walked to the far left-hand side of the cottage wall – further than Leah would have been comfortable with. 'I'll take a look round here, scaredy-cat. Best to check there's nothing waiting to jump out on us.'

A sudden sound halted them. A footstep on the pathway, just out of view. Then another.

Everyone froze; Debs darted back several paces and passed the butcher knife from hand to hand before her. 'Come on then, bitch!' she hissed. 'Why you getting all shy, now?'

The horse's head peeked around the corner, then it came forward, snorting.

Toni tittered. She covered her mouth. Then she laughed out loud. Leah tried to remember at any point when Toni had actually laughed out loud – naturally, that was, not the affected gibberings she'd emitted when Debs had been taking a pop at everyone.

Now she laughed and kept on laughing, at the top of her voice.

'Stop that,' Leah hissed. When she got closer, she saw that something was badly wrong with Toni. Tears leaked down her face. She was actually, properly hysterical.

'Sorry, but you have to admit... it's funny. Straight from the horse's mouth! Oh Jesus!' She was gone again, tears dripping off her face.

Leah didn't hit her, but did grab her wrist. 'Never mind spooking the horses – you're spooking us all. Stop it. Right?'

'You're hurting me!' Toni said it mid-laugh, but she got the message, and calmed down. Leah let go of her wrist.

Debs scratched the horse's nose. 'At least there's a friendly face. Here, boy...'

'You know each other?' Shell said, incredulously.

'Oh yeah. I've been on this one, day one. Derek, his name is.'

'Is there anything on this island you haven't ridden?' Shell said.

'Thing looks a bit agitated,' Debs said, ignoring the barb. The horse snorted appreciatively. 'Reckon it's normal for a horse to be out loose, around here?'

'Let's keep our eyes open. Don't let it distract us, if you can't get rid of it.' Leah knocked on the front door. There was a stained-glass window, a minimalist effect of bright red and navy blue that reminded Leah of boiled sweeties. The knocker was a lion, looking somewhat pleased with itself rather than ferocious, grinning despite the brass bulb suspended from its mouth.

Leah snapped it several times back and forth. Then she tried the handle.

'Nothing.'

'So what, we just bust in?' Shell said.

'Last resort. Let's go around the side. There's a patio door – it might actually be easier to break the window.'

The garden was tidy, except for a hut at the bottom with a bush or privet hedge beside it – recently shorn of branches, to go by the tangle of debris and sharp ends piled up near it. Something was heaped under bright blue tarpaulin beside the shorn branches. Leah didn't like the look of any of this. She stepped onto the decking, somewhat wary of lingering surface water.

A single glass lay on the decking, tucked in tight against the patio door.

Behind the glass lay a generous kitchen area, completely empty except for furniture. An opened bottle lay on the worktop; a chopping board lay on the centre of the circular table, but there was no sign of food or recent habitation.

Leah tried the door. It slid open.

'Hello?' she called. She peered inside, and stepped in, staring round an alcove.

Then she flinched, and dropped to her knees. The others gasped.

'What is it?' Toni squeaked in her ear.

'There's someone there.' Leah had to repeat herself – the first time she uttered that sentence, it had been too low to hear.

'Who? Did you see a face?' Shell's voice was hoarse with the tension.

'They're sat down, in the next room. There's more than

one... In the dining alcove... They're sat to dinner...' She got up and called out, loudly, bravely: 'Is there anyone in there? We need help.'

'It could be an ambush,' Debs hissed.

'Just keep watch behind me,' Leah said.

Shell gripped her by the arm. 'They must have heard you by now. I don't like this.'

'I'm going to get their attention. Stay in the doorway. Anyone attacks me – don't hesitate. Just run.'

'Shut up, Leah,' Debs said, irritably.

Leah moved into the dining room and rounded the corner. Then she screamed. Properly screamed – not a fairground scream, or a scary movie scream, or a mouse-darting-over-your-shoe-in-a-cellar scream. A guttural, full-throated, frightening cry of fear and despair. She sank to her knees. She clamped her hands over her eyes. But it was too late. She had seen it all.

Debs and Shell moved forward. 'Don't,' Leah said, dragging them back. 'Just don't.'

37

Leah had read about people retching or outright throwing up upon receiving a shock, or seen it in the movies. But she had never thought it was something that actually happened, right until that moment. She staggered out of the vestibule and into the garden, feeling a spasm of nausea end in a tight clench in her gullet. She retched, hardly bringing anything up, knees and palms bitten hard by the paving stones.

'Don't,' she managed to say to Toni and Debs, 'don't look. Don't go in there.'

'What is it?' Toni asked. Her shoulders quivered; she let the knife she was holding drop. It landed on its point, right in the laminated flooring at her feet, just an inch or two from the toe of her boot.

Shell had seen it. She came out, staggered, then sat down hard on the doorstep.

'There are bodies in there,' Leah said, wiping her mouth. She placed a hand on Toni's shoulders. 'The old couple...' She swallowed. *Don't tell Toni about Roy. She doesn't need to know.* 'One or two others. They've been murdered. Slashed. Their faces, necks... One of them was gutted.' She slapped herself hard in the face. *Don't say the worst thing. Don't tell them about the absolute, final atrocity.*

'Mouse is in there,' Shell said, rocking back and forth. 'Mouse is there. She's there. They got Mouse!'

'Shut up,' Leah said.

'What do you mean, "Mouse is there?"' Debs wailed. '*Dead?* Mouse is *dead?*'

'She's on the table,' murmured Shell. 'Someone carved her. And they wrote something on the walls...'

'Get away from here,' Leah said. The whole world seemed to vibrate. She couldn't articulate any sadness or emotion, although her heart was beating harder and faster than she would ever have felt possible. *This must be what shock is like*, a distant part of her mused. She felt her veins, her blood, roaring in her ears, pulsing at her wrists and neck. Her legs quivered. But not to run. 'This was left for us to find. Whoever did it must still be around, nearby.'

'I want to see,' Debs said. 'Is Eoghan there? Oh God...'

Toni grabbed her arm. 'Don't. Leave it. It must be a trap!'

'Get off me! Is Eoghan there? Please tell me Eoghan isn't there.'

'Eoghan isn't there,' Leah said. But Debs wrenched her arm free, and took those fatal two steps beyond the patio area.

A second later she ran out, sobbing.

Toni followed her, aghast, running well beyond where Shell was still sat on the decking, raking her dirt-encrusted fingers through her hair.

'"Owl Society dinner",' Debs shrieked, pointing towards the patio. 'That's what she wrote.' She began to hyperventilate. 'This isn't just revenge, this is a fucking maniac! A psychopath... God in heaven, we are going to die out here.

We were meant to see that. Fiona fucking Halfpenny is going to carve us up. Someone help us!'

'That's not going to help,' Leah said. 'Toni, sort her out.' Her voice was unnaturally calm. *Numb*. She took several unsteady steps back through the patio door.

Shell got up. 'Are you mad? Don't go in there!'

Leah shook her head. She turned to the right, and lifted a heavy set of keys from a hook in the wall. 'There's a car key here. One or two others... Let's look for the car and get out of here.' She unzipped her jacket pocket and placed the keys inside.

'Leah, look out!' Shell's face, stricken, lunged forward. She grabbed Leah, her fingers biting into her shoulder.

Leah stumbled. 'What are you doing?'

'There's someone moving in there!' Shell screamed. 'Get out, get out!'

They ran. 'Head towards that shed,' Leah wheezed. 'Don't panic. Don't split up yet. Stick together.' She dared a glance over her shoulder; there was no sign of any pursuer.

'That's a trap, surely,' Debs wheezed, as she stopped halfway between the patio, the shed and the bushes. 'If I wanted to trap someone in this garden, I'd force them over here.'

'There's something hidden,' Leah said, feeling in her pocket. The keys were there. 'Look. The blue tarp. At the side of the shed. What's under that?'

'A bomb, probably,' Toni said. 'That's what this bitch has got in store for us. She'll blow us all to hell.'

'Not her style,' Leah said. Debs sagged, for a moment. Leah caught her by the shoulder. 'It's OK. It's OK, love.'

'It's not OK,' Debs said. 'I can't believe what I saw, there. It was a fucking slaughterhouse! Mouse…' Her eyes widened. 'And I'm sure there was…' Her eyes flickered towards Toni.

'Not now,' Leah said. 'Right? Not now.'

Toni was oblivious. She pointed at the blue tarp, a shocking, aquamarine contrast to the branches and trees. 'There could be a car under there.'

'Why would they hide it under tarp, beside a load of branches and garden crap?' Shell said. 'I think Toni's right. It's a trap. If it's not a bomb or something, they could be hiding in that shed.'

'We are running out of options,' Leah said. 'I'm having a look. Shell – keep an eye on the house. Toni – keep an eye on the shed. You see any movement at all, you shout. Debs… Debs, you with us?'

Debs blinked. Her eyes were bright red and puffy. She clenched the butcher knife tight to her chest. It occurred to Leah to take it off her. She parked that thought for now. 'I'm with us. With you. I'm here, I mean.'

'Good. I need you to look sharp. If anyone makes a rush at us, we're going to stick together, and we're going to fight them off. They can't take us all out. Got it? Whether it's Fiona Halfpenny, Freddy Krueger, or Christ knows who else. All right? We can't get separated. If we're a team, we'll survive.'

'Mummy Owl,' Debs whispered. 'That's the Mummy Owl I remember.'

'And that's the fox I remember.' Leah smiled kindly. Then she approached the tarp and the piled branches, giving the shed a wide berth. A shuddersome memory came to her – the chainsaw blade, spitting sawdust and razor-tipped splints, slicing through the wall. This shed looked sturdier than the hut at the Spindling, though it was much smaller.

No face appeared at the window; no blades, motorised or otherwise, appeared.

Leah gripped the tarpaulin. The muscles and tendons groaned in her arm as she extended it. Her fist had been clenched, and she hadn't realised it. Every nerve poised to spring.

Was she hiding under there? Waiting to fly out? *It would mean I'm next. All she has to do is take me out, and escape. Just one stab, faster than you can blink. And that's me out. And then there were three...*

Leah pulled back some of the conifer branches and evergreen fronds. They spilled over, leaving a more obvious car-shape underneath.

'God's sake, Leah!' Toni barked. 'Don't piss about.'

Leah pulled the tarp. It came away easily.

Shell gave a yelp. 'That's my car! My car's under there! I had no idea what she did with it... I couldn't see it out at her house.'

Leah approached the side doors. *Wouldn't put it past her... Would not be completely astonished, here, if the door should fly open...*

She pulled out the ring of keys. There were all sorts on the fob – some of them were labelled with coloured stickers, wrapped around the metal. One looked like a car key, but was bright yellow, with a single black stripe down the middle. Looked. sporty. *Be funny if there was a Ferrari somewhere about here... Banana yellow, and God help Fiona Halfpenny if she got in the way...*

'Any of these your keys?'

Shell shook her head. Then she grimaced, nodding towards the 4x4. 'Someone's bashed it up... Look at the headlights. The windscreen's smashed at one corner, too.'

It was true – a single crystalline detonation stretched out from the driver's side corner, a latticework of cracks that stretched all the way down to the opposite corner. The headlights had all been taken out, and the grille had also been stoved in. Dents and dings pocked the bodywork like bullet holes, and one of the side windows had been completely shattered. Leah could see the shards glistening on the seat inside.

Leah peered in. There was no one inside the 4x4. She reached out for the passenger-side door handle.

'Leah!' Shell cried.

Leah stiffened.

'Be careful. Remember what Toni said...'

'Shell, don't say a word unless you see someone approaching us,' Leah barked, anger surging. 'We're walking on eggshells as it is. You're keeping watch, right?'

'Right. Sorry.'

Leah gripped the handle. The door opened.

'Not locked...'

Toni pointed to the bonnet. 'It's open... I think even if any of us did know how to hotwire a car, it's going nowhere.'

There was a dark gap underneath the bonnet. Leah lifted it. The pipes, pistons, wiring and God knew what else was smashed and disrupted. Oil spattered the superstructure and the underside of the bonnet. A second's glance told her all she needed to know.

Inevitably, the tyres were slashed, too.

'OK,' Leah said. 'This car can't start. But it can still move.'

'What do you mean?' Debs asked.

Leah pointed to the pathway, which led down an incline towards the gate, the one they'd driven past on Friday night. Beyond that was the main road. 'We just need some momentum, to make the wheels turn. The road goes all the way down to the lake. There's boathouses there, and Steve and Pete's workstation... I suspect we've got the key to a boat.' She brandished the yellow key. 'Failing that, we can break into Steve's shack down there. There's all sorts. We've got options. At the bottom of the hill, when we hit the main road, someone will come past. Even if they don't, we're closer to the pub, the houses... someone can help. As long as we steer this heap of shit – no offence, Shell – we'll just roll down the hill. And we're safe.'

'It's a plan. It's doable,' Debs said.

'Damned right. OK. Let's get the glass cleared off the seat, and everyone get in. We'll give it a push. Once it gets moving, I'll steer us down the hill. Piece of cake. What could go wrong?'

Silence answered her – and worried faces.

'Just before I do that...' Leah got to her knees and checked underneath the car; then she popped the boot, knife at the ready.

Nothing there, except a half-empty bottle of screenwash, muddy wellingtons, baby wipes, blankets, forgotten toys – the bric-a-brac of a family car. And no sign of a hidden assailant, coiled and waiting to spring.

'Just checking,' she muttered. 'Right. Everyone in.'

38

Debs rolled up her sleeves. 'I'll shove, you drive. If you see a maniac... please shout something. Beep the horn. Scream. Anything.'

Inside the 4x4, Toni and Shell sat in the back, while Leah was in the driver's seat. Shell had shown little desire to be at the controls of her own car; she'd blanched upon the sight of the front seat, the slash mark down the side, the spilled upholstery. She'd simply shaken her head at Leah.

'OK,' Leah said, 'handbrake's off. Shouldn't take much...'

Debs' eyes were wide as she pushed at the back of the 4x4. It moved, fast. Leah felt a thrill travel through her as she grappled with the steering wheel. If there had been an immobiliser system, it was completely disengaged with the electrics smashed. This meant an end to the power steering, too. Leah wondered briefly if this is what steering cars had always been like before the technology had come in – a wrestling match of sorts, or like a captain out at sea, fighting the helm.

'We're off, Debs, come on,' she bellowed.

Debs sprinted to the open passenger door and got in, shutting the door and belting herself in. 'We're moving. It's happening,' Debs said. She sobbed, entirely without warning, shoulders hunched.

Leah placed a hand on her shoulder. 'It's OK, honey, we're out of here, now.'

'Watch the road, you berk!' Debs palmed a tear from her cheeks.

The 4x4 rolled down the incline towards the driveway. Leah clenched her jaw. Surely now, this was the time. This was when the figure in black would appear, scuttling out of a doorway, peeling away from the wall, dropping from the roof. It would have a blade or a buzzing saw or perhaps even a gun, braced and poised, ready to end Leah with a single bright spark and then oblivion.

No one came. The trees closed in around the 4x4 as it built speed, bouncing over a bump in the surface and giving everyone inside a jolt.

'Easy, rally driver,' Toni stuttered.

'Never mind easy – get us around and out of here,' Debs said.

Leah kept the clutch down and her foot poised on the brake out of habit. The end of the driveway loomed. Everyone held their breath and braced, ready for the shadow to appear.

There was nothing; just the road curving down and around the mountain.

Debs cheered. 'Don't stop – there's nothing coming.'

Leah turned the wheel to the left, and the 4x4 built up speed. The mountain spiralled round slowly as the 4x4 descended. Their ears popped. Air blasted in through the broken window, caressing Leah's forehead, cooling the perspiration there.

'We're through,' Shell said, her voice thick. 'We're out.'

Leah shook her head, peering past Shell's darting eyes

to the road behind them. 'She's got a motorbike. I think I damaged it, but it's hard to tell. She's mobile, and she tried to chop me in half with a chainsaw. We're not out of this yet. We can't be.'

'Look at that,' Toni whispered. 'What a view.'

The sea loch sparkled in a patch of sunlight, though the waters looked troubled. Steve's boat shed was a stolid white lump by the shore, matchbox-sized for now. The pub was nowhere to be seen, hidden by the treeline near the shore. Then the road dropped into the valley. They were travelling a good forty miles per hour or so; Leah applied the brakes gently to each turn, some of them hairier than she remembered.

'You said you saw people in the house.' Toni stared out of the passenger-side window. 'What people? Mouse was there, you said?'

Leah swallowed. She had an image. Mouse's face criss-crossed with slashes but still recognisably Mouse. 'Mouse was there. She's dead.'

Toni covered her face with her hands. The sound she made was more of a wheeze than a recognisable cry. Had Leah ever heard Toni cry? 'Poor Mouse. I can't believe it. Fucking maniac.'

'We can't think about Mouse now,' Leah replied, her voice steady. 'We've got to get out of here, in one piece.'

'Leah. Was Eoghan there?' Debs pulled at Leah's trousers, a gesture the latter found inexplicably infuriating. 'Steve was there, wasn't he? Anyone else?'

Leah met her stare. 'No. Eoghan wasn't there. It was Steve, and the old couple... Their throats had been slashed.'

Toni started, as if she'd been jolted awake. 'What about Roy?'

'I didn't see Roy.'

'You sure? You don't sound sure.'

'Roy wasn't there.'

'I saw the bodies, too,' Shell said, calmly.

'Roy wasn't there,' Leah said. 'I'm sure of it.'

'There were more than four bodies there,' Shell said.

'You had a split second to look. We had to get out of there. We have to get off this island. There was no one recognisable.' *Oh, you're such a clever clogs,* Leah chided herself. *Lying off the top of your head, that's a good one. "No one recognisable". Meaning his face was hardly recognisable after someone had carved it up. Is this right? How would you feel if it was John, and Debs wasn't telling you that your husband was lying there?*

Leah felt a pang at the idea of John and David – miles away, and hopefully oblivious. Then she felt a quick blade of fear slide between her ribs. *Was* David far away? Fiona Halfpenny had lured the other halves over, surely – making Shell contact Ewan, and then Eoghan and Roy coming over at the same time. Making them part of the plan. Had Ewan come with Roy and Eoghan? Surely he would have got in touch, if so. Surely he would have been there at the house, with Eoghan and Roy. *John wouldn't just have shown up.*

Surely.

'Are you sure you didn't see Roy?' Toni asked. 'I swear to God, if you're lying, I'm going to carve you up.' Toni's face loomed large in the mirror. Leah flinched; the car lurched a little.

'She said she didn't see Eoghan or Roy,' Debs said. 'You

were telling the truth? Weren't you, Leah? You were telling the truth, right?'

'That's right. Eoghan and Roy will be at the pub. We'll find out in a minute.'

'So, we're going to the pub?' Shell said.

'Yeah. Quickest way out of here.'

'Isn't that what she might be expecting?' Shell glanced over her shoulder, as if the motorbike might appear at any moment.

'I think she might be done,' Leah said. 'Probably making her escape. We should keep an eye out for a lone female. Any advantage she had on us was the element of surprise. It's gone, now. She's going to struggle to sneak up on us. If she is, we're ready.'

Leah had allowed the car to roll free. It picked up speed as the road straightened out. The loch glittered through the trees. There were no other cars on the road, which still had enough of a decline to keep the 4x4 buckling and bumping on its own momentum.

The signpost came up; there was the turn-off for the lochside marina, the Gaelic name pleasant to look at, impossible to pronounce. Straight on was the beach, with its sign for the inn.

'Shit!' Shell cried.

Leah almost bounced out of her seat in shock. 'What?'

'Turn! Turn! There's someone in the treeline!'

'Where?'

A finger stabbed out beside Leah's face. 'There! There! For God's sake, she's pointing it right at us!'

'Pointing what?'

'A gun!' Shell shrieked.

She blundered over Leah's shoulder, forcing her against

the door. Shell jerked the wheel. 'Get off the road! She's got a shotgun!'

'We can't... Get back, Shell!'

The 4x4 shivered as it made a sharp turn down the left-hand exit... but the arc was too sharp, the speed too much, and the trees came close.

'Get down!' Shell screamed.

Leah ducked her head, wrenched the wheel to the right, and tore down the left-hand road towards the marina, the boathouse, the workstation. Debs placed her face down between her knees, as if braced for an air crash.

No crash came; no roar, no sputter, no tinkling of shotgun shells. Leah raised her head. The water was dead ahead – the road turned to the right, heading towards the marina. The water was grey, uninviting, the surface without form or character in the dull light. In the centre of the water was the diving platform, the scene of the almost ill-fated race.

The place they'd been watched. The moment they should have realised they were in danger.

Leah turned the car towards the shed. The 4x4 was still travelling at pace, lurching alarmingly over the uneven road.

'Need to slow down, Leah,' Debs said, as the green double-doors approached.

Leah braked – but only a little.

'Way too fast, Leah,' Debs said.

The green doors loomed, dead ahead. The 4x4 was still going too fast.

'Leah, stop! What are you doing? Stop!' Debs shrieked.

Leah did not stop.

Someone – maybe Toni – screamed at the top of her voice.

The 4x4 crashed into the green doors, then was still.

39

Toni broke the silence. 'What are you playing at?' She rubbed her forehead, then punched Leah on the shoulder. Then once again, in Leah's ear, teeth clenched: 'Are you trying to kill us? Shit... is it *you* that's done all this?'

Leah grabbed Toni's fist, and held it. 'Don't do that again.'

'An explanation would be good though,' Shell said, in more of a gargle than a voice.

'It's not rocket science,' Debs panted. 'Though it's not exactly making a cheese sandwich either. She's breaking into the shed. We didn't have any keys.'

'Ram-raiding. To give it its technical term.' Leah gave a tired smile and let go of Toni's fist, then cranked the handbrake. 'Always fancied doing that. Right. Let's get in there and see if there's anything we can use.'

'Well you better do it quick,' Shell said, out of breath. A cut on her forehead trickled blood onto her nose. 'There is someone out there. It looked like they had a shotgun...'

'"Looked like"?' Debs said. 'We were just about home and dry and you go and spook the horses because it "looked like" someone out there had a shotgun on us? Are you kidding?'

'Well what else was I supposed to do?' Shell shrieked.

'That's what I saw! Haven't you noticed? We're being stalked here! Unless this is the best TV prank show in history, we're being stalked! Someone kidnapped me and put a knife to my throat. The same person killed God knows how many people!'

Toni flapped her hands as if trying to rid her fingertips of something nasty. 'I get the confusion, I really do. But we've got to get out of here. If there's someone on the road trying to kill us, they'll be here any minute!'

No further discussions were needed. They piled out of the car.

Leah had turned the wheel slightly just before impact, judging the angle perfectly. The doors to Steve's shed had flown open, leaving enough room for them to get in past the bulk of the 4x4. Leah flicked on a light. A riot of sports equipment appeared under the blinking bulb, a disturbing strobe effect that took a moment or two to settle. Shadows weaved and dodged the eye. Kayaks, paddles, and a row of ancient hiking boots in a rack confronted them. At the far end of the shed was a cartoon crocodile's head, carved from wood and painted bright green. The head was turned to one side from a faux trophy mount, and it winked as it grinned at them.

'Quickly,' Toni hissed. She had taken up a position by the waterline, scanning the building, and anyone who might approach. 'This isn't a shopping trip. Grab whatever you need, and let's go!'

Leah said: 'I wouldn't want to get trapped in here, either. There's no way out apart from the front doors.'

'This'll do,' Debs muttered. The archery target had been stored at the far wall. There were no arrows embedded, but it was the same one they'd been practising on twenty-four hours before. She picked up the bow she'd used to win the tournament and slid it over one shoulder. The leather quiver, a novelty item that Debs had branded 'Robin Hood's jockstrap', had a glossy brown sheen in the dim light. It was filled with arrows. Debs hooked that over her other shoulder. 'This feels better,' she said, grimly. 'This is more like it. Knife's OK. But if that clown gives me something to shoot at, she's going to grow some feathers.'

'How about those kayaks?' Shell whispered. 'Maybe we can get out on the water.' She pulled at some of the kayaks on the rack. 'Give me a hand with these, Leah, would you?'

'You want to paddle out of here?' Leah asked.

'Yeah. Didn't you mention it earlier? It's as good a plan as any. Anyone wants to shoot at a moving target out on the water... good luck to them.'

'I was no good at the lesson, though. And you weren't here for it, in fact.'

Shell hesitated. 'How hard can it be? Water's calm. Just keep your balance. Any problems, we stick together anyway. If one of us upends, then the other one puts us right. The smaller ones will do, I guess? Maybe the medium-sized one for Toni?'

'OK. Let's go for it. And hope she doesn't have a speedboat.' Leah paused. 'Shit. She probably *will* have a speedboat.'

'Let's keep to the open water,' Debs said, 'paddle down to the far end of the island where there's people, get out, and then we just pop into the pub. Job done. They can't all be maniacs. Well...' Debs' eyes lost focus for a moment. She was imagining the same thing Leah was. Everyone at the pub being a maniac didn't seem like a far-fetched idea at this moment.

'Hurry up!' Toni yelled from outside. Framed in the stoved-open doors, in the sliver of the gap to the side of the 4x4, she was an anxious figure, arms folded, shifting her weight from foot to foot.

'OK... Let's do it,' Leah said. 'There are four kayaks – let's drag them out.'

All three lifted a kayak, and a paddle from the rack. Leah emerged first, heaving the orange hull onto the gritty surface. 'Right... I'll go back in and get one for you, Toni, once the others have...'

Toni was gone. There was only the shoreline, the lapping water, a faint breeze and the cold sunshine.

'Toni? We're leaving. Right now. What's going on?'

Someone grabbed her by the arm. Leah flinched and dropped the kayak and paddle.

It was Debs. 'Leah, we can't stay here,' she whispered.

'Where'd she go?' Leah said, panic rising. 'She was there two seconds ago!'

'It doesn't matter where she went,' Debs hissed, teeth gritted. 'She was like a startled rabbit – she's probably run off into the woods. We can't do anything about that. Let's get on the water and get out of here.' The arm tightened.

'We can't just leave her. Toni!'

Debs clamped a hand over her mouth; Leah twisted away from her, then shoved her. Debs fell heavily, blinking.

Shell emerged from the shed, scraping her kayak along the floor of the shed. 'Hey, I found something else... What's going on? For God's sake, we don't have time to fall out, here.'

'Toni!' Leah yelled. 'Come on! We're leaving!'

'...Don't...' said a small voice, from the trees to the left of the shed.

'Toni?' Leah squinted.

Toni's face appeared, low to the ground, next to one of the trees. She waved frantically. 'Down, down,' she hissed, 'on the ground, now. She's here; she does have a gun, for God's sake!'

Then the first shot rang out.

40

They all flinched. Debs, already on the ground, turned to the right and laid herself flat, the arrows and the bow jutting from her back, an awkward sail. One of the kayaks spun, the orange hull erupting in orange shards and splinters. Shell blinked, staring at her arm. Blood slicked her wrist and dripped off her fingertips in thick, dark drops.

'Shot. I've been shot!' She spoke in a whisper.

Leah launched herself forward, taking Shell by the shoulder, and pulling her behind the boot of the 4x4.

As she did so, the gun boomed again, spiderwebbing the windows on the right-hand side. There was a clear ting of the bodywork being peppered.

Shell blinked rapidly, clutching her arm. Blood oozed through her clenched fingers. Leah gripped her by the shoulder.

'It's OK,' Shell said, 'nothing major, nothing fatal, just the old, you know, the skin at the side... Look...' She turned her arm, where part of the hooded top had been torn away, revealing raw flesh underneath. 'Shotgun pellets, but like I'd been scratched by a branch, you know, nothing...'

Leah leaned close to Shell's ear. 'I need you to stop speaking.'

'But I've got something; I found something...'

'I need you to stop speaking. We need to listen...'

Someone cannoned into Leah's side, and she yelped. It was Debs, huddling in close. She had the bow in her hands. 'She's got to come over here,' Debs whispered, close enough for Leah to see her lips tremble. 'If she does, I'll get her. I'll get her.'

'No – we have to run,' Leah said, peering over the edge of the 4x4's boot as far as she dared. 'Into the trees. Maybe split up. It's the only chance we have.'

'She'll pick us off,' Shell said. 'She'll have a gun on us, right now.'

'Think about it,' Debs said. There was a terrible fixity in her expression; Debs had gone into fight mode, whereas all Leah wanted to do was give in to the tremulous, cowardly urge to sprint, as far down the beach as she could, increasing the pace and the distance and getting away from whoever was out there. 'If she's shooting at us from that side... she's doing it from an angle, near the path we came down, probably from the trees. We can use the angle of the car and get out of here. Head along the beach. Or, go to the trees, where Toni is. If I can get a bead on her, it's game over.'

'There's this other thing,' Shell said, trying to speak without moving her lips. Leah noticed that all colour had fled from her cheeks; the only remnants of colour were the scabs and bruising left over from her earlier encounter with Fiona Halfpenny. 'I found this other thing...'

'Shut up,' Debs said. 'Listen to me. This is what we have to do. All she has to do is walk around the other side, and she has a clear shot at us. Staying here is not an option. We can't go into the shed – she'll burn it down. We'll get barbecued. You following me?' She grabbed Leah by the shoulder and shook her, staring into her eyes. 'You both following me? This is life and death. Let's move out, now...'

'Hang on. If she shot at us from that side, maybe she'll have gone around the back of the shed,' Leah whispered. 'That's what I would have done.'

Debs bit her lip. 'You're probably right. Either way it's a gamble. Either way, we have to get out of here, and do it fast. She can't shoot all of us.'

'OK,' Leah said. 'Maybe we should split up – gives us a chance of getting out of here. One of us, anyway.'

'Or we stick together, draw her out, and I drop the bitch with this.' Debs shook the bow. 'After that, we get busy with the cutlery we've got stashed on us, and that's the end of the story.'

'Will you please listen?' Shell cried. 'I've got this other thing, from the shed.'

She unzipped her jacket. Leah gasped.

'I can't, not with this arm... One of you will have to do it,' Shell said. Some focus, or clarity, had come into her eyes, now. The bleeding seemed to have stopped; certainly it wasn't oozing out from beneath Shell's fingers any more.

'I'll do it,' Leah said. And then the screaming started.

41

It came from the right-hand side of the 4x4, as Debs had predicted – to the left of the three cringing women. It was a high-pitched squeal, almost unearthly in tone. The sound of a maniac. A maniac approaching fast.

'We have to run! Now!' Shell cried.

Leah grabbed her. 'She's trying to flush us out. Wait…'

Shell twisted out of her grasp, and got to one knee. 'Wait, nothing!'

As she prepared to lurch forward, a deep thump concussed the air, seeming to grip all three by the scruff of the neck. The tyre to the left of Shell erupted, just like the kayak had, belching blackened shreds. It deflated instantly, the vehicle sagging.

'Now we run!' Debs cried. 'She has to reload! Run!'

Panic and an instinctive sense of opportunity seized them. They ran in the opposite direction, Shell's arm swaying uselessly at her side, streaked with crimson, her hands red.

The screaming devolved into giggles, behind them. 'That's right!' a voice croaked. 'That's it! Fast as you can, girls?'

Leah glanced over her shoulder. There was a suggestion of a figure running behind them, someone in a yellow coat.

It darted into cover at the edge of the shed, close to the wrecked car.

'She wants us to run that way!' Leah yelled. But it was too late; Shell and Debs had taken off, sprinting on the shingle stones, crouched low, their feet kicking up clumps of stones like tracer fire – which was then joined by actual tracer fire as the gun discharged again. Leah felt a soft rain falling on her hair. It had been close, close enough for her to feel the air displaced as the shotgun pellets whizzed past her.

'That's it!' the voice sneered behind her. 'You hesitate now, Mummy Owl! You wait a little second, there. Let's get acquainted.'

Leah saw a flash of yellow over her shoulder – then she took the chance and ran after the other two. They had already disappeared into the treeline, the budding branches snapping back in their wake. There was no sign of Toni either.

Leah checked her run and stopped. She heard footsteps crunch along the path at the back of the shed, where the others had gone. As Leah had suspected, the hidden person with the gun had run around the back of Steve and Pete's workstation. The figure was to the left of the outer wall. There was a sudden, sickening silence. Leah waited, fumbling with her jacket pocket.

An eye appeared at the edge of the building first – a dark, unblinking eye, with a suggestion of short, spiky dark hair just above it.

'Oh,' keened the voice, 'Mummy Owl's being a big brave owl, isn't she? Or is she just a coward? Frozen to the spot? Too scared to fly away?'

'Come out and find out,' Leah said. But her voice was so

dry, and her fear was so great, that the line came out as a squeak.

'Know how many people I've killed, just in the past couple of days? Do you?' The eye blinked. She cocked her head, awaiting an answer.

When none came, Fiona Halfpenny answered herself. 'All of them.'

'You're the one hiding, not me. Why don't you come out and show me your face?'

'Yes, why don't I?' The figure stepped out. She had the gun raised to her shoulder and sighted along the barrel to her face, above the yellow raincoat, with only the eye and a pale forehead prominent. 'I had hoped to do you last, Leah. Shame. I had plans for you, too. I might have to take care of you now, though. Debs or Toni will fill in for you, though. It's all one, now.'

'Or maybe you'd better just drop it?' Leah said. Her entire body was aquiver – her arms, hips, knees – and she had to clutch what she held in her right hand tightly to stop it from slipping out her hands.

The thing Shell had passed to her from the workstation.

The flare gun.

Shell had loaded it, but hadn't thrown the safety catch. Leah did so now, dropping to her knees, and aiming right at the woman holding the gun on her.

Leah saw her mouth drop open. Then the figure darted back into cover behind the shed.

Leah ignored her. She pointed the flare gun into the air, grit her teeth, and fired.

For a moment she was sure it had exploded in her hand; that she would see a gushing stump on the end of her wrist.

But the hiss told her that it had been a near-perfect shot, vertical, and still travelling, a white scratch turning to flaring red, high overhead on the chilly blue.

A sound that might have been screaming, might have been swearing accompanied this. Leah threw the flare gun aside and ran, back around the 4x4, back onto the path, and then streaked into the trees.

The gun fired once, in response. Leah saw, heard and felt no impact; her pursuer had missed by a long way. She rebounded off trees as she charged into a thicket; a burrow threatened to snap her ankle when Leah's foot was briefly lodged there; and she was sure that someone followed up behind her, screaming in rage. Or it could have been the wind, her blood, her pulse pounding somewhere just above her ears.

Leah dodged and feinted, turning slowly but surely towards the road. The trees scrolled past her as she reached the path, converging and gathering and scattering in thin naked rows. She was exposed, on the road, briefly. Long enough to hear the buzzing sound.

She flashed back to the chainsaw. Then she ran back into the treeline and crouched low.

A motorbike. The same one Fiona Halfpenny had ridden at the Spindling – though Leah couldn't be sure, crouched in tight behind the stout girth of an oak tree. The bike whizzed past; Leah traced it by sound, moving around the trunk of the tree so that she was forever out of sight. As the sound of the bike faded, she peered out, in time to see a yellow flare disappearing up and around the road.

Leah had a moment of pure relief, sunk on her haunches, and she sobbed. Her cheeks were already wet with tears she hadn't been aware she had shed, during her moments of breathless panic. For a few blissful seconds there was only the wind, stirring her hair, chilling her skin.

Then came the sound of the plane.

Leah saw it through a gap in the trees; the yellow and blue plane climbed overhead, heading out of the far edge of the loch. Seemingly heading towards her.

Towards the flare.

She got up and ran through the trees towards the shoreline. By the time she got through the woodland, far to the right of the workstation, she saw it coming in low – and close, maybe four hundred yards away. It was close enough to make out the serial number on the side.

Leah leapt up and down on the shore, crossing her arms (hope to die) – and then throwing her arms out, again and again, a ludicrous TV workout there on the shingle beach. 'Please! Please, come in!' she screamed.

The plane came past. The wings didn't dip, like in the war movies. But it came around again, banking sharply.

'They've seen me,' she whispered. 'They've seen me! And they're coming!'

The plane rose sharply and made another pass. This time it was lower, lower still, and then, yes, it was landing. The water rose in plumes as the plane touched down gracefully, the loch surging in pure white in its sudden wake. The plane headed towards a jetty, maybe three hundred yards away.

Leah wiped the tears from her eyes, and began to run. 'It's over. Thank God, it's over!'

42

The sun broke through as Leah ran along the shoreline, illuminating the sea loch in a beautiful dark, almost regal blue, still disturbed by the impact of the plane. The Nordic colour scheme of the Sgian Dubh Air plane's fuselage was perfect in front of the craggy hillsides to the north, gleaming in the light.

Pete the pilot was in front. He waved. 'Hey! You all right?'

'My friends,' she tried to say, choking as if she had run through a dust cloud. 'They're here. They must have seen...'

She collapsed before she got to the jetty, where the plane was tied up. Peter sprinted over, his face pinched tight. 'Leah! They're here; it's all right love. Step on over. They're here; it's fine.'

She saw the stones on the beach fly away from his shoes. His hand was heavy on her shoulder. She clung to him, like a child spotting its mother at nursery. 'There's a maniac... She killed people. She's here, somewhere, on a bike.'

He pulled her to her feet. 'Come on – they're all in the plane. They ran out the trees when I landed. I followed the flare... Was that you? One of the lasses said you had a flare, out of the workstation... I was coming in for the overlap.' He guided her over to the plane. Faces at the window;

Debs and Shell and Toni, all crying; Toni clattering the window as if she was a teenybopper catching sight of her idol. She began to run for the jetty, the open door.

'She's still out there,' Leah croaked, as she made for the open door, the water slapping at the boards of the jetty.

'Sounds absolutely insane.'

'What about the police? You called them?'

'On their way.' His hand was firm at her back, as she stepped on board.

The other three were manky, their hair matted, and Shell smelled like a butcher thanks to her new wound in the arm, but they all hugged close, sobbing, when Leah got inside the cabin.

'Thought she'd got you,' Toni moaned in her ear. 'We were sure she'd shot you!'

'She bottled it,' Leah mumbled, through a curtain of Toni's hair. 'Saw the flare gun and got spooked. I didn't shoot her with it, though. Made sure I got the shot away... got help.'

Pete closed the door, his face set. He peered out the window for a second. 'Best we get going. You said she had a shotgun? What did she look like?'

'Hard to say,' Leah said. 'Short spiky hair, I think. She had a gun on me; I was focused more on that.'

'She's mental,' Shell wheezed. She still hugged Leah far too close. 'Pure muscle, though. She packs a punch – I can tell you that.'

Pete donned his headset and buckled himself in. 'I've untied us – everyone get buckled in, now. I won't bother with the flight checks – get in, and stay away from the windows. Oh – I'll need you to put the bow and arrow and the knives in front. Turbulence, deadly weapons... I'll have to store them. Leave them by my seat. I'll get us in the air in a minute.'

The propellers began to turn. Pete guided the plane away from the jetty as the four women buckled themselves in. Leah stared hard at the waving trees, washed in the bright sunshine. She watched for a flicker of yellow; a hunched figure on the little bike, matching their movement from the road. She saw nothing.

The plane built up thrust; then came the lift. Leah kept her attention on the shore, even when the plane was surely too high to hit, unless the bitch had a rocket launcher. Can't rule it out, she thought. Perhaps she would streak through the water like the shark in *Jaws*, jumping high enough to bite them. Or maybe the final horror was more prosaic, the killer squeezed into a locker like a rat stuffed up a drainpipe, maybe. Or crouched in the passenger seat beside the sole pilot. Where they'd left their weapons.

Leah peered over the edge of the seat, just in front of her. Empty, of course.

'We're safe,' Toni said. 'Oh thank God. Is there a little gin 'n' tonic I could have?'

Someone laughed at the joke; Leah wasn't sure who. If it was Debs, then the laugh had broken her. She sank forward into her seat, fingers running through the back of her hair, shoulders heaving, but not in mirth. Leah reached across the aisle and laid a hand over Debs'. Debs didn't look up, but she clutched it. Sobbing.

'Mouse,' was all Debs said. Leah screwed her eyes shut.

A crackle sounded. It was a radio channel; a woman's voice. 'Pete? You there?'

Pete clutched his headphones. 'Just getting airborne now. Over.'

'Thank God.'

'I'll be back at ours in two minutes, Gwen.'

'Thanks. Dear God. What a mess.'

'Are the police on their way?'

'I called them. Think they'll bring a helicopter over. Heavy mob.'

'Sounds like we'll need them. Thanks, see you soon. Stick the kettle on. Over.' He turned round. 'My wife. Gwen. Not sure if you met her? She was scheduled to take you home.'

The plane levelled out. The sea loch lost definition, became a great grey mirror. At its mouth was the open sea, dappled with sunlight through brief clouds. Houses appeared as the plane banked slightly. Leah remembered someone saying, *This north end has all the houses on it.* Maybe it was Steve.

'Steve's dead,' Leah said.

Pete's face registered surprise; he turned to her, briefly, then shook his head. 'Later,' he said. 'Talk about this later.'

He brought the plane down; the water below grew more distinct. They were maybe fifty feet or so from the water – uncomfortably low, Leah thought. Then the radio pinged again.

'Pete – this is Harry at the petrol station. What's going on up there? I saw a flare. Over?'

'Hi, Harry – false alarm,' Pete said. 'All under control. It's the group I had out with me over the weekend. Old school party. I'm bringing them in. Over.'

'We all good? Over.'

'All good. Over and out.'

Toni leaned over and tapped Pete on the shoulder. 'What was that? False alarm, did you say? There's no false alarm.'

Pete sighed, pulled off his headset. 'Can you come over here for a second? You're in my eyeline.'

'What?' Toni frowned.

Pete flicked a switch, then let go of the controls. The aircraft continued on its path, skimming low over the surface of the water but on a flat plane. Then Pete swung his legs over the seat, and grabbed Toni by the neck.

Leah reacted first, getting out of her seat. She hesitated when Pete glared at her. His other hand groped for the door. A flick, a simple twist, and the air blasted in, drowning out her screams.

'You're very talented,' Pete sneered. 'Let's see if you can fly.'

Toni couldn't. Leah grabbed out for Toni's outstretched hand; missed, then had a glimpse of her face, mouth gaping, screaming.

Pete hurled her out, kicking her as she tried to grip the edge of the door.

Leah saw her drop, a pinwheeling figure, then finally landing, the water erupting around her. She was lost to view as the plane surged on.

Then Pete twisted the door shut, and clambered back to his seat.

'Any more complaints?' he said, grinning. 'Thought not. We're coming in to land, so do behave yourselves. That was to stop any of the rest of you getting ideas. The jetty we're going to is just over there. I'm sure you can see it. And you'll see my wife, too. I know her as Gwen. I think you know her by a different name, though.'

Leah, her hand pressed to her mouth, sank back into her seat as far as she could go. Out the window she could make out the boardwalk jutting into the water. At the edge of it, leaning on a dirt bike on its kickstand, was a figure in a yellow mac.

43

'Rush him,' Debs said, just loud enough for Leah to catch it above the engine's low, descending notes. 'Now. It's our only chance.'

'And then what?' Leah said, watching the water come closer, and closer again. 'Crash the plane? Try to get out while it sinks? We've no chance.'

'We've got weapons. In the front. The bow and arrow... the knife.'

'We'll never get the chance.'

'It's this or nothing. There's two of them to deal with – we are not going to get out of this unless we try something!'

Panic rising, she tried to think of one single good reason not to go along with Debs' suggestion. But their pilot put paid to any further speculation.

Pete, concentrating hard on the water, spoke in the flat tones Leah remembered from their first day at the riverside in Glasgow. 'Um, if any of you girls are thinking of doing anything silly, there's an easier way for me to bring things to a halt.' He reached into the well at his feet, and then waved a pistol. Leah had only ever seen a handgun like that in films and TV shows; she had no idea if it was real, but was in no mind to question him. 'No problems with depressurisation, now, whatever you might have seen in the movies. Just sit down and relax. While you can.'

'Means nothing,' Debs whispered. 'I'll go first. His back's turned to us. Get the gun off him!'

'He'll just shoot you,' Leah said. 'We'll get our chance on the ground!'

Shell had her head in her hands. 'Toni... I don't believe it. I just don't... He threw her out! He threw her out of the plane!'

'We have to forget about it.' Leah placed her hand on Shell's back. 'We'll have to take our chance when it comes.'

She cried out, surprised, as the water kissed the underside of the plane.

A flicker of yellow as the plane came to a stop, and Pete guided the plane towards the jetty, where the bright candle-flame figure was already busying herself with ropes.

Pete rose from his seat, eyes twinkling with amusement. 'Out your seats when I say. Slowly. Hands up. Any sudden moves, and it's a sudden ending. More sudden than Toni's.' The gun turned towards Leah; she flinched. 'You first... what are you called again? Mrs Owl? Yeah, you. Up. Hands up, I said.'

Pete opened the door, and Leah shivered in the sudden influx of the colder air.

The person they'd known as Gwen looked up and grinned. The side of her face was swollen and purple – from the crash, Leah supposed.

'Well hello there!' Fiona Halfpenny yelled, at the top of her voice. 'Come on down and give us a hug, Leah!'

Leah hesitated. Pete shoved her and she stumbled down the stairs, landing in a heap on the planking. It swayed at her feet. She got onto her hands and knees, and looked up into the twin barrels of a shotgun.

Gwen smiled. Here, Leah saw the resemblance, at last; the wide eyes, a downward angle where the brows met. 'Grace and poise, Leah, grace and poise. That's what you're best at. Now, you and the other two bitches, walk towards that shack, just over there. Do it slowly. Or you die.'

44

The place of execution had a desk, a closed laptop computer, a 'Scottish colourists' calendar scored and asterisked with thick black marker pen, and several chairs. One of the windows looked out onto the plane, still gleaming and dripping, and the choppy waters. With the intermittent sunshine and some bruised clouds by the mountains in the background, the image might have made a good calendar shot itself. By the other window there were only trees.

Inside the shack, Shell and Debs were fastened to the seats with masking tape – too tight for them to move. Debs had made an effort to topple over the seat at first, but Halfpenny had laughed at her and set her straight. Debs had tried to spit, but her mouth was too dry.

'I'd save my breath, if I was you,' Halfpenny said. 'While you've got it.'

Shell had descended into sobbing and pleading. 'Please… I've got three boys, you have to find it in your heart…'

Halfpenny shook her head. 'Oh good God, give it a rest. I've heard all this before, remember?' Here she changed her tone to a somewhat brash American twang. A touch of Brooklyn, perhaps. 'You remember? In the car? And everywhere else? Pitiful. Isn't it? The pleading and whining.

It's really hard to listen to. But it's fascinating how they plead, all the same. All of them. Even the tough nuts. They all do it.'

'Please let me go,' Shell snivelled. 'I've never done anything to you! Please, I have a family...'

'Shut her up,' Halfpenny said, all mirth vanishing from her face.

Pete obeyed her on the instant. A strip of silver tape was pulled with a sharp shearing sound, then it was placed over Shell's mouth. Her blackened eyes went wide as he did so, spilling huge crystal-clear tears over the thick material and then onto her chin.

'Glad you could all make it,' Halfpenny said, leaning on the desk. She spoke confidently and brightly. It was easy to imagine her employing this patter while she was preparing nervous fliers for the journey. 'I'll save you the bother of asking questions, stalling me, that kind of thing. Basically I made a bunch of money with my art, I found Pete here, we started a little business because we really like these islands, plus I always wanted to fly... and then little squeaky Mousie Mouse got in touch. And that gave me an opportunity. I hacked into your emails and social media and I prodded you all into coming here. That's it, all explained. You can go to your graves happy. Now... I will admit, you gave me some trouble. We've had to bring forward our plans a bit – Shell escaping was a bit of a curveball, I have to say. But no problem, really. I have to skip forward to the main event. And that means me and you, Mummy Owl.'

Leah had not been tied to one of the seats. She stood in a corner, where Pete held his pistol on her. She hugged herself, partly to stop herself shivering, partly because she felt completely exposed, out in the open and in harm's way, as if she was naked. Pete had barely blinked, while he was holding the gun on her, like a guard dog that might turn nasty with the slightest movement. He chewed the side of his mouth, and his eyes were bloodshot. He seemed to seethe, utterly on edge. Leah couldn't look at him.

'Haven't you done enough?' Leah said. 'Haven't you wrecked our lives enough? You've killed Mouse. You've killed Toni. There's no need to go on with this.'

'Aw, put a sock in it. Mary bloody Poppins,' Halfpenny sneered. 'Come on. Out with you, Leah. We're going for a little walk. The other two... well, Pete'll keep watch on you while we're gone. He'll take really good care of you.' Halfpenny raised the shotgun. 'Let's go, Mummy Owl.'

'Leah, run,' Debs said, simply. 'Forget about us, and just run.'

Halfpenny scratched her chin, holding the shotgun casually in the crook of her elbow. 'Interesting thing about Debs, here, Leah... while I thought you were the queen bee – or Mummy Owl, to coin a phrase – this cow here was the one I actually liked. I had good memories of her. She had a bit of chutzpah, you know? Some moxie. She was like a really feisty best friend character in a cartoon, the crazy one. I think I wanted to usurp her, in a way. Not you.'

'Leah, she's going to kill us,' Debs said, matter-of-factly. 'Don't let her kill you as well. You know this makes sense. Run.'

Halfpenny crossed over to the far corner, depositing the shotgun onto the table. Then she turned to the corner where Pete had deposited the weapons he'd taken off the others as they got on the plane – their blades, and the bow and arrows. Halfpenny selected an arrow, and tested the serrated point on her finger. 'Ouch! No messing with these things. They're made to kill, never mind hitting the bullseye. I like it.'

'Run now, Leah. We're dead anyway,' Debs said.

'No, don't, Leah. All that's going to happen in that scenario is – I'll kill you first. Then the other two. Won't I?'

Before Debs could reply, Halfpenny stabbed down with the arrow. It pierced the tape that had been used to bind her legs to the chair, and travelled a fair distance before Halfpenny let the shaft go. Halfpenny bent low and watched it quiver as Debs screamed. Leah clapped her hands to her head, unconsciously.

A well of blood formed where Debs' thigh was, spilling over the masking tape in thick red drops.

'You bitch,' Debs said through gritted teeth. 'Absolute bitch. You pathetic, cowardly bitch.'

'Stick around,' Halfpenny leered, sticking out her tongue.

'Don't hurt anyone else,' Leah said. She took a step forward, despite the gun Pete was holding on them.

'Oh, that's so noble of you,' Halfpenny said, then shrieked with laughter. 'Come on. No more messing about.' Halfpenny brought out her knife – long, tapering off to a razor point that reflected the light. 'Come with me, Leah. Or I'll start cutting them. Know how many people I've killed with this?' She raised the knife, allowing the light to play on its surface. 'All of them. Barring poor old Toni.'

'OK,' Leah said. She raised her hands. Halfpenny motioned her to move towards the door, and she complied, her knees proving stubborn as they quivered. 'I'm going.'

'Hey,' Debs said. 'Wait up a second.'

Leah paused. Her breath whistled through her nose. She felt faint; lights danced at the very edges of her periphery, as if purple flares were gradually eating away at her vision; caterpillars gnawing a leaf from the outside in.

Halfpenny turned her head to the left – only slightly. *The shotgun was within reach.*

Then Pete lunged, jabbing the barrel of his pistol into Leah's cheek. 'Yeah. I could hear what you were thinking, you know. You shouldn't think out loud.'

Debs' face had gone the colour of porridge. The arrow was still embedded in her leg, but the blood had stopped flowing. Her whole body seemed to be shaking, though. She licked her lips and said, in a trembling voice: 'Before you head on outside, I want to tell you a couple of things.'

'Go on then...' Halfpenny said, genuinely interested. 'Who were you again? In the Society? The badger? The piggie?'

'Whatever. Debs is my name. That's what my friends call me.'

'I'll just call you a miserable slapper, then, if it's all the same to you.'

'You remember that night? Halloween? The initiation ritual? The one where you lost your mind?' Debs tried to smile.

'Yeah. That's why we're here. Do keep up.'

'You know my mother spoke to yours, not long after they locked you up?'

'Couldn't care less, bigmouth.'

Debs' gaze moved to Leah. Leah read the expression, the intent. Leah shook her head, once.

'Yeah,' Debs continued, 'she told my mother that it was a relief, when you got locked up. Know why?'

'I'm sure it's really relevant, and something you have to get off your chest.'

'It is. I want you to know before I die, that your mother was relieved when you got put away. Relieved. You were a burden, she said. You were an embarrassment. You didn't know whether it was day or night. You couldn't read or write properly. Just drew your pictures. "Thank Christ that halfwit is gone," she said. "I can begin my life." She did begin her life, too. Got out and about. Shagged half the men on her street. She was delighted with it.'

'Fascinating,' Halfpenny said. She actually yawned. 'Oh, I'm sorry. Carry on with this great piece of fiction.'

'Know what else? She said your art was shit. Piss-awful. She said that there was one thing that she would have been happy never to see again, other than your stupid face, it was your stupid paintings. Having to humour you. Having to stick them on the fridge.'

Halfpenny smiled. 'I'm supposed to hit you or something now, right? Big sock on the jaw. Maybe a backhander. Hollywood stuff, right? Instead… I think I'll just rest my hand, for a little bit.'

She opened her free hand, as if she was a conjuror showing an honest empty sleeve, then rested the meat of her palm on the quivering flight of the arrow stuck in Debs' leg. Then she leaned down, hard.

Debs threw her head back and gritted her teeth. She intended to repress the scream but could not altogether succeed. A fresh trickle of blood edged down the massed strips of masking tape as she cried out.

Halfpenny moved the arrow this way and that, utterly expressionless. Then she stood up abruptly. Debs' head went limp for a moment, and her eyes grew dull, her breathing shallow.

Halfpenny brightened up. 'Just something to think about, action girl, while we're away. Right. Shell – you OK where you are?'

Shell's eyes were streaming tears. She clamped her eyes shut while Halfpenny addressed her, unwilling to countenance the scene before her. Halfpenny shrieked laughter at her own joke.

'Right. Out we go.' She handed Pete the shotgun, then slipped in behind Leah.

Leah gasped as the knife prodded her lower back, right in the base of her spine.

'Now open the door,' Halfpenny said, brightly. 'Let's you and me step out.'

45

'Down towards the water, please,' Halfpenny said. 'Away from the plane.'

The razor tip prodded Leah in the back. This time it pierced the skin, and Leah cried out. 'I'm going!' she said. 'You don't need to do that.'

'Just reminding you I'm still there,' Halfpenny said. 'Come on. Nice and steady, now. You won't do anything I don't like, will you? Just keep parallel to the shore. We're going over towards that pier. You see it? It's going to be extended, you know. Turned into a wharf. Tour boats can berth, there.'

'You think you're going to be running a tour?' Leah said.

Halfpenny paused. 'Nah, absolutely not. We'll be in jail for this, no doubt about it. I might blame Pete for it; it's not out of the question. People will automatically blame the man, score on for the patriarchy. I've made some preparations. But you've got to be realistic when it comes to slaughtering people, haven't you? Well, would you look at that scenery? This is a great place to die, you have to admit.'

Leah's throat constricted. She could think of nothing to say. The worst thing: it *was* now a beautiful day. For the first time, under the sunshine, Leah didn't feel chilly. There were intimations of summer on the early spring glow, a warm caress on the cheek. Leah thought about David and John. That she might not ever see them again. That she might not ever get to hug her boy anew, hold him close. They might never snuggle up under their blanket again, watching the cartoons. No more Christmases. She tried not to sob; her lips and chin wobbled, but she made no sound.

'Oh incidentally,' Halfpenny continued, 'I wasn't going to kill you. Earlier on. With the chainsaw. I wanted to push things forward a bit, make you run back to your buddies. So it worked out all right in the end. Things did get complicated with the husbands showing up, I have to admit. That threw me.'

'Was John there?' Leah dared to turn and look.

Fiona Halfpenny grinned. The look transformed her face. Her pupils had grown large, like a cat zeroing in on its prey, preparatory to pouncing. She seemed to be sweating – an ugly sweat that had nothing to do with exertion, and more to do with some terrible inner mechanism, perhaps her roiling mind.

Insane. She is insane.

'I didn't see John, I must admit,' Halfpenny said, finally. 'You were lucky, in that respect. Maybe he doesn't love you enough to drop everything and come over? He might end up being the sole survivor. I got Ewan, though. Shell's husband. He was first. He came to the right place – the lodge near the top of the mountain. I was waiting for him. I strung him up from a rafter. Might do the same with his wife. So, they're a matching pair, into eternity. Well, until the forensics or whoever find them and cut them down. Shame, isn't it? Three boys, they have. Shell told me. She told me all about it. She pleaded, in the car. That's her speciality. But it's nothing special, really. They all plead, you know. Did I say that before? Probably did. It's funny. You'll plead, too.'

'Why did you do this? You killed all those people... You killed Mouse... And now Toni's dead... Because of something that happened when we were *kids*?'

'Pretty much.' Halfpenny sniffed. 'What can I say? When something rankles, it *rankles*.'

'Was it the party? Halloween? The box? It was a shitty thing to do, we all admit that... But we were kids. It happens.' Leah was strangely calm. She sucked in breath and her heart was God knows how many beats per minute, but her voice was level, coherent.

Halfpenny nodded. 'I know. Kids' stuff. But the thing is, it clings to you. It *stains* you, forever. I couldn't stop thinking about it. I tried, over the years. But it's not just trauma. There's something else. Something that's always been there.'

'You can get help. I heard...' *Choose your words carefully, for God's sake.* 'I heard that you had difficulties.'

'Difficulties?' Halfpenny barked the word.

'Yes. You can get help for it – you can stop it. Even now, after all this. We can help you. I can recommend someone. And we can come together and help you, as a group, the way we should have done...'

Leah's words were running away with themselves, too fast, too desperate, too much like begging. Halfpenny chuckled. 'I could have believed you for a second. Very touching. Yes, we could get the band back together. How nice.'

A sharp prod in the back. Leah gasped. That one hurt, and if it hurt that much, it hurt enough to bleed.

'No, I'm not talking about those difficulties. They're under control. That's not why I'm here. My basic problem is... I'm a wrong 'un. I like hurting people. I was like that before I met you. Torturing animals, all the classics, really. That's why we had to move from our last town. I was caught setting fire to rabbit hutches. It all fits, I suppose, if you are a psychologist or something. If you applied a bit of rationality to the irrational. I recognise this about myself, no denial here. So, I don't actually need revenge as a motive, but you know what? It sure helps. I couldn't do it all alone, though. I found Pete. Isn't that nice? I found my partner, a bit like you girls did. The internet's amazing, you know. You can find your other half – it can be done.'

'Yeah. I bet you're a regular Fred and Rose.'

Halfpenny's footsteps halted, while Leah's continued. She stopped and half turned, but before she could get a look behind her, a fist smacked into the back of her head.

Leah was on one knee, before she could process what had happened. She moved a quivering hand towards the back of her skull.

Another hand got there first, clutching Leah's hair and pulling her head back.

Leah couldn't see the blade, but she felt it against her neck, where her pulse jitterbugged under the skin. Just the merest touch.

'No more cheek, Leah,' Halfpenny hissed, at her ear. 'That's mild compared to what's going to happen.' Then she let go.

Leah got to her feet, feeling her head throb and swell where she'd been punched. 'Don't do that to me again,' she said. She mustered the courage to say it, but she couldn't quite muster the courage to face Halfpenny. As she was before on the outset, her nemesis remained a blurred figure in yellow, as if viewed behind a veil of water.

'Not that being a basket case hasn't been good for me. I turned it into art. Did you like the portrait, incidentally?'

'What?'

'The portrait,' Halfpenny said, in a sing-song voice that was as frightening as it was uncanny. 'That's a picture, dum-dum. The owl. That's you. The one in the Halt.'

'Lovely,' Leah murmured.

Halfpenny kicked her in the backside, hard. 'You're a shit liar. Move. I'll tell you when to stop. Yeah… as I was saying, I tried to put it all into art, conquer the demons, that sort of stuff. Didn't work. You see there's madness, but it's not a concrete thing, you know? However you express it. But a grudge… That's something you can put into form and shape. That's something you can be sure of. You know you remember stuff and it just… twists you… *up*?' The last word was screeched, and punctuated with a fresh punch on the back of the head. Again, Leah sprawled onto her hands and knees on the tufted grass at the head of the stony beach.

Halfpenny helped her up, gripping her by the shoulder. She spoke in a genial tone once more. 'Yeah, so, I had therapy, I had medication. I had problems, I had treatment. I had all kinds of things going on, and I made a conscious decision one night. Funnily enough, the trigger was when I had a model who liked cutting herself. I asked her why she didn't just finish the job. Genuinely baffled me, that. Anyway, that was quite a nasty scene. I didn't kill her, if you're wondering, but I did use her blood for a project. But I realised the question was one for me to answer, like all the best questions. It was my thing, just for me. Why don't I just finish the job? If I do, maybe I can stop thinking about it after I settle the accounts. When I start to slice you bitches up. When I make you understand what it felt like for me in the fucking *box*.

'Your little pal – Mouse, they call her? She got in touch with me around about this time. Now I don't believe in fate, destiny, karma, anything like that. If it existed, God would already have paid you back. And in that case, my rage would be gone. I'd have exorcised it. But that isn't the case. Karma is bunk. But coincidence is very real. So I treated it as if it was karma. After Mouse got in touch, I found out you scumbags are all nice and cosy with your la-di-dah middle-class lives.'

'That isn't true,' Leah said. Her head was aching, now, and she felt sick. Her voice sounded faint, too. 'My life hasn't been la-di-dah. I had an accident… My boy, my son, had an accident. He was injured. He needs me. He's severely disabled. I'm his carer as much as his mum. Please. You have to let me go back to him.'

'Hm. That's a tough break. Is he mentally disabled, you know? Brain-damaged? Think he'll be able to process what's happened to Mummy, or will you just be a big confusing absence in his life?' Halfpenny started to giggle, as Leah sobbed.

Leah saw him, then. She saw David without her. Lost. His father, despite his calm nature and his skilled hands, struggling without his wife there to guide the boy. She saw his every issue overcome so far – the chair, the sign language, the nappies and the washing, the knowledge that when he reached adulthood he would need the same – reversing itself. And she loved him, every atom of him. She needed him, and he needed her. This could not be the end. 'You can't do that. You can't do that to me. I have to help my son. I can't leave him alone.'

Halfpenny's laughter grew shrill, her tone mocking. 'Can't I? Bitch I've just carved up… how many is it? I forget! I've already heard this from Mouse. She pleaded, too. She pleaded for her little one.'

'Don't speak. Just don't fucking speak.' Leah blocked her ears with her fingers.

'Never mind all that,' Halfpenny said, brightly. 'This is all about you. Here we are. On the pier. There's our boat. That's the finish line. That's where you and me will sort things out, Mummy Owl.'

Leah saw the boat, moored up fast. A rowing boat, it looked like.

At the stern was a cardboard box.

46

Pete sat down on the empty chair. He tossed the roll of masking tape up and down in the air, catching it perfectly as it fell every time. 'Now, girls, what shall we do in the meantime?'

'If I was you, I'd worry about the cops showing up anyway,' Debs said. Her face was still pale and she dared not move her leg, which remained transfixed by an arrow, a vertical line jutting out of her flesh. 'Nice effort by Leah, firing that off. Shame she didn't think to barbecue your girlfriend with it, though.'

Pete smiled. 'Shall I let you into a secret? I've been given a job to do out here. Can you guess what it is?'

Some of the old snark came into Debs' voice. 'Oh, I don't know, mopping the floors? Doing the ironing? It looks like you basically do whatever you're told. Interesting relationship you have, there.'

'It works,' Pete said. 'You can say that for us. We like the same things. And we're in it for life. More than I can say for you. Bit of a tramp, aren't you?'

'Oh, please. I'm having my lifestyle choices criticised by a murderer. Give me a break, Pancho.'

'What did you just call me?'

Shell, her mouth still taped shut, could only form an approximation of an expression with her bloodshot eyes and a turn of her head. She clearly indicated to Debs: *No.*

'Pancho,' Debs went on, unabashed. 'You know, the moustache. It may be that you've just not shaved in a couple of days, but it looks like you're growing a mouser, there. I had to check the calendar when I first met you, thought it was Movember or something. But no. It's a *choice.* Moustaches are never an accident. I get that some people have beards, but a moustache... that's niche.'

'Please don't waste your breath,' Pete said. 'You might not have much of it left.'

'Tell me – what's the plan after you kill us? I mean there's a very narrow window between us all going missing and the cops getting involved. Every single bit of evidence is going to point at you. What's your plan?'

'We've got one – that's all you need to know.'

'Whatever it is, it's going to fail. You know that.' Debs paused. 'If you got out of here, right now, on the plane, you could get away with it. Pin it on her. We'd even back you up. Just give us a chance. Let us get away.'

'You're not in any position to make deals.' Pete sniffed. 'And as for what you said about our plan not working... we're relaxed about that. This is a work of art she's embarking on, you know. Something that people will discuss for years to come. We put in a lot of preparation.'

'Here we go, the megalomania plan. Mate, you won't be discussed. No one will find you fascinating. You'll pop up in a weirdo documentary on a channel you always, always flick past. And at that... you'll play second fiddle.

You're an accessory, a sidekick. Any attention you get, it'll be a fraction of what she gets. You have to understand that.'

'I do. I'm counting on it. She is a genius. I'm happy to play the supporting role. She's everything I ever wanted in a woman.'

'Anyone ever call you a bitch, Pete?' Debs sneered.

'Anyone ever mistake you for anything else?' He laid the roll of tape aside and clapped his hands – startling Shell. 'Anyway. Here's the plan,' Pete said. 'I have to kill one of you before Fiona gets back. I know which one it's going to be. I'll let you think about it.'

Debs tried to speak, but her throat seemed to constrict. Finally she spat out: 'Just get it over with then, creep. Errand boy. Go on. Get it done.'

'I will,' he said. Pete laid his pistol down on the table, beside Fiona's shotgun, and crossed over to a cupboard. It was unlocked; inside was some gardening equipment, including what looked like...

Pete smiled as he brandished the chainsaw. 'Ever wondered what it'd be like to saw through a person with one of these? If you haven't, I bet you're lying.' He came forward, the blade balanced in his hands. 'They never really showed you that in the films, you know. The true effect. It was Fiona's idea, actually. She took this out to scare your friend, Leah, earlier on. I think she wants the spray effect, to use it as a basis for a painting.'

Debs could think of no comeback, no defiance. Her legs began to shake, and a terrible thought struck her: how much better it might have been to expire from blood loss, had Halfpenny ruptured a pipeline somewhere in her leg. To simply fade away and pass out. It seemed it was only a flesh wound, though. Hadn't passed through any major roadworks, hadn't gone through the bone. Left her alive.

Worse luck.

'Now, I'm not going to do it right now. I just want you to have an idea. A little taste...' He cranked it up. Shell and Debs flinched in the sudden, brutal, mechanised howl as the blade whirred. Pete's eyes glittered as he moved the blade towards Debs' face. The child-like, furtive expression of enjoyment was perhaps the worst indicator that this man had no conscience, no pity and no sympathy – worse than Fiona Halfpenny's manic, bulging-eyed, almost camp displays. Here was the real Pete, unmasked.

Shell's eyes rolled up in her head, and she tried to shift away from Pete. She only succeeded in upending the chair, and she crashed over onto her side.

Pete shut off the chainsaw. 'Well, we've got a man down, here. You don't get out of games that easily, my lady. You'll need an excuse note from Mother.'

'Don't hurt her,' Debs said.

'I'll hurt who I like, when I like. You've probably guessed, I'm doing Shell next, though. Know why? So I can get you all to myself afterwards. I've been promised some time with you, before Fiona finishes the job. Shame it wasn't Toni, but, you know, orders are orders. I don't think Fiona cares what I do with you, but she didn't want Toni around. Funny how someone can get jealous like that. Too bad she couldn't fly. Not much of an Owl Society, was it?'

'She can't fly,' Debs said, 'but she can sure swim.'

Pete then heard a sound behind him – a simple shift, a creak of the floorboards. He spun around, still with the chainsaw in his hands, and spluttered in astonishment at the sight of Toni stood in the centre of the floor, with the bow, and an arrow nocked in the centre. Toni, dripping wet and shivering. Toni, who'd crept through the door under cover of the sound of the chainsaw. Toni, still alive, despite hitting the water at a height of fifty feet; Toni, who'd grabbed the one weapon she was able to use with confidence; beautiful Toni.

'I...' was all he managed, before Toni released the arrow.

It pierced his chest with a sharp report, and he wheezed, rather than screamed, clawing at the flighted shaft that had gone right through him. An arc of blood passed through the bright sunshine spearing through the window, a sudden pulse of bright red before he crashed to his knees, the chainsaw clattering alongside him, silent and useless.

Toni, hands shaking, took another arrow from the quiver and struggled to fix it. Pete crawled towards the table, where Fiona's shotgun and his pistol lay.

'Don't fuck it up now!' Debs shrieked. 'Be quick!'

Toni nocked another arrow at last, and aimed straight at Pete. He cowered, face pale. 'Wait,' he gurgled, raising one bloody hand. 'Wait...'

But she didn't. The second arrow went through his throat.

47

'Shame about Toni,' Halfpenny said, conversationally, as she led Leah towards the boat with the box on the stern. 'I'd like to have done the job myself but we had to make an example. What a nice person she was, eh? Except, she wasn't really. I saw what went on at the Halt. Screwing that skinny rake of a pilot in his stupid board shorts. Forty going on fourteen. Who was he trying to kid anyway? God knows he tried it on with me, too. A joke. The great hedonist. Both of them were too pathetic to live. I hope it was worth it for them.'

Focus, Leah thought. *Look ahead.* Thinking, thinking all the time. Options on the beach ahead? Make a sudden leap for the water? Run for the trees? Hope a car's passing? Signal a passing airliner?

I guess I signalled a passing plane. See how that worked out?

Then her internal voice grew harder.

You'll have to do it. At some point you have to take the gamble. She is going to kill you.

Halfpenny could outrun her, certainly at short distances. Perhaps she could outswim her, as well. Leah imagined striking out hard into the centre of the lake, then turning her head to see that grinning face streaking towards her like a torpedo with an obscene image chalked on the front.

As Leah had suspected upon first sight, it was a rowing boat, a decent size, simple but expensive-looking, varnished wood inside – a burnished, rich colour – and whitewashed on the outside. Its name was *Twilight Runner*, according to the blue paint on the side.

Leah swallowed. The cardboard box was big – too bulky to be carried easily, no matter what the weight was inside. As they came close, Leah fancied she heard something moving inside.

That's when raw fear kicked in. She stopped, but Halfpenny shoved her.

'In we go, sweetie,' Halfpenny said. 'That's it. Step inside. Sit at the front. Don't you worry about the box. That's for later.'

Leah did as she was told. There was a strange effect; her brain had automatically expected the boat to lurch, but there was only the mildest creak as Leah sat on the cushioned slat, her hands on her thighs.

Do it now? Back over the side, into the water?

'Just sit comfortably,' Halfpenny said, as she untied the boat and prepared to push into the water. Then, perhaps reading some subtle change in Leah's posture, she quickly brought up the knife.

'Filleting knife, this,' Halfpenny said. 'Not sure what sort of fish it's meant for – shark, I guess, going by the size of it. Perfect for filleting people, as it turns out. It's been modified. I got it on an online marketplace, would you believe. Some dude just selling one off from his front door. Cash in hand. Ripped himself off beautifully, too. Sometimes I wonder if he was punting it because he murdered someone with it and had to dump it. That'd be ironic. Anyway. Don't get any silly ideas about going in for a swim. Even if you did, I don't fancy your chances. You had a bit of a turn out on the water yesterday, didn't you? I thought I was going to have to run in to save you, so I could execute you later. Did you go into cold shock?'

'Cramp,' Leah said.

'Well, there you go. Be a pity if you just dived in and drowned. That'd be so disappointing. Anti-climax, they call it.'

Halfpenny pushed at the pier, and the boat moved out into the water.

Then they were afloat, and Halfpenny leapt in the seat facing Leah. The cardboard box was behind her.

Something shifted inside. Leah's stomach traced its movements, her guts twisting. *Dear God. What's she got in there for me? Is it alive?*

'Grab the oars, Leah. You're rowing.'

'Where?'

'Out in the middle. The deep blue sea.'

Leah did what she was told. She hadn't handled oars since she was a teenager, and grappled with them awkwardly before settling into a rhythm of sorts. Her chest twinged along the lateral lines of her ribs, and she gritted her teeth against the pain. Had she cracked them?

In trying to muffle her cries, Leah focused on David. A barely controlled grief and sorrow began to cloud everything, even her immediate peril. David... Would she see him again? How would he react when he was told Mummy wouldn't be coming home?

Put a stop to it. Take a chance. Be ready.

'Not too good at this, are you?' Halfpenny sneered. 'The rowing machine at some hoity-toity gym isn't quite the same as the real thing. This is not one of your talents, Mummy Owl.'

Leah pulled harder, feeling a nasty twinge in her lower back. The shore withdrew, fast, and the motion made her slightly nauseous.

Leah glanced over her shoulder, to make sure she was heading in the right direction. She was slightly off course, tracking parallel to the shore; she altered it by using one of the oars to straighten up.

Then she had her idea. And her pulse quickened.

Halfpenny suddenly jammed the knife into the wooden slat in front of her. 'Let's go through some of your other options,' she said, conversationally, 'apart from diving over the side. The next best guess is to rock the boat. Ah... I can tell by that reaction that this was either your exact plan, or you hadn't thought about it at all. Either way, I'll punch you through with the knife before you can get enough of a sway going to knock me overboard. Or knock me off balance enough for you to steal the knife. So I wouldn't bother with that. After that... Hmmm. You'll probably be thinking that you'll get a fair chance when we get to the middle of the loch. But the same applies. If you end up in the water, you won't be swimming underneath it for too long. Then I'll spear you like a nice fat tuna. So, you're sort of out of options, really.'

'Best I go along with it,' Leah said.

'Yeah, best you do.' Halfpenny nodded and grinned. 'You're clever. So clever, as well as good-looking, as well as being great at sports, and passing your little tests and exams, and flirting with the boys, and having them fall in love with you, and having all the friends... Not daft like me. Except the daft one has the knife.'

'You've got me,' Leah said. 'Hands down. So, what's the story with the box?'

'I'm glad you asked. I thought this one up especially for you, Leah. The other ones won't get the star treatment, but you will.'

Again, the scraping inside. There was something alive inside the box. And maybe more than one thing.

She knew what they were, before Halfpenny spoke. 'Good old Mouse. We had a really good deep conversation going on email. I almost forgot that I was supposed to hate her, too. She told me so much about you guys. We spoke about the Halloween trick, but I made out that I had a good sense of humour about it now. So much easier to do these things by email. I don't know if I could have said that in person. Anyway... I asked Mouse what her scariest thing would be. She said "sharks", which I can't really work with, though it might have been interesting to get her out in the water. And then I asked what yours were. You know – what you might have written on the piece of paper, for the demon. Was she lying? We're about to find out.'

Leah could picture them. How many would there be? Pink tails, twitching noses, the horrible, all too human-seeming hands...

'They're inside another box in here – they'd have gnawed out of this box in about two minutes, otherwise. See, this is my plan for you, Leah. This might be a comfort; might not. I want you to live. I want someone to get out of this. I'm not saying I want you to be unharmed. But I do want you still breathing. I want to see how you'll handle having done to you what was done to me. I want to see how you'll get on with the same situation. Except it won't be rubber rats, like you gave me rubber spiders. It'll be real ones. Not pet shop rats, either. Shit-house rats. Filthy. You can probably smell them if you have a sniff… No? Their fur's revolting. Full of fleas. You know that way a meadow or a wheatfield will move in the wind? That's what they look like with the fleas. Vermin on vermin. And soon they'll be on you. They're hungry – a few of them have been in the trap a few days. Surprised they didn't eat each other. In fact I'll be surprised if they don't eat you. Scream if it gets too uncomfortable, won't you?'

'I am not getting in that box.'

'You are,' Halfpenny said, nodding eagerly. She retrieved her knife. 'You so are. And you're going to do it now.'

'You're absolutely right about that.'

'Remember what I said about the tricks, now.' Halfpenny let her hand drop. The blade was poised, ready to dart forward. 'One little twitch and you're history. This is a big moment. The time I had you in my absolute power. I want you to remember it.'

'I'm going to cherish it.'

'You almost sound convinced!'

'I am. Convinced that you're thick. One other thing – we can't be friends any more.'

Leah pulled hard on the oars – then dipped her right hand. The paddle rose from the water, slick and dripping. Then she slammed the handle as hard as she could to the right, dropping to the side with the same motion.

Leah felt, as well as heard, the colossal crack as the paddle hit Halfpenny in the jaw.

Now the boat rocked, all right. Halfpenny fell, completely stunned, jarring the box. The cardboard tumbled over the back of the boat and into the water. Then it began to sink.

Leah got to her feet, and grabbed what she had spotted in the bow of the boat when she'd turned to adjust her position.

An anchor, new and shiny but old-fashioned in design, with curved, sharp edges at the top, attached to a coiled length of rope. Heavy; needed two hands to lift; just the job.

Halfpenny lay on her back, blinking, blood surging from her ruined nose and mashed lips. The knife lay in the bottom of the boat. Leah paused for less than a second, wondering if she should make a grab for the weapon.

Then Halfpenny sat upright, blood gushing from her ruined face. She snorted, spraying warm blood into Leah's face, then sprang forward with a roar.

Leah heaved the anchor overhead, then swung it down, going with the momentum, getting all her weight behind it.

The anchor punched into Halfpenny's chest, and stayed there. She gasped; her eyes bulged; blood streaked the yellow jacket. The anchor was lodged in her chest, deep, just below the collarbone.

'Fancy a swim?' Leah shrieked, and shoved Halfpenny hard with both hands.

Halfpenny fell over the side; Leah, stumbling forward, saw a bloody hand groping for her arm as she leaned over.

'No,' was all she managed to gasp, before they both plunged into the freezing water.

48

Leah struggled to get free, but Halfpenny's grip on her was absolute. The anchor dragged them into the freezing black water, the line taut beside her.

Fiona Halfpenny's face was a smudge in the dark. She screamed something, one final curse, as her blood pumped out fast and warm against Leah's face.

Leah brought her knees up; she grabbed the line, and Halfpenny's grip slipped off her. Then Leah kicked out hard at the pale face, like an unearthly flame in the darkness. It disappeared, dragged into the depths by the sinking anchor.

Leah clawed at the line, but it slithered out of her hands. She couldn't move; she choked, lungs filled with water. Cold shock; she could only float, lying on her back, but the surface and the light were no closer. Spears of light began to streak across her vision. After all this. All this. No. She thought of David. His smile. His brightening expression when she came into the room. That was all she could do.

Then the hand grabbed her, hard. Bubbles escaped, precious air.

Surely not Fiona Halfpenny, somehow freed, an unkillable revenant.

Leah was dragged to the surface, whooping, coughing, a hand striking her back once, then once again.

'Got you, you berk,' Toni gasped.

49

John was actually wringing his hands when Leah spotted him making his way through a throng of hi-vis vests. Tall, troubled, his glasses threatening to tip off the end of his nose – the same as any other time, really. She called out to him, and he ran.

'My hero,' Leah said, into his neck. 'Just in the nick of time.' And she began to laugh. She knew the laugh was all wrong, wrong place, wrong time, wrong pitch. He sat beside her on a huge stone placed on the beach – probably to stop boy racers tearing up and down the shale and shingle, as much as any sense of public amenity. He held her tight, and let it descend into sobs.

'David,' she said finally. 'Tell me. They say he's fine. But I need to know from you. Is David all right?'

'With my parents. He's absolutely fine,' John said. 'We're going to get you home soon.'

'I'd be dead if it wasn't for Toni... God knows how she survived. She came back for us...'

'That's for later,' John said.

Out on the sea loch, the police launch had berthed alongside the empty rowing boat. They were hauling up the line at the anchor, and Leah thought, in a curiously cold and clear way: *this is when the anchor is pulled up, and it's empty, and she's still out there somewhere. This is when it happens.*

But the anchor was still snagged on something – a burst of yellow appeared, with limp arms inside it, and a lolling head. John turned her head away. 'Don't look at it.'

'Why not?' Leah sniffed. 'I want to be sure she's not coming back. She had rats, you know. Rats. Rats in a box, for me.'

Leah did turn her head away, though, and stared at the others. Shell had been taken away. Something in her blank stare had frightened Leah. *Someone turned the lights off,* she thought. *Will Shell ever come back? Have they told her about Ewan?* Leah heard that voice, again. *'I strung him up from a rafter.'*

Someone howled; Leah turned to see Debs sitting on the beach, stupefied, while a police officer placed a hand on her shoulder. She began to sob, her whole body convulsing, her head in her hands.

Eoghan. They must have got Eoghan, too.

'I missed the boat,' John said, absently. 'I missed the sailing the others got. I was held up in traffic; I might have made it if I'd rushed, but David didn't want me to go. Said he didn't want to be left alone. So I stayed.'

'Thank God he did.' David had saved him – stopped him from coming over, from becoming a victim. Maybe he'd saved her, too. In her most extreme moments of danger, when death was close enough to touch, thinking of David had given her the clarity and strength to go on. And the very idea of him would give her everything she needed from now on.

On the shore, Toni moved with the same poise she always had. Like Leah, she'd been given a change of clothes but was covered in a blanket. Her face was blank, like Shell's. She sank down on her haunches and placed a hand on Debs' shoulder.

'Just a minute,' Leah said, extricating herself from John. 'I'll be back in a second. Got something to do, here. Just wait a minute.'

Leah cast off the blanket and joined Toni and Debs. They held each other tight.

Acknowledgements

Many thanks to Greg and all the team at Head of Zeus, and to my agent Justin and his fellow saints at Kate Nash. Thanks once again to Claire, Helena, Rory and Elaine for putting up with the late-night and early-morning typing, as well as the occasional screams of anguish. Writing is a solitary occupation, but, strangely enough, you can't do it alone.

Thanks also to the entire editorial team for picking up my many, many bloopers. I thought I was unembarrassable when it comes to literals but I plumbed new depths with the first draft of this novel. 'The Bikini Mistake' will haunt me forever, but, looking on the bright side, it's a great book title...